KILLING SEASON

Faye Kellerman is the author of thirty-one novels, including twenty-two *New York Times* bestselling mysteries that feature the husband-and-wife team of Peter Decker and Rina Lazarus. She has also penned two bestselling short novels with her husband, *New York Times* bestselling author Jonathan Kellerman and teamed up with her daughter Aliza to co-write a young adult novel, *Prism*. She lives with her husband in Los Angeles, California, and Santa Fe, New Mexico.

Also by Faye Kellerman

FAYE KELLERMAN
KILLING SEASON

HarperCollins*Publishers*

HarperCollins*Publishers* Ltd
1 London Bridge Street,
London SE1 9GF

www.harpercollins.co.uk

Published by HarperCollins*Publishers* 2017
1

First published in the USA in 2017 by
William Morrow, an imprint of HarperCollins*Publishers*

Copyright © Plot Line, Inc. 2017

Faye Kellerman asserts the moral right to
be identified as the author of this work

Designed by Diahann Sturge

A catalogue record for this book is available from the British Library

ISBN: 978-0-00-814867-6

Printed and bound in the UK by
CPI Group (UK) Ltd, Croydon, CR0 4YY

MIX
Paper from
responsible sources
FSC™ C007454

This book is produced from independently certified FSC™ paper
to ensure responsible forest management.

For more information visit: www.harpercollins.co.uk/green

RAINSTORM

As the casket of a young girl, aged sixteen, was lowered into the ground, her sister, through tearful eyes and a choked voice, sang "Amazing Grace." Her brother stood awkwardly in a suit and tie, dry-eyed and stoic. Her parents sobbed and wept and clutched the loose earth, desperately trying to hang on to something physical. All four knew that there was no longer a silver lining to dark clouds, that life had unalterably changed and there was nothing anyone could do to ever make it whole again.

PROLOGUE

NO WONDER THE *South lost the war.*

No one could tolerate this kind of sweltering heat, with afternoon temperatures rising above the hundred mark and humidity off the scale—blistering and relentless. It was the kind of heat that charred the lungs and seared the skin. It burned his eyes and cracked his lips.

In the city, the people around him kept apologizing: telling him that it was a heat spell, that usually the humidity wasn't this bad, and that it usually cooled down at night. But the night was just as hot, with radiant heat coming from the asphalt in shimmering waves. The road had been periodically illuminated as he drove to the woodlands, but once inside the miles of untamed terrain, it was black as tar. And sticky. From where he stood, drenched in sweat, he was miserable and tired and dealing with a multitude of bugs.

Mosquitoes, the palmetto bugs known to most as cock-

roaches, and the clouds of gnats. The forest hummed with bugs especially since he was near water. The insects were merciless: buzzing his ears, dive-bombing his nose and mouth. And the chiggers, clinging to his socks and trousers, smelling the salt and sweat, waiting for the hem of his pants to ride up or the tops of his socks to fall down to sink their teeth into his flesh.

Because of his heavy dress, his tools, and his knapsack, he was overloaded. He was having trouble breathing. He was having trouble moving. He had always been steady and meticulous. He had always been painstaking. This time, he was just plain sluggish.

Too bad because he wanted to relish the final phase of his handiwork. Tonight, if he was smart—and of course he was very smart—would be the last time he went digging.

Tonight should be the last time. Tonight needed to be the last time.

Except for the tedious niggling fact that despite his best efforts, things hadn't worked out perfectly. And that preyed upon him more than the heat, humidity, or any of the carnivorous insects.

Sweat in his eyes, dripping off his nose. He was clothed head to toe, from shoe covers to his hat: a living sauna.

He plodded on.

Hunting for the right spot that was clear enough, close enough, and soft enough. Lugging the shovel over his shoulder, he had to squint hard to see the flashlight beam, giving him barely enough illumination in the smothering darkness. Using his ears, the sound of the river as his guide.

He was getting too old for this. After this, he would stop. He had to stop.

He paused, took a deep breath in and out. Put down his

knapsack and opened the front pocket. He took out his measuring tape and cordoned off the spot—a perfect three-by-five. He'd go four feet deep, maybe more if the ground was soft enough. It would take him hours to get it right. It would take him all night. He would finish before daybreak.

Always finish before the sun came up.

He plunged the shovel into the ground. The crypt had to be precise.

He'd be back to fill it up.

For the last time.

Maybe.

CHAPTER 1

THEY WERE WHISPERING about him, this time to the new girl.
She had arrived at River Remez along with the New
Mexican monsoons of summer. He had been out driving—
running an errand for his mom—when he had noticed her
with Chelsea and Shannon and Lisa Holloway walking down
Arroyo Way. It had been four in the afternoon, the typical time
for the mountain skies to open up, but the storm that day had
been particularly strong. Blustery winds and blinding lightning
strikes were followed by ear-shattering thunder, the distance
between sight and sound growing shorter as millions of volts
of electricity loomed dangerously close. The rains were flood-
ing the sinewy roads and hillsides, red clay soil oozing from
the mountains. It was coming down so fast that he had almost
pulled over as pea-sized hailstones bounced off the windshield
of the SUV. But the wipers were batting the hail away with
rhythmic efficiency.

The girls were soaked to the skin, dodging ice pellets, running with their T-shirts pulled over the tops of their heads, showing inches of tanned bare skin along the belt line. He was about to offer them a lift, but at the last moment they beelined under the portal of JD's house.

Their hushed voices in the school's lunchroom howled like a tempest. Not that he could hear them—they were too far away—but he knew what they were saying because it's what everyone said. Shannon and Chelsea were talking in tandem.

"That's Vicks over there sitting by himself."

"He's kinda weird. A lone wolf. Especially after his sister died."

"Raped and murdered."

"Strangled."

"She was only sixteen."

"Almost seventeen."

As if her age mattered. But it was always the addendum because Ellen had almost been seventeen. The new girl would be shocked and scared. "Who did it?"

"Unsolved for over two years."

"Lots of suspects, no one ever arrested."

"Some people, at first, even thought that Vicks did it."

The new girl's eyes would get big. "Did he?"

"Nah, Vicks is just Vicks. Weird but harmless."

"He rides his bike everywhere even though he can drive. It could be pouring outside and there's Vicks pedaling his bike up the mountain."

"You know how it is. Those nerdy math types."

"He's a genius in math."

"Yeah, if you need help for your SATs, just put on a smile and he's a sucker."

Giggles all around.

Then suddenly the whispering would stop and they'd move on to gossiping about someone else.

His eyes moved back to his book, some ludicrous sci-fi thriller, but his concentration wasn't there and his mind shifted into default mode: thinking about his sister . . . both sisters, but mainly Ellen. Ben was now older than his sister had been when she passed.

That day when his mom got the phone call, they'd been driving back from Albuquerque. At fourteen, he had maxed out in high school math and was taking college calculus at UNM in Albuquerque. The school year was days away from over. He was tired, grumpy, and hungry, and traffic was a bitch on I-25. Between rush hour and construction, the highway had become a parking lot. He'd been arguing with his mom when Dad's call cut through the Bluetooth. The day: Wednesday. The time: ten after five.

"Do you know where Ellen is?" he asked.

"She isn't home?" Mom waited a second. "She should have been home two hours ago."

"She's not home, Laura." An awful pause. "How far away are you?"

"I don't know . . ." Panic had seeped into her voice. "I guess about forty-five minutes."

"Just get home. I'll keep making phone calls."

The ride home was unbearably long and silent.

Four hours later, the police were sitting on the living room couch. Detective Samuel Shanks did most of the talking. Back then, Ben had thought Shanks a big man: tall as well as hefty. Three years later, they were around the same height, although Shanks still outweighed him by fifty-plus pounds.

The detective spoke earnestly. He asked questions: Has she ever done this before? Any problems at home? At school? What about with her friends? With a boyfriend?

Ellen had no problems with anyone. Everybody loved her.

Ben's younger sister, Haley, sat stone-faced with her best friend, Lilly. They were two little eleven-year-old sticks, huddled together. Finally, Mom noticed their terror. "Ben, take the girls outside."

"Outside?" he said. It was dark.

"No, not outside." Mom was flustered. "Call up Lilly's parents and tell them to pick her up." Then Mom changed her mind again. "Ask if Haley can stay over there." And a third time. "No, just have them pick her up . . . Lilly." Finally, she had lost it. "Just . . . go to your rooms right now. I need to think."

Then Sam had asked to speak to their son privately. His father seemed confused. "Ben? Why?"

Shanks didn't answer the question. "Just for a few minutes."

Once in the privacy of his room, Ben felt numb. Shanks tried the sympathy approach. "I'm sorry this is happening to you. A lot of times, these things just work themselves out."

Ben nodded, but he was dubious.

"You know, brothers are kind of protective of sisters, right?"

"Ellen's older than me."

"But she's still your sister. I bet you notice things, being closer in age than your parents. Do you think your sister might be keeping something from your parents?"

"Like what?"

"You tell me."

"Nothing to tell. Ellen doesn't do drugs. She doesn't have a secret boyfriend. She doesn't have a secret life. I'm not making her perfect, but everyone loves her." Ben locked eyes with the detective. "This isn't like her. Something's wrong."

Shanks moved to his desk and picked up a picture. "Your friends, Ben?"

"Yeah."

"This one over here." He pointed. "He's big for fourteen."

"He's fifteen."

"Yeah?" A pause. "Being your friend, he must have known Ellen."

Ben felt himself stiffen. He knew what this Shanks guy was implying. "No."

"No what?"

"Just no." End of private talk.

Lists were made—phone numbers and addresses of friends and acquantainces. Then Sam passed out cards with his cell number. It was dutifully entered into all of their contact lists. Within a day, Ben had committed it to memory. His former life ceased to exist. He was hurled into overdrive.

First was the passing-out-flyers phase: HAVE YOU SEEN THIS GIRL?

Next was the endless-searches phase: on the hiking trails, in the mountains, and at the riverbeds, in neighboring towns to Albuquerque and beyond.

Mom calling Shanks ten times a day; Dad calling him twenty. Shanks became a household word—what he did, what he didn't do, what he was doing. Shanks this and Shanks that.

"Ben, call up Shanks and tell him that she was seen on the Plaza in Taos."

"Ben, call up Shanks and tell him there was a sighting of her at the caves in Carlsbad."

"Ben, call up Shanks and tell him someone spotted her in Las Vegas."

He called and reported the latest sighting to Shanks.

"New Mexico or Nevada?" Shanks asked.

Ben cupped the house-phone receiver. "Mom, was it Las Vegas, New Mexico, or Las Vegas, Nevada?"

She yanked the phone from his grip. "I'll do it myself."

Hundreds of calls along with hundreds of leads that went nowhere. Every weekend, Ben rode his bike to the mountains and searched, hiking on and off the trails until almost every square inch of the Sangre de Cristos had been trampled. Most of the time the searching became ritualistic, done without conscious thought. Always on his own, always alone. And then after Ellen was found—

"Hey, Vicks."

Ben jerked his head up from his book. He'd been on the same page for the last five minutes. Back to the present. Exactly where he didn't want to be. "JD."

"You busy?" He sat down without asking.

Ben studied the guy. Over the summer, he had really grown into his quarterback status: six three and muscular as hell. Remez High was all about football and JD was the football god. He could pass, he could run, he could anticipate, he could fake, and he could score because JD was smart. He won a lot of games in his junior season. Senior year was here and everyone was waiting for the sweep. JD was being scouted by almost every major university. Not just scouted—wooed. JD was the BMOC with his brown feathered hair falling across his forehead, his cleft chin, his swagger, and his white-toothed smirk. JD's favorite line was "After JC, it's JD." The guy wasn't really a friend, but he wasn't an enemy either.

Not that Ben had any enemies . . . or any real friends, for that matter.

Unless you considered Sam Shanks a friend.

"How'd your summer go?" he asked.

"'S'right. I saw a lot of suits going in and out of your house," Ben told him.

"What can I say?"

"You make a decision?"

"Schools are like girls. So many options, so little time."

"It's a hard life but someone has to live it."

"Exactly." JD smiled with his white teeth. "I'm leaning toward Duke."

"Good choice. Free ride?"

"All the way."

"Sweet."

"I still want to keep my options open for the Ivies. Most of them don't give athletic scholarships, so I'll need merit. Which means . . ." JD handed Ben two sheets of paper filled with calculus problems. "It's for entrance to AP Calc. Twenty-four problems. Could you look them over?"

"You're not supposed to get help on the entrance exam." JD waited for a more favorable response. Ben said, "So you want me to cheat for you?"

JD said, "Hells yeah." A pause. "Just look over my answers and say yes or no."

Ben took the papers. Ninety-three seconds later, he said, "Look over eighteen and twenty-four. The rest are right." He handed the test back. "Who's teaching AP Calc this year?"

"Lowen."

"He's a good guy."

"I'm just looking for the A for the first grading period.

Then it's party time." A wide shark's-tooth smile. "Are you TA-ing for him, Vicks?"

"For Lowen, yes, but not AP Calc. This year I'm doing regular calc and geometry."

"Which regular calc?"

"Afternoon session."

"Ro's in that class. Say hi for me."

"Ro?"

"The new girl who moved here in June."

"The blonde."

"So you've noticed her." JD smirked.

Not many girls here were blond. Besides, she was exquisite—around five six with long hair and long legs. Big, round blue eyes. It would take a moron not to notice. Ben said, "So her name is Ro? Like the Greek letter?"

"*R-O* not *R-H-O*. No matter how you spell it, she's on fire." JD touched an imaginary flame and made a sizzling sound. "Hot! We're an item." He held out a twenty. "For your efforts."

"Nuh-uh," Ben said. "You're not buying me off. Besides, I didn't do anything."

"Up to you." JD pocketed the bill and left.

The bell rang. Ben got up and dumped his paper-bag lunch into the garbage and headed for his TA calc, where no doubt Ro—not the Greek letter—would be looking at him with a strange expression on her face.

TUCKED INTO THE front corner, Ben sat about five feet from the teacher's desk, trying not to pay attention to the new girl. She, on the other hand, was brazen, clearly sizing him up. He wasn't much to write home about: five ten, one-forty with pale brown eyes and dark curls that brushed his shoulders.

He needed a haircut. His looks qualified him as boyish except when he didn't shave. School prohibited facial hair and that meant that every other day he had to plow through a sizable amount of stubble.

Lowen came in and class began. The first week was review starting with Algebra 2. Ten minutes before the bell rang, Teach told everyone to close their books.

"Let's see who was really paying attention," he said. "Everyone get out a sheet of paper and a pencil. Five points to the first one to solve the problem I put on the whiteboard." When he was sure all textbooks were closed, Lowen wrote the problem and then turned to Ben. "Take over, Vicks. I'm grabbing a cup of coffee." As soon as Lowen left, the noise level went up. Not that anyone was cheating, but talking was another thing.

Ben stood watch, which gave him an excellent chance to look the girl over. She was working like a devil, layers of honey-blond silk covering her face as she scribbled furiously. Within a minute, her hand shot up. He walked over to her, and wordlessly, she handed him her paper. He said, "Uh, you got Z, but you need all three variables."

"Right." She snatched the paper from his hands.

A moment later, it was Manny Martinez's turn. Ben was checking his work just as Lowen came back. "We have a winner."

"Very good, Mr. Martinez, you're off to a fine start," he said. "You can record it, Vicks."

As he opened the grade book, Ben's eyes scanned down the list—twenty names with a clean slate where scores would soon be posted. Quickly he looked for Ro's last name but couldn't even find her first name. But that was an easy fix because the only name he didn't recognize was Dorothy Majors.

Then he got it. Dorothy as in Do-ro-thy. Just as Lowen

was giving out the homework assignment, Ben felt his phone vibrating. Checking the text, he felt light-headed—his heart thumping as he tried to stave off panic. Catching Lowen's eye, he pointed to his watch while making a walking motion with his two fingers. The teacher waved him off and he raced out of the classroom.

He made it to his locker as his chest seized up. He debated making a quick call to Shanks, but decided it was a bad idea. This conversation needed a face-to-face. Whatever the results, the day was shit.

Open the locker, get the books out, and get out of here.

"Hi."

Ben whipped his head around while balancing an armful of books. "Oh, hi."

"I just thought I'd introduce myself." She held out her hand. "Ro Majors."

"Uh . . . Ben Vicksburg." He shuffled his books so his right hand was free to shake hers.

"Vicksburg? Like in the Civil War battle?"

"Yeah, somewhere in my background is Rebel blood." More shuffling of books. "Way down there, though. My family's been here for five generations."

"Whoa. That's a long time to be in one place. You must have a lot of relatives around."

"Uh . . . sure. Not all in northern New Mexico." He was trying to find his English lit notebook. It seemed to have disappeared. "I've got relatives here. I've got a lot in Albuquerque, some in Durango, some in Roswell."

"*The* Roswell?"

"*The* Roswell."

"Have they seen any aliens?"

"Only when they look in the mirror."

She smiled and said, "Do you have those big family reunions?"

Man, she asked a lot of questions. "Uh, yeah, every year around August twelfth . . . which is Santa Clara feast day." Voilà, he found the notebook. His mind wasn't on the conversation, but for once he made an attempt to be polite. Probably because he liked looking at her face. "You were that close to the answer."

"Yeah, just a little slow."

"Maybe next time."

"He gives those five-pointers a lot?"

"Every week."

"Okay. I'll have to move quicker. I'm not bad in math, but I am deliberate."

"Math requires deliberation. Patience is a good thing." He stacked the books he didn't need back in the locker. Shanks's text was still burning in his brain. He had to get out of there.

". . . you're done with calc?" She was still talking to him.

"Yeah, a long time ago. I'm kind of a math nerd."

"So I've heard." He stared at her and she blushed. She said, "Not the nerd part, just that you're a math brain."

"Right." A pause. "JD says hello, by the way."

"When did you see JD?"

"In the lunchroom." He closed his locker with a thud. "Just after you left with Shannon and Chelsea . . . who were no doubt giving you the skinny on me as well as everyone else in this little school."

"Four hundred isn't small. At least by private school standards."

"Ah, you're from private stock?"

"Scarsdale, New York."

"What brings you here?" Why was he still talking to her?

"Parents. Not my idea, believe me. Who wants to leave high school in their senior year?"

"Yeah, that's pretty bad."

"Beyond bad. It took me two weeks to talk to them again. This is like the polar opposite of New York. I bet you know, like, everyone in the school."

"Just about." Ben shrugged. "JD gleefully told me that you two are an item."

"That is true."

"He's a lucky guy." Ben forced a smile. "Nice meeting you, Ro."

"Are you coming to the kickoff game next Friday night?"

"Don't think so." Ben made a not-so-subtle glance at his wristwatch.

"Are you in a hurry?"

"Kinda."

"Sorry about all the questions. I'm a little nosy at times."

"Nothing wrong with being curious. It's just that I've got to meet . . ." *A homicide detective.* "Someone . . . it's kinda important."

"Then I won't keep you." She gave a nice smile, and waved.

Ben watched her walk away, her hips sashaying down the hall in a gait that said confidence. She and JD were well matched in that regard. Talking to her had momentarily calmed him down. As soon as she was gone, his heart started racing once again. He slipped his backpack onto his shoulder and jogged to his bike.

He was in too much of a hurry to even feel sorry for himself.

CHAPTER 2

THOUGH SMALL IN population, River Remez was spread out, bleeding into hundreds of miles of flat earth, mountains, and riverbank. Streets were stuck in between the natural features, which made the town beautiful but not terribly efficient. Roads stopped and started, and housing developments meant three homes on one street and ten on another. Some had river views, some were perched atop the ridges, and some were right outside the plaza, which wasn't much more than a square block of green space surrounded by tourist shops and the Hyatt Hotel. The real town shopping was on Sierra Road, an ugly strip of asphalt that had whatever people needed: Walmart, Lowe's, Albertsons, Gap, Starbucks, Trader Joe's, strip malls, and movie theaters.

Like Santa Fe, River Remez's saving grace was the architecture. Almost everything was low rise and adobe style, which gave the town a uniform appearance. Even the police station was fashioned from the same brown stucco. It sat alone, a one-story office building across the street from a Rite Aid drugstore.

The parking lot of RRPD was half empty and so was the bike rack. Ben was so frazzled when he arrived that he hopped off his bike and just laid it on the sidewalk. Then he went back and locked the wheel to the rack.

Even small towns have theft problems.

As usual, Maria was behind the desk. In her midthirties, she was short and stocky with bobbed dark hair and brown eyes. Her uniform was always perfectly pressed. "Hey, Vicks."

"Detective Shanks is expecting me." Ben took off his backpack and handed it to her for inspection. "He just sent me a text."

Maria gave the insides of the rucksack a nominal glance and handed it back. "Go ahead."

Inside the door, Ben was in the sprawl of the River Remez PD. It was a small police station in a small town that was an offshoot of a slightly larger town. Since there was only one building, uniforms and plainclothes detectives shared a common space. Shanks was the senior detective and had his own office in the back.

As Ben passed desk after desk, he was greeted by name.

"Hi, Vicks."

"Hey, Vicks."

"What's cooking, Vicks?"

"Hey, Vicks."

Everyone avoided eye contact. Not good.

Ben knocked on Shanks's door and then went in. Sam was on the phone but he motioned to take a seat. He also refused to make eye contact.

Shit. Really not good.

Sam hadn't aged all that much in three years, but every year there was added strain on his face. White temples that had once been black, bags under the gray eyes, more creases every time they talked—most of the wrinkles put on his face by Ellen's murder, the only homicide in the district within the last ten years. Shanks was a big man and his shirts always seemed to strain across his chest. His usual dress was a white shirt, a tie— blue, black, or red—dark slacks, and scuffed oxford shoes.

He got off the phone and spun his chair. When he didn't talk right away, Ben said, "It's not the Demon."

"Vicks—"

"It is the Demon?" When Shanks paused, Ben said, "It's not him. I know it's not him. Just tell me, for God's sake."

"It's not the Demon aka Billy Ray Barnes." Shanks could barely contain his emotions—a mixture of disappointment, sadness, and fury. "I'm sorry." Ben didn't speak. "His DNA didn't match . . ." An awkward pause. "What we found on your sister. Now it could be that he was working with some- one else with your sister—"

"Her name is Ellen, and that's ridiculous."

"Sorry. Of course her name is Ellen. And don't dismiss it so out of hand. We haven't even begun to scratch the surface with Billy Ray Barnes. It's still a possibility."

"He didn't kill Ellen," Ben told him. "What about Katie Doogan?"

Shanks groaned out loud. "What about her?"

"Did her name come up with the Albuquerque PD?"

"Of course her name came up."

"So, Albuquerque thinks that Billy Ray shithead murdered Katie Doogan?"

"Possibly, but without a body, we can't make any assumptions."

"I'll make an assumption. He didn't kill her either."

"Ben—"

"He didn't kill Katie and he didn't kill Ellen. But the same person who murdered Ellen also murdered Katie. I'm going on record, telling you this right now, right here, and I don't care what the Albuquerque PD or the FBI or the CIA or VICON or any other initialed suit has to say."

Shanks said, "I know that you're upset."

"I'm not upset. I'm just mad that I got sucked into believing what I knew wasn't true."

"There are differences," Shanks said. "Maybe I should have seen it coming. Ellen's case happened way farther north of where Barnes worked. So it makes sense that he didn't murd—"

"That's not what you said at the time, Sam."

"Ben—"

"You sat right there and I sat right here, where we are right now. And when the whole Demon/Billy Ray Barnes story broke, you told me that you and everyone else were ninety-nine percent sure that the Demon murdered Ellen, and I said to you, 'No, you're wrong,' and then you said to me, 'Ben, it looks like it's over.' And I said to you, 'I hope it's over, but I don't think it's over.' And then you said to me, 'Ben, there's no sense in prolonging this whole thing if it's over,' a statement that I found very offensive—"

"I apologize—"

"And then I told you I have no stake in being right or wrong. Just that I know what makes sense and what doesn't make sense. And this didn't make sense!"

"You know, Ben, I almost didn't tell you because I knew this was going to happen."

"What was going to happen?"

"That you would say 'I told you so,' and frankly I didn't want to hear it because now I still have a three-year-old open murder case that I'm absolutely sick about. So I apologize to you if I don't have time for your gloating."

"I'm not gloating! I wish to God I was wrong. But I knew I wasn't."

"Fine, Vicks. Go to the academy and I'll be the first one to recommend you for homicide detail. You're plainly smarter than anyone else on the force or in the state police."

"I'm gonna go home now."

"Sit." Shanks put his hand on the kid's arm. His eyes were wet. "I'm sorry, Ben. I'm sorry I can't do better. And I'm sorry I didn't do better. I meant it when I said you're smarter than me and everyone else. That's just a plain fact. No disrespect meant."

Ben looked away. "He didn't do Katie Doogan either."

"Let's look at it logically," Shanks said. "Unlike Ellen, Katie lived in Albuquerque. That was Barnes territory. APD has him on *four* murders down south."

"I don't care what other murders he did. He didn't kill Katie Doogan. And when they find the body, you'll see that I'm right."

"How can you be so *sure*?"

"Because Barnes's other victims were older women—"

"One was nineteen."

"My sister and Katie were sixteen. Besides, the nineteen-year-old was hooking. The Demon's victims were prostitutes or transients or women who were skunk-drunk and made terrible decisions. That wasn't my sister, that wasn't Katie."

"Psychos can be opportunistic—"

"Barnes worked at night, both Ellen and Katie were abducted during the day."

"Vicks—"

"And the way the other bodies were positioned . . . that wasn't my sister."

"Your sister wasn't staged."

"That's exactly it, Shanks. She wasn't staged. She was dumped in a grave, and a deep grave. Someone planned it out. It took a while to dig a hole that deep. It was not like the Demon, who really was opportunistic. None of the Demon girls were buried. They were dumped but not buried."

Ben stood and started pacing in the small office.

"I know not all killings by the same murderer are identical. Sometimes killers change depending on the situation. But Ellen's was clearly planned. Stalked. I just know it. I'm a math head, Shanks. I see patterns, and Ellen's didn't fit the Demon. Not to mention that physical resemblance between my sister and Katie—same age, same height, dark hair, dark complexion for Caucasians: Katie's Black Irish and Ellen had more Indian in her than either Haley or myself. And when you find Katie's body, you'll see I'm right."

"Sit down, Vicks, you're making me nervous." Ben stopped pacing and finally sat. Shanks said, "I'm listening very carefully to what you're saying. And like always, if you have any ideas, I'm open."

Ben threw back his head and exhaled. "God, I'm tired."

"I know you are."

Then he sat up. "Did you tell my parents yet?"

"My next phone call."

"It's going to be horrible at home. Reliving it all over."

Shanks softened his voice. "What can I do for you now, Vicks? Want to go out for coffee?"

"No." Ben looked up. "No, thanks . . . but if you want to do something for me, let me see the file."

"No."

"Why not? Because you're not feeling kindly toward me?"

"Vicks, c'mon. I see you more than I do my own daughters."

"Much to your chagrin."

"If I didn't like you, I'd tune you out. But I do like you. I'd adopt you if you didn't have two wonderful parents. I care about your welfare. Why do you keep torturing yourself?"

"It's what I need to do."

"What you need to do is be a teenager, Ben. Chase girls, drink vodka, smoke a little weed . . . God, I can't believe I'm saying this."

"I want to look at the file."

"Just sit back and close your eyes. I'm sure you know it by heart."

"I like to read it. I like to see the print because every time I see it, I see something different—not necessarily new but different. That's what I do. I'm relentless so you don't have to be."

"Now who's insulting who? You know Ellen has been my priority one since that day."

"You said I was gloating."

"You're right. That was terrible. I'm very sorry."

"And I'm sorry for maligning your diligence. But I still want to see the file."

The usual pause before Shanks would cave. He was, above

all, a good guy. He said, "I'll pull it, but first you need to get me some coffee."

"Done."

Shanks handed him two mugs. "Get yourself some coffee too. As long as you're going to hang around, we might as well make it official. Happy birthday."

Ben's birthday had been almost a month ago on July 31—same as Harry Potter. He had turned that nothing age of seventeen. Shanks had taken the time to remember. "Thank you." He managed a small smile. "Thanks a lot."

"Stop staring and get me coffee. I'm losing my caffeine high and you're making it worse. And make a fresh pot."

After being the errand boy, Ben was finally rewarded with his sister's files: boxes of them, well worn and dog-eared, his sister's homicide recorded in notes, pictures, and futility. There were some words that were always the hardest to digest: manually strangled and sexually assaulted.

His sister—his flesh and blood—broken down into organs, flesh, and bones by the autopsy report, the pictures taken postmortem. Snapshots were also taken at the grave although the body was unrecognizable as Ellen. In any big city, there would have been no way Ben could have gotten access to privileged material. But this was River Remez—a small town.

He read until his eyes gave out and it was clear that Shanks was waiting to go home. Slowly, he returned the files he had read back to the boxes. Shanks stowed them away and got up. "You need a lift?"

"I have my bike."

"I have a bike rack. It's getting dark."

"There's enough sunlight to get me home. But thanks." Ben paused. "Did you tell my parents?"

"I called your mom. You were too busy reading to notice that I left the room."

"That sounds like me." The two of them walked outside. The sun was still above the horizon, but not by much. Ben sighed. "Okay, then."

"Ben, I'd be happy to come over and talk to her in person."

"Don't put yourself through it. I know my mom. She'll just hole up in her bedroom."

"What about your sister?"

"I'll take care of her. She'll be functioning in a few days. I'll see you next time."

"What next time?"

"C'mon, Sam. You know me. Until he's caught, there is always a next time."

"Ben, you've got to stop."

"Is he gonna stop, Sam?" When Shanks didn't answer, Ben said, "I'll stop when you know without a doubt whatsoever that *he'll* stop. Until then, it's business as usual."

CHAPTER 3

USUALLY THE FAMILY ate at seven, but Ben knew that tonight would be different. Haley and Lilly were sitting at the dinner table. They had either finished the meal or hadn't even started. His sister was twirling strands of curly auburn hair with her forefinger.

"Did you ladies eat?" Ben asked.

It was Lilly who answered. "No."

"Where's Dad?"

"Working late," Haley said.

"Where's Mom?"

Haley pointed to the kitchen.

Mom was at the stovetop, stir-frying vegetables. Next to the stove were cubes of cooked cold chicken on a paper plate. She was wearing a black apron and an expression to match. Her graying brown hair was pinned back, and her face was bathed in steam.

Ben knew he had to say something. "I'm sorry, Mom."

She didn't answer.

"I know how hard this must be—"

"Ben . . ." She turned around and her eyes were dry. "I'm not feeling my best. Would you mind taking over?"

"Of course."

She put the pan down and retreated to the bedroom. His mom slept a lot. On weekends, it was rare to see her up before ten. He finished up cooking, added the chicken cubes, and then dumped the stir-fry onto three plates. Not very appetizing but it was hot and fresh. He took it back into the dining room with knives, forks, and napkins. Water was already at the table.

"Here we go."

All of them started nibbling, but no one was really eating. Haley continued to twirl her hair, her gold eyes focusing on a distant spot. Lilly, with her dark eyes and smooth mocha complexion, chewed the same bit of chicken for five minutes.

After a half hour, Ben said, "Well, I see how well my culinary skills went over. Anyone up for ice cream?"

Haley shook her head. Tears formed in her eyes. "Gonna take more than a sundae to make it go away." She got up and headed to her bedroom. Lilly looked in the direction of Haley's bedroom, then looked at Ben.

"Go, hon," he told her.

"You need help cleaning up?"

"I'm fine. Go."

Lilly got up and went to comfort her best friend. After the kitchen had been cleaned and everything had been put away, Ben went to his room and lay down in darkness. His head throbbed and his bones felt sore. He tried not to think, but the images came anyway and he was too tired to fight them. He fell asleep still in his clothes. His slumber was fitful. The next morning his head was on fire and his T-shirt was soaked in sweat. He stripped and showered, but still felt like garbage. He took three Advil, donned a clean shirt, a clean pair of jeans, and sneakers without holes. He needed a shave, but couldn't muster the energy.

Again, there were Lilly and Haley at the dining room table. Lilly had obviously slept over, probably because no one had offered to take her home. But she slept over a lot; the house was her second home.

"Hi, ladies." Ben looked around. "Where's Mom?"

"She's still sleeping." Haley regarded her brother. "You don't look well."

"It was a hard night."

"No, you really don't look well." She got up and felt her brother's forehead. "You're burning up for real. Go back to bed. I'll wake Mom up."

"Where's Dad?"

"He left early. He wasn't in a social mood."

Ben loved his parents dearly, but he didn't always respect them, both of them checking out when times got tough. They were needed now and they had become background noise.

"Mom will take us. Just take care of yourself."

His sister was right. He crawled back into bed.

His dreams were bathed in a fog of memories and delirium. Not Ellen this time, but Katie Doogan. The sixteen-year-old had disappeared three months before Ellen's body had been found, nine months after her abduction. He had thought that with his sister missing, he had hit the nadir of his existence.

He was wrong.

He had lived through the whole thing again, this time with enough knowledge to know what was in store for the family. His mother and father had fallen apart again, leaving Haley and him without supervision and guidance a second time.

In solidarity, Ben and his family attended the candlelight vigils during the first two weeks of Katie's disappearance. They dared not introduce themselves right away, lest they automatically link their current situation with Katie's family's. Because at first there is always that hope. But by the third vigil, it was clear that the Doogans knew who the Vicksburgs were. Margot came up to Ben's mother, Laura, and without speaking, the two of them hugged. Dad and Alan Doogan hugged as well. There were two other Doogan children: Bryan was seventeen and Kevin was thirteen. Eventually Ben noticed Bryan staring at him and nodded, thinking to himself: *Buddy, your hell is only beginning.*

At first, whenever Bryan was home from college, he and Ben searched together. Sometimes in the mountains. Sometimes on riverbanks. They went down south and hunted through the endless stretches of emptiness that encompass the flatlands of southern New Mexico. Their personalities were completely different. It was obvious that Bryan coped with his tension by talking compulsively. Ben remained quiet and methodical. The endless chatter became elevator music, something in the background that Ben ignored except for the occasional "yeah" or "uh-huh." The months of Katie's disappearance stretched to a year, and beyond.

Ben stayed in bed for two days running, thoughts weaving in and out of nightmares. By the third day, his fever had broken. He was weak but well enough to drag himself out of bed and into the world.

"Keep moving" was his motto. Otherwise, he'd curl up and die.

Arriving at school, he realized he hadn't done homework for three days. Not that it would affect his grades, but he hated being irresponsible even with an excuse. He opened his locker, took out his homework notebook, and frantically searched for past assignments. Nothing was written down. Normally that wasn't a problem because his memory would carry him along. But the last few days had thrown him off balance. He spotted Ro, who was in his lit class. She was talking to Chelsea and Shannon, the three of them gossiping like little magpies. Both Chelsea and Shannon were cute girls. Chelsea had curls, dimples, and a nice smile. Shannon was lithe and even-featured. But Ro was so damn polished-looking that she put them to shame. She also seemed perpetually cheerful. Somewhere in the back of his mind, he pegged her for a middle child.

Once he had been a middle child.

"Hey, Ro," Ben called out. The three girls turned around. "Do you have the lit homework?"

Her expression was one of surprise. "You mean the five-page essay comparing *A Tale of Two Cities* with Thomas Paine's 'Common Sense'?"

"Oh shit! That's right. Thanks."

"Where've you been?" she asked him.

"I had a bug, but I'm okay."

Chelsea said, "You didn't do the essay?"

"She assigned it to us the first day," Shannon said. "You know how Jackson is with essays."

Ro stepped in. "You want to see mine?"

"No, no. I read the material. In my feverish state, I forgot about the essay."

"I'm sure she'll give you an extra day."

"I hope she doesn't," Shannon said. "The curve will be better."

There was nothing to say to that. Ben walked away, figuring he'd knock the essay out during recess. When the morning bell rang for the break, he balled himself into a corner, flipped open his laptop, and wrote furiously. Fifteen minutes later, it was done—spell-checked, the grammar proper, and somewhat, if not entirely, cohesive in thought. He ran to the computer lab to print it out.

A minute before the bell rang, Ben sat down and plopped his essay on the desk for Jackson to collect. As Ro walked by, she picked up the paper without asking. She went through the first page and then looked up. "When did you write this?"

"During break."

She put down the assignment and went to her seat up front.

Class passed by slooooowly. Finally, it was lunch. Ben didn't hate school, but now that he was a senior, Remez High had nothing more to offer. He found an empty corner table, took out a book, and tried to zone out, getting his mind off school and death.

Ro came over. "Can I sit down?"

"Uh . . . sure." He knew his face was red. God, it was embarrassing . . . getting moony over someone else's girl. "Do you need something?"

She sat. "Your paper . . . or what I read of it . . . was pretty brilliant."

Ben laughed softly. "See, I have an unfair advantage over you. I've had Jackson before and I know how to write to her taste."

"It was a good paper, Vicks. Just say thank you. Did you make your important meeting?"

"Pardon?"

"A couple of days ago when I introduced myself. You said you had an important meeting with a mysterious someone." A pause. "Or was that just an excuse to end the conversation?"

"No, no. I did have a meeting."

"College interview or something?"

"Uh, no, nothing like that. Sure I can't do anything for you?"

"You can correct my math homework."

Aha. Finally, the real reason. "Sure. Let me see—"

"I'm kidding, Vicks." A brief smile. "I just came over to say hi. Although if you're dying to correct my homework—"

"Let's see it."

She rummaged through her backpack and handed him her homework. Ben said, "Number three and number twelve." He gave it back to her.

"Thanks." Awkward silence. Ro said, "Um, I've heard you don't do school spirit, but I'm throwing this out anyway. It would be nice if you came to the kickoff game."

Ben frowned. "Why?"

"Because it's important for the school to get a good turnout—" She stopped herself. "Actually, it's a personal invitation from JD. I'm coming as an emissary."

"Well, if I had the slightest notion to come, that just killed it."

"Look, Vicks. I know you guys aren't best friends, but he doesn't dislike you."

"Nor do I dislike him."

"He said thanks for the help. He made AP Calc. So he's asking you to come."

"No, *you're* asking me to come."

"He thinks I might hold more sway." When Ben didn't answer, she tried another tactic. "What about your sister? Correct me if I'm wrong, Vicks, but didn't she just start River Remez High?"

"How do you know my sister?"

"Don't be paranoid. She happens to be in my brother's class. He said she was real friendly. In my mind, that immediately put her at odds with you. Just because you're a wet blanket doesn't mean you can't do something nice for her."

"You really know how to charm a guy."

"My charm would be lost on you." Ro was begging. "Come to the game. It'll be fun."

"It won't be fun, but . . ." He paused. "I suppose it wouldn't kill me to take Haley. That means I also have to take Lilly—that's her best friend."

"Best friends are important." She gently slugged his shoulder. "C'mon! Get yourself out of your comfort zone."

"My comfort zone doesn't exist." Ben frowned again. "If I do come and if I have a rotten time—as I suspect I will—you will have to shoulder the blame."

"Okay with me. I have strong shoulders, Vicks." She smiled. "You know, making that pyramid with the girls and everything."

"You made cheerleader?"

"I made the first cut. I realize it's probably a little lowbrow for your taste, but superficialities are important to me." When he laughed, Ro said, "I'm serious. If I played myself in a movie, I'd hate me. I'm really not a mean girl, but I am kinda shallow."

"You can't be shallow if you admit you're shallow. That shows depth."

"You're adding attributes where there are none. That's why JD and I are so well matched . . . that and we're possibly the most gorgeous people on earth."

"One of you is."

She didn't even blush. She stood up. "If you come and if I make cheerleader, you can look up my dress when I cartwheel."

Ben burst into laughter. "Who *are* you?"

"I know what guys are thinking. I'm just out with it." She gave him the stink eye. "C'mon. It won't kill you to go just this once."

"I will give the idea, although initially abhorrent, some thought."

"Do that. Get your mind off elevated thoughts and put it in the gutter where it belongs."

CHAPTER 4

I F BEN HAD read the files a hundred times, Shanks had read them a thousand. Even now, after it had been confirmed that Ellen Vicksburg's body had no traces of the Demon's DNA on it, Shanks couldn't shake the feeling that he'd missed something—more like years of missing something. One goddamn homicide in ten years and Shanks was as impotent as a capon.

The kid kept harping on Katie Doogan. Maybe it was time for Shanks to take a second look at that case. He was about to pick up the phone to call down to Albuquerque when the kid decided to make an appearance. Ben was standing at the open door. "Need some coffee?"

Shanks handed the teen two mugs—his mug and the kid's birthday present. While Ben was gone, Shanks looked over the cases on his desk. There were plenty of burglaries to justify his salary. Two fresh ones: a break-in at the liquor store and a break-in at the discount electronics store. Both places had video surveillance. Shanks had caught a break.

The kid came back ten minutes later with two fresh cups. Shanks said, "What took you so long?"

"Got roped into being the coffee boy for the squad room." Ben sat down. "At least I'm good for something."

"You've lost weight."

"I've been sick."

"You need some calories." The kid was reed thin. Shanks checked his watch. It was almost five. "What are you doing for dinner?"

"Thanks, but I have to go home."

"Understood. How are your parents?"

"Coping." Ben sipped his coffee. "I was kinda a jerk to you a few days ago."

"You were kinda under stress. I meant it when I said you're smarter than anyone else." When the kid didn't answer, Shanks leaned forward. "Vicks, tell me—in your opinion—what am I missing?"

The boy looked at him. "I was going to ask you the same question."

"Okay." Shanks closed his burglary files and took out a notepad. "If Ellen's murder was a stranger one-off, I'm never going to solve anything. He kills, he's done, and he's gone. If it's a serial killing, we're both overlooking someone. You lived with your sister. You were there, bud. Anyone tweak your antenna?"

"No one you haven't talked to."

"What about Timmy—the boy who had a crush on Ellen? Do we know what he's up to?"

"He's a student at Missoula. He was in Montana when Katie Doogan was abducted."

"You're sure about that?"

"Yes. I checked."

"And you don't like any of Ellen's friends for suspects?"

"No."

"What about your friends?"

"I don't have friends."

"You did back then. Kind of protective of them, as I recall. Maybe now that you have some distance, you might feel differently."

"It wasn't any of them. Besides, didn't you get DNA off them?"

"No. They were minors. State labs are always backed up, and I would have needed a good reason to process their DNA. Do you think I should reinterview any of them?"

"None of them did it. I'm positive."

"Do you think it was a stranger abduction?"

"Yes."

"And this same guy abducted Katie Doogan?"

"Most likely, yes. Things match: the age, the physical similarity, the way they were abducted. This guy knew what he was doing, at least with Ellen. Like I said a million times before, a grave that deep takes time to dig. If it's the same guy, Katie's body is going to be found in a deep grave near water."

"So we're back to a serial killer."

"Yeah." Ben was quiet.

Shanks said, "What's on your mind, Vicks?"

The kid sighed. "I blew it, Sam. I really did miss something. It came to me in a dream. I feel like an idiot."

"If you missed it, I missed it too, which makes me a double idiot." Sam sipped coffee. "Tell me."

"Ellen was abducted on June twenty-second. That's a day away from the summer solstice."

Shanks stared at him for a moment. "You're right. Katie Doogan was abducted in the wintertime. There was snow on the ground."

"Up here in the mountains there was snow on the ground, but not in Albuquerque. According to the calendar, it was spring. Near the vernal equinox—March twenty-first. The summer solstice is usually on June twentieth or the twenty-first. Me, being a stickler for dates, didn't even think about those dates. Then I read the chart and we talked about Katie Doogan and I thought a little bit more. And then it hit me."

Shanks buried his head in his hands. "I'll check it out. See if we have other homicides that take place on these . . . earth days." A sigh. "Trouble is we might pull up quite a few incidents on those days, Ben. The dates are ripe for satanic rituals."

"Right." The kid threw his head back. "I didn't think of that."

"So . . . what do you think about the murder being done by a satanic cult?"

"If it was a cult, it wasn't your typical teenage satanic ritual. My sister's grave was way too neat and organized for a bunch of tweaking adolescents. But that doesn't change what I told you. I think the murderer liked those dates—earth days as you call them."

Shanks nodded. "I'll post a bulletin and send it out to other police departments. See if anything comes in."

"Thank you."

Shanks eyed him suspiciously. "Do you have anything else to tell me?"

"No," Ben said. Too quickly. "If I come up with anything else that looks good, I'll let you know."

"What do you mean if you come up with anything else?"

The kid stood up. "I don't want to waste your time. I tell you things I think are important. Thanks for taking me seriously."

"Ben, I always take you seriously."

"I aggravate you."

"And that's proof that I take you seriously. It would be much easier if I could blow you off." Shanks eyed him. "Where are you going next year?"

"Going?"

"For college?"

"Oh. Probably UNM. Maybe St. John's."

"The college where you read the classics?"

"I do know how to read."

"Don't you have, like, a perfect grade point average? Why aren't you thinking about other schools like the big ones?"

"Not interested."

"Ben, it's a big world. Experience it. If you don't like what you see, you can always come back."

He stood up. "I'd better get going."

Shanks stood as well. "Eat something."

"Going home for dinner right now."

When the teen held out his hand, Shanks drew him into a bear hug. The kid resisted, and then melted. "Keep that great brain working in fine order, okay?"

"Sometimes I wish I could turn it off," Ben told him.

"It can be done, kiddo. That's why God invented streaming."

AT DINNER THAT night, Ben witnessed a cheerless meal for the thousandth time. He could set his watch to it: twenty minutes for gulping down the food that no one really tasted. Though Mom always offered, no one ever wanted dessert. Afterward everyone retreated to their own private spaces. After he polished off his homework, Ben began his real work in earnest—checking the current police cases, specifically homicide cases, that were available online. He'd enter in facts and figures, trying to make sense out of meaningless deaths. Sometimes he was able to hack into actual files, sorting through postmortem photographs, witnessing gray faces and expressionless eyes. That he missed those earth dates, as Shanks had called them, for so long ate at him like battery acid. It gave him a little insight into the frustrations of a detective.

At around eleven, Ben closed his laptop. He had no desire to go to a high school football game, but there were other people in his life. He went to Haley's room and knocked on the door.

"It's open."

Haley was on the computer. She looked so young and vulnerable, wearing Santa Claus pajamas and with fuzzy slippers on her feet. She had pulled her curls into a ponytail. Ben said, "What are you looking at?"

"Milquetoast is coming to Sandia in February. Tickets go on sale Friday at midnight."

"Do tell." Silence. Ben said, "If you bag them, would you like a ride?"

"Yes." Haley jumped up and kissed his cheek. "Can you take—"

"Yes, I can take Lilly too."

"You're the best."

"Nonsense. I am nothing but an Uber, but that's what big brothers do." He paused. "Speaking about big brothers, would you like me to take you and Lilly to the kickoff game on Friday?"

"O! M! G! That would be amazing! I wanted to go but was afraid to ask you because I know how you feel about football."

"Not all football, just high school football, specifically my high school."

"You're weird, but wonderful. Lilly was working up the courage to ask her mom if she could go. You know how protective her mom is. But if you go, she'll be cool with that. Just don't hang around once we get there."

"Okay, now I'm getting a little insulted."

She kissed his cheek. "I'm going to call Lilly now. You can leave. Thanks, Vicks."

"It's Ben."

"I know your name. No one calls you Ben. Why is that?"

"I really don't know. Lots of guys are called by their last name. I guess 'Vicksburg' is too long. 'Benjamin Vicksburg' is way too long. Every time I fill in my name for a standardized test, I run out of little boxes. Mom must have been on crack. I heard you made friends with the new kid."

"Where'd you hear that?"

"From the new girl, Ro. She's a friendly person like you are. What's the kid's name?"

"Griffen . . . he's actually okay."

"Cute?" When Haley didn't answer, Ben said, "His sister's cute."

"No, she's gorgeous. You two are friends, then?"

"Haley, I do not have friends. You know that."

"I know." A pause. "Don't you ever get lonely?"

"Sure, but lonely isn't the same as solitude." He looked at her cat clock with its swinging tail. "You should go to bed."

"I'm old enough to determine my bedtime."

"Yes, you are. But you're still too young to drive. In a few years, that'll all be gone and I'll no longer serve any purpose for you. I'll just be that weird math guy who lives in his head."

BEN WAS IN somewhat of a good mood, which, in and of itself, was unsettling. He walked up to Ro, who was at her locker, and tried out a smile. It was a strange sensation. "You talked me into it. I am bringing the girls to the kickoff game."

"Great." Her own smile was forced.

He said, "Or is that not a good idea?"

"No, it's great that you're coming."

She was clearly bothered. He said, "Are you pissed or something?"

"You're gonna think it's silly." Ben waited. She said, "They just posted the spots on cheerleading for this year. I made it. Varsity."

"Wow. I know that's fiercely competitive. Congratulations."

She said, "I didn't make captain."

"Okay." He shrugged. "Sorry."

"See, that's why I didn't want to tell you." She stomped off.

"What'd I . . . ?" He had to jog a few steps to catch up with her. "I said sorry."

"You think I'm acting like a spoiled brat." She stopped walking and clamped her fingers on to his arm. "Don't deny it. If you deny it, I'll know you're a first-class phony like I am and I'll never speak to you again."

"You're not a phony."

"Of course I'm a phony. I am the premier phony. I went up to Shannon and congratulated her like I was all excited and happy and all I could think was, How did this happen? I did, like, way better than she did." Her eyes welled up with tears.

Ben was stunned. Even living with Haley, he had absolutely no understanding of girls. "Jeez, Ro."

"See! That's the 'you're a spoiled brat' look. Don't deny it."

Again, she stomped off. Ben followed her. "It's just that you come in here like gangbusters, snagging the alpha dog. You make the varsity squad, which is unheard of for a newcomer. What I'm really thinking is, how about a little deference for the homegirls, you know?"

"I can't help the way I feel. Oh God, that's Shannon. Don't say anything."

"I'll catch up with you later," he said.

But again Ro grabbed his arm with a firm grip. "Hey, Shannon. Congrats."

"Thanks. Can I talk to you for a minute?"

"You can talk in front of Vicks. It's just Vicks."

"Plain old Vicks," he said.

Ro nudged him. "What is it?"

"I just don't want you to be upset."

"Me?" Ro pointed to herself. "Why would I be upset?"

"Because you were obviously better than I was and the only reason I made captain is because, like, I live here. I mean, you live here too, but you just came to the school. I got the spot because I . . . you know."

"You did great. You deserve it."

"No, I don't. I wasn't half as good as you. I do have eyes."

"Look, we're a team—"

"There's no 'I' in team," Ben said.

Ro elbowed him again. "C'mon. Stop talking nonsense. You deserve it, Shannon. Honestly."

"No, I don't. But thanks for saying that." She was still reticent. "So you don't think JD is mad?"

"No. Why should he be mad?"

"Because you're his girlfriend and all . . ."

Said wistfully, Ben noted. Shannon used to be JD's girl-friend. When Ro came, she was relegated to Ron Weekly—a first-class jerk—and the number two spot. But if she harbored any ill will toward Ro, she was masking it well.

Ro said, "I'm sure JD doesn't care at all."

"Okay. Good." Shannon smiled. "Practice every day after school. We've got four days before Friday's game."

"I'll be there." Ro saluted. "I've got a few things to work out with Vicks. See ya."

"See ya." Shannon cartwheeled down the hallway then jogged away.

Ro zeroed in on Ben. "Don't say anything, okay. Just listen. I know what I am. I'm competitive, but I also want to be popular. Why is that important to me? I have no idea, but it is. I'm a mass of insecurities."

Ben started to say something, but instead just laughed. "You're nothing if not honest."

She shrugged. "I like talking to you."

"That won't get you far in the popularity department."

"You know, I've got everyone's ear here. You're not as low down on the food chain as you'd like to play yourself."

"I'm not a freak, if that's what you're getting at."

"Well, kind of a freak. You're not on Facebook or Insta-gram or Reddit."

"You looked me up?"

"I wanted to friend you."

"Yeah . . . I don't do social media."

"You're so busy that you don't have a minute to catch up with friends?"

He smiled, but said nothing, thinking to himself: *What friends?*

She smiled back. "Want to watch me at practice after school?"

"I can't. I have to take Haley and Lilly to Santa Clara Pueblo today. It's Lilly's grandfather's birthday and there's a big communal celebration."

"Lilly's Native American? She looks Chinese."

"She is half Chinese, half Santa Clara. Both of her parents are senior scientists and work at Los Alamos. The Tafoyas live in River Remez, but Dr. Tafoya has an ancestral home there. I mean, the homes aren't ancestral but the land is. You can come if you want . . . to the celebration. It should still be going on way after practice."

"Where is the Santa Clara pueblo?"

"Thirty-eight miles from here. I could come and pick you up. I think I'm taking your little brother too. Haley said something about a new boy wanting to see it when Lilly told him about her family and the pueblo. Griffith?"

"Griffen. Yes, that's my brother. I don't think I'm going to be done with practice until like eight or nine."

"Up to you. Give me a call if you change your mind."

"I don't have your phone number."

"That can be remedied." Ben gave her the number. "I might actually rack up minutes on my calling plan if you decide to use it."

Ro smiled at him. "Did you ever read *Winnie-the-Pooh*?"

"Eeyore, right?"

"Absolutely. Like you, there's something adorable about his gloominess. I think underneath that morose façade is—"

"Someone very depressed?"

She laughed. Then she smiled and waved good-bye. For a brief moment he really wished he could come to her practice. He would have loved to look up her dress. But once he got up there, he wouldn't have a clue about what to do.

CHAPTER 5

THERE WAS NO direct way to get to the Santa Clara pueblo from River Remez. Ben decided that rather than take the roads—most of them rutted pathways of dirt and gravel and mud after the recent rains—he'd take the highway, which meant backtracking into town. That was okay. Lilly and Haley and their new friend, Griffen, wanted to shop for groceries for the party.

Ben liked the kid. If Ro was superficial, Griffen was plainspoken. He liked hiking and skateboarding and was always moving. He reminded Ben of himself, a glimpse into what he might have been had Ellen not been murdered.

After the three of them returned with a cart full of groceries, Ben slipped onto the 285/84, where the ride to Santa Clara was a straight shot until Española. Within a minute, the land spread out into miles of wilderness, the blacktop cutting through rock and mesas, formed of ancient earth and ritual.

They were heading west into a strong sun with a very strong glare.

Exits from the highway were miles apart: the Santa Fe Opera, the Tesuque pueblo, Camel Rock—where Griffen noted that the rock formation really did look like a Bactrian animal—until the highway slowed at Buffalo Thunder, a monolith of hotel and casino and water-drinking golf courses. The drive through Española was backed up with traffic. The city was a mixture of ethnicities and sat between two counties: its own county and Santa Fe. Whereas the city of Santa Fe had a stable population of sixty thousand—it could swell to over a hundred thousand during the tourist season—Española was three times as large. It had the regular businesses: fast food, movie theaters, family-style restaurants, a bowling alley, garages, drugstores, tattoo parlors, and the ever-present Dairy Queens.

At I-30, Ben went west, passing San Ildefonso and on into Santa Clara. Abutting one another, the two pueblos had much in common, from a tradition of pottery making to language. Over the years and through his grandmother, Ben had learned a few words of Tewa. At some point—long, long ago—he had meant to learn more, but other things got in the way.

Santa Clara was a large pueblo. Lots of its land was dry and dusty, but the acreage also included miles of piñon forest. The place was not Ben's home but he felt at home there. He parked in an unpaved area and everyone got out of the car, carrying grocery bags into the small adobe house. A mutt the size of a German shepherd came out to greet them, its tail wagging like a windshield wiper.

"Hey, Baker," Haley said.

The dog ran back and forth with each trip to and from

the car. Once everyone was inside, Griffen and Haley helped
Lilly's grandmother, Grace, put away the groceries and set up
for the meal. Lilly had disappeared into one of the three back
bedrooms. Although the Tafoyas were a well-known pottery-
making family, Lilly had always directed her artistic bent toward jewelry.

Grace was in her sixties, elegantly dressed in black slacks
and a silk tunic. She had a round face with skin stretched over
pronounced cheekbones. Her eyes were black, her hair was
coiffed and gray, and she smiled with ivory-colored teeth.
"Thanks for bringing the girls . . ." She looked at their male
companion. "The kids."

The teen stuck out his hand. "Griffen Majors."

"Pleased to meet you, Griffen."

"I like your house. Lilly said you made all the pots."

"Me and members of my family."

"Cool."

Ben said, "Something smells good and I'm hungry. What
time is the shindig?"

"Seven thirty."

"I'm gonna say hello to Henry but I'll be back." He heard
Lilly call his name from the back bedroom. "I'm coming." He
looked at Grace. "You need anything?"

"No, I'm fine. Not that Papa Joe will appreciate any of this.
And tell Henry he's welcome as long as he behaves himself."

The teen laughed and went to see what Lilly wanted. She was
hunched over a table, her fingers already blackened by silver
polish. She showed him a bolo tie clip. "What do you think?"

"It's gorgeous." He turned it over in his hands. "Finished
on both sides. I love your stonework, Lilly. You keep getting
better and better."

Lilly smiled. "Papa Joe wears bolo ties and loves stones."

"It's perfect. I know Joe's a grumpy guy, but if he doesn't love it, there is no hope for him."

She smiled. "You're gonna stick around for the party, right?"

"Are you planning on thumbing a ride home?" When she blushed, Ben said, "Of course I'm sticking around. I'm just going to say hello to Henry."

"Make sure he doesn't get you drunk."

"Heaven forbid. I'm driving."

He was leaving when Lilly said, "Ben?"

"Yeah, hon?"

"I hate to bother you but I need help with math."

"*You* need help? There's a first. What is it?"

She showed him her book and pointed to the troubling problem. "We're supposed to calculate the area of all of these figures. It's eighteen that I'm stuck on."

Eighteen was a figure that looked like a cloud with a point. He said, "Let me see what you've done so far." She showed him a blank piece of paper with her name, the date, and the class assignment on it. "You haven't done any work. There's nothing on the paper."

"I've done them in my head. Except eighteen. I can't visualize it. I keep visualizing shapes but there's always leftover area that I can't break down into simple polygons."

"You're looking at geometric shapes. Think of other shapes."

"Like what?"

"Ice cream cones?"

She stared at the picture, then she hit her head. "Each cone sharing an edge with the bottom and the common point."

"That'll work." Ben smiled. "Is that how you always solve problems—in your head?"

"Yep. Is that weird?"

"No, it's very scientific actually. Especially in physics. It helps to have a visual before you apply the actual numbers. I do it all the time." Ben patted her back. "We geniuses think alike."

She blushed and went back to her bolo. "Thanks so much."

"You're welcome." Ben pointed to the bolo. "And I mean it. If Joe doesn't want it, I'll take it."

"I can make one for you, you know."

Her eyes were filled with expectation. Ben graced her with a gentle smile. Lilly's siblings were a generation older than she was because her father had been married before. For the last four years, Ben had become her surrogate big brother. He had taught the two girls how to ride a bike, how to swim, how to read a compass, how to follow tracks in the mountains, how to skateboard. But puberty did what puberty does, and for the last few months, Lilly had become shier with him. He still viewed her as a little girl, of course, and he was careful not to give her the wrong impression.

Rather than answer yes or no, he said, "I'll see you later, hon."

Lilly's face fell, but she masked her embarrassment by working on the bolo clip. Ben wondered if he should say something, but he'd only open up another can of worms. Right now, he had enough worms to start a tackle and bait shop.

HENRY NARANJO WAS a third or fourth cousin. Ben forgot the specific details, not that it mattered. Everyone was related distantly or otherwise in the pueblo. Henry's studio was in the back section of the plaza, a dim, yellow light on over the door. He drank like a fish, smoked foul-smelling cigars, drove a souped-up BMW, and had had his license suspended twice for speeding. He'd been married twice with two kids and had remained on decent terms with both women. He was as American as they come, serving in the marines for two tours, but he wasn't beyond doing the Indian thing if it meant showing customers that he was authentic. He wore a beaded headband and his black hair was braided and fell down his back. He was seated at his worktable, shoulders hunched over, squinting in the electric lighting, working on a red clay bowl. Henry, like a lot of Indian potters, worked freehand, considering it cheating to use a wheel. Music was blasting as loud as the volume button would allow. Ben turned it down and Henry looked up.

"Someone has to take care of your eardrums."

"Sit down, Vicks." Henry tossed him a glob of adobe clay. "Do something with those hands instead of jerking off."

The blob was wet and sticky, oozing red all over his hands. "I have no talent for this kind of thing."

"It's practice."

"You say that every time, and every time, I suck. It'd be like me giving you a problem in topology."

"Just go with your heart, Vicks. Squeeze it, shape it, mold it . . . feel the energy." A pause. "Have you gotten laid yet?"

"Grace wants to know if you're coming tonight."

"Of course." Henry took a peek at Ben's work-in-progress. "Looks like a turd."

Ben rolled his eyes, threw the glob at him, and washed his hands. He checked his cell. Plenty of bars for reception but no calls. "How've you been?"

"Got a few commissions from Indian Market."

"That's good."

"I'm not complaining," Henry said. "Who's calling you? Or not calling you. You keep checking your phone."

"No one important." Ben stowed the phone in his pocket.

"You still bugging that poor detective?"

"Always."

"How's the college search coming?"

He was taken aback. "What?"

"George Tafoya says you should make something of yourself."

"Of course I'm going to make *something* of myself. I'm going to college."

"Where?"

"Henry, why do you give a shit?"

"I told George I'd talk to you. He thinks you should go to Caltech or MIT. You should listen to him. Get out of here, Vicks."

"Who'd watch over you if I did?" Ben turned to him. "So you talked to me. Now you can shut up."

"Don't get pissed. River Remez is a small town in a small state. People think you're destined for bigger things. It's a compliment, idiot." When Ben didn't answer, Henry said, "So you're scared?"

"I'm not scar—stop talking, okay. You're pissing me off."

"Maybe." He pointed a red-clay-covered finger at Ben. "But I am telling you the truth here."

"You never left here for the big city."

"I make pots, Vicks. I live here because this is the capital of pottery making. I don't do nuclear physics." A pause. "Is it because of Haley? You overprotect that girl. She doesn't need your help."

"I know that. I'm not staying for Haley. I'm staying for myself. I like it here."

"You're looking at your phone again."

Ben hadn't realized he had taken it from his pocket. He put it away again. "I'm gonna go see if Grace needs help. She says you can come if you behave yourself."

Henry smiled. "I'll behave myself. I'd do anything for her pozole."

AS THE CAR pulled up to the curb, the porch light went on. Ro came out a moment later, bounding down the walkway to the car. She opened the door for Griffen. She put her arm around her brother. "Was it fun?"

"Super, superneat. Lilly's grandfather showed me all his costumes. Some were like a hundred years old."

"Wow. Are you hungry?"

"Are you kidding? I'm stuffed. They make a lot of stuff with beans. I'm gonna be dangerous tonight."

In the backseat, the two little girls cracked up.

Ro stuck her head inside the car. "Anyone want to come in?"

Ben declined for the trio. "I'm a little tired. Besides, I promised Lilly's mother I'd take her directly home. How'd practice go?"

"It went well. I just got home twenty minutes ago."

"Well, I'll see if your hard work paid off at the kickoff game."

"You're still coming?"

"I told you I would. I keep my promises."

She said, "I'm sorry I couldn't make it tonight. I was disappointed actually."

"It was really nice." Ben tried to act casual, but the melancholia was obvious.

Ro said to the girls, "He told me that he'd take the two of you to the game. Make sure he doesn't renege."

"We'll be there, Ro. Good night."

"Good night." Ro rubbed her arms, but didn't shut the door. "See you in class, Vicks?"

Ben leaned over and took the door handle. "Sure." He waited until she stepped back before he shut the door. He wasn't mad or even disappointed. It was just the way of the world.

Sometimes you lose and sometimes you lose.

CHAPTER 6

IT WAS FOGGY and wet, but under JD's guidance, Remez was smearing the competition 28–0 at the end of the third quarter. Ben sat off to the side, away and alone, wondering why he came where he neither fit in nor wanted to fit in. People kept telling him he was allowed to have fun. Trouble was he'd forgotten what fun was. He used to like skating and snowboarding, but after Ellen died, that all went to hell.

The crowd began to roar again. JD had just made a brilliant pass to Mark Salinez, who timed it perfectly. Ballet for jocks, but it was pretty impressive. Ben looked away from the field and saw that Lilly was coming toward him, her stick legs climbing each tier until she got to the top. Impending womanhood was years off with her. Haley already had a few feminine curves, and he wondered if it was a sore spot between them. Lilly had chosen to don school colors in a show of solidarity:

a red T-shirt, gold scarf, and jeans. High-tops on her feet. "I brought you a hot dog and a Coke."

"Thanks." Ben took a bite. "I'm actually hungry."

"Mind if I sit down or are you solving the world's energy crises in your head?"

"Have a seat. How are you?"

"Good. It's a good game. Thanks for taking me, even though you had no choice. Where Haley goes, so do I. And now it's also Griffen."

"Yeah, I've taken to calling you yin, yang, and yang."

"More like yin, yang, dot, dot, dot, and yang."

"Ah . . ."

"It's cool," Lilly said.

But clearly it wasn't. Ben said, "Lilly, boys come and boys go, but a best friend is forever."

Her eyes were far away. "I don't begrudge either of them, you know. I think they're perfect for each other."

"They're fourteen."

"You can fall in love at any age."

"You can fall in love, yes, but maybe not stay in love."

Lilly was still unconvinced. "I just wanted to give them some privacy. That's why I'm interrupting yours. Why don't you sit with the rest of us, Ben?"

"Lilly, I'm not a huge football fan probably because I'm jealous of the guys who play and get the attention. I'd rather sit alone because it's less noisy, and every once in a while, I can look up at the stars. They put on an even better show than JD."

She smiled. "You're such a dreamer."

"I'm a loner," he corrected. "A lone wolf."

Haley was bounding up the steps. To Lilly she said, "Where'd you go?"

"I'm right here."

"Come back. Just because he doesn't want to be part of it doesn't mean we can't have fun."

"I thought you told me not to stick around," Ben said.

"I don't want you hovering around me, but you don't have to alienate yourself." Haley paused. "I talked to Ro at half-time. She's going to show me some moves so I can try out for cheerleading next year. She also invited us to pizza with a few of the players after the game."

Ben was suddenly at attention. "Uh-uh. No way."

"Ben!"

"You know what pizza after the game is, Haley? They go out to Ochoa parklands and get drunk and smoke weed. Sometimes they throw up in the trash cans. Not my idea of a good time, and it better not be your idea either."

"Please?"

"Mom would kill me. Beer is bad enough, but Weekly's a pothead. No."

"Mom's not here. Please? Ro asked us to come."

"Fine. Go with Ro and be her responsibility. I'm not having any part of this."

Haley made a big point of sighing. "You'll come with us?" she asked Lilly.

"Not without Ben. I don't trust those guys."

"You show solid judgment," he said.

"Please, Ben? Just this once?"

"Why are you always asking me to do stuff I don't agree with?"

"Why don't you ever do stuff that's fun?"

"Getting stoned is stupid, not fun." She didn't answer and he was torn. Go and have a rotten time or leave Haley to her own defenses?

"Just this once?" Haley pleaded. "It'll give me status with my classmates. I promise I'll never ask you again."

She was Ro in miniature. Ben shook his head. "This is a mistake, but I'll do it this one time and only for a few minutes. That's the deal. If you complain, the answer will be no."

She kissed his cheek. "You're the best." She grabbed Lilly's hand. "Come on! We're going to miss the fourth quarter."

Lilly turned and waved good-bye. He didn't bother waving back. The night had been a bust and he just knew it was only going to get worse.

A FEW MINUTES turned into an hour. Ben sat in the darkness watching Ro sip her second beer while Griffen looked on in a little discomfort. JD was on his fourth bottle, but he was a big guy and always handled his booze well. Mark Salinez was also good-sized. He could down a six-pack with little effect. Shannon had chosen to remain dry while Chelsea had been nursing a single bottle for over an hour.

It was Ron Weekly who was plastered. Weekly had one of those kinds of cute faces that girls went gaga over, the kind of looks that would turn womanish in his fifties. He was smaller than Manny and JD, but wiry and scrappy. Weekly was also not very good at holding his hooch and, of course, was drinking more than anyone else.

The park was black, the sole illumination coming from a couple of flashlights. Manny had brought along a CB radio, and whenever a cop was in the vicinity, the lights went out and people hid behind the trash cans.

Ben kept checking his watch. He had promised that he'd have the girls at home by eleven, which meant around thirty more torturous minutes.

Weekly pulled out a joint. "Anyone interested?"

Chelsea raised her hand. "Less calories than booze." Shannon laughed a little too loud, then laid her head on Weekly's shoulder. He brushed her off as he lit up. He passed the joint around and JD took a hit. He passed it to Ro. She locked eyes with Ben and then inhaled deeply. By the time the joint came to Haley, Ben's eyes were daggers.

Haley dutifully passed it to Lilly, who passed it to Griffen, who passed it back to JD, who took another hit.

"Someone call the doctor," Salinez told JD. "'Cause tonight you gave me one sick pass."

"Call the ambulance," JD said. "A real sick pass for a real sick catch." Another hit, then JD downed a wedge of pizza, washing the whole thing down with a beer. "But in all fairness, we could have mowed them down with a rolling pin. They were pussies."

"Yeah, they really sucked." Weekly took a hit. "Sucked the big one." He grabbed his crotch and laughed.

Ben said to Haley, "Ready to go?"

"Few more minutes," Ro told him. "She's my bud." She put her arm around Haley. "My little bud."

"It's a weekend, bro," JD said. "What's the hurry, Vicks?"

Weekly said, "Where's the fucking john? I need to take a wicked piss."

"Locked up at this time of night," JD said. "Just use the bushes."

"Gross," Shannon said.

"Hey," Weekly said. "I'm marking my territory, dude. Just

like the ca-yotes." He howled and broke up at humor no one else saw as funny. After he urinated behind a trash can, he stumbled back into the crowd, tripping over Haley. He prevented himself from falling flat-faced into the dirt by catching himself with the palms of his hands.

Haley stood up. "Are you okay?"

Weekly went over to her, picked up her hand, and kissed it. "I am fine, my fair maiden."

Ben was on high alert. *Drop her hand, asshole.* Instead Weekly kissed it again. "How does such a douche like Vicks have such a charming, lovely sister?"

With Weekly still holding her hand, Haley began to squirm. Ben stood up. "Take your hands off her."

Weekly turned, grinned, and threw his arm around Haley's shoulder. "If she doesn't like it, let her say something, asshole."

Haley blushed and tried to move away, but Weekly had a good grip on her shoulder. Ben went nose to nose with him. "Take your goddamn hands off my sister." A hard shove. "Now!"

Lilly gasped and Haley's eyes got wide. Weekly recovered and shoved Ben back, his arm making a swing toward his face.

He ducked, but the asshole still clipped him on his cheek. Ben, being quicker and sober, kneed Weekly where it hurt. As Weekly doubled over in pain, Ben grabbed his jacket lapels and threw him into the trash cans. In the background, some of the girls were screaming. Shannon had rushed over to Weekly while Ro was screaming to stop. It was JD who ran interference, something he was good at on and off the field. He towered over Ben by a good four inches and fifty pounds. "Go home, Vicks."

Ben locked eyes with Ro. *Say something!*

Silence.

He backed away and grabbed Haley's hand. "Don't worry. We're out of here!"

Weekly had gotten back on his feet, but was still woozy. "Don't fucking come back!" he slurred out.

"Shut the fuck up, Weekly," JD told him.

Lilly and Griffen exchanged glances and left to catch up with Haley and Ben.

Ro shouted out, "Where are you going, Griffen?"

"I came with him, not you."

"Griff?"

But the boy was already at the car. As soon as Ben took off, Haley lit into him. "I could have handled myself."

"Yeah, I saw how well you did that."

"I coulda done it if you hadn't butted in. Why did you do that?"

"'Cause he was drunk and he was pawing you and you're too stupid to see it."

"He wasn't pawing me and you're too stupid to trust me."

"Haley, shut up and let me drive before I have an accident. I can't see too well, okay?"

Lilly said, "How's your eye?"

"It hurts."

The rest of the ride was silent. When they got home, Haley stormed away. Still in pain, Ben waited a few seconds to get his composure back. He went inside the house. Mom took one look at him and her eyes got very wide. "What in the world happened?"

Haley said, "What happened is my brother is an idiot!" She stalked off to her room.

"Oh my God!" Mom exclaimed.

His father said, "Laura, go get an ice pack."

Mom hurried into the kitchen. Lilly looked at Griffen. No one moved.

Ben said, "I'm all right. C'mon, guys, let me take you home before it swells shut."

Laura came back with a bag of ice. "Benjamin, what happened?"

"Little difference of opinion. No big whoop."

"You got into a fight?" Dad was incredulous. "You?"

"With who?" Mom turned to Dad. "Hold this under his eye, William. I'm going to get some Advil."

Dad did as instructed. "Who punched you?"

Ben took the ice pack from his father. "It's not important."

"Ron Weekly," Griffen said. "He was acting like an idiot."

"Ron has always been an idiot," William said. "Why were you fighting with him?"

"He was goading Ben by disrespecting Haley," Lilly said.

Dad whipped around. "What'd he do to my daughter?"

"Nothing, honestly," Ben blurted out. "It's not important."

"He *punched* you?" Dad was furious. "I'll kill him."

"I overreacted." Ben stared at Lilly and Griffen with one eye. "Sorry if I embarrassed you guys."

"If you had gotten clobbered, it would have been embarrassing," Lilly said. "But you left on a high note."

Griffen grinned. "Man, you shoulda seen the look on Weekly's face when you threw him halfway across the field."

"What?" Ben's mother said.

"You really clocked him!" Griffen said. "It was cool!"

"It's nothing, Mom. It's just part of being a guy."

Griffen said, "Man, that was supercool! I'm glad you

decked Weekly." Anger had seeped into his voice. "He's a real asshole." The kid looked at the adults. "Sorry."

"He is an asshole," Dad said.

Ben adjusted the ice pack. "C'mon, kids. Let's get home. It's late."

"You aren't going anywhere." Dad stood up. "I'll take them home. And if that jerk ever touches you again, I will sue his family until they're begging for mercy."

Ben smiled. That's how lawyers attacked. They sued.

Laura said, "Is this going to come back to bite you, Ben?"

"Nah, it was off campus. But even if it were on campus, no one's gonna say anything. It's just guys being guys."

"Especially because Weekly was drunk."

"You took Haley to where there was alcohol?" Mom was aghast.

Lilly said, "If Ben didn't go, she would have gone with Griff's sister. I told her she was being stupid, but who listens to me?"

"It's true," Griffen said. "Ben had to go to keep a watch over Haley."

"He should have brought her home and let me deal with her anger," Mom announced. "I am going to talk to that girl right now!"

Ben held her arm. "You don't need her crap. Let me handle it."

"I'm her mother!" Then she deflated. "I am so tired of all this!"

"C'mon, Mom. It doesn't happen very often. You relax and let her yell at me."

"He's right," Dad told her. "Don't stress. If she starts screaming at you, you'll get upset."

"I'm already upset."

"It's late, Mom. I have to talk to Haley anyway. She's furious at me."

"Why is she so mad at you for defending her?"

"Because at the moment she thinks I'm ruining her life."

"Oh, for God's sakes!" His mom's eyes were wet. "You think that after all that has happened, at least we could all get along."

"We do get along. This is normal stuff. And unlike the real problems, this will pass." Ben readjusted his ice pack. "Go rest, okay?"

Defeated, she retreated to the bedroom and slammed the door. After his father left with Lilly and Griffen, Ben knocked on Haley's door.

"Go away."

"Open up the door or I'll pick the lock." A moment later the lock sprang back and Ben walked inside. Haley's face was full of utter contempt. "You had to pick on the most popular boy in school."

"Second most popular. JD is number one."

"Well, he's a lot cuter than JD. I hate you."

"Haley, he was disrespecting you."

"If he's disrespecting me, let me handle it. Not you. Me!" She threw a pillow at Ben. "Now I'm gonna get tortured by everyone and it's all your fault! It's bad enough you're a geek. Why do you have to bring me down to your level?"

"I may be a geek, but Weekly's an asshole."

"It's my life, Ben. Just butt out."

"I know Weekly much better than you do. He's an ass. Most boys are asses."

"You're an ass."

"I'm an ass but I love you."

She threw another pillow at him. "God, how am I going to show my face on Monday?"

"I promise I'll keep a low profile, all right?"

"Too late for that." Her fists were balled up in fury. "God, why did Ellen have to die?"

Her words hit him like a wrecking ball. Even if he had a comeback, his voice would have stuck in his throat.

In the few seconds of ensuing silence, Haley realized what she had blurted out. She was genuinely horrified. "I didn't mean it that way, Ben." Tears formed. "I just thought about sisters and—"

"'S'right." Ben stood up. "No explanation needed. Sometimes I wonder about that myself." He left, gently shutting the door behind him.

He collapsed onto his bed with searing pain in his head. Haley was knocking at his door a moment later. He still couldn't talk.

Haley said, "Ben, open up." She was crying audibly. "Please? I'm so sorry."

Exhaling, he got up and opened the door. Then he plunked back down on his mattress. When she turned on the light, he told her to turn it off.

Haley was at the foot of his bed. "I didn't mean it like that." She was sobbing between breaths. "I just . . . sometimes wonder . . . what it would have been like to have a sister . . . but not instead of a brother." She was digging the knife in deeper. More sobs. "I'd die if anything happened to you." She attempted to hug him. Teardrops fell on his shirt. "I'm so sorry."

"It's all right, Haley. I'm not mad. And I'm sure that Ellen would have handled it better than I did. She was socially adroit."

"I'm so sorry!" Haley wailed.

Ben was too tired to be patient. "Look, I know I get on your nerves sometimes. It's okay. Go get some sleep."

"I hate myself."

"Just shut up. You're acting silly."

"Why does everything bad have to happen to me?"

Ben had no answer for that one. "Go get some sleep. Come on. I'll walk you to your room. Let's both get some rest."

His mother caught him just as he was about to close the door to his room. "You're going to have a big bruise." She gave him a bottle of Advil. "You may need this."

Ben managed a sick smile. "Thanks."

"How's Haley? Are you two still fighting?"

"Nope. I told her to get some sleep. You do that too."

Mom sighed. "Ben, I know that sometimes I'm a little absent—"

"Mom—"

"No, let me get this out. I really appreciate all that you've done. Sometimes when Dad is working late hours, I know I lean on you. It's a big burden."

Her insight surprised him. "Truth is, it makes me feel useful."

She kissed his cheek. "Try to get some rest."

"Sure." In the privacy of his sanctuary, he stripped off his clothes, put on pajamas, took three Advil, and crawled into bed. Ten minutes later Haley knocked on the door.

Shit.

"It's open."

She came in. "Are you still mad at me? I'd hate you if you said that to me."

"That's the difference between us. I'm mature and you're not. Go to sleep."

"Can I sleep here tonight? On the trundle?"

"Haley, either you're eleven or fourteen. Which is it?"

She sighed and left.

Peace at last.

Ben closed his eyes. He knew he'd eventually fall asleep because that's what the body did. As far as restorative sleep went, well, that was as elusive as good dreams.

CHAPTER 7

ON MONDAY, BEN felt the whispers behind his back, feeding his already hyperdeveloped paranoia. He avoided people by coming into classes a few minutes late and bolting out as soon as the bell rang. Lunch was the problem. If he showed up, there'd be a confrontation. If he didn't show up, he'd look like a pussy. In his mind, action was better than avoidance.

Sitting at his table, he watched them watch him, their chairs arranged in a tight circle around their table. None of the guys had ever been shy about using their fists. Finally, JD slowly got up and walked over, his height and girth meant to intimidate.

Without looking up, Ben said, "Yes?"

JD spun a chair around and sat down, leaning his chest against the splat. He kept his voice low. "What the fuck is wrong with you?" When Ben didn't answer, he threw his head back. "It's Weekly, dude! You're fucking wack!"

"Any other good cheer you care to spread, Santa?"

JD looked at him with lazy eyes. "Say something to Weekly, Vicks." A pause. "Not for me, for Ro. She's . . . conflict phobic."

Ben fixed his eyes on JD's face. The dude wasn't a bad guy. Nor was Weekly. Ben did overreact. He glanced at Haley, who was looking at him.

The things he did for his siblings . . . both of them.

"Okay," Ben said. "I'll say something, but not for you, Ro, or Weekly or anyone else in your posse. I'll do it for my sister because I embarrassed her."

"Whatever." Neither of them moved. JD said, "What's with you and Ro anyway? Why is she always talking to you?"

"She's a friendly girl. If it bothers you, I won't talk to her."

"It doesn't *bother* me. I'm just curious."

Ben didn't answer. He stood up and, without waiting for JD, walked across the room. Ro had been sitting between Weekly and JD. Ben saw her push her chair away from Weekly to make room for him. Instead he sat behind Weekly on the outside of the circle.

Ben said, "You're an asshole, but I was an idiot."

Weekly said, "Yeah, I was an asshole, but I was drunk. I had an excuse. You're just an asshole."

"An idiot maybe but not an asshole," Ben said.

"Open to debate," Weekly said. "If you ever knee me like that again, I'll kill you."

"Have you seen my face?"

"Think about it, Vicks. A black eye or your dick?"

A protracted moment of silence. The guy was making a

point. Reluctantly, the two of them fist-bumped. "Enjoy." Ben got up and walked out of the room.

Just get through the rest of the fucking day. When the final bell rang, Ben was determined not to act like a fugitive. *Walk slowly. Be calm.* He missed the combination to his locker on the first try. The second time was the charm. As he was sorting through his books, he heard Ro's voice.

"Hey . . ."

He turned around. "What?"

"You're mad at me."

"JD doesn't like me talking to you." Ben threw his books in his knapsack.

"He said that?"

"Go ask him. I've gotta go."

She followed him out to the bike rack. "Can we talk for a second?"

"No, we can't. And thanks for sticking up for me, by the way. I really enjoyed feeling like an ass at your behest."

"My behest?"

"You asked me to come. I came. Now I'm not only a weirdo, I'm an idiot. Please leave me alone, okay." He missed the combination on the bike lock and started over.

Ro said, "So you always have to agree with someone to be friends?"

This time the lock took three tries. Ben stood up, brushed off his jeans, and extracted his bike from the rack. Ro gripped her fingers around the handlebar. "Look. Weekly is an ass, but he wasn't really doing anything to your sister. Yes, he's a jerk, but he isn't a pervert—"

"Stop!" Ben lowered his voice. "Just . . . stop!" He focused on her baby blues. They were wet. "Stop defending Weekly, stop telling me I'm wrong, and please stop talking to me, okay?"

She didn't answer.

Ben dropped his hands to his sides. "I don't know why you've taken me on as your pet project. Well, I do know why. Everyone knows why. I don't need your pity or anyone else's pity, okay?"

"That's true. You have enough self-pity for the entire world."

Had she been a guy, he would have decked her. Instead he made himself look at her face. "That's not just cruel, that's bordering on unforgivable. No one is that *horrible*. What the hell is going on with you?"

She suddenly deflated. Her eyes gushed water.

"Oh God . . . don't cry . . ." Ben hated when girls cried. When anyone cried, for that matter. He had witnessed enough tears for a second flood. He took in a deep breath and let it out slowly. "I know it's hard coming to a new school—"

"It's not *that*!" Fat wet droplets were pouring down her cheeks. "I'm not crying for myself . . . well, I am crying for myself. I mean, who better to cry for than me? But it's not because I was uprooted." She wiped her eyes on the sleeve of her blouse. She paused to steady her voice. "I lost my sister, Vicks. I thought I might have found someone who could relate . . . for my sake, not yours. I told you I'm selfish."

"Stunned" was an okay adjective but incomplete for the way he felt. Ben brought his hand to his mouth. When people discovered his situation, they never knew what to say. It was strange to be on the other side. He stuttered out, "When?"

"Two and a half years ago." Ro wiped her eyes again. "June sixteenth." When he continued to stare at her, she said, "I know. Effectively, we lost our sisters who were the same age at the same time."

"How . . . do you know? The date, I mean? My sister's date." He knew he was rambling. "Not your sister. I mean, you know your sister's date."

"I looked up the case as soon as Shannon told me about you." She dried her eyes again on her shirt. "It was like someone socked me in the stomach. I don't think I heard too much else after that."

Neither one spoke for several seconds. Then Ben said, "How'd she pass? Not that it matters. I mean . . . forget it. You don't have to talk about it."

"She had cancer. Osteogenic sarcoma. It's a bone disease. I'm not saying that it was as horrible as what happened to your sister . . . well, it was pretty horrible, but in a different way. It wasn't as shocking, maybe. Anyway, the end result was the same."

"Oh please, let's not compare misery. I certainly don't have a monopoly on grief."

"No, you don't." She was dry-eyed now. "I shouldn't have laid it on you like that. Sometimes I have no filter . . . like all the time."

"It's okay. I'm glad you told me."

"I'm not glad. It makes you look at me differently. You know what I'm saying."

"I do, but I won't. I mean, I won't pity you." A beat. "Unless you want me to pity you."

"Don't be stupid." She exhaled. "You can't tell anyone." A beat. "Really. Promise?"

"It's not a problem, Ro. I don't talk to anyone."

"You have a sister and parents. If anyone found out, my mother would kill me. She handles the whole thing by blanking it out. Of course, you can't ignore anything so monumental. She was this close to a breakdown." Ro pinched off an inch with her thumb and forefinger. "My father found a year-long job here as a lawyer with the government just to get her away from her old life. He offered to let me stay back home with my best friend, but I couldn't leave my brother alone to deal with their shit."

"I totally get it."

"I know you do. That's why you reacted like you did Friday night. And that's why I didn't say anything. I do have a point to all this drama. After my sister died, my mom was obsessed with my health. Understandable, but it didn't make her any easier to live with. Vicks, every time I had an ache or a pain or even an itch or a twitch—*anything*—Mom whisked me off to the doctors. She was convinced I had cancer too. I was X-rayed so much I probably glow in the dark. Finally, the doctors told her she was doing way more harm than good. But she couldn't stop herself. That's when my dad knew we had to leave. He packed us all up and moved us to this hick town . . . no offense."

"It's not a hick town, but it *is* a small town."

"Anything smaller than Manhattan is a hick town to me. Ever been there?"

"Once, for a math competition."

"What did you think?"

"I was in and out of an auditorium. I never really saw the city."

"Why am I not surprised." Ro smiled slightly. "Look. I know your little sister is really none of my business, but, like most New Yorkers, I'm overly pushy. I'm gonna say this whether you want to hear it or not. I'm staging an intervention. For Haley."

"Whatever."

"Not whatever, Ben. Your overprotective behavior is going to warp her. Weekly is an idiot, but he's not a perv. And if he flirts with her and she's okay with it, let it go. Not all males are bad. Not all boys are bad. You're a boy. You're not bad. You've got to let her be a normal fourteen-year-old girl. You've got to let her giggle and flirt and bat her eyelashes. Let her grow up and develop and be a wonderful, beautiful, superficial girl like I am."

Her cell beeped out an Adele ringtone. She looked at the screen.

"JD?" he asked.

"Why don't you like him?"

"I came over to the table when he asked me to."

"You didn't answer the question."

Ben shrugged. "I have nothing against the dude. We don't have much in common."

"How about me? I like you both."

"Like I said, he doesn't want me talking to you."

"You made that up."

"Ask him." When she didn't answer, Ben said, "Miss Mc-Peacemaker. Okay, just for you I will try not to irritate JD. It will be hard because the guy is really irritating."

"Yes, he is conceited."

"I'll be cool with JD, but Weekly's off the table."

Ro smiled. "JD thinks you're a genius in math. He said you tutored him."

"Both statements are correct."

"JD got over seven hundred in math."

"I'm a very good tutor." Her phone rang again. "Go talk to your boyfriend. We'll catch up later."

"We're on speaking terms again?"

"Yes . . . if you want."

"To be determined. Just don't say anything to anyone, okay? My mom really would kill me."

"I'm great at keeping secrets."

She gave her famous little wave good-bye and started to walk away.

"Ro." When she turned around, Ben said, "What was her name?"

"Gretchen." A pause. "Thanks for asking."

"I'm sorry she died. That really sucks."

"Right back at you, Vicks."

CHAPTER 8

FOR THE NEXT few weeks, Ro avoided him. Disappointing but not unexpected. Often people told him stuff, to express empathy at first, but then they started talking about themselves. Afterward, they usually realized they'd said too much and would shut down. Ben was used to it, but with Ro, it felt like betrayal for the second time.

He had wanted her to leave him alone. He had gotten his wish.

As fate would have it, he saw way more of Griffen than of Ro. He and Haley and Lilly had become this tight little triad. The kids hung out all the time. They spent way more time sparring than getting along, but that was sexual tension. Despite what Lilly had said, Ben really couldn't tell which one Griffen liked better. At present, he seemed to be basking in the dual female attention.

The days became dull: a routine hour after hour even

though the classes differed. He didn't mind TA-ing because Lowen usually let him go early—sometimes he could skip the class altogether. One day, five minutes before calculus was due to start, Lowen motioned Ben over with a crooked finger. "Go to the supply cabinet. I need the Boswell instruction books, twenty of them. While you're there, get me some paper and twenty calculators." He handed him a cloth bag and a key. "You'll need these."

"Sure."

Down the hall, a right turn, and over to the supply room. He inserted the key in the lock and opened the door while turning on the lights. It took him a second to process what was going on. A figure thrusting and grunting. The pants puddled at his ankles. A pair of legs clasped around his waist.

Ben quickly shut the door, leaned against the wall, and started panting. He knew instantly who it was because of his size and muscle. A minute later the girl came out fully clothed, clutching her coat to her breast. Her dark hair was a mess. They eyed each other for only the briefest moment.

Lisa Holloway.

It was an image that Ben didn't want in his head, but knowing it wasn't Ro made it a little better. He caught his breath, knocked, and then went into the supply room. JD had his pants back up.

"Hey, Vicks."

"JD." He started going down the list of supplies while sneaking in a quick glance. For once, JD looked sheepish.

"Hey," JD said again. "Look, Vicks, it isn't what you think."

"No?" Silence. "Look, JD, if you want to be a jackass, that's your business."

"It's just not what you think," he repeated.

"It is what I think, but it's none of my business." Ben reached for some elementary calculators and put them in the canvas bag.

"She came on to me. Swear to God, she cornered me and pushed me in the closet. Stuck her hand in my pants—"

"Not my business."

"What was I supposed to do? Tell her to stop?"

Yes, you shit. That's what you were supposed to do. "It's not my business, JD."

"I don't make a habit of doing things like this." His voice was desperate. "I really like Ro. I'd feel bad if . . . you know."

Ben held up a hand. "Stop begging, okay. I wouldn't rat you out. You know me better than that."

"I'm not begging." But of course he was. "I'm just explaining."

"Fine. You're explaining. Gotta go."

"She's not all that you know . . . Ro isn't."

"Don't know her that well to say yea or nay." Ben shrugged. "Maybe she is all that, and you're not."

He left the closet with two armfuls' worth of supplies. He wasn't even angry. Had he and Ro been talking, carried on where they left off a few weeks ago, he might have hinted at something. But she hadn't given him more than a few passing words. As tempting as it was, it felt dishonest to blow JD's cover. He wasn't going to sneak into her life through the back door. She had to want it, and since that wasn't happening, she had made the decision for him.

Still, he felt bad for Ro. And in a perverted way, he also felt bad for JD. He wasn't a bad soul. He was only eighteen. He was just another horny guy at Remez High. No one knew who the fuck they were and what the fuck they were doing. High school was purgatory until they all earned enough indulgences to reach the vaunted era of independence.

A NUMBER OF seniors were applying for early admission to colleges and universities. Ben was not among them, so he didn't have the November 1 application deadline hanging over his head. Still, the college counselor, Tom Gomez, had scheduled an appointment with him mid-October at eleven in the morning. It was a waste of time, but it was school policy and it was easier to go with the plan than to question it.

The counselor's office was a small room on the second floor of the administration building. There were multiple college flags pinned on the back wall along with a map of the U.S. When Ben came in, Gomez pointed to the chair opposite his desk. The man was in his fifties, short and stocky, with gray hair, high cheekbones, and a wide mouth. Like Ben, Gomez had come from solid New Mexico stock. Their families were friends but not close friends. Talking to him was like talking to an out-of-town uncle: the relationship was a little closer than normal but not close enough to feel entirely comfortable.

"How are you?" Gomez asked.

"Fine."

"The folks?"

"Pretty good."

"Good to hear. We missed you at Nambe feast day."

"Yeah, I'm sorry I couldn't make it. School and all."

"You? Worried about school?"

Ben gave him a sheepish smile. "Not really."

"Yeah, not really. Okay. What schools are you considering?" When Ben handed him a slip of paper, Gomez read the list. He said, "This is it? St. John's and UNM?"

"They're good schools."

"They are very good schools. But why are you limiting yourself? You have the entire world at your feet."

Ben looked at the floor. "All I see is gray tile."

"You can deflect the obvious with humor, but I've known you too long to be distracted. With your scores and your grades and your recommendations and where you live, you could walk into any school you want. Why isn't MIT on the list? Or Caltech? Or Chicago? Or even Harvard?"

"I'm not interested, Mr. Gomez."

"Since when have you started calling me 'Mr. Gomez'?"

"Just trying to be respectful."

"You're trying to create distance between us."

Ben tried another tactic. "My scores were not perfect."

"Stop nitpicking, Ben. You know they're exceptional. You know you're exceptional."

"With schools like the Ivies, you have to have four years of a foreign language."

"Who told you this nonsense?" Gomez paused. "Or are you making it up so you don't have to put yourself out there?"

"I'm just telling you what I've heard."

"You've heard incorrectly." Gomez gave him a reproving look. "I repeat. With your grades, your scores, your recommendations, and where you live, you can go anywhere—especially considering your background."

"What about my background?"

Gomez stalled. Then he said, "I just meant that you've gone through a lot. A lot of guys would have cracked under the circumstances."

Immediately Ben felt anger boil in his chest. "So . . . like I should write on top of my application in red: 'this guy has a dead sister'?"

"Ben—"

"Or do you mean the essay? To whom it may concern: take me as a pity case because my sister was murdered and I'm still alive and functioning."

"Ben—"

He got up. "I think we're done." He bolted out of the office, filled with fury, his heart beating through his chest. Leaning against his locker, fist clenched, he tried to catch his breath. He did manage to get the combination on the first try. When the door opened, his books came tumbling out. He banged the locker next to his, and then bent down to pick up the books. When he stood up again, he hit his head on the open door. "Fuck!"

Ro was there. "What's wrong?"

"Well, hello, stranger, fancy meeting you here."

"Stop it. What's bothering you?"

"I just got out of a counseling session with Gomez."

"He wants you to apply to other schools."

"How did you know?"

"'Cause I know where you're applying and you're selling yourself short. If I had your scores, I'd be wearing crimson as we speak."

"How do you know my scores?"

"Haley told me."

"How the hell does she know?"

"Perhaps you told your family. Perhaps they discuss you when you're not around. Perhaps she overheard. Whatever the reason is, you're still selling yourself short."

"That isn't what made me mad."

"Okay. What made you mad?"

"He implied that I should like . . . write an essay about me and what I've gone through . . . meaning that I should exploit my sister's death. Like some ridiculous college essay is worth stooping so low. God, can you believe that idiot?"

Ro stared at him, then shook her head. "You know the trouble with you, Vicks? You don't live in the real world." She turned tail and stalked off.

"Wait! What did I . . . shit!" He slammed his locker door shut. "Shit. Shit. Shit."

"Ben?"

He whirled around. Lilly had a slightly stunned look on her face. Her cheeks were red. "You dropped your book."

He looked at the lit book in her arms. "Right . . . thanks."

She backed away, and then waved from a safe distance.

He went looking around for Ro. She was at her locker, wiping her eyes with her shirtsleeve.

"Okay," he said. "What'd I do wrong this time?"

"Nothing."

JD had suddenly materialized. "What's going on?"

"Nothing," she repeated. "I don't want to talk about it."

"Is it something I did?" JD asked.

Ro slammed her locker. "You know I can be sad without it having anything to do with you."

"Of course." JD turned to Ben. "I've got it from here, Vicks."

Ro grabbed Ben's arm. "He doesn't have to leave just because you say so, okay. You're not the center of the universe."

"If I'm not, I should be," JD said. Ro rolled her eyes, but couldn't help but smile. He put his arm around her. "You shouldn't ever have to cry. You're the hottest-looking girl in the entire school. Probably the hottest girl in the entire state . . . maybe even the hottest girl ever. And you just happen to have the hottest boyfriend ever. What's there to cry about?" He turned to Ben. "Am I right about this?"

Ben said, "I would contest a lot of what you're saying, but not her hotness quotient."

"He's complicated." JD pointed to himself. "I'm not. Sometimes simple is better, right?" When she didn't answer, he said, *"Right?"*

"Sometimes being alone is even better than simple." She walked away.

When she was gone, JD said, "What the fuck just happened?"

"She's pissed at me. It might have to do with college essays but I'm not sure. I'm kinda dumb when it comes to girls."

"Let me tell you something, Vicks. That ain't ever gonna change." JD shook his head. "You got shit on me, so you don't have to answer this. But what . . . exactly is your relationship with her?"

"I think we're friends . . . loosely defined."

"Friends?"

"Loosely defined."

"Awesome." JD slapped his back none too lightly. His voice dripped sarcasm. "Benjamin Vicksburg has finally made a friend."

CHAPTER 9

THE TWO BOYS were nervous. As Ro looked in her rearview mirror, she saw that they weren't talking much, but they were punching each other a lot. Even though Griff had gone out with Haley and Lilly tons of times, Ezra's presence made it an official double date. The girls were no longer friends, they were love interests.

Ezra Rael was half Hispanic, half Jewish. He seemed like a nice kid, although Ro had only met him a few times. She was happy that Griff was making friends with a boy. It showed he was integrating and probably doing a better job at it than she was—taking his time to pick the right people: kids whom Griff liked, not just those who'd serve him well.

She grew tense as she approached Vicks's house. Like most of the homes in the area, it was fashioned from brown adobe, a sprawling one-story home fronted by a free-form adobe wall, short piñon pines, and silvery Russian olives. It sat on undulating land in the midst of the Sangre de Cristo Mountains. The one thing this state had was lots and lots of land. That kind of space was something that Ro wasn't used to. Sometimes she found it liberating. Most of the time the vast expanse scared her as if the bogeyman was just waiting to come out from behind a rock. She hadn't had a conversation with Ben in a very long time. If he was upset about it, he hadn't said anything. But she was attuned to nuances. They both knew what was going on and it made her feel small.

When she pulled over, Griff said, "Thanks for the ride."

"I'll walk you to the door."

Griffen sneered. "Seriously?"

"Just gonna give Vicks a quick hello."

Griffen sighed. "Please disappear quickly, okay?"

"Fine."

They walked up the pathway and Griffen rang the bell. The two little girls came out. Although their outfits were the standard uniform of jeans and a T, both of them had done up their hair and had put on makeup. Ro would have liked to snap a picture, but it would totally embarrass her little brother.

Haley said, "We've got a little time before the show starts. Wanna come in?"

The two boys nodded like bobbleheads. Haley could have suggested anything and they would have agreed. Ben's mother came out. She was a pretty woman with hair streaked with silver. She had wonderful smooth skin and full lips. Her eyes were chestnut gold, like Haley's and Ben's. And like Ro's own mother's eyes, Mrs. Vicksburg's showed eternal sadness.

She said, "Thank you for bringing them over. I'll drop them back off after the movie."

"Only if it's convenient," Ro said. "Griffen can call me."

"No, no. I'm happy to do it."

An awkward silence. "I'm Dorothy Majors, by the way." Ro held out her hand. "I'm in Vicks . . . Ben . . . I'm in Ben's class. Is he here? I thought I might say hello."

Mrs. V looked surprised. "He's in his room." Another silence. "Come in."

Ro followed her into a neat living room, unadorned except for family pictures and a piece of pottery here and there in a shelving unit. There was a leather couch, a couple of kilim chairs, and a sofa table with a few paperbacks. In the corner was a small beehive fireplace, common to this area, called a kiva. The floors were oak and the ceiling was made up of latilla strips vertically and big, whole log beams called vigas that ran horizontally. New Mexico had its own architecture and architectural terms. Ro had had to learn an entire new vocabulary once she got here.

There were four rooms off a small hallway. Two doors were open—the master bedroom and Haley's room. Two doors were shut. The mother knocked on one of those.

Ben's voice. "Busy."

The mother said, "You've got a visitor."

They both heard shuffling. Ben opened the door and peeked his head out. When he saw Ro, his eyes widened.

Ro said, "I just dropped Griffen and Ezra Rael off. Apparently, they are having an afternoon with Haley and Lilly." Still no response. She said, "I just thought I'd say hi."

Ben's eyes shifted between Ro and his mother. He said, "Hi."

There was an electric stare between them. His hair—unruly at times—was a nest of interlocking waves and curls. She thought he looked as though he just rolled out of bed, except the eyes were on hyperalert. Sometimes the color morphed from gold to muddy green, especially when he was angry. Ben's complexion darkened and Ro knew she was blushing because she was hot. The mom was still appraising them, her eyes moving back and forth between their faces.

Haley called out, "Mom?"

The sound broke the trance. The mom said, "I'd better see what she wants."

As soon as she left, Ro butted her way inside, past Ben, before he could stop her. She had a wide smile on her face. "What are you doing so secretly, Vicks? Watching porn—"

Her mouth dropped open and her eyes became saucers. She put her hand to her lips as she looked around the room in astonished silence.

It seemed like every square inch was covered in paper: on the bed, on his desk, on the floor, on top of his dressers. Stacks and stacks of files, dossiers, folders, reports—some of them printed text, but there were others with pictures . . . revolting pictures.

Murder cases—at least fifty of them. Glancing at the pages Ro saw young girls who had been slaughtered, shot, sliced, burned, trussed, and tortured. The first picture that caught her eye was of a blonde who appeared to have been scalped. All of them were graphic . . . explicit in their violence. Up close and personal.

She looked down, then looked around again—like witnessing an accident, she couldn't stop staring. Along with the pictures were horrendous words—"rape," "sodomy," "sexual mutilation." It took all her strength not to upchuck her breakfast.

She knew she was breathing rapidly. Her head felt light.

Focus.

Her eyes found the sole exception to this house of horrors. There was a corkboard above Ben's desk and on it was a collage of photographs of the same girl: gold eyes, dark hair, olive complexion, and a sunny smile. Her stare engaged from any point in the room, and maybe that was the point. The happy pictures were in stark contrast to everything else. The living and the dead . . . or maybe it was the dead and the dead. Whatever it was, it made her nauseated.

It was a gorgeous day outside—low sixties, crystalline air, and the bluest of skies that can only be seen in mountainous regions. And this was how Vicks chose to spend his Sunday.

He said, "Let me get rid of—"

"Don't."

Ben said, "At least let me shut down my computer."

Ro's hand was atop his. "Don't do that either." She took the mouse and scrolled down. More cases and more gruesome pictures. A moment later she heard a loud click. Her head spun around. Vicks had locked the door behind them.

"I don't want my mom coming in. It would upset her."

"Y'think?" She gawked at him and he looked away.

He said, "If you feel uncomfortable being alone with—"

"Stop it. I'm fine being alone with you, okay?"

"Surprising . . . seeing as you haven't talked to me for the last two weeks."

"I talk to you all the time." But her defense sounded lame to her ears. She had been avoiding him, but not for the reasons he thought. She had wanted to talk to him, but she wanted him all to herself. She didn't want Shannon or Chelsea seeing them together, asking questions. She especially didn't want JD to be around. He was always quizzing her specifically about Vicks.

Why do you talk to him? he would ask.

Why not?

'Cause it's weird. He's weird. He's not interested in you, he's not interested in the world. He's on his own planet. Let him be.

His own planet. That was an understatement. Ro said, "It's true. I was avoiding you. I get tired of people staring when we talk."

"I do have a phone and you do have my phone number."

She nodded. She looked again at the corkboard. "Ellen?"

"Yes."

Looking at his dead sister made her eyes get wet. But the entire room was so filled with disgusting images it was hard to tell where the tears were coming from. She knew that some of Ben's obsession had to do with survivor's guilt, but this went so far beyond. She picked a file and read another case—fourteen-year-old girl strangled, burned to a crisp with gasoline, and then dumped in a rural road.

"I'm not saying this to criticize you or pass judgment. That's the truth." She turned to him. "But why are you doing this to yourself?"

"Keeps me busy." His voice was a hush. "I don't have a plethora of friends."

"No, that's not it." She managed to meet his eyes. "You don't have friends because you choose to sequester yourself and concentrate on your sister's murder. So I repeat. Why are you doing this to yourself?"

"I dunno . . . really."

"Yes, you do. You do know. Why?"

He exhaled forcefully. "Okay. I'll tell you. But you've got to listen."

"Okay. I'm listening."

"Suppose . . . suppose you could find a cure for osteogenic sarcoma. It would be too late to save your sis—to save
Gretchen—but you could prevent other teens from suffering what she went through. Wouldn't you give it your all?
Wouldn't you work every single neuron of your brain to stop
this disease from ever killing again?"

"Of course." She nodded. "I understand what you're saying, Vicks, but I'm not a doctor. And even if I were a doctor,
I'd never be smart enough or lucky enough—or both—to cure
my sister's disease. And even if I turned out to be a brilliant
doctor, I couldn't do anything about it now, right?"

"Of course."

"The difference between your case and my case . . . is
really the difference between you and me. I know I'm helpless. But you . . . you believe that you can do this better than
the professionals."

He didn't answer.

"Am I right about this, Ben?"

He said, "I understand what you're saying and maybe there
is a bit of truth in that. The real story is the professionals here
are overworked and underpaid. Detective Shanks is a good
guy. He's worked the case for over two years and he really,
really wants to solve this. A suspect would be a good start.
His heart is in the right place. And I've been doing nothing
but pestering him since my sister went missing. But he's not
getting anywhere. This newest arrest—Billy Ray Barnes—was
sort of his last hope. I saw it, Ro. I saw the wind knocked out
of his sails . . . the boat capsized, actually. He doesn't have it in
him anymore. Someone has to fight for Ellen."

"Who's Billy Ray Barnes?"

"A serial killer. The Albuquerque Demon."

"The guy they arrested several months ago."

"Yes. He's responsible for at least four murders in the Al-buquerque and southern New Mexico regions. Shanks was hoping that he was responsible for Ellen. We were all hoping he was the one, although I knew he wasn't. I was right. None of the biological evidence matched."

"How did you know he wasn't the one?"

"That would take a while to explain. It's a little bit of intu-ition and a lot of inconsistencies. And now this Demon thing has done nothing but obfuscate my sister's case."

"Obfuscate . . ." She raised her eyebrows. "Sounds like an SAT word. And yes, I know what it means."

Ben explained, "One of the cases—practically the only one—that looks like it might connect to Ellen's is a missing girl down in Albuquerque named Katie Doogan. She went missing about three months before my sister's body was found." He had to take a moment before he could continue. "I think they're related. But Katie is still missing. Until her body is located, I can't go any farther with her."

"And what do you propose to do? Go look for her body?"

"I've already done that about a bajillion times. My parents connected with her parents, Margot and Alan, at one of the many candlelight vigils for Katie. Her older brother and I used to go looking in the woods for her every weekend for about six months. God, it was like reliving my sister . . ." He paused. "After Ellen's remains were found, Margot and Alan came to the funeral. They are such good people."

Silence.

Ben said, "It's been a while since I've looked. Maybe I'll try again over Thanksgiving. The problem is even if we found Ka-tie and she still retained biological evidence like foreign DNA, it would take a while to process because the New Mexico state lab is jammed, working the Billy Ray Barnes case. What am I supposed to do, Ro? Wait until we get a lucky break? And how many other girls will be murdered in the meantime?"

Ro didn't answer, still staring at the morbid files strewn across his bed. Her mouth was dry. A small shudder traveled down her spine.

When she had first arrived in New Mexico, she found out pretty quickly where the power was. Within a few weeks, she and JD were an item and that was exactly what she wanted. She liked JD. He was hot, he was built, he was smart, he was funny, and he had the kind of status that gave her status. With JD, she could be popular and respected. She made cheerleader when ordinarily that wouldn't have happened. She had a good shot at being homecoming queen. She would have the best-looking date for the prom. The guy had it all. But the best thing he had going for him was his lack of seriousness. She was happy to date him, happy to be physical with him. She'd never *do* him, but she'd do enough that he'd be happy and he could brag to his friends. When they parted, it would be fine.

So long, it's been good to know ya.

They'd probably never meet again, but if they did—like twenty years from now—JD would probably still be good-looking with a little paunch and a receding hairline. And she, of course, would still be hot. And it would make JD feel good to know she had been his girl a long time ago.

That's who she was: beautiful, competitive, phony, and a big user of people. She was always the one who demanded to be noticed.

Look at me, look at me.

And people did look at her, because she was gorgeous. It

was Gretchen who was quiet and studious. Gretchen who won the academic awards. Gretchen was cute, but she wasn't a beauty queen. Ro was smart, but she wasn't brilliant. God had divided the assets fairly. Gretchen was always well respected. Ro was always well liked. Still no one ever said, if only I could be like Gretchen. But a lot of people said, if only I could be like Ro.

Vicks wouldn't do her any good in the popularity department. He was a step down from JD. Her friends would desert her because JD would mash her into the ground if she dumped him. It was JD who had the power, and without him, she couldn't compete. But that really wasn't important to her anymore. The problem wasn't losing JD. The problem was being with Vicks. She didn't want to become attached to him. With Vicks, it would be different because Vicks had passion. He cared.

She had wanted a boyfriend whom she liked and a friend who cared. Unfortunately, that friend happened to be a boy whom she was developing feelings for. She didn't want to care back. Caring was painful. Caring hurt. Caring meant when it was time to part, there would be tears and feelings and all that bad stuff.

". . . thinking?"

"Pardon?" she said.

Ben said, "I asked . . . what are you thinking?"

"That you can't solve the world's problems."

"I'm not trying to do that. I'm limiting my rather poor resources and gray matter to my sister's case. Yes, I'm crazy and obsessive, but I can't help it. I need to find out who did this and then stop him from doing it again."

"Okay." She picked up a file and put it down. She took in

a deep breath and let it out. "Okay." She made some room for herself on his bed. "Fill me in."

"No, no, no. I don't need help. I just want you to understand that I'm not some weird ghoul with a fascination with death. It's just Ellen's death."

"I understand. You're not a ghoul. But you do need help. At the very least, I'll be a fresh pair of eyes."

"No. Absolutely unacceptable."

"Stop being paternalistic." She gave him a weak smile. "See, I know big words too." Another file showed some post-mortem shots. This time the girl's throat had been severed so badly Ro could see her backbone. She remained resolute. "Stop arguing. Fill me in."

"Look. Let me just shut down my computer. It's a beautiful day. We'll go for a walk—"

"No," Ro told him. "No, no, no. Just . . ." She patted the mattress next to where she sat. "Sit down next to me, Vicks. Get it all out. I want to know what you know."

"You don't really want to be part of all this ugliness, Dorothy. It's the stuff of nightmares."

"I've had plenty of nightmares. I'm not delicate. Even before I lost my sister, I wasn't delicate. I was always conniving and political. I'm not arguing with you anymore, Vicks. Sit down and fill me in."

He sat down and then he spoke to her. Haltingly at first, then like an open sugar canister on the edge of a counter—one small nudge and everything just spilled out.

CHAPTER 10

"THERE'S A REASON for so many files."

His pacing was driving Ro bonkers, but she didn't say anything.

"I have duplicates because I have them arranged in different ways depending on what I need," Ben was saying. "From the date of the murder—earliest to latest—alphabetical order, region, and method. Whenever there are matching dots on the files, I think that the cases might be related. For instance, these three yellow dots on these three folders, I think there's something that ties the cases together."

"Like what?"

"Physical characteristics, age of the victim, the way the victim was murdered, if there was sexual activity, the time of day, the season, where the victim was found, if she was posed or not, how deep the grave was . . . My sister was found in a deep hole. It was just chance that I found . . . that she was found. An animal must have been digging around the area. Just enough to expose . . . her hand."

"You *found* her?" Ro asked.

"On the anniversary of her abduction." He stopped pacing, his eyes very far away.

Twenty people had volunteered for the search, walking through the mountains in a grid pattern. The group split into two, and one group chose to explore the area near the river. Ben went with the river group at first, but a couple hours in, he strayed from the party, electing to look by himself.

Twenty minutes later, something metallic glinted in the filtered sunlight: a small ring sitting on a finger. The hand was half skeletal but still retained some flesh. Ben's breath shortened and his eyes became blurry. Something deep rose up in his throat. He threw up with such force that he hit a tree five feet away. After that, things became hazy. He remembered sitting on a rock, shivering even though it was in the seventies in town. By the river, it was cooler, shaded by the mountains, the tall cottonwoods, the sycamores, the aspens, and the pines. His shakes had nothing to do with the temperature.

The mud and the cool soil along the water had preserved some of the body. More important, deep inside Ellen's body, the riverbanks had preserved biological evidence. Surely an arrest would be imminent, Shanks said.

Imminent had been going on three years.

Ben whispered, "It was beyond horrible, but what made it even worse was the police. I was too stupid to realize it, but they were actually questioning me."

"Shanks?"

"No. Shanks came in later. A guy named Chelly. When Shanks found out what was going on, he reamed the guy's ass.

Lucky for me, I don't remember too much of that day. Not like the day Ellen was abducted. That day I remember very well."

Ro was trying to keep her train of thought. Ben's attention was scattershot. He'd look around his room as if it were unfamiliar territory, and then he was back in reality. Normally, he was hyperfocused, the anti-ADD. She knew she was making him nervous. Finally, someone had outed his secret and he didn't know whether to be relieved or mad.

"So . . . like . . ." He started rooting through the cases laid out on his bed. He pulled up six files. "Okay . . . all these files have orange dots. I felt they weren't related to Ellen, but they were related to each other. I put them together like . . . like a year ago for these two files."

"Are they related?" Ro asked.

"Four of the six have been linked to the Albuquerque Demon. If I had anyone's ear, I'd say that the police should be looking into these two victims as well."

"So call the police."

"I don't know anyone in Albuquerque except maybe the primary on the Doogan case—Milton Ortiz. And I don't know him that well. I have been questioned enough to know I don't like it."

"Then call up Shanks."

"Still debating whether or not to do it."

"You don't trust him?"

"Yeah, I trust him. He knows I'm obsessive but he doesn't know the extent of it. In my head, what I'm doing is totally normal. To anyone else, it is odd."

"Let me say something . . . just get it out, okay?"

"Okay."

Ro said, "Everyone copes with things in a different way. If this is what you've got to do, then do it. I won't pass judgment."

Ben nodded. "Did I tell you I loved you?"

"No, but I just assumed it from the start."

Ben laughed, then grew serious. "Anyway, serial killers . . . a lot of them like to relive what they did."

"I know. I've seen a lot of bad TV."

"It is bad TV but it's also true. I'm trying to figure out how they'd relive my sister's murder in hopes that I can figure out patterns."

He tucked his hair behind his ears.

"Sometimes I do step back. I suffer when I read about this stuff. Instead of feeling bad, I try to immerse myself in details so I don't see the big picture."

"Like doctors working with cancer patients," Ro said. "They give you these minute details of the progress of the treatment or the disease . . . when all you want to know is if she's going to be okay."

"Right. Think of me as a forensic oncologist."

"You know what an oncologist is?"

"Not until you told me about your sister. When I looked up osteogenic sarcoma, I found out what an oncologist is." He shrugged.

Ro shrugged back. She picked up some files and began reading them to herself. Seeing her occupied, Ben went back to the computer.

A half hour passed.

Ro said, "You have so much organized information. Take these three burgundy files. You've got this girl, Janina Nuñez from Arizona, associated with Nicole Lafey from Louisiana and Nancy Jimenez from Las Cruces. Has anyone else ever put these three together?"

"I have no idea."

"Vicks, this is a gold mine of data. Put it to good use. Think of the families." When he didn't answer, she said, "If you're worried what the police will think, I'll come with you. Nancy Drew and the Hardy boys."

"You nailed it. I don't want to be the wiseass kid who shows up the professionals. Shanks is tolerant of me—very nice actually—but I don't want to be an asshole."

"But you did get it right with the Demon."

"So did Albuquerque and state police."

"But they've only linked four. You have six."

"They're still testing others. They may have a lot more links than I do."

Silence. "I'd like to meet him . . . Shanks."

"No way. I'm not bringing you into my psychopathology."

"You already have."

"That's because you barged into my room."

"Vicks, I just keep thinking of all the families you could be helping."

"I'm not ready to talk to Shanks. I just don't want to do it yet, okay?"

"Fair enough. Let me see your sister's file. I should have read that first."

"Okay."

Two hours later, Ro was done with Ellen's file. She moved on and kept reading. "What's with this folder, Vicks? You have two red dots on it."

Ben spoke as he scrolled down on his computer. "Julia

Rehnquist. She has some points in common with my sister's death."

"More than Katie Doogan?"

"I can't make that assessment until Katie has been located." He turned to face her. "About three weeks ago it came to me, stupid idiot that I was. Look at the dates of all three girls, Ro. Julia was abducted on December nineteenth. My sister was abducted on June twenty-second. Katie was taken on March twenty-first. Do you see the pattern?"

Ro studied the three girls on paper. Different months, different dates, different places. "They're all in the latter half of the months. But I have a feeling that's not it."

"The murders happened a day or two away from the equinoxes or the solstices."

"Wow." Ro felt her heart beating. "That's really creepy. Like the Zodiac Killer."

"You know about the Zodiac Killer?"

Ro felt her face go hot. "At one time I wanted to go to California for school. You know . . . sun and beaches. You research San Francisco, you learn about the Zodiac Killer."

"Ro, that was like forty years ago. How would that pop up in a superficial search of San Francisco?"

"Okay. I've got a confession to make. Don't you dare throw it back in my face." She cleared her throat. "All those crime shows on TV? I'm addicted to them. Not the fiction ones . . . the true crime."

Ben was trying to hold back a smile. "There are a lot of them."

"I like them all: *Reasonable Doubt, The First 48, 48 Hours on ID, 20/20 on ID, Scorned, Snapped, Grave Secrets, Sins and Secrets, Nightmare Next Door, Swamp Murders, Nothing Personal, Dateline on ID, Forensic Files, Cold Case Files, Murder by the Book, Watching Evil, City Confidential,* old reruns of *Watching the Detectives* and *Manhunters* . . . I have a mad crush on Lenny DePaul. Sometimes I fantasize about being Michy."

Ben stifled laughter. "No comment."

"I used to watch like all the time. Now with my busy schedule I treat myself to a few before I go to bed."

"Sweet dreams," Ben said.

"Seriously. I mean, the stuff really scares me, but I keep coming back to it. Like maybe if I saturate myself in such horror, it'll no longer scare me. Or perhaps I'm a little off like you are."

"Those shows are popular. Maybe there's something a little off in all of us."

Ro said, "The Zodiac Killer was always the bogeyman to me because of the taunting of the police, all those charts, and the case was never solved."

"Yeah, we got ourselves an astrological monster. These aren't random dates, that's for sure."

"It's creepy."

"Yeah, when I pointed this out to Shanks, he was thinking about something satanic."

"That's even creepier." A chill went down Ro's spine.

"I don't think it was satanic," Ben said. "Julia Rehnquist's body wasn't carved up or mutilated like you would expect in a satanic murder. At least I don't think she was. I've never seen the police file. My sister was also . . . whole."

"I hear you." Ro started skimming Julia Rehnquist's file. It was a year-old case. She had been sixteen years old, jogging on a hillside on a Saturday in Berkeley, California. She was found eight months later, sexually assaulted and manually strangled, buried in a four-foot grave in Mount Diablo State Park. The closest town was Diablo, California, which had a tiny population. Vicks had also written down Alamo, California, a town of fourteen thousand, and Danville, California, population fifty thousand.

"How far are Diablo, Danville, and Alamo, California, from here?"

"Around nine hundred miles."

"I know that serial killers travel a lot. They drive around all the time looking for victims."

"You really have seen a lot of true crime. And you're right. Rehnquist is in a different geographical locale. With Katie Doogan, I thought I was dealing with someone unique to New Mexico, but now I don't think so." He looked up from the computer. "Berkeley is similar to Santa Fe—very liberal and really kooky. It attracts all kinds of people. That's a point in common."

"What does that mean, Vicks? We've got a ravaging reactionary who's killing girls?"

"As ludicrous as it sounds, you never know."

Ro said, "Okay, both Ellen and Julia were buried in the mountains. Which makes sense. If you're going to take the time to bury a body, you don't do it in a populated area. Was Julia buried near water?"

"I don't know without walking the terrain. There are streams in the area."

"Is there something significant about water?"

"Maybe. Or it could be that he used riverbanks because it's easier to dig a deeper hole in muddy soil or he uses water as a geographical guide. Whatever the reason, the murderer didn't want these girls to be found. The graves were deep in both cases."

"Hard to dig a deep grave in the mountains in the heart of winter."

"It's a California winter."

"Ah, that's right." Ro thought a moment. "You said the graves were deep because he wanted the bodies to permanently disappear. But the bodies were found."

"Animals smell bodies. They dig. Sometimes they make a hole just deep enough for erosion to start working its magic."

Ro said, "Have you told Shanks about the Rehnquist case?"

Ben gave a pained look. "No."

"You have to do that. If you're wrong, so what?"

"I don't care if I'm wrong. I don't want to drag Shanks into something that would make him look stupid."

"Vicks, if you're not going to do anything about all this data, why do it?"

"Because at least I'm doing something. I'll talk to Shanks . . . eventually." Ben started to gather up the files from his bed. "I've been at this for hours. I can't think anymore. Let's get out of here."

"Where to?" She saw him look at her feet. "What?"

He said, "You're wearing boots but not the right kind. What size are you? Your shoe size?"

"Seven and a half."

"I'll see what I can scrounge up." He checked his watch. "But we have to leave now."

"Where are we going?"

"You'll see." He unlocked the door and opened it, leading Ro into the kitchen, where his mother was setting up a tray of snacks: guacamole, salsa, corn chips, flour tortilla chips, and a plate of fresh fruit. She smiled when she saw the two of them. "You've been in there for a while. I thought you might want a snack."

"What's your shoe size, Mom?"

"My shoe size?"

"I want to take Ro to see Aspen Vista before all the leaves fall off. Maybe we'll even have enough time to hike a little of Big Tesuque. But she can't walk in what she's wearing."

"Ben, it's after two."

"We've still got some sunlight left. I promise I'll be back by dinner. What's your shoe size?"

"I'm an eight," his mom said.

"Close enough. Can I borrow your hiking shoes?" When his mother smiled again, Ben spoke out. "Ro is JD's girlfriend but we talk sometimes. You know how it is. Some guys get all the luck."

Silence.

"Can I go in your closet?" Ben asked her.

"Of course." His mother's voice had turned quiet. "Give her the brown high-tops."

"Great. Could you wrap that up for us?" He pointed to the food. "We'll take it in the car."

"Of course." She gave a brief smile to Ro. "You and Griffen are welcome to stay for dinner."

"Thank you, but I have other plans."

Ben had gone looking for the shoes. His mother was talking with her eyes down. "Well, I guess I'll go wrap this up."

"Can I help?"

"No, no." A sad smile. "Just make yourself comfortable in the living room."

Ro waited until Ben came back with two pairs of hiking shoes. "Either of these should work. Try them on."

"You upset your mom."

"By telling her you weren't my girlfriend? I'm sure I did. No sense letting her wallow in delusion."

Ro tried on a pair of shoes. "She invited me for dinner . . . your mom."

"You can stay. I won't kick you out."

"I told her I have plans . . . which is true." She laced up the high-tops. "These fit."

"Then let's go." He took her hand and pulled her to her feet. "It's time for you to see what New Mexico is really all about."

CHAPTER 11

AFTER LOADING THE backpack with water, food, a first-aid kit, and a flashlight, Ben rummaged through the coat closet for warm outerwear and gloves. When they got outside, he asked for her keys.

"I can drive." Ro was offended.

"I know you can. But I know where I'm going. Don't argue for once. Let's just go."

Her Explorer handled well, especially on Hyde Park Road where the road was paved. He wasn't exactly going pedal to the metal, but he made good time, looping around curve after curve, leaving the city and entering national forests with steep mountains filled with pines and scented air that wafted upward from the detritus. They twisted around miles of untamed nature: ponderosa and piñons, sycamores, cottonwoods, Russian olives, red sumac, and golden aspens. When he was closer to the spot, Ben slowed down, allowing Ro to take in the scenery.

"This is beautiful," she admitted. "I never knew this existed. You do this often?"

"I like to hike, especially at this time of year. Just wait. You ain't seen nothin' yet." Climbing higher until traffic suddenly backed up to a crawl, they ascended the two-lane highway at a snail's pace until the car made the twist around the final bend and the mountainside came into view.

Ro gasped. And even though Ben had seen it many times before, it never failed to impress.

The entire surface above and below was covered in pure gold—acres upon acres of deep yellow quaking aspens. The richness of the hue was otherworldly but it was especially brought out by an intense blue sky. It was an abundance of pure color. Cars had slowed down to gawk, allowing Ro to drink in unadulterated artwork provided by nature.

"Are we getting out?"

"Not yet, but we will."

"How could anything be any prettier?"

"All we have to do is add water." He drove for an additional fifteen minutes until they reached Big Tesuque. Parking, as expected, was hard to find, but someone pulled out just as they arrived. Ben backed into the spot, turned off the motor, and they got out. He slipped on his backpack and checked his watch. "I think we'll be okay. You can use the john if you need to."

"How long will the hike take?"

"Couple of hours maybe."

"Two *hours*?"

"You're such a city girl." He grinned. "Bathroom, yes or no?"

"Is it gross in there?"

"It's a park, Ro."

"Flushing toilets?"

"Dream on."

"Ugh." She used the facilities and came back out. "Ugh times two."

He took her hand. "C'mon."

The rise of the trail was in gentle steps surrounded by amber aspens and the music of Big Tesuque Creek. At this time of year, the level was high, water rushing down the mountain rather than in its usual trickle. Though the trail was a corridor of yellow, there were other hues to break it up: the deep red leaves of the sumacs, wild daisies, deep burnt-orange Indian paintbrush, and white columbine. The chamisos were shedding the last of their canary flowers. The ground still held some greenery and some scattered wild alpine strawberries, tiny and dry.

Off the hiking trails was the usual queue of small tents near the creek. There were also artists with easels painting poor representations of nature. The trail wasn't packed but there were plenty of people—common at this time of year.

"Okay?"

"I'm fine." Ro walked with deliberation, grabbing Ben's hand and latching on to it for support. As they climbed the mountain, her breathing quickened.

"How far is it?"

"We've just begun."

"I dunno about this. How high is this?"

"Around nine thousand feet."

"Good God!" She was huffing and puffing. "People are actually breathing and talking at the same time."

"Rest a moment. We've still got a long way to go."

"Seriously?"

Ben smiled and waved at a couple in their seventies.

"Gorgeous day," the white-headed woman said.

"Don't get better than this," he answered.

They resumed the hike, climbing upward as the path twisted and turned, the ground beneath them damp from the rains, until a line backed up at the first stream crossing. The logs were almost submerged but there was enough wood visible to cross without a problem if one was careful in stepping. Ro's eyes got big. "I'm not doing that."

"You're not exactly fording the Mississippi," Ben told her. "It's like six feet across."

"I'm not doing it," she repeated.

He pulled his hand away. "You have two choices, Ro. You go up with me or you go down by yourself."

"I really don't like you."

People were lining up behind them. He said, "Up or down."

She grabbed his hand. "If I fall in, I'll kill you. You go first."

"I can't help you if I'm in front of you." He picked her up by the waist and placed her on the log. Then he came up behind her, holding her hands outward like they were walking on a tightrope. Ben smiled to himself. It was ridiculous because the distance was so short, but there was a first for everything. "One foot in front of another. Almost there."

"This is embarrassing."

"You're fine. No one cares."

When she reached the other side, she hopped off. She looked upward. "That's kind of a steep incline."

"No, it isn't. Keep going."

She sighed and plowed forward. Upward, upward, upward.

It was comical. Dogs were bounding up the pathway. People in their nineties with canes were passing her by. Toddlers were passing her by.

"I have a cramp," she said.

"Where?"

"Everywhere. Why is this considered fun? It's got nothing to recommend it at all."

"Nothing?"

"Okay. It's pretty."

"Yes, it's pretty," he said. Especially when the trail widened into an open meadow filled with autumn wildflowers. The line grew sluggish. People had stopped.

"What's going on?" Ro asked.

Ben pointed to a black furry thing sitting in a pile of bushes about fifty yards from where they were standing. "Black bear over there. He's storing up for the winter. Probably some berries still on the ground."

She went pale. "What do we do?"

"Nothing. It's happy. It won't bother us. Just keep going."

"What if it likes my perfume?"

"If anything, he'll eat me first."

"You have no fat on you. He'll eat me first."

"You're lean yourself. Maybe he'll take that guy over there. He's got a gut."

Ro laughed. "How about that woman over there?"

"Way too scrawny."

"How old is she? About a hundred?"

"Maybe more."

"She's in better shape than I am."

"A lesson for us all," Ben said. "Keep going."

They climbed up until they reached a second stream crossing. The trailhead ended at a paved service road. Ben pointed
to the left.

Ro was aghast. "We're not done?"

"Nope. But this is mostly level."

"How high are we now?"

"Around ten and half, but we're going down to about ten."

"If we go down to ten, when we return, does that mean we
go back up?"

"You can do math. Go on."

The service road was filled with people. Below, the mountains were deep gold. The sky was cerulean and completely
without clouds. It was colder here, in the forties, but the sun
was strong and felt good on her face. Ro rubbed her hands
together.

"Cold?"

"Just my fingers."

Ben reached into a jacket pocket and handed her a water
bottle and a pair of gloves. "Drink. You don't want to get de-
hydrated."

She put on the gloves. "You're not cold?"

"I'm fine."

She drained half the bottle of water. "It really is spectacular."

"A rare burst of positivity."

"Is that what we do, Vicks? Bicker back and forth like an
old married couple?"

"Truce?"

"Truce, but probably not for long."

He smiled. They walked without talking until the entire
vista was nothing but gold. Two elderly women were sitting on
a view bench. When they got up, he snagged the seat, slipped

off his backpack, and opened it up. He took out the food, opening the Tupperware, careful not to spill. "Hungry?"

"A little." She took a chip and dipped it in the guacamole. "Good."

"Try the salsa."

She tried it and coughed. "What'd she put in there? Gunpowder?"

"This?" Ben made a face. "This is nothing!"

"You must have sandpaper in your mouth." She gulped water. "That's hot." She coughed again.

"Eat some tortilla chips. Water will just spread around the heat."

"Do you have any taste buds left?"

"Jalapeños are considered pretty mild over here. Take the guac."

She did, slathering the roof of her mouth with avocado. "This place is nuts. It's the only city I know that has a dedicated chili shop."

"Like the Eskimos with snow, we have a zillion words for chili. Stop kvetching and look at the scenery."

"Kvetching?"

"If you go to Las Vegas, New Mexico, there's a Jewish cemetery with a bunch of Weils in it. My grandfather Ed on my mother's side is a Weil."

"I take it he's still alive?"

"Yes. He lives in Albuquerque."

"What does he do?"

"He was originally trained as an engineer, but worked as a patent lawyer for Sandia Labs down south. He's always worked for the government. He's retired now but he still does a lot of tinkering in his garage."

"Do you see him?"

"Every time I go down to Albuquerque. He and my grandmother come up for the holidays. My dad lights Chanukah candles for him. It's really funny because he says the blessing in Hebrew and he can't make the guttural *Ch* sound. He's a cool guy, my grandpa Ed. His own father, my great-grandfather Abe, was a physicist who worked at Los Alamos during World War Two with Oppenheimer and Teller."

"Wow. You have pedigree. How about your father's parents?"

"They're alive. I see them at holidays too." He turned to her. "What about you?"

"All my grandparents are alive."

"Good genetics."

"English, Scottish and Irish and Welsh. Believe it or not, even with that kind of homogeneity, there are blood feuds."

"The English and the Irish? No!"

"And my Scottish grandfather fights with everyone. We have a rather contentious family." Her eyes stared straight ahead. The sun was beginning to sink, casting gilt shadows on a gold carpet. "It's really gorgeous."

After she finished off the guacamole, Ben got rid of the trash. The road was less populated as the hour grew late. The air was cold and still except for the quaking of the trees. Ro was beginning to shiver.

Ben said, "We can go whenever you're ready."

"Just a few more minutes."

He sat back down. "Habit-forming . . . right?"

"It's just so peaceful." She sighed. "It was nice of your mom to invite me for dinner. I really do have plans. We're all going to the movies."

"Sounds wholesome . . . except for the inevitable weed and boozing and other things that take place afterward."

She didn't deny it. "Ben, why don't you come?"

"Not a chance."

"You know, Lisa Holloway really likes you. And she really is cute, despite the Goth thing."

Don't say a word. "I'm not interested." He focused on her eyes. "I know you mean well, hon, but please don't try to fix me up. And please don't try to integrate me into your clique. I'm happy with my status. I know I'm a lone wolf—as Lilly tells me all the time. And I always tell her that no great discoveries were ever made at parties unless it was a formula written on the back of a napkin. The truth is, people like me, we live a lot in our heads."

"I hope it's a good place."

"Sometimes it is. Sometimes it's very dark. And when it's dark, I go outside and see what the sun looks like. And right now, it looks like the sun is going down. We should go. The critters that you don't see in the daytime are starting to hunt now."

She stood up and they started walking. The hike down was silent. When they reached the bottom of the trail, the sun was sinking behind the mountains. Ben leaned against the hatch of the Explorer and together they saw the fireworks spread in the sky, a brilliant display of gold, pinks, deep corals, and lavender. By the time he pulled out, the Explorer was the only vehicle in the parking area.

Ten minutes later, on the silent trip home, the stars began to come out. Ro rubbed her shoulder, turned on the heat, and fished her cell from her purse. Ben said, "You might have to wait to get reception."

She nodded and held her phone in her hand. "Can't say the entire day was a hoot and a holler, but it ended with a bang. Thank you for what was probably the most interesting time I've had since I got here."

"You're welcome."

"You are really an enigma . . . wrapped in a puzzle . . . wrapped in a riddle . . . wrapped in a mystery."

"You forgot conundrum." A pause. "And what are you?"

"I've already told you that, Vicks. I'm self-centered, egotistical, shallow, competitive, and if I need to be, a real scheming bitch."

"I don't see you that way at all."

"Okay. I'll bite. How do you see me?"

"You're lonely."

"Me? I'm like the most popular girl in the school. I'm around people all the time."

"Who said you can't be lonely with people all around?" He was staring out the windshield. "That's why you talk to me. If you had someone else who you could tell your secrets to, you wouldn't be talking to me at all. It's fine, though. I like being your temporary confidant. In a year, you'll be gone and I'll still be here and we'll probably never see each other again."

Tears formed in her eyes. "You know, Vicks? You have this way of just bringing everything down."

"Maybe, but at least I don't find you scheming and bitchy and shallow."

"Do you like me?"

"Ro, as pretty as you are, I wouldn't put up with your mouth if I didn't like you, okay? I think you're smart and funny and nice to be around. So think about that the next time you get mad at me."

She didn't say anything. A minute later her phone sprang to life. Ben knew she probably had a million missed calls and a million texts. She didn't make any phone calls, but she began to attack the texts.

He wouldn't know from experience, but he supposed that once in a while it was nice to be in demand.

CHAPTER 12

THOUGH BEN RARELY spoke to Ro at school, she did show the following Saturday to help in his research. This time there was no banter back and forth and no hike in the mountains afterward. She was all business and that was fine with him. In the weeks that followed, she proved to be very helpful. That she was a crime junkie made it easier. Ben no longer felt so ghoulish. They became a good team.

The previous month, he had started searching for murders that occurred near the equinoxes. The first spate of material that he had pulled up mainly referred to a chain of gyms. Then he plugged in "vernal equinox" and "autumnal equinox" and pulled up thousands of hits. Some were names, some were scientific articles, but there were more than a few blogs about things that go bump in the night. He read and he learned. For instance, when the star Algol (known as the Ghoul) was in proper alignment, it was key to mischief and mayhem. He pulled up charts and graphs that reminded him of the Zodiac Killer. And he also got more than a few book titles—*Blood on the Equinox, The Equinox Killer, Equinox at Daybreak*. There were lots of conspiracy theories and murders—even some terrible mass murders—but nothing that fit the particular patterns Ben was focused on. The vernal equinox seemed to generate more iniquity than the autumnal equinox, although both were popular themes in crime fiction.

The solstices turned out to be different animals. Ben got the conspiracy theories, along with the titles of novels and movies, a few made-for-TV specials, and a couple of true-crime segments.

But Shanks was right.

The solstices appeared to attract a lot of ritualism and witchcraft. Some of the witchcraft was benign—Wiccans celebrating mother earth through dance, song, and orgiastic rituals. But then there were the Goths, and when they were involved, the tenor went from bacchanalia to satanism. Some of the rituals were completely silly. But lots of what he read was disturbing, with rites that included murdered cats. When the talk about animal sacrifices morphed into human sacrifices, it was just plain frightening.

He continued on, compelled by justice, he told himself, but it was also compulsion. He and Ro met every Saturday for two to four hours depending on how much homework she had. She was also studying for the SATs, and whenever she needed math help, he was more than happy to oblige, getting away from all the ugliness. But often they worked straight through until Ro looked at her watch and said she had to head to cheerleading practice, leaving him alone with his witches and warlocks and lovers of Lucifer.

A couple of weeks before Thanksgiving, just as their session was reaching the three-hour mark, Ben got a beep on his computer.

Ro looked up from her laptop. "What was that?"

"Hold on." He clicked a few keys and navigated until he found the site. "A new case."

"What case? Something related to Ellen?" A pause. Ro got up and read over his shoulder. "Where is this from?"

"The *Knoxville News Sentinel*."

"A murder in Knoxville?"

"Cosby."

"Where is Cosby?"

"Tennessee. A girl . . . Jamey Moore . . . seventeen-year-old . . . disappeared two months ago . . . shit. She was abducted on September twenty-first."

"Yikes. That's right near the autumnal equinox."

"Yes, it is." Ben read aloud. "'She was from Knoxville . . . possibly a runaway . . . a body was discovered two days ago near Cosby, Tennessee, in the Great Smoky Mountains National Park.'"

"I feel faint, Vicks."

Ben whipped around. Ro was sitting on the bed, sweating. "Jeez, you're white." He ran to the kitchen to get some water. When he came back, her head was between her knees. "Drink."

"I can't get up without my head tingling."

He massaged her back while she waited for blood to rush back to her brain. This was all his fault. "Enough of this horrible stuff. I'll turn off the computer and we'll go for a ride."

"You can't turn off the computer now." She was still talking with her head between her legs. "This is like superimportant.

Go back to the computer and tell me about it." Slowly, she lifted her head up from her knees. She was still pale. "Go!"

He read the article for a third time, then a fourth. Ro sat up and said, "You know what this means. He's gone through all the seasons."

"I know." Nausea crept into Ben's stomach. "Ellen's was the first, three years ago, the summer solstice, then came Katie's disappearance on the vernal equinox, Julia Rehnquist was a year ago, the winter solstice, and Jamey Moore . . . right near the autumnal equinox. Four murders in three years. He's completed a cycle."

"He's going to repeat it," Ro said. "And this time he's going to be more precise."

As soon as she said the words, Ben knew she was right. He threw his head back, sweating and shaking, in a full-fledged panic. Haley would be fifteen next year. Ripe for the picking. *Breathe in, breathe out.* "It's four murders in four locations." He was trying to calm them both down. But he didn't believe his own words. "Maybe if he repeats it, he'll pick a new place. Somewhere he hasn't killed before."

"But where?"

"I don't know, Ro. I don't . . . since we don't know what's going on, exactly, let's concentrate on what we do have." A pause. "We have abductions in Knoxville, Tennessee, Berkeley, California, and Albuquerque and River Remez, New Mexico. The first two abductions were here. Then he went west of here. Then he went east of here."

"You think he picked the places randomly?"

"No, I don't," Ben said. "But I don't know what these four places have in common."

Ro said, "They're all close to mountains."

"Yeah." Ben nodded. "Good. Right. First point in common. All of the bodies were buried either in or close to state parks. Except Katie. We don't know where she is officially, I'm thinking she's probably somewhere in the Sandias. If this monster picks a new place, it's not going to be in the plains states."

"Unless it's the Ozarks," Ro said.

"Fuck!" He pounded his fist on the desk. It made Ro jump. "What am I missing?"

"How far is Cosby from Knoxville?"

He typed the cities' names into the computer. "As the crow flies, forty-one miles."

"How far is it from Berkeley to Mount Diablo?"

Again, he tapped the keyboard. "This site isn't giving me anything for Mount Diablo. Let me try Alamo." He made some adjustments. "Sixteen miles from Alamo . . . nineteen miles from the town of Diablo. Let me see if Google Maps . . ."

More clicking.

"To get from Berkeley to Mount Diablo, you take the . . . it looks like the Interstate 80 south to a Highway 24 to Interstate 680 to the town of Alamo. Then maybe you have to take streets—Stone Valley, Green Valley, to Alameda Diablo. There may be a more direct route." He felt a hand on his shoulder and looked up. "Hi. Feeling better?"

"A little. How are *you* doing?"

"I dunno, Ro. With this new case, it's getting too close to home."

"We're only a little over a month away from the winter solstice. You've got to tell Shanks."

"Let me sort this out first."

"Vicks!"

"Nothing's going to happen in a few days. Let me get my head on straight."

"I'll give you two weeks . . . to the end of November," Ro said. "But if you don't say something by then, I will."

"Okay. I'll talk to Shanks."

"When?"

"Right after Thanksgiving. I swear I will go into his office and show him this article. Just let me get myself organized. Can we go back to what I pulled up in Tennessee? Let me try to make some sense out of . . ." More Google Maps. "Gatlinburg is also in the Smoky Mountains and is much closer to Knoxville . . . ten miles as the crow flies."

"That's about thirty miles closer to Knoxville," Ro said. "So why did he choose Cosby?"

"Cosby is close to Dollywood."

"What?"

"Dollywood." He regarded Ro. "You know . . . the Dolly Parton theme park?"

"Who is Dolly Parton?"

"God, you are so city. She's an old-school country-music star with a great voice. Wears big blond wigs and has ginormous breasts."

"We have a killer who likes country music? Or maybe ginormous breasts? That would be half the population of the flyover states."

"Uh, you're living in a flyover state."

"Not by choice."

"Stop being such an elitist. There is something beyond Manhattan."

"Yeah, there's Boston, I suppose."

Ben rolled his eyes and enlarged the map. "Okay . . . here

we go. It looks like Cosby is closer to Interstate 40. To get from Knoxville to Gatlinburg might not be as direct. Might be more appealing for him to drive on a big highway. Less likely to be spotted than on some country back roads. But I'm not familiar with the place, so I could be way off." He rubbed his eyes with his fists. "I can't concentrate anymore. I'm too shaky."

"Then let's quit." Ro looked at her watch. "I've got to go to cheerleading practice. To be honest, I'm glad to be going. It'll feel very good to do something so insignificant. This is just . . . it's too big for us to handle, Vicks."

"I'll go to Shanks. Just give me . . ." He sighed. "I'm a jerk for dragging you into this. I don't know why you're doing this with me, but you've been a huge help. Thank you."

"Wanna pay me back?"

"Anything. What do you need?"

"Homecoming's in two weeks. It would mean a lot to me if you came."

He groaned inwardly. "Dorothy, I know you're going to be homecoming queen. And I'm really, really happy for you." A pause. "You don't want to make me suffer, right?"

"No, but I still want you to come."

"It's like two weeks away. I don't have a date."

"I could get you a date. I'm sure Lisa Holloway—"

"I have no interest in her, okay?"

"What do you have against poor Lisa?"

Keep a lid on it, Ben. "Why is this so important to you?"

"'Cause I like you more than anyone else in the entire school and I want you to be there in my moment of glory."

How could he resist such a naked plea?

"If it's that important to you, Dorothy Majors, I will come to see you in your moment of glory." He grimaced. "Do I have to come to the game *and* the dance?"

"Yes. I'll get you a date for the dance."

"No, I am going stag."

"You can't go stag."

"Then I'll take Haley."

"You can't take your sister. That is so loser."

He thought a moment. "I'll take Haley *and* Lilly."

"Vicks, they're fourteen!"

"But together they're twenty-eight." He grinned. "If I take Haley and Lilly, I'll have to take Griffen . . . and then I'll have to take Ezra for Lilly."

"So that leaves you stag again."

"I'm going stag. That is not up for negotiation."

A sigh. "Okay. Go stag. Sit by yourself in a corner. See if I care."

"For as much as we talk in school, I might as well be hidden in a closet."

Ro looked hurt. "I'm not embarrassed to be your friend." When he didn't answer, she said, "Maybe it's the other way around."

"That's ridiculous."

"I'm always inviting you to be with me and my friends. You never ask me to sit with you. You never ever call me up."

Ben knew he was trapped. Silence was his best option.

Ro tossed her hair back, waves of golden amber. "Then it's settled. You'll be at the game and at the dance for me. No backing out."

"God. Okay. I'll go."

She grinned. "You really are my favorite person."

"And you're mine as well. Let's get married."

"I'd make you miserable, Vicks."

"I know. And I'd make you miserable. But it would be fun while it lasted."

CHAPTER 13

THANKSGIVING, FOR BEN, was the most tolerable of the holidays because it was filled with relatives and there were no expectations about his behavior. It used to be that Mom hosted the meal, but after Ellen's death, she lost her flair for cooking and entertaining. No matter. There were plenty of kinfolk to pick up the slack. The Vicksburg and Weil clans were on a rotating schedule. This year dinner was in Albuquerque with Grandpa Ed and Grandma Pauline. Mom came from a family of four children, who in turn produced families of three to four children. Ben's dad's parents—Louise and William Sr.—would be coming in from St. Louis. Ben had tons of aunts and uncles and even more cousins—some married with kids of their own. The amount of people varied—never fewer than fifty and sometimes as many as eighty. Henry usually drove down from Santa Clara, often with a kid in tow from one of his ex-wives.

This year, as always, the feast was a mix of traditions. Santa Clara cuisine used the traditional triad of corn, beans, and squash as well as yams and potatoes. Grandma Louise and Grandpa William drove in with the turkeys—two deep-fried and one barbecued—and two honey-glazed hams. The cousins did a spread of southwestern specialties. Grandma Pauline baked all the desserts and the corn bread. Grandpa Ed's specialty was latkes—potato pancakes traditionally served during Chanukah. Since most of the family wasn't Jewish, he felt he had to get his own heritage in somehow. Ben's family was in charge of the flowers and the table decorations.

Festivities started around two and lasted until midnight. Ben loved being surrounded by the swirl mainly because he never had to explain himself. He could talk with the relations or sit and read in a corner. Haley always thrived in the commotion. She had cousins in her age range. The little-little kids would always put on a show that usually ended in tears and a meltdown.

Of all the relatives, he identified the most with his grandpa Ed. The old man was seventy-four, but as quick-witted as a man a third his age. After the meal, while others were involved in football, Grandpa would steal him away to his laboratory, better known as a three-car garage, and show his favorite grandson his latest invention, some variant of a rocket and rocket launcher. Then they'd talk about how to improve it, making drawings, doing calculations, redesigning body shapes to reduce friction and wind drag, and increasing the horsepower of the engines to accept bigger payloads and improve efficiency. Lost in a sea of numbers, neither one brought up the elephant in the room.

When it was time to go, Ben always felt a wisp of sadness.

It was silly. He could see his family anytime, but he rarely did. The forced intimacy was good, but he couldn't quite figure out a way to make it happen on his own. He was constantly fighting against an inclination to isolate himself.

Man was a social animal. Some animals were more social than others.

IF HE WAS going to have to suffer through a high school football game, he wanted to make the kickoff, being precise and methodical. The two little girls had gone shopping on Black Friday and had come back an hour late, loaded down with bags of bargains, adding clothes to their already stuffed drawers. It was their first homecoming dance and Ben knew it was a big deal. Still, he hated being late. The kickoff was at two. They had ten minutes before the official clock started.

He pounded on Haley's door. "When?"

"One minute!"

Nothing made him more edgy than waiting, and his eyes darted around with unspent energy until they abruptly focused on the door to Ellen's room.

Something spiritual grabbed him. He turned the knob and went inside.

Pink bedspread, heart-shaped pillows, three stuffed animals—her elephant, her monkey, and her teddy. The white bookshelves were filled with young-adult paperbacks popular three years ago as well as some classics—Jane Austen, Alexandre Dumas, Victor Hugo, Charlotte and Emily Brontë, Daphne du Maurier, and Edgar Allan Poe.

Ellen always had a penchant for gothic literature.

There were scattered candles and lots of pictures showing family vacations in Colorado, Arizona, Montana, and even one in L.A. when his parents took them to Disneyland. He and his sisters stood in front of the Mickey Mouse flowers at the entrance to Main Street—three kids in shorts and T-shirts ready to have fun. There was her eighth-grade graduation photo, her smile one of genuine glee.

He looked away.

The closet still contained her clothing, and her shoes were still lined up perfectly and with compulsive neatness. Folded sweaters and sweatshirts were in the drawers. There was her iPod in her pink iPod case. There was her cell-phone case. There were her pens, pencils, scratch paper, knickknacks, and leftover money that she'd never spend. Posters as well as pithy sayings still hung on the walls. Her schoolbooks and her sheet music for choir sat on her desk. He swept his finger across the top. Not an ounce of dust. Mom cleaned the room regularly. But no one had the heart or the energy or the desire to do the obvious. The shrine remained intact. He closed the door behind him and leaned against the wall.

He no longer cared if they were late or not. The girls would come out when they were done. The main thing was that they'd come out.

BECAUSE IT WAS the homecoming game, empty seats were hard to find. There was no way he was going to sit with a bunch of fourteen-year-old girls. Equally unattractive was sitting with his classmates watching James David massacre the opposition. The man had talent and Duke was a good choice. In a couple of weeks, he'd get the acceptance letter. Then he'd be gone: a new city and a new life. Ben wasn't envious, but at times he did wish he was more like JD.

He had only come for the halftime show and the announcement of homecoming queen. Everyone knew that Ro had a lock on it. Nevertheless, Ben braved it out in the top tier of the bleachers of the visiting team, figuring that no one from his school would see him consorting with the enemy. Although it was sunny, the temperature was in the forties. It would drop as soon as darkness fell, about an hour away. He hadn't brought gloves, so he stuck his hands in his jacket pockets to keep them warm.

Halftime finally came, and with it, the cheering when Ro's name was blasted over the PA. The noise was loud and boisterous. Ben hunched over, watching as the open-car parade began to circle the football field. The Rolls-Royce convertible, on loan every year courtesy of the Levy family, was given over to the queen. And there was Ro in her cheerleading costume and leg warmers, waving a white-gloved hand, her blond hair blowing in the wind as if she were gliding on a cloud. She exuded magnetism. Everybody wanted a piece of her.

Ruefully admitting the truth, he knew he was no exception.

Lilly suddenly materialized.

"Hey there." He noticed that she didn't look happy. "What's wrong?"

"Ezra crapped out. He has a cold. Can I sit down?"

"Uh, someone's sitting there but I suppose you can sit until he comes back."

She sat. Ben regarded her. "You're pissed at him?" When Lilly said nothing, he said, "He can't help getting sick."

"I'm not mad at Ezra." She sat down. "I like Ezra. Ezra likes me. But we both don't like each other in that way."

"I see."

"I don't know why Haley insists that I have to have a date wherever I go." She crossed her arms over her chest. "If she doesn't want me around, that's okay. But if I do go, I don't know why I have to be paired up with some boy who doesn't want to be paired up either."

"That's a valid point."

"I hate being a third wheel. I have a life beyond Haley Vicksburg." But there were tears in her eyes.

Ben held back a smile. "Well, Lilly, this is the situation. You are now stag and so am I. Would you do me the honor of being my date for the homecoming dance?"

Lilly wiped her eyes. "You don't have to do that. I'll be okay."

He held back a laugh. "You're rejecting me?"

"Stop it!" Her smile was shy. "I know I'm being ridiculous. And I really am glad that Haley is happy. Really."

"I believe you." A pause. "You want to see real happiness?" Ben pointed to the open car carrying Ro. Her smile was ear to ear. "Now that right there is the picture of happiness, Lilly."

"That right there is Haley in three years," Lilly muttered. "I sound jealous, right?"

"A little."

"I hate being jealous. The thing is, I don't really know who I'm jealous of. Sometimes it's Haley. Sometimes it's Griffen. Sometimes I just want him to go away and have things like they were before he came here. But I really do like Griff. And he's perfect for Haley. I don't know why I'm so unhappy. It's not like they exclude me. I just feel so pathetic."

"They don't include you out of pity," he said. "They're fourteen. You're probably a good buffer." Ben smiled again. "You know, Haley's still your best friend. Nothing is ever going to change that." His eyes went back to the football field. "How'd you find me?"

"I just looked for the most remote spot in the stadium."

"Good call." He saw the guy who was sitting next to him approaching with a tray of hot dogs and soda. "You're about to be displaced."

Lilly stood up. "I gotta get back. Haley hates when I skip out on her. She thinks I'm mad." She got out of the way so the man carrying the tray could sit down. "Where are we meeting after the game?"

"At the car. We'll go home, change, and go back to the dance."

"Whoopee!" She twirled her finger in the air. "I'm not gonna embarrass you by being your date."

"You won't embarrass me. Can't speak for you."

She smiled. "See you later."

"Bye." Ben went back to staring at the Rolls; a silver Corniche with a red interior. It would have been worth it to be homecoming queen just to ride in such a beautiful vehicle. He blew warm air on his hands. He was cold, hungry, and more than a little depressed. When the third quarter started, he got up and bought two hot dogs and a big cup of coffee, and drank and ate in the car with the heat blasting on his face. No longer cold. No longer hungry.

Two out of three ain't bad.

EVEN LILLY HAD ditched him. At the dance, Ben had left her alone to go find Ro and congratulate her, but the crowd around JD and her was too thick to penetrate. All he wanted to do was show his face so Ro would know that he'd kept his word. But hanging around the perimeter of fans and well-wishers, he began to feel like the paparazzi.

When Lilly caught up to him, she was beaming. The little

girl was wearing a black strapless dress that covered a nonexistent chest. She was built thin and boyish—taller than her petite Chinese mother, but not at all hulking like her father. Around her wrist was a corsage.

"Nice flowers, young lady."

"Ezra decided to come."

"He did, did he." Ben nodded approvingly. "What happened to his cold?"

"He still has it. Haley put powder on his red nose so it wouldn't show up in the pictures."

"Nice of him to come when he was sick."

"Yeah, it was." Lilly looked down. "You look very handsome."

"Thank you. And you look very pretty."

"I look like I'm playing dress-up."

"The dress is lovely, Lilly. And so are you."

"Thank you." She was blushing. "I have to get back to Ezra. It's awkward to dance with him. I don't want to catch his cold."

"The things you do for love."

She gave him a playful shove and skipped off. Now that she was taken care of, Ben could finally retreat without guilt. Overpaying for a large hot tea, he warmed his hands on the paper cup and then stepped out of the tinsel-covered gym onto the adjacent patio. People were milling around. He kept walking until he was alone. The night was cold and the sky was studded with stars. He stood against a cottonwood and felt chilled air going through his lungs, converting to mist when he exhaled. Five minutes later, Tom Gomez appeared, smoking a cigarette.

"Mind if I join you?"

"No, not at all." Ben sipped his tea.

"How's it going?"

"Same as last time." A pause. "Sorry for running out like that. I dunno . . . sometimes I get a little crazy. I apologize."

"I offended you," Gomez said. "I apologize for that. But not for the rest of what I said."

Silence.

"Ben, our families have been friends for a very long time. I'm speaking to you like I would speak to one of my own kids . . . if I had a kid as gifted as you are."

"Not interested."

"It's my job to make you interested." He took a drag on his cigarette. "I don't want you to look back ten years from now and see the terrible mistake you're making. I don't want you here twenty years from now, feeling like you're trapped because you sold yourself short."

"Is that how you feel?"

"Sometimes. But I suspect lots of men at my stage of life feel a little trapped. I love my life. I just wish I experienced more of it on my own."

"Then why'd you stay here?"

"UNM was very good to me. I wanted to give something back to my community."

"Ditto."

"I have family here going back hundreds of years."

"Ditto."

"And then . . . sometimes . . . on clear starry nights like this one, I can't think of anyplace else I'd rather be."

"Ditto, ditto, ditto."

"But there's a difference. I'm a man of limited funds—"

"Ditto."

"Now, that's not true. You could get a full scholarship to lots of places. Besides, that's not the point."

"You brought it up."

"Ben, I'm a man of limited funds and also limited talents. That's not you."

Ben said, "I'm happy here, Tom. I'd like to go to St. John's just for a change of pace. But I'd do fine at UNM."

"You've taken a lot of courses there."

"It's got a decent math department and a good physics department. I could actually attend both places at the same time—St. John's and UNM."

"One's in Albuquerque, one's in Santa Fe."

"I could go to the UNM campus near Santa Fe. Or I could commute. It's only an hour. Plus, I've already been offered a paying internship with Circuitchip."

"I can see you're determined not to have a social life."

"All I'm saying is this area has plenty to offer. Hell, we've got all the major labs here—Los Alamos, Sandia—"

"You'll need a PhD."

"So maybe when it's PhD time, I'll go somewhere else. In the meantime, what's wrong with sticking around close to home?"

"Just tell me you're not staying for Haley."

"Nah, Haley doesn't need me." He said it unconvincingly, especially after the latest development with Jamey Moore. But he pressed forward. "I'm staying here because I want to stay here."

"So, it's either St. John's or UNM or both."

"That's the plan."

"Okay, Ben." Gomez stubbed out his cigarette with his heel, then picked up the butt and threw it away in the garbage. "If that's what you want, it'll surely happen."

Ben stared up at the sky. "I appreciate it, Tom."

"I think someone's looking for you." Gomez was referring to Ro, who had just come outside onto the patio. He said, "You know the dating pool is much bigger at other universities."

Ben laughed. "You'll try anything."

"I'm an old dog, but I haven't quite given up. I'll leave you to your thoughts."

Ro had on a bright red ball gown and was protected from the cold by only a shawl. She spotted Ben and came running, holding up the hem of her dress, looking like Cinderella when the clock struck twelve. "There you are." She kissed his cheek. "Come inside. It's freezing!"

"I'd be cold too if that's all I was wearing."

"I'm serious." She rubbed her arms.

"I know. But I like it out here."

"Vicks!"

"I showed up for your event—both of them. Isn't that enough?"

"No."

Ben smiled and rubbed her arms to give her warmth. "You look breathtaking."

"You don't look so bad yourself." She straightened his tie and smoothed his shirt. Then she tucked an errant piece of hair behind his ear. "Very handsome."

"Not bad for a penguin. But I'm glad you approve."

"Can you come in now? I want to dance with you."

"After you dance with JD."

"I have to have the first dance with JD. Don't be mad at me. I really want to dance with you."

"Ro, I'm happy for you. I really am. This is what you wanted." He kissed her cheek. "But I don't like being filler."

"I can't be happy unless you're happy."

"That's the issue here. I'm happy right now and you're not. And if I go in there, you'll be happy but I won't be. Let's just let it rest and we'll both be happy."

"Or unhappy."

He lowered his head to kiss her cheek but she turned and gave him her mouth. It was just a gentle peck on the lips, but it sent electric shocks through his spine. He pulled away. "Go back to your king."

She exhaled. "Um, I've got a favor to ask you."

"I'll be happy to tutor you anytime and free of charge."

"Not that. God, you always think I'm after something." She smiled. "Of course I usually do have ulterior motives. Uh, can we meet on Sunday instead of Saturday?" She gave another smile. This one was forced. "Got some plans . . ."

"Go ahead, Ro. Enjoy yourself. This is your time, baby."

"I'll see you on Sunday?"

"Uh, no." He looked away. "I was planning on hiking Mount Baldy."

"Oh . . . much better than looking at murder folders. I'll go with you."

"I'm leaving at six in the morning to capture the daylight. It's a rigorous hike at twelve thousand feet in frigid air. It's definitely not for you."

Her face fell. "So why don't you hike it tomorrow instead of Sunday?"

"Tomorrow?" This time *he* smiled. "Got some plans . . ."

She failed to see the humor. "You don't want me to come."

He stalled, trying to think of a lie. "I think I need a little space."

"You have space all the time. You're always by yourself. What is with you?"

Just then Ben saw JD come onto the patio, his head turning in all directions. "Your Highness awaits."

When Ro saw him, she sighed. "You're impossible." She hurried back to JD. The two of them were fighting, arms gesticulating back and forth. But they resolved things pretty quickly. Within minutes, he had his arm around her bare shoulder and her head was on his bicep. They walked in together—king and queen.

And the jester stood alone.

CHAPTER 14

BY WAKING UP at five, Ro hoped to catch Ben before he left for his marathon hike. It was pitch-black outside, and as she wended her way to his house, she felt her heart beating in her chest because she knew he'd be angry.

She had come prepared, dressing in layers with a warm coat, warm socks, gloves, a hat, a parka, and a fresh set of clothing. She had brought loads of food, a flashlight, and a GPS that she didn't know how to use but Ben could figure it out.

Having looked the hike up on the Internet, she was nervous. It was rigorous, it was at a very high altitude, and it was going to be freezing. Ben was crazy. And she was crazy for going with him. She was especially crazy for going with him when he didn't want her. But she couldn't help it. There was something about the boy that kept sucking her in: his spirit, his sadness, his passion. It was ridiculous. They weren't even a couple. They fought as much as they got along. They were totally ill-suited for one another. But Ro needed him. She also needed him to need her.

She parked in front of his house and was relieved to see that both of his parents' cars were in the driveway, which meant he was still home. She blew out air, walked up to the front door, and knocked softly. It was twenty to six. The door swung open. She steeled herself for the onslaught. "Hi."

Angry eyes looked at hers. "Are you nuts?"

"Happy to see you too. Can I come in?" She didn't wait for an answer, walking past him and into the kitchen, where his mother was preparing sandwiches. "Hi, Mrs. Vicksburg. How are you?"

His mom looked shocked. "Ben, you can't seriously think of taking Ro hiking on Mount Baldy."

"Of course not—"

"It'll be fine!" Ro showed off her multiple sweaters and her hiking shoes. "All dressed and ready to go." She sneaked a glance at Ben. Then she looked away and grimaced. He was furious but working hard at maintaining calm because they both knew there was no sense in getting his mother upset. She said, "I've come prepared."

He said, "I appreciate you wanting to come, but like I told you in school, it's a tough hike."

"Then would it kill you to do a simpler hike?"

His mom said, "Amen to that."

Ben took in a deep breath and let it out. "Okay. This is what we'll do. We'll start out, and when you start to flag, we'll turn around."

"Now that sounds like a plan." Ro held up her rucksack. "I've got everything I need in one neat package." When she grinned, it enraged him. No matter. She'd calm him down once they were alone.

His mother said, "Are you sure you have everything you need, Ro?"

"I made a list and checked it twice. I have sandwiches and water and a poncho because I know it gets wet. I've got gloves and a scarf and a change of clothes." She smiled at Ben, who didn't smile back. She threw him the keys. "You drive. You know the way."

He caught them with one hand. "I'll be right back."

"Where are you—" But he was out the door. A minute later he came back, holding his knapsack by the strap. He gave his mom a set of keys. "At least you'll have your car."

"This is a foolhardy idea, Ben."

"I'll be home by six." He was clenching his jaw. It was giving him a headache. "Let's go."

Silently they walked into the frigid darkness and climbed into Ro's car. Ben stowed both backpacks in the rear seat. As soon as he put the key into the ignition and turned on the motor, Ro cranked up the heat. "Wow, it's cold."

Ben slowly eased the car into the street. The first few minutes were agonizingly silent. She finally said, "You're mad."

"Give me a few moments, okay?"

The intensity in his voice told her she had gone too far. "Look, I promise I'll keep up. And I won't kvetch. I'm a lot stronger than I make myself out to be. I can do this."

"Ro, I'm not mad. I just need to think, okay?"

She looked down. "I just wanted to see you."

"A few minutes? Please?"

She said nothing. They drove through the gravel streets

until he merged onto the asphalt of Sierra Road. Ten minutes later he accelerated onto I-25 south.

Ro said, "Is this the right way? I thought Baldy was north."

"I know where I'm going, okay."

"Sorry. Can I turn on the radio?"

"It's your car."

"What kind of music do you like?"

"Doesn't matter."

She turned on rock, then thought better of it and turned on easy listening. "A little intense for heavy metal."

Ben was silent. He turned down the heat so he could be heard. "Uh, let me get a couple of thoughts out, okay?"

"Sure." Her voice was timid.

"Dorothy, I know it's been hard for you being here. But it's been a real boon for me. I want to thank you for making the effort to be nice to me." He glanced at her. "I'm glad you came to River Remez. And by the looks of your popularity, so is everyone here . . . glad you came. It certainly was good for Haley. She and Griffen . . . they're really cute together."

Her smile was heartfelt. "Those two really are a pair." A grin. "Ah, young love."

"Yeah, it's sweet." His voice grew soft. "Ro, you've given me a lot of insight and you've also given me the push to say something to Shanks."

Ro got excited. "You set up an appointment with him?"

"I'm going to do it this week, as promised."

"Can I come?"

"No."

"Why not? I want to meet him." She punched his shoulder lightly. "We're a team."

"We're not a team, but you've helped me tremendously. Thank you."

"Vicks, there is no one on this planet that I admire as much as you."

"Thanks, but let me finish, okay?" A protracted silence. "Next semester I'm changing my schedule. I'm not going to be around much. I mean, I'll be around if like you need help in math—"

"Stop it already." Ro felt her heart beat a little faster. "What's going on?"

"I'm taking some upper-division classes at UNM. They're scheduled Tuesday and Thursday. On Wednesdays and Fridays, I'm going to be interning at Circuitchip."

"The computer chip maker?"

"Yeah, they are the largest business in Albuquerque—Rio Rancho actually. It's a big opportunity for me. Like working for Google or Amazon, but closer to home. That means I'll be down south Tuesday through Friday. That's what I was doing yesterday. Working it out with the school."

Ro felt her eyes go moist. "You're done with high school?"

"No, I've got government and an English class. I've talked to Mr. Gomez and a couple of the teachers. They've agreed to give me independent study. I'll be there all day Monday, but I'm not doing any more TA-ing or stuff like that."

Panic hit her and she had no idea why. She barely saw Ben at school. But in the back of her mind, she always knew he was there. "How long have you known about this?"

"Like I said, most of this happened yesterday, but I've been thinking about it for a while."

"You never said anything."

"I wasn't sure. You know, doing the adult thing . . ." He

gave her a forced smile. "If I lived in River Remez, I'd need a car. I didn't want my dad to fork out the money. It's a car, it's gas, it's insurance. I won't be living at home. In Albuquerque, they've got buses to Circuitchip and my grandparents don't live too far from the university. I'll be staying with them."

Ro stared out the windshield. "Will you be here over the weekend?"

"Yeah, my grandparents have a spare car that's not great for a daily driver but it's fine for the weekends. I'll have to come home on Sunday to go to school on Monday. So I'll be here a couple of days." He touched her arm and she jumped. "You okay?"

"Yeah, I'm fine."

He said, "Take care of my sister for me, okay? I'm serious about this. She'll be fifteen this summer. She looks even older. I'm worried." Panicked, actually. "I'll see what Shanks says, but regardless, I won't rest until this monster is caught. Take care of her, take care of Lilly too. They're much more likely to listen to you than to me anyway."

"Of course I'll watch over them. They're my buds." Ro looked down. "Are you going to attend graduation?"

"I'm planning on it. Anyway, you know how twelfth grade is. Everyone's just about checked out. I'm just doing it a little early."

"That's good, Vicks. Sounds like you've got it figured out."

"I'm trying my best." A pause. "And I'm sincere about helping you raise your SAT math score. Any of the Ivies would be lucky to have you."

She didn't answer.

He said, "Ro, I know this guy. Grant Statler. He's really wealthy. His family used to be in the hotel business." No response. "Uh, his dad works for a hedge fund in L.A. He just finished his first semester at Ha-vard, of course."

Still no response.

"His grandparents have a summer home in Santa Fe. We used to go to camp together. He's probably the closest friend I have, and that's not because of me. He's a great guy. If you go back east, I'll give him a call. I'm sure he'd love to take you around." When she didn't say anything, Ben tapped the wheel again. "I've got something else to tell you."

"What? You're gay?"

"No, I'm not gay." Ben was taken aback. "I'm a little nerdy, but why would you think I'm gay?"

"I dunno. The car's beginning to feel like a confessional."

Not far from the truth. "I lied to you on Friday. I never had any intention of hiking Mount Baldy today. I made up something to tell my mom because I didn't want to tell her the truth. I *am* going hiking, but my plan is to look for Katie Doogan. Give it one last shot before I go to Shanks. I didn't want her to know. And I didn't want you to know. This is not something that I want you to be a part of."

"Well, Vicks, I'm here and unless you intend to turn the car around, it looks like you're stuck with me."

"Ever been to Albuquerque?"

"Not really."

"It's an interesting city. It's got some good art museums—"

"No, no, no," Ro said. "I'm coming with you."

"You'll distract me."

"So I won't talk, okay? I'll stay ten feet behind you like a good squaw. Or is that politically incorrect to call a Native American a squaw?"

Ben didn't answer anything.

"This is all a mess!" Ro shook her head but refused to cry. "It's because of JD, right?"

"That I'm looking for Katie Doogan?"

"That you're leaving the school."

"It has nothing to do with JD or you or high school. It's about me doing what I need to do to jump-start my life."

"Would you stay in Remez High if I broke up with JD?"

"Absolutely not."

She crossed her arms. "Then it doesn't matter to you one way or the other?"

"What matters to me doesn't count. It's what you want." Silence. "Do me a favor, okay?"

"I'm not doing anything for you. I'm pissed at you."

"Why? Because for once I didn't follow your script?" She didn't answer. "If you ever do break up with JD, let me come with you."

"I don't need you. I can handle my own affairs."

"I'm asking you this one thing, okay. Let me come with you."

"I'm not breaking up with him."

"Then there's no issue."

"At least not until after the winter dance." A pause. "I already bought the dress."

Ben laughed. "Well, there's a reason to stay with a guy."

"Shut up."

"JD's a big guy, and with a big temper to match. I just want to make sure nothing bad happens."

"All guys have tempers." She turned to him. "If I decide to break up with JD, you can come with me, but only if I come with you to look for Katie Doogan."

"You don't want to do this."

"Excuse me, but I do." A beat. "Where are you searching? In the mountains?"

"Yes."

"I'm dressed for that. And what's the likelihood that we'll find her?"

"The null set."

"So basically, we're taking an all-day walk in the woods. Do you even know where you're going?"

"That's insulting."

"I'm just curious if it's like a random thing or—"

"Of course I know where I'm going." He sounded aggravated. "Something like this, you don't just pick random spots. I've been doing this for a while. I've charted it all out—where they've previously searched, where they haven't searched, where the riverbanks are, where the lakes are. It's anything but random. I carefully plotted out these pathways yesterday."

"When you weren't planning on ditching me next semester."

"Stop taking it personally. It's not like I'm going to Timbuktu. I'll be an hour away."

"I'll never see you in school."

"You don't anyway." When she huffed, he said, "Can we stop bickering?"

Ro turned up the volume of the music. Then she turned it down. "How much longer to get there?"

"Around an hour."

"Will you miss me?"

"I'll miss seeing you the two minutes we talk every day." Ben tapped the steering wheel. "How about if I tutor you on Sundays so I get a chance to see you." When she didn't answer, he said, "When's the next time you're taking the SATs?"

"Mid-January."

"We've only got a month. You're quick. A little bit of tutoring and you'll rock it."

She gave him a smile that was tinged with sadness. She sighed. "Thanks. And I'll pay you."

"Not a chance. This is my way of giving something to you. So when all those college boys are chasing you, you'll think fondly of me."

Her eyes watered up. Ben handed her a tissue and she dried her eyes. She sat up and stared out the window. "Tell me about Grant Statler."

"That was a quick change of heart," Ben noted.

"That's me, Vicks, in a nutshell. I may get down, but I'm never out."

CHAPTER 15

THE SKY BEGAN to lighten, changing from charcoal to deep, evanescent pinks and intense lavenders right before the brilliant golds of sunrise. As they headed toward downtown Albuquerque, the highway was empty, the horizon obscured by the multistoried buildings of a real city. With its steady growth and a population topping the half-million mark, Albuquerque had pushed New Mexico into the twenty-first century. In many ways, Ben thought of it as a small town from the Wild West. If crime rate was any indication of lawlessness, the image fit perfectly. Because of the wide-open space, New Mexico was always a perfect hiding place for fugitives, drug dealers, and transients making their way across the continent.

Ben drove deep into the preserves of the Sandias, keeping a close watch on time because daylight was short. He parked at the trailhead, but kept the motor idling for heat. "We should eat before we go."

"Nothing like baloney and cheese first thing in the morning."

"Is that what you packed?"

"Excuse me. No one was up to fix my Niçoise salad."

Reaching around to the backseat, he opened his knapsack. "I have egg salad. That's kinda like breakfast."

"Sure."

"Coffee? It's black."

"Yeah, motor oil is fine."

He poured two cups and gave one to her. She wore a blue Cornell sweatshirt and a pair of jeans. Her complexion was alabaster white except for rosy cheeks enhanced by the cold. Without makeup, she had a sprinkling of freckles over her nose that he'd never noticed. Her hair was tied back into a ponytail. The November air was cold and parched and had been that way for a while. Her lips, though rubbed with something greasy, were chapped. Her eyes were moody blue.

They ate quickly and in silence. After a quick bathroom run, Ben handed Ro a walking stick and adjusted it for her height. The trail he had mapped out contained several estuaries that emptied into the Rio Grande. Though rescue parties had searched the area many times, Ben just had a feeling that Katie's resting place was near water.

The sky was pale and there was a cold breeze as they started up the trail. No talk, which was good. He could focus, hearing the burbling of the water, the rush of wind, the other noises of nature—scampering, cracking, and birdcalls. The trail was compacted dirt—hard under the foot—whereas the ground beside it was filled with brown and gold organic material, all of it sodden. Whiffs of wet paper and pine wafted through the air. After a half hour of hiking, Ro decided to talk.

"Why'd you pick this spot to search?"

"Soil is looser around water, so you can dig a deeper grave. But also . . . when you do this long enough, you have to start thinking like the killer. It's real easy to get lost off-trail. Everything starts to look alike especially in the dark and in this terrain. It's impossible to navigate without tools. Unless you have compasses or GPS, which doesn't work too well here, you need some kind of guide to get back to where you parked your car. The shores of a riverbank are a natural conduit. If you're burying bodies, you're probably doing it at night, so it helps if you're following natural landmarks."

"What are you looking for?"

He stopped walking and glanced around. "I look at the topography. I'm looking for sunken ground. You have to look really carefully because at this time of year everything is covered in leaves."

It was weird—explaining what he did. He took out his compass and marked the location in a notebook. "Okay." He used his walking stick as a pointer. "We can cut through here to the creek and follow it north. If you go up the trail, the rise is pretty quick. If you're carrying a body in the dark, you're going to choose a route that's direct. Let's go. Use your stick. There are tree roots you're not going to see."

"How many times have you explored this area?"

"Twice." She stumbled and he caught her. "You okay?"

"Fine."

"I'll go slower."

"Appreciate it." Ro walked with care down the hillside. With each step, her boots sank into piles of leaves. The ground was soggy and irregular and some of it was muddy. She appeared nervous. She said, "Then you think that Katie Doogan is buried in a deep grave."

"Yes. That's what happened with my sister and I think the cases are related."

"You think he planned it—premeditation."

"Yes."

"And he's someone from the area?"

"Someone who was familiar with the locale. A lot of local people were questioned. Nothing came of it."

She tripped again and caught her balance. "Maybe I should concentrate on walking instead of bombarding you with questions."

"It's not you. I trip all the time." Ben took her arm and led her down to the riverbank. "This way."

The waterway was less than a full-fledged river but more than a creek. Whitecaps swirled as cold, crystalline water rushed over the boulders and tree roots. Empty skeletal trees reached up to the skies. Pines dripped dew as the sun began to warm the air. Sometime later Ben picked up the conversation. "There were lots of interesting possibilities for suspects. But like I said, nothing panned out."

"Anything remotely promising?"

"Shanks put most of his energy behind this boy—Tim Sanchez. He was a year older than Ellen—seventeen. He had a car. He had a wild crush on her that wasn't reciprocated. Everyone at school told Shanks the same story. He followed her around . . . not exactly stalking her, but staring from afar."

"Did your sister ever say anything to your parents?"

"Nah. That wasn't Ellen. People at school said she was nice to him. Maybe that was her mistake, they all said. Plus, he didn't have a good alibi for when she was abducted. For a while he looked real promising."

"What happened?"

"They searched the house and his closet and his shoes and the Dumpsters around his house for torn clothing or blood or whatever. They also took his DNA. No evidence against him. They let him go."

"How were you with that?"

"In the beginning, I didn't like it. When the DNA didn't match, I knew it wasn't him. Now that patterns are emerging, I *really* know it wasn't him. It was hard on Timmy and his family. They felt the heat of everyone staring at them. They moved to Montana."

"What happened to him? Or did you lose track?"

Ben stopped walking. "You never lose track of a suspect, even one who was exonerated. You always think about the possibility that maybe there was more than one murderer. Timmy's in Missoula. He's a sophomore. When Katie Doogan was abducted, he was taking an exam in American history. I've actually talked to him a few times, asked him what he thought about what happened."

"What'd he say?"

"He didn't know anyone who'd want to hurt Ellen. He was devastated when she was kidnapped. Even more devastated when people were looking at him like he had something to do with it. He fully cooperated with the police. It's not him."

The water began to roil as the distance across it narrowed. They climbed upward. The air was thin, cold, and dry.

"The thing is . . ." Ben looked around. "If it *is* someone local, that means he's still around. That's what's really scary. He kills here, then he goes west, then he goes east. It's crazy."

Ro stopped and took out a bottle of water. "Sorry to slow you down. I've gotta catch my breath."

Ben felt guilty. "You feeling okay? A little light-headed?"

"I've been here long enough that I should be used to the altitude." She tightened the scarf around her neck and covered her mouth and nose. "It's cold."

"You want to turn back?"

"We've only been walking for a couple of hours." She took a breath in and out. "My lungs are feeling it. I'll be okay in a few minutes."

"I can come back another time, hon. It's fine. This is my personal issue, not yours."

Ro took another gulp of water. "Yeah, it is. But now I'm here and involved, and we might as well look for the body. It must be hell on the family—the Doogans. Until they find their daughter and have a proper burial, they're carrying a heavy weight."

"That's why I didn't want you to come. Not that I don't appreciate the company." Ben noticed she was still pale. "Maybe you should have a Balance Bar or something."

"That might be a good idea."

"For both of us." He took out the snacks and they ate without talking. When she told him she was good to go, they continued onward. The time went by quickly, an hour of walking and looking until he heard something. He grabbed her arm. "Stop. Don't move."

She froze. She whispered, "It sounds like a bear . . . not that I know what a bear sounds like."

"It's late in the season, but . . ." Ben slipped his backpack from his shoulders. He took out a gun, ammo, and bear Mace. "Don't worry. Got it covered." He dropped ammo into the revolver.

"You have a *gun*?"

"I always carry a gun when I go into the backcountry. But don't tell the cops. I should be nineteen."

"You actually know how to shoot that thing?"

"I do and so does your boyfriend. We used to go to the range together."

"When was this?"

"The summer before last." They heard the growling again. "Yeah, that sounds like a bear. It's definitely warning us off."

"What do we do?"

"We turn around and go the other way."

"What if it comes after us?"

He didn't answer, took her hand, and they reversed direction. "Stop looking back. We're fine."

"I have come to the conclusion that the only fur I want to see is hanging in the Bergdorf salon. And faux fur at that." She was walking too fast and she stepped in a pool of mud. "Oh God!"

"It's dirt. It'll wash off."

"Ugh, it's so squishy."

"I thought you weren't gonna kvetch."

"Ursa Major changed my mind." She made a face. "You actually went shooting with JD? Meaning you two were friends at some point?"

Ben sidestepped the questions. "Hold on a moment." He unloaded the gun and rechecked to make sure the chambers were empty. Then he stowed the gun in his jacket. He kept the bear Mace within reach. "You should drink. The humidity must be in single digits."

She took out her water bottle. "You can't hate JD if you went shooting with him."

"I never said I hated him." He pulled her in a different direction. "Let's try up this way."

"What's here?"

"Don't know. I've been around here, but not at these coordinates."

"You keep coordinates of every place you've been."

"Of course. Why should I retrace something unless I want to retrace?"

"Are there bears here?"

"We'll find out. Go."

"Ugh. It's uphill?"

"We're going toward the trail. We'd have to go up anyway."

They walked without talking, two sets of eyes sweeping over the ground, asking it to give up its secrets. An hour more of searching with nothing to show for it. Ro said, "I have to go to the bathroom."

"Lots of bushes out here. Take your pick."

"I'm not gonna go in a bush."

"If you'd prefer a tree, go for it."

"That's disgusting." She sighed. "I'm fine."

"Ro, we're about an hour away from the car. Just do it. I promise I won't look."

"That never even occurred to me."

"Don't be stubborn. Just go over there and do your business. You'll feel much better."

"The only thing that's going to make me feel better is a marble bathroom and a tub filled with hot water and bubbles. You were right, Vicks. I'm a wuss. I'm not doing this again."

"A smart person knows her limitations." He opened up another bottle of water and drained it. Maybe the best thing to do was to show by example. "You can do what you want, hon, but I need to piss. I'll be right back."

"You're leaving me alone?" She grabbed his wrist. "I'll go with you. I'll close my eyes."

"It's like twenty feet away." He gave her the bear Mace. "Please don't use this on me by mistake."

"Where're you going?"

"See that tree and that bush?" Ben pointed with his stick. "Right there."

"I want to go with you."

"You're being ridiculous." As he started up the hill, she came after him. "Stop it! C'mon!"

She stopped. Gorgeous girl, but a sissy. They made them soft in the city. She was rooted to the same spot and gripping the Mace when he returned. "Uh, I can take this back now."

She didn't answer, remaining as still as stone. He had to pry the Mace from her fingers. Her face had turned from white to gray. Ben said, "What's wrong?"

Slowly she lifted her stick, the tip pointing to an area on the ground about fifty feet from where they stood. She tried to talk, but the words clogged her throat. She didn't need to say anything. He saw it: a near-perfect seven-by-five-foot leaf-covered rectangle lying below the surface of the ground.

Don't think, Vicksburg. Do!

He took out his cell. No reception. He took out the GPS. That wasn't working either. The mountain was blocking the signals from satellites. He'd do it the old-fashioned way, compass and pencil.

He wrote down the coordinates. He drew a map. He made landmarks. He took pictures with his camera. He needed to be able to lead the police back to the spot. Ro hadn't budged from where she was initially standing.

"Let's go." She wouldn't or couldn't move. "Ro, we have to call the police." He took her gloved hand. Even through the suede, her fingers felt icy. "You're cold. Let's go warm you up."

He tugged and eventually she followed like a puppy being leash-trained, walking very slowly without conversation. Ben was worried. Her face was bloodless, her lips were chapped, and she was shivering. The front of her pants at the crotch was marked by a big piss stain.

It appeared that fear had overcome her sense of propriety.

CHAPTER 16

AS SOON AS they were in her Explorer, Ben cranked up the heat. Ro sat on the edge of the passenger seat, her knapsack still hanging on her back. He took it off and then rummaged through the contents. She had brought along a change of clothes—a pair of knitted leggings, a thick argyle white sweater, and a pair of Uggs. He took out the clothing. "You might want to change. Maybe be a little more comfortable before we go back."

Ro looked down at her lap. Her lower lip began to tremble. The tears started a few moments later. He handed her the Kleenex box. "You need help, Dorothy?"

She nodded.

He came over to the passenger door, took off her muddy boots and wet socks, and stowed them in a plastic bag. Hoping to motivate her, he unzipped her jeans. She was heat-welded to the spot. "Let's get the jeans off. Turn around and lift up your butt."

She did as she was told and he pulled the sodden denim down. Her legs were slim and long. Her panties were white lace and probably soaked as well. He gave her the leggings. "I think you can handle it from this point. I'll turn around so you can take your underwear off."

She didn't answer, but he could hear her moving. A few minutes later she whispered. "I'm okay."

He went back to the driver's seat. Her complexion had taken on a greenish hue.

"I feel sick," she told him.

"Do you need to throw up?"

Without answering, she threw open the door and barfed without leaving the car. When she sat up, her eyes were watery and goop was leaking from her mouth. She took a tissue and wiped her face.

"Water?"

"Yeah. Is it her?" Her voice dropped. "Katie Doogan?"

"I have no idea. But we have to call the police." His brain was reeling. "I don't know anyone in the Albuquerque PD other than Milton Ortiz, who was assigned to the Doogan case. I'll try to get him. He knows me. But there's a good chance that we're going to be questioned by someone else."

"Questioned?"

"You as a witness, me as a suspect." He smeared his lips with organic lip balm. "'S'right. I've been down that road before."

"A suspect?" A pause. "Why?"

"The police are going to wonder what we were doing hiking in the backcountry. This is what I want you to say." Silence. "Are you listening?"

"Yes."

"Tell them that you'll be happy to answer any of their questions. But you won't answer anything until you have a lawyer present. In this case, the simplest thing to do is to call your dad. They're not going to mess with anyone from the state attorney general's office." She didn't answer. "Ro?"

"I hear you."

"Okay. Once your dad is with you, then just tell them the truth. That you just came with me. And you can tell them that I was here looking for Katie Doogan's body. Because that's what I'm going to say. If they start asking you pointed questions, your dad will be there to protect you."

"I don't need protection. We didn't do anything."

"I know, Dorothy. It'll be okay. But still, ask for a lawyer. That way they can't question you."

"Doesn't that make you look like you're hiding something?"

"No, it makes you smart. That's exactly what I'm going to do. As soon as we get reception, I'm gonna call my dad to come down. Then you call your dad. Then we call the police. Say nothing until your dad is with you. You can tell the police I'm obsessed with my sister's case. You're not revealing anything new."

"Okay." Her eyes were on her lap. "What about the files and everything you have in your room?"

"Uh, good question." He weighed his options. "Don't volunteer anything, but if it comes up, tell them. You don't have to protect me. I don't need protection."

"Why would they even think you were doing something wrong? Katie Doogan's been dead for two years."

"Let me explain something," he told her. "The police suspect everyone. When I found my sister's body, they grilled me, implying that I knew all along where she was . . . and that by finding her, I was trying to be a hero to my family. At the time I was too naive to realize where they were going. Shanks helped me out. I'm wiser now. I know I'm gonna catch heat."

"Vicks, I was the one who found the spot."

"You can tell them that, but they probably won't believe you. Just stick to the truth. Don't let them rile you. And don't say anything unless your father gives you permission to talk."

"Okay." She took his hand and squeezed. "I'm with you all the way."

He managed to smile, then turned on the ignition and put the car into drive. "Let me know when you get reception."

It took twenty minutes. Finally, her phone sprang to life. "We've got bars."

Ben was driving on a two-lane highway and it took a little maneuvering to pull the car over onto a slender gravel shoulder and completely off the blacktop. He pulled out his phone and punched in his dad's cell. When it clicked in, he said, "Hi, it's me. I got a problem."

"What's wrong?" Panic in his father's voice.

"I'm fine, Dad. I was hiking in the woods. I think I might have found a body."

"At Mount Baldy?"

"No, I'm down in the Sandias—"

"You went looking for Katie Doogan! Again!"

"Dad, I've got to call the police. I need you to come to Albuquerque like right away."

"God, when are you going to stop?"

"You need to come to Albuquer—"

"I hear you, dammit." Dad was beyond aggravated. "I'll come as quick as I can. I don't have a car."

"I left the car with Mom."

"I know. But she's not here and I'm with a business associate. I've got to get a ride home and get the car and explain everything to Mom and get her all upset. Ben, you have to stop with this nonsense!"

"Dad, right now I have to call the police. Come down as quick as you can."

"Call up Grandpa Ed. He can get to you in twenty minutes."

"He's a patent lawyer, Dad."

"Just shut up and do what I say."

"I'm not going to bother Grandpa, okay. He's an elderly man. Whenever you get here, you get here. I won't talk until you're with me."

"Fine." A pause. "I am so damn frustrated with you."

"I know you are. I'm sorry. I've got to hang up. Ro has to call her parents."

"Ro?" A gasp. "Ro Majors is with you? Are you out of your mind, taking her down to search for bodies?"

"She needs to call her father, Dad."

"Tell her not to say anything either until her father gets there."

"We've been over it. I'll talk to you late—"

"Where should I meet you?"

"Uh, I have to wait for the police at the trailhead. Then I have to lead them down to where we saw the grave—"

"You didn't find a body."

"We found what might be a grave."

"So you don't know if it's a grave or not." When Ben didn't answer, his father said, "Where should I meet you?"

"Just go directly to the Albuquerque PD main headquarters, okay. I'm going to try to find Milton Ortiz. At least he knows who I am. Oh, and maybe you should call Shanks."

"Sure. Ruin someone else's day."

"Dad, if it's Katie, do you realize what this will mean for the Doogans?"

"Don't you lecture me—"

"I'm sorry. I really have to go now."

"Ben, don't say a word, okay?"

"I get it."

"I love you."

"I love you too." He hung up the phone. "Call your dad. He's going to be furious with me. He may even forbid you to see me again."

"I can handle my dad." But the minute he came on the line, Ro burst into tears. She handed Ben the phone. There was no getting around the truth, so he didn't even try. Ben explained as concisely as he could why he was needed in Albuquerque.

Andrew Majors, Esq., was shouting into the phone. "You went with my daughter to search for a body? How could you do that to her, Ben? What is wrong with you?"

"Sir, I'm very sorry—"

"So damn irresponsible as well as creepy!"

Ro pulled her cell from his hand. "He didn't want me to come. I insisted."

"Stop defending him!"

"I'm telling you the truth. Ask his mom. He didn't even know I was showing up this morning. He told me not to come. It was totally my idea, okay, so stop screaming at him."

A long pause. Then Ben heard her father say, "Why did you do this?"

"Because I like being with Ben. He lost a sister and I lost a sister, and for the first time since it happened, I could talk to someone about Gretchen without feeling like I was revealing something shameful. God, do you know how horrible it is keeping her death bottled up inside? Like her dying was a criminal act?"

Another pause. Her father shouted, "What in the hell does that have to do with looking for a body?"

"He knows the family of this missing girl, Daddy. This was important to him. And he's important to me."

"He's not even your boyfriend!"

"He's better than my boyfriend. He's a friend. And if you don't want to help me, I'll find someone who will."

"Dorothy, will you please stop being so dramatic?" A pause. "I know lots of people in Albuquerque. I'll make some calls. Don't talk to the police until I get there. Understand?"

"We've been over this before. I get it."

"How can you get it if I just told you what to do?"

"Ben told me the same thing. Not to talk to anyone until you get here."

"Wait. Just hold on, okay? Does Ben need any help?"

Her eyes started watering. "No, he's already called up his dad." A pause. "Thank you, Daddy. I'll see you later." She hung up. "Okay. Call the police."

"You know, this is just the tip of the iceberg."

"I'm not made of spun sugar. I won't melt. Call the police."

This was a call he truly didn't want to make. To stall, he gave her a black-humor grin. "Now *this* would make a great college essay."

She hit him.

"You have some time before January applications are due."

She hit him again.

"I guarantee you, you have undergone a unique experience. No one else will be writing about it. It's even better than a dead sister."

She hit him a third time . . . hard. "Only you can say that without my hating you."

"Don't lose a golden opportunity, Ro. It'll get you in anywhere you want to go."

"Maybe." A pause. "As long as I can leave out the part about peeing myself."

CHAPTER 17

BEN HID THE gun and ammo under the backseat. He said, "Unless they take apart the car, they won't find it. If they do, I'll tell them I hid it so you won't get into trouble. Originally, I was going to drive my mom's car. The gun wouldn't be a problem. It's registered and my parents have a concealed weapons permit."

"So why are you hiding it now?"

"Because the law says I need to be nineteen to use it without an adult present except in certain circumstances. Since I was using it for protection on a hike, I think I'd be okay. But right now, I don't want to explain away another issue. Do you mind?"

"Whatever you need."

When that was done, he started scanning his contact numbers. "Here we go . . . Milton Ortiz."

"He's the one on the Katie Doogan case?"

"The lead detective." He punched in the numbers. "He isn't going to be in on Sunday unless—uh, hi, Detective Ortiz?" What luck! He gave Ro a thumbs-up. "This is Benjamin Vicksburg. I met you last year at Katie . . . yeah, yeah, that's right . . . I'm fine . . . they're fine, thanks. Um, I really don't know how to say this, so I'm just going to come right out with it. I was hiking with a friend in the Sandias and we found something that looks suspicious . . . no, no remains. It's sunken ground that looks like a grave . . . yeah, really regular . . . no, I didn't touch anything. But I did note where I found . . . no, not on the trail. We were off-trail . . . yeah, I know . . . I know . . . um, I'm about a half hour away from the Master's Park trailhead. This is the first place I got reception. But I can meet you there and show you what we saw . . . okay . . . okay . . . bye."

Ben blew out air. "That was fortuitous. He's meeting us at the trailhead. Much better than some random patrol-car officer. You stay warm in the car. I'll take him down."

"Uh, no way I'm going to be alone, Vicks."

"Okay. How about this? Take the car and meet your parents at the Albuquerque PD. I think Ortiz works at headquarters on Southeast. Let me find you the address—"

"I'm not driving in this area by myself. Are you crazy?"

"Ro, if you're going to hike down, you'll have to change back into hiking boots."

"Ugh. They're disgusting."

"I'll put them on for you so you don't have to get your hands dirty, little Miss Princess." He started the car. "Call your dad while we have reception and tell him to meet you at the division on Southeast. I'm almost positive that's where Ortiz works."

Ro did as she was told. When she was done, she said, "How well do you know him? Ortiz."

"Not well. He didn't approve of my hiking in the back-country. The only people who do that are mountain men, hermits, vets with PTSS, misfits growing MJ, tweakers with meth stills, fugitives who are hiding from the law, and kill-ers dumping bodies. Dorothy, you really need to disassociate yourself from me."

She was staring out the passenger window. "When I'm with you, I don't have to be on."

"Ro, you know what's going to happen. Your parents are going to forbid you to see me. I'm a little creepy. Even my own father thinks what I do is a little creepy. I've got this plan next semester—I really do think about my future—but until the monster is found, nothing else matters to me."

She was quiet. "How about if you had a girlfriend? Would that matter to you?"

Ben shook his head. "I am so not boyfriend material. Ro, people like you make others happy; people like me make oth-ers squirm. I am definitely an acquired taste."

She changed the subject. "What do you know about Ortiz?"

"I met him a few times during some of the searches for Ka-tie. He was at one of the vigils. I know he's part Acoma. My grandpa Ed has some distant cousins who are Acoma."

"The Jewish grandpa?" When he nodded, she said, "How did *that* happen?"

"In the 1800s, the tribe had a Jewish chief named Silver-man. He was a cousin of my great-grandfather Abe, Ed's fa-ther. I think the Silvermans were related to the Weils."

"So you might be related to this dude?"

"If you stay here long enough, you're going to be related to everyone."

She exhaled. "How long do you think this will take?"

"To get back to the trailhead? Fifteen minutes."

"No. The interviewing."

"Right. For me, it'll take a while depending on what kind of mood Ortiz is in. You'll be out in no time. Once they get wind that your father works for the attorney general, they'll let you go. My state has honed the fine art of back-scratching."

Ben was trying to act casual, but his stomach was churning. He didn't want to talk, so he turned on the music and Ro took the hint. The next twenty minutes passed in tense silence until they reached the trailhead. It was almost two in the afternoon and both of them hadn't really eaten since eight in the morning. Plus, Ro had upchucked whatever she had eaten. "You need to get something in your stomach."

"Not baloney and cheese. What else do you have?"

Ben went through his backpack. "I have cheese sandwiches, PBJ—"

"PBJ is fine."

He doled out the sandwiches. The peanut butter tasted like glue and the jelly was sickeningly sweet. But he ate anyway. Fueling up before the battle.

IT TOOK A half hour to reach the suspected spot and the only reason it took that long was Ro. She was deliberate in every step and needed to be. There were lots of hidden roots and rocks, ways to twist an ankle. Ortiz was dressed in slacks and a dress shirt and tie, but he had on a parka and hiking shoes. He was around five eight, with a weathered face and broad shoulders. He had mocha skin, black eyes, and a mop of black hair combed straight back. When the trio reached the clearing, it was Ro who spoke first.

"Right there."

Ortiz's eyes fell on the spot. For the next minute, he stared at the spot, arms folded across his chest. "How'd you come across this?"

Ben said, "I'll answer any question that you want, Detective, but I've called my dad and he's instructed me not to talk until he's with me. Ro's been told to do the same."

Ortiz stared at the kid. "You need your dad to talk to me, Ben?"

He shrugged.

Ortiz kept gazing at the sunken ground. "That does look like something."

"I found it," Ro said. When Ortiz looked at her, she said, "I found it. Not Vicks . . . Ben."

"Was it your idea to hike in this area?" Ortiz asked.

"Sorry," Ben interrupted. "She isn't talking until her dad gets here."

"I didn't ask you, I asked her."

Ro said, "The answer is still the same."

"How old were you when Katie Doogan was abducted, Ben?" Ortiz smiled in a cop's way. It was supposed to encourage him to be relaxed. "It's a simple question. Surely you can answer that."

"Fifteen."

"I know it's been a long time, Ben, but do you remember where you were when you learned about her abduction?"

"Clear as a bell. I was with my cousin Henry Naranjo at Santa Clara. He had the TV on. I even remember the broadcasters—Adrianne Jamison and Frank Peoples."

"Pretty good memory."

"At the time my sister was still missing. It hit a nerve."

"Do you remember where you were the day before the announcement?"

He thought hard. "That's the day she was abducted, right?" Ortiz didn't answer. He said, "Nothing's coming to mind."

"Anywhere near Albuquerque?"

"No, I was in River Remez."

"Positive?"

"Not a hundred percent, but I was fifteen. I didn't drive. I can't imagine why I'd be in Albuquerque unless I was with my parents and we went in for dinner or something."

"Then there is a possibility that you were here?"

"Ninety-nine percent sure I was in River Remez ... unless I was taking a class at UNM. But that wouldn't happen because Katie was abducted on Saturday and there wouldn't be any school. There was no reason for me to be in Albuquerque unless I was with my parents."

Then it dawned on him.

"Henry's daughter's birthday was on that Saturday. My family and I spent the entire afternoon at Santa Clara. I didn't want to go home with my parents—the less time I spent with them, the better. Henry let me sleep over. He took me home the next day."

"You were fighting with your parents?"

"Just the opposite. No one talked. Home wasn't a happy place."

"How about now?"

"Better. My little sister's fourteen now. She's a live wire. It's a pleasure to have some energy."

"Do you remember what time Henry took you home?"

"No, but it had to be after the TV announcement. Since I remember the names of the news anchors, you can backtrack." A forced smile to Ortiz. "How's that for being cooperative?" When the detective didn't answer, Ben said, "Look, sir, I don't care about answering your questions, but my old man does. I don't want to rile him. He has enough to contend with."

Ortiz turned his attention to Ro. "You mind telling me why you two went hiking here? Off-trail?"

"I'm a respectful daughter."

"Detective Ortiz, we're on your side." Ben's eyes went back to the grave. "I don't know anything more about that than you do."

"Wait here." Ortiz trod up to the perimeter.

For the ground to sink that deeply and that uniformly, it was clear that the area hadn't been disturbed in years. Deep down, Ben knew that Ortiz didn't really suspect him. But finding the grave automatically made him a "person of interest."

The detective walked back to the kids. "Okay. Let's get some reception so I can call it in. You said you'd be willing to talk to me when your father gets here?"

"Absolutely."

"Willing to give me a DNA sample, Ben?"

"Yep."

"What about taking a polygraph?"

"Tell me when and where."

"Not that I suspect you." But of course he did. "Do you still see Detective Shanks?"

"All the time."

"You should know the drill. Let's go back." As they were walking, Ortiz turned his attention to Ro. "Are you Ben's girlfriend? Or won't you answer that?"

"Just friends."

"Your clothes are a little thin for hiking."

Ro turned red. "My hiking clothes got dirty. This is a change that I brought along."

Ortiz nodded. "Ben, how extensively were you questioned about your sister's death? I mean, you are protecting your butt here. You do see that."

"Of course I'm protecting my butt. My father would kill me if I talked to you alone. He's an attorney."

"Could you answer the question or won't you do that?"

"Informational questions. 'Who'd your sister hang out with? What's the talk in the school? Did your sister ever talk about someone bothering her?'"

"There was a guy for a while, right?"

"Tim Sanchez. He's in Missoula. Nothing came of him. He didn't do it."

"You found your sister's remains if I recall."

"Yes, I did." Ben tripped over a tree root but caught himself. "That's public record. I'm not going to talk anymore, Detective. I seem to have trouble speaking and walking at the same time."

"I'm not talking either," Ro said.

The lack of conversation helped Ben think. The depression could be anything—from a dog or horse grave to a hiding place for human remains. Ortiz was intense and solemn. Ro still looked vaguely ill. Ben, on the other hand, felt a range of emotions—from dread and agitation to anticipation. Now that the cop was here, the fear had worn off. All that was left was the adrenaline rush of discovery.

CHAPTER 18

AS SOON AS Ben pulled into the parking lot of the Albuquerque PD station house, he said, "You know they're going to separate us."

"That's okay," Ro said. "One thing that I have is a big mouth. I'm not easily intimidated."

"I know. Wait for your dad and then just tell them the truth."

"Got it." She gave him a forced smile, and then reached out. He intercepted her arms in a big bear hug. Ro said, "I'll be fine."

"I know you will."

Time to face the music.

The building, like most of those in New Mexico, was dun-colored, low profile, and architecturally in sync with its brown surroundings. The Albuquerque PD had six divisions and Ortiz had worked the southeast part of the city for a number of years. The Doogan family lived in the district.

Ben and Ro sat like two displaced people in reception; Ortiz was still at the trailhead waiting for the Scientific Evidence Division. A half hour later, a woman came in, introduced herself as Detective McLaren, and escorted Ben into an interview room—a small windowless cell consisting of a table, several chairs, and a video camera. Detective McLaren was short with black hair and dark eyes. "Detective Ortiz is on his way. Do you need anything in the meantime?"

"Just my father."

"Yeah, Detective Ortiz said something about you wanting your father." McLaren peered at him. "How old are you?"

"Seventeen."

"You don't need your father to answer questions, you know."

"He's my father and he's also my lawyer."

"Okay. Got it. I'll be back."

"Thank you." He sat upright even though he wanted to put his head on the table and go to sleep. But that behavior was typical of criminals. Innocent people were supposed to be too nervous for sleep. Twenty minutes later his family charged into the room: Mom, Dad, and Haley, along with Lilly. Mom's eyes were smoking. Dad seemed more sympathetic. "You okay?"

Ben gave them a practiced smile. "Fine."

Detective McLaren came in. "We're going to have to clear a few people out."

Mom said, "I need a moment with my son."

"Uh . . . sure," McLaren said. "Call me when you're done."

Mom was dressed in a flannel shirt and jeans with heavy boots on her feet. She looked ready to do some logging. "William, take the girls out. I need a few moments."

"Just a few, Laura."

"I get it." Once they were gone, she turned to her son. "You lied to me, Ben."

"I'm sorry."

"Ben, if something had happened to you or Ro—an animal attack or a busted leg or a fall—we would have been looking in Mount Baldy instead of where you actually were. Don't ever, *ever* do that again."

"I won't. I promise."

She stared at her son's face. "Do you honestly think your father and I don't know what you're up to? Every time I come into your room, you slam your laptop shut. I'm not stupid. Behavior like that is going to arouse my curiosity. I'm your mother."

"I'm not doing anything bad."

"I know what you're doing, Ben. I've been on your computer."

"You looked at my computer?" He felt bile rise up in his throat. He could barely contain his outrage. "I can't believe you invaded my privacy!"

"You're my son. You're seventeen. You still live in my house and I have a right to know if you're doing something illegal."

"I'm not doing anything illegal." He was beyond furious. "Did you go through my drawers also?"

"Stop being so indignant. I know what you're doing. Am I telling you to stop? If I told you to stop, would you listen?" She tapped his forehead. "You lock me out of there, so I do what I have to do. I know that boys your age don't confide in their mothers. But don't *lie* to me."

"I said I won't." He was still pissed. "Don't look at my computer anymore, okay?"

"It wouldn't matter anyway. You'll encrypt everything as soon as we get home. So you're mad at me." She kissed his forehead. "Hate me. I can take it."

"I don't hate you . . . c'mon! I can be pissed at you without hating you."

She sighed. "I'll get your dad. Don't give him grief."

As soon as his father walked into the room, Ben turned his frustration on him. "She looked at my computer. Can you *believe* that?"

"You actually expect me to be on your side? She's your mother. She can do whatever the hell she wants. Now let's go over this before the detective arrives. What happened?"

Ben was furious with both his parents, but this was a battle he wasn't going to win.

Forget about the battle, just win the fucking war.

THE GIRLS WERE sitting on hard plastic seats staring at their laps. Laura Vicksburg sighed. They deserved more, way more than what Laura had given them for the last two and a half years. She composed herself and then walked over. "C'mon. Let's go for ice cream."

Haley looked at her mom. "It's like forty degrees outside. I'd rather shop."

"No shopping. Your clothes are falling out of your drawers as it is. If it's too cold for ice cream, we'll do coffee and bagels. Let's go."

As soon as the girls stood up, Ro's mother, Jane Majors, came out of a second interview room with Griffen. He waved to the girls and the girls waved back. Laura eyed Jane—always dressed up like a lady who lunched. She wore dark slacks and a red sweater. Fashion suede boots hugged her feet. Several gold chains were draped around her neck, and two gold hoops adorned her earlobes. Laura had met Jane only briefly, when dropping off or picking up the girls.

Protectively, Jane linked her arm with Griffen's. The boy was taller than her by several inches—around five eight. She was trying to steer him away from the girls, but Griffen broke away to talk to his friends. The blond, blue-eyed, shaggy-haired teen always appeared to have a sloppy ease about him that was alarmingly different from his mother. His decision to talk to the girls forced contact between the mothers.

"Hello, Jane," Laura said.

"Laura," Jane said.

"We're going for coffee and bagels," Lilly said. "Would you like to come with us?"

"Sure," said Griffen.

Jane said, "Griffen, I have things to do at home."

"So go home. I'll come back with Haley and Lilly."

"I'd prefer you come home with me."

Laura said, "Another time, then."

Griffen said, "No. Not another time. I want to go out with the girls." When Jane stiffened, he said, "Mom, I'm fourteen. It's coffee and bagels! Lotta guys my age are smoking pot and screwing girls."

"Griffen!"

"Stop pretending I'm a kid. I'm in high school. And if I want to go out for coffee with my friends, you should say, 'Of course, Griffen. Have a good time.'"

Laura said, "Maybe this isn't the right time for this, Griff."

"There's never a right time," Griffen protested. "Mom, I like Haley. I like Lilly. I also like Ben. Ro likes Ben. I know you don't like Ben, but you should. He's a good guy. A lot better than JD, whom you're enamored with because he's a football hero and brought you flowers at homecoming."

"This is not appropriate, Griffen," Laura said sternly.

Jane was red-faced, but she managed to keep some dignity. She held up her hand. With wet eyes, she said, "You're right, Griff. You are old enough . . . to determine . . . if you want to go out for coffee or not." A forced smile. "I'll see you all later."

Laura put her hand on Jane's wrist. "Come with us. And don't be embarrassed about Ben. He's different. There are times I'm not too crazy about him myself."

"I really do have things to do at home."

"Okay." Laura gave her a strained smile. "Another time."

"Of course." Jane's eyes were still moist. "Laura, I never got a chance to tell you this. I never made the time . . . but I am . . . truly sorry about what happened to your daughter."

"Thank you." Laura's eyes watered. "I appreciate your words."

"I don't know how you cope." Tears rolled down Jane's cheeks. "All the pitying looks—"

"Mom!" Griffen spat out. "Put a sock in it."

"Doesn't it drive you crazy?"

"Shut up, Mom!" Griffen told her.

Jane kept on: "The way they look at you like you did something wrong!"

Laura had stiffened, but kept calm. "You deal with everything one day at a time."

Jane clutched her arm. Then the words just came tumbling out. "I lost my daughter, Laura."

"Oh my!" Laura was taken aback. "Oh my goodness, you never said anything." She drew her into an embrace. "I am so sorry, Jane!"

"Can . . . cer." She was actively crying. "She was . . . sixteen."

Dumbfounded, Haley gawked at Griffen, who simply shrugged. She said, "Why didn't—"

Griffen shushed her and pointed to his mother, who was sobbing on Laura's shoulder.

"Oh," Haley said.

"Yeah." Griffen rolled his eyes. "Oh."

Lilly took them both aside. To Griffen she said, "I'm sorry. How long ago?"

"Almost three years ago. I was eleven." Griffen folded his arms across his chest. "To her, I'm *still* eleven."

Haley was dry-eyed. "I was eleven also."

"I know." Griffen looked down. "Haley, my mom swore us to secrecy." He shuffled his feet. "I'd appreciate if you didn't tell anyone else. I know my mom. After the confession, she'll be all embarrassed."

"I won't say anything," Haley said. A pause. "Does Ben know?"

"Yeah, Ro told him."

"But you didn't tell me."

"It never came up and I didn't see the need to talk about it." He was irritated. "To tell you the truth, Mom is right about some things. I hate the pitying looks. I know I wouldn't get them from you guys, but it's nice to be just Griffen. A plain dude. Not Griffen with the dead sister."

"Is that why you became friends with me? Because I had a dead sister?"

"No!"

Lilly said, "Guys, don't fight." She looked at the mothers. Laura and Jane were deep in conversation. "Why don't we let them stay here and we'll find a coffee shop or something." A beat. "I'll go tell them the plans."

Haley looked at Griffen. "Ro tells Ben but you don't tell me?"

"Ro is Ro and I'm me, and if you don't like it, that's just too bad."

"Fine." Haley became wet-eyed.

Griffen looked away. "C'mon, Haley. This is crazy." When she didn't answer, he said, "C'mon. Pinkie truce?"

"Oh, fine!" Haley huffed. "Pinkie truce."

He offered her a pinkie. She hooked his little finger with her own. Then they both dropped hands. Haley said, "So who do you know that's fourteen who's doing it?"

"Just talking."

"No, you're not. Who?"

"Russ Lopez. He's doing Shawnie Baker. You can't tell anyone. Russ would kill me."

"He told you?"

"Maybe it isn't true. He could be bragging. Don't say anything."

Lilly came back. "Okay. I told them we'll be back in a half hour. Let's go."

Haley said, "Did you know that Russ Lopez and Shawnie Baker were doing it?"

"You won't tell anyone, huh?" Griffen said.

"Lilly doesn't count."

"I already knew it." Lilly hooked one arm with Haley and the other with Griffen. They walked out the door linked together. "Stop being so immature. My father's first wife was sixteen when they married. She was already knocked up. Sex is just part of life."

"I like that," Griffen said.

"Shut up, Griff!" Lilly broke away and linked Haley and Griffen together, hand in hand. "I know the score, guys. I know destiny when I see it."

Haley blushed and so did Griffen. But they remained holding hands. Lilly grinned. "Let's get some cappuccinos. I'll pay."

"No, I'll pay," Haley said.

"No, I'll pay," Griffen said. "I'm the guy."

"No, *I'll* pay," Lilly insisted. "I'm the only one here who can't trot out the pity card."

CHAPTER 19

ORTIZ HAD FINALLY made it back an hour later. He was dirty and exhausted, but for the first time in a long time, hopeful. When he came into the interview room, the kid was sitting near the wall with his father on the left. The man introduced himself as William Vicksburg and hands were shaken all around. The father's suit was pressed and his shirt was wrinkle-free, but his face looked haggard. Not that he appeared nervous, just worn-out. Kids could do that to you in a heartbeat.

"Are you comfortable?" Ortiz asked Ben and his father.

"Fine."

"Feel better now that your father's here?"

"Yes." Ben was grinding his teeth. He was being given the honor of having two detectives to grill him—Ortiz and McLaren. "Thanks for waiting for my dad."

"I had no choice." Ortiz smiled.

"No, you didn't," William Vicksburg added. "Not that Ben needs me. He's pretty independent. But I wanted to be here."

"No problem with that." Ortiz focused in on Ben. "Can you just walk me through the day?"

"Okay." The kid unfolded then refolded his hands and set them on the table. "I left the house around six."

"With the girl? Can you give me her full name?"

"Dorothy Majors."

"So, the two of you decided to go hiking together."

"No, she wasn't originally part of the plan," Ben said. "She just showed up at my house at five in the morning. I told her a couple of days ago that I was hiking Mount Baldy. It was meant to discourage her from coming to see me. She's not a hiker. But she just kind of forced her way in."

"So why didn't you just tell her to leave?"

"I should have." Ben cleared his throat. "But it seemed easier to let her come. Not to deal with the drama."

"Yeah, girls are like that sometimes. They can make you mad." Ben didn't say anything. Ortiz said, "Go on."

"We left around six."

"For Mount Baldy?"

"No. I never had any intention of hiking Baldy. I lied to her because I didn't want her with me. I wanted to be alone."

"You hike alone often?"

"All the time. It helps me think."

"What do you think about?"

William said, "That might be getting personal and I don't see the point in it."

"Okay," Ortiz said. "Now, you arrived at the trailhead at what time?"

"Around seven thirty."

"With Dorothy Majors, the girl."

"Yes."

"You decided to hike with her anyway."

"I didn't have much choice."

"Because you didn't want to deal with her drama. Go on."

The kid was grinding his teeth again. "We ate something and then we started to hike at Master's trailhead."

"But you didn't hike the trail. You hiked in the backcountry."

"I hike in the backcountry all the time. It's more interesting."

"That's not a smart thing," McLaren told him.

"I'm prepared. I can read a compass, Detective. I had bear Mace even though it's late in the season."

"Do you carry a gun?"

William said, "He's not answering that."

Ortiz said, "If you had this girl with you and she wasn't an experienced hiker, why would you hike in the backcountry?"

"Okay." Ben threw up his hands. "I'm done with the dance. I was looking for Katie Doogan."

"I know you were."

"Maybe I found her."

"Maybe." Ortiz was casual. "It's an odd thing to do, Ben."

"If you don't look for something, you'll never find it, right?"

"Why are you so interested in finding Katie Doogan?"

"Because I think her abduction might be related to my sister's case."

"You're trying to solve your sister's case?"

"In a word, yes. I think you know that. And I've been about as successful as the police."

Ortiz paused. The kid was trying to get under his skin. It was working. "Why do you figure that your sister's case is related to Katie Doogan's? Katie may even be alive. We don't have a body."

"Well, you just might have one now. So how about a thank-you?"

"You like being a hero?"

William put his hand on his son's arm. "Do you have a point?"

Ben said, "I know you're in contact with the Doogans. You must know that I went with Bryan almost every weekend for about six months to look for his sister because the police simply gave up."

Despite himself, Ortiz bristled. "No one gave up, Ben."

"Excuse me," Ben said. "You were allocating your resources to other cases."

"Katie Doogan is still an active case," McLaren said.

"That depends on your definition of 'active.'"

"Ben, take a breath," William said.

Good advice for all of them. Ortiz said, "Detective McLaren is correct. Katie Doogan is still an open and active case. And just like Detective Shanks is in contact with you and your family, I am in contact with the Doogan family. You don't sweep something like this under the rug, Ben."

The kid looked away. "Glad to see all of us are on the same page."

Ortiz said, "Bryan Doogan is in college now."

"I know. We keep in touch."

"I know you do. And you're telling me that you came here to look for Katie Doogan? With the girl."

"Dorothy Majors. She tagged along. I really wish she hadn't done that."

"Is she your girlfriend?"

"No."

"So, what's the deal?" McLaren said.

"We're friends."

"Would you like her to be more than a friend?"

William said, "This isn't relevant, Detective."

"Maybe it is . . . looking for a body," McLaren said. "Maybe you were trying to impress her?"

"He's not going to answer that," William said.

"I wasn't trying to impress her," Ben said. "I didn't want her there, but I'm happy she came. She saw the area first. Once she pointed it out, I knew we had something."

Ortiz said, "When was the last time you searched for Katie Doogan?"

"I have to think." A pause. "I went twice in the summer."

"And?" McLaren asked.

"And I didn't find anything, obviously. As soon as I did spot something, I called the police." He looked at Ortiz. "You specifically, because it's your case."

"I appreciate that, Ben. Where do you look for Katie? I mean, the Sandias are vast."

"I have a log, Detective. Places I've tried before. I try not to duplicate my searches."

"You have a log?"

Ben closed his eyes. It was a mistake to mention that. "Yes."

"I'd like to see it."

Ben turned to his father. William said, "Do you have any objections? If you do, say no."

"I don't like people looking at my stuff." Silence. Then Ben said, "It's in my backpack."

"Can I look inside your backpack?"

Ben kicked it over to him under the table. Ortiz bent down

and sorted through the teen's belongings. Ben kept his material organized: walking sticks, compasses, pens, pencils, a camera, an analog waterproof watch, a notebook, a poncho, a change of socks, and a cooler bag of food and water. There was a Swiss Army knife that the police didn't find when they initially searched his backpack. But it didn't set off any alarms in Ortiz. If the boy hiked a lot, it was something he'd use all the time. He took out the notebook and scanned the contents.

Lots of diagrams and coordinates, each one of them with a date and time. There were some notes, and the printing was meticulous: no cross-outs or smears.

"Can I keep this?"

"No," Ben said. "But I'll make you a copy."

"Can I have a copy made while we're talking to you?"

"No one touches my stuff except me. I'll make you a copy later. Please put it back."

Ortiz paused. "You're pretty possessive." When Ben didn't answer, the detective put it back and said, "Make me a copy. I did notice that the dates go back to over a year ago."

"When Bryan and I first started looking on our own."

"What about your sister?"

William stiffened. "What about her?"

"Hold on," Ortiz said. "Just let me get the question out. You must have searched for her many times before you found her."

"Is there a question here?" William asked.

"I kept my sister's searches in another notebook," Ben said.

"Where's that one?"

"Burned it once we found her."

"Once *you* found her."

"Once the police verified that it was her."

"That must have been a shock . . . finding her remains exposed like that."

Ben sent a quick glance to his father. "Do we *really* have to talk about this?"

His father said, "Answer the question, Ben."

"It was horrible. By the way, there were about fifty people looking for Ellen, so I wasn't alone."

"But you were alone when you found the remains."

"I was looking by myself. Increases the odds, the more places you look."

"You seem to have a good track record for finding bodies."

Ben sat up. "Did you find a body in the depression, Detective?"

Ortiz pulled back. "I don't know what's in there, and that's the truth. It's going to take time. All I'm saying is you're good at finding things."

"Not if you calculate it like a batting average. I just take a hell of a lot more at-bats than the police. My actual stats wouldn't even qualify me for the minors."

Ortiz was stoic. "Okay. So why were you looking in that particular spot, Ben? It wasn't random."

"No, I never do things randomly. I hadn't tried that area."

"That doesn't answer the question," Ortiz said. "Why did you choose that spot?"

A long pause. "I have some theories."

"I'd like to hear them," McLaren told him.

"It'll take a while. I don't want to keep my father here longer than necessary."

"I'm sure your father won't care."

Ben said, "I want Detective Shanks to be present."

"Why?" Ortiz asked. "You don't like my charm?"

For the first time Ben smiled. "This is the deal. I've got a mountain of data just sitting in my room. I'm sure you have a mountain as well. It might be good to compare and contrast. If I'm going to open a vein, I'd like to do it properly. I'll come back if you want. Or you can come up to River Remez and we can go over it in Shanks's office."

"A mountain of data on what?" McLaren asked.

"You don't have to answer that," William told him.

"Can I answer it?" When his dad was quiet, Ben said, "My sister was murdered and her killer hasn't been caught. I know you have a backlog of current cases. I also know that the Demon is taking up a lot of your time. And we know that the Demon didn't kill my sister. So, until Ellen's killer is either fried or behind bars for life, I'm going to do whatever it takes to find him."

"Which is what, Ben?" Ortiz said.

"Well, since I have no idea who it is, I do what I can, which isn't much. I collect data."

"Which brings us back to the original question. What kind of data do you collect?"

He looked at his father. William said, "Do you do anything illegal? If you do, don't answer it."

"Nothing illegal. I'd just prefer to do this another time."

William said, "I know what you've been doing."

"That may be. But I'd really prefer not to talk in front of you."

His father stood up. "I'll go grab a cup of coffee."

When he left, Ben said, "I look at unsolved murder victims like my sister—young, female, in their teens, with dark hair, that were sexually assaulted. Innocent girls—not runaways or hookers or girls doing high-risk behavior. No one deserves to be killed, of course, but I think my sister's killer was looking for a different profile than someone like the Demon.

"Even so, I look at everything. When. Where. How. If the victims were the same age, if they were murdered in the same way, if the time of abduction was the same, where they were murdered, how they were violated. Fact upon fact upon fact. I enter all the data into the computer and see what it spits back. If something's related geographically, like Katie and Ellen, I make a note of it. If the age is related, like Katie and Ellen, I make a note of it. If appearance is related, I make a note of it. If they were kidnapped in daytime or on certain days, like Katie and Ellen, I make a note of it."

"And you insist that Katie Doogan and your sister are related cases even though there's no body."

Ben leaned forward. "I was looking for Katie near water because Ellen was found near water. When Katie's remains are found, it's going to be near water. That depression is about a hundred yards from the riverbank."

Ortiz nodded, hoping to encourage the kid to keep talking. Instead Ben sat back and crossed his arms over his chest. "When would you like to meet to look at my stuff?"

"My schedule is probably more open than yours. Pick a day and a time."

"I'll look at my school schedule. After the New Year, things will open up for me. Plus, I'll be down here most of the time."

"Doing what?"

"Going to school and working."

"Going to school where?" McLaren asked.

"UNM."

"You graduated."

"No, but I've been taking math classes there since I was fourteen."

"Where will you be working?" Ortiz asked.

"Circuitchip. Some people consider my talents an asset to their businesses."

The kid was definitely an odd duck, but Shanks had always said that. Ortiz said, "Ben, I want to ask you something about your data. Do you just have information on murders like your sister's or do you also have other kinds of information?"

"Not all the murder cases link up to hers. Very few of them do link up."

"How many?"

"Those that are really similar to Ellen?"

"Yes."

"Katie Doogan links up. Maybe there are a couple of other cases. We can talk about them when we go through the data. It's easier when the facts are in front of my face. Besides, I'd really like to talk to Shanks first."

Ortiz wasn't going to let him off the hook. "But you have investigated other murder cases that have nothing to do with your sister's death."

"I don't know how they're related until I read them. But I've read through a lot of unsolved murder cases, if that's what you're getting at."

Ortiz cleared his throat. "With the other murder cases that aren't related to your sister's . . . do any of them link up to each other?" When Ben's shrug was noncommittal, he said, "Specifically do you have anything that might help us with the Demon? If you do, son, now is the time to spit it out."

Ben's foot started tapping. It was obvious that he knew something. He said, "I'll take a look."

"Because if you do have information, I'd appreciate it. We know there are other bodies out there. If you're not comfortable with me alone, talk to me and Shanks."

"I'd prefer to talk to Shanks first. No offense."

"I'm very offended." But Ortiz was smiling. "Sure, go talk to Shanks. But do it soon . . . this week."

Ben's father came back, cup of coffee in hand. "How much longer?"

"I think we're okay right now," Ortiz said. "If we find something in the depression, I might have a few more questions."

William said, "Then we're going to go."

Ben said, "Could I talk to Ro for a moment? It doesn't even have to be in private."

"I don't know if she's done or not."

"I'll go check," McLaren said.

Five minutes later she came back. "Gone."

Ben blew out air. "I was hoping to catch Mr. Majors to apologize."

"Yes, that's exactly what you're going to do." To Ortiz, William said, "If you need anything else from Ben, call me first."

"I understand." Ortiz shook Ben's hand. "I'll talk to you later."

As Ortiz watched them leave, his mind went into overdrive. Was Benjamin Vicksburg a strong suspect in Katie Doogan's murder? No. Was he a suspect at all? Couldn't rule him out even with the alibi. Was he a suspect in his own sister's murder? Even less likely. But until those crimes were solved and the killer put away, he had to consider everything.

The infinite possibilities made Ortiz depressed as well as hopeful.

CHAPTER 20

RO'S PARENTS HAD chosen to rent an upscale house perched on the ridge of the Sangres. It was a one-story, free-form adobe that sprawled over the top of the crest and faced southwest, giving the interior a peek of distant downtown Santa Fe and the Jemez Mountains beyond. Ben had never been beyond the hallway—waiting to pick up Haley and Lilly—but it had a big picture window and the view from it was incredible. It was cold outside, probably in the thirties. Clear to the south, cloudy to the north. He knocked on the door, but then decided to ring the bell.

Griffen answered. "Hey." He walked outside and closed the door behind him. He was in his pajamas. "If I were you, I'd think about turning around. It's a little dicey inside."

"They're pissed?"

"Well, put it this way. My mom's pissed at me, I'm pissed at my mom, and everyone's pissed at Ro."

"Did my name come up?"

"Yeah, Vicks, you're pretty much at the top of the shit list. Your saving grace is my mom told your mom about Gretchen. She may have bought you a hall pass with that one."

"I'll take whatever I can get. How'd that go . . . with your mom talking about Gretchen?"

"Emotional. We all walked away and got coffee and bagels. I went home with you guys, as you know, so that pissed my mom off."

"That's why she's mad at you?"

"I embarrassed her in front of your mom. I try to be patient with her. I know she's gone through a lot. But I'm not going to die on her. I'm in high school. Just . . . leave me alone."

"I hear you." Ben paused. "Is Gretchen's death still taboo?"

"Today she talked about it. Tomorrow?" Griffen shrugged. "My mom's gonna need a serious twelve-step program. You don't unwind overnight when you're wound up as tight as she is."

"I need to see Ro."

"That may be a toughie. My dad's still yelling at her."

"It's important."

"You go at your own risk."

Just as Ben was about to go inside, Jane Majors opened the door. She had on navy slacks and a thick white sweater. Her hair was impeccable. Her face was made up, piercing blue eyes focusing in on his face. "Hello, Ben."

"I'm very sorry for what happened, Mrs. Majors. It was never my intention to get Ro in trouble or put her in danger. I apologize."

"I appreciate your words." She looked at her son. "You

should come in, Griffen. It's cold and you aren't properly dressed."

He threw his hands up. "You want to knit me a cap with earflaps?"

Ben gave him a gentle shove forward and he disappeared into the living room. Mrs. Majors took in a deep breath and let it out. "I spoke to your mother today, Ben. She's a lovely woman."

"Thank you. I'll pass along your words." Ben tapped his toe. "If it's not too much trouble, could I have a word with Ro? I wouldn't bother you except it's important. I think I left my notebook in her car."

Mrs. Majors's sigh was long-suffering. "Wait here." Then she seemed to think better of it. "It's cold. Come inside."

"I'll wait here. I'm fine." He was dressed warmly, but even so, thirty-plus degrees gets real chilly when standing around. He jumped to keep some circulation going. It took about ten minutes. When Ro came out, her eyes were red and swollen. She was dressed in jeans and a red sweater and fluffy slippers. Her mother was hot on her tail.

"Hi," Ro said.

"Hi. I think I left something in your car."

"I don't think so. I didn't find anything."

Ben zeroed in on her eyes. "I'm positive I left something." As subtly as he could, he extended his forefinger and pressed his thumb on top of it. Ro's eyes got wide. "Oh . . . sure. Maybe. Hold on. I'll get my keys."

Jane said, "I'll go with Ben. You go back inside."

"No, no, no," Ro insisted, a little too vociferously. "It's my car. It'll take a minute."

Andrew Majors came out. He was still dressed in a suit and

tie, his blond hair slicked back and light eyes holding malice for all. He was not a happy man. "What's going on?"

Ben said, "I came over to apologize."

"You certainly should apologize. I realize that my daughter has a way of pushing herself into situations, but c'mon, Ben. Use some common sense."

"You're right."

Andrew turned to his wife. "Would you mind if I talked to Ben for a moment?" Without waiting for an answer, he threw his arm around the kid's shoulder and led him away from the front door. "Were they hard on you . . . the police?"

"No, not too bad," Ben said. "I'm sure they asked Ro a lot of questions about me."

"They did. They think you're an oddball. You arouse their suspicions."

"I know. I suppose if the tables were turned, I'd be suspicious of me as well."

"Your father is a general lawyer. He's not a criminal lawyer." His eyes bored into the kid's. "Do you need a criminal lawyer?"

Ben's face went hot, but he managed to keep eye contact. "No. Not at all."

"Now's the time, son. We all make mistakes. Don't tell me what happened, but you can tell me if you made a mistake. I've hired myself as your pro bono lawyer and we have confidentiality."

"I've made a lot of mistakes, sir, but crime isn't one of them." He should have been offended. Instead he was just tired. "I don't need a lawyer. But I appreciate your asking."

Majors patted the kid's back. "Okay, I believe you. Personally, I think you're just one of those weirdo math types. I knew a few of them at Princeton. Ro thinks you're a genius. She told me your scores. Are you considering Princeton?" He didn't wait for an answer. "You should."

At that moment Ro came out holding the car keys. She regarded her father. "He left his notebook in the Explorer. You can go inside, Daddy. I think I can handle this."

"Give me the keys."

"Daddy, don't be ridiculous." She pushed him toward the house. "Mom's waiting for you. Go inside and think about other ways to make my life miserable."

"Dorothy, stop it. You deserve all the grief that we've given you."

"I'm a good kid. I don't deserve any grief, FYI."

"I'm not saying you're not a good kid. But you can be infuriating."

"Can you give me a few minutes alone with my friend without embarrassing me, please?"

Mr. Majors shook his head. "Remember what I said, Ben. Princeton has a great physics department."

"Dad, stop!" She pushed him again. "Go away!"

Ro waited until her dad was inside, then she unlocked her car. Ben climbed into the backseat, retrieved the gun and ammo, and placed them in his jacket. As he exhaled, a cold cloud of mist surrounded his face. "Sorry."

"For what? I insisted that I go with you. I'm not sorry about it. I found the grave."

"Yes, you did. Good eyes, girl." A pause. "I'd better go."

"See you in school tomorrow?"

"Uh, no, actually. I'm playing hooky. I'm going back down to Albuquerque tonight. They're digging up the spot. The Doogans got wind that something's going on and . . ." He threw up his hands. "They're probably there right now. I need to be there too. But this time I'm going to meet up with Shanks at the spot and be official."

"I'm coming!"

"Ro, you know that's not happening."

"I'll talk to my dad."

"I'm not taking you."

"I have a car. And I don't need your permission to come down, Vicks."

Andrew Majors came back out, the porch light bathing his face in a yellow glow. With his blond hair, he looked like he was frozen in amber. "What's going on?"

"Nothing," Ben said. "I was just leaving."

Ro held his arm. "Ben's going back to Albuquerque. They're digging up the spot we found . . . that I found. I want to go with him."

"And I told her no," Ben said.

Mr. Majors said, "Ro, come inside and stop pulling a tantrum."

"I wouldn't pull a tantrum if you wouldn't treat me like a child. I'm going to be eighteen in three and a half months."

"But you're not eighteen yet." Ro's dad rolled his eyes. "Come inside. Let's not create a spectacle."

"Dad, did you know the age of sexual consent in New Mexico is seventeen?"

Ben hit his forehead. "I'm going."

Ro kept her hand clamped on his arm. "If I'm old enough to have sex, I'm old enough to go with Ben. Besides, I found the spot. Why can't I go?"

"I don't want you to go," Ben said.

"Okay. Don't take me," Ro countered. "I'll go myself. I'll

flounder around in the mountains and probably get lost and be eaten by a bear."

Mr. Majors said, "Give me your car keys now."

Ro dropped them into his palm. "I will remember this."

"You're not going to the mountains by yourself and Ben doesn't want you to go with him."

"Only because he knows that you don't want me to go."

"Um, Shanks is expecting me. I really do have to go," Ben interjected.

"Sam Shanks, the detective? He's going with you?" Mr. Majors asked.

"No. I'm meeting him at . . . where we were hiking today."

"See? I'll be under police protection." Ro looked at her father. "Please!"

"Ro, I'm not coming back tonight. I'm sleeping over at my grandparents' house."

"I've always wanted to meet them. Or I can come back with Shanks. Please, please?"

"All right, all right." Mr. Majors waved her away. "Just take her with you, Ben. To tell the truth, I'm too damn tired to deal with her histrionics anymore. Just watch her like a hawk. She's your responsibility."

Ben didn't want that responsibility, but the cosmic wheels were turning and fate did what fate always did to screw him up. Ro let go of his arm. "I'll be right back. I've got to go put on shoes."

"Hiking shoes," Ben shouted out.

Mr. Majors said, "Son, I'm giving you a chance to redeem yourself. Don't disappoint me. And think about Princeton. If my daughter had your scores, it would be a done deal."

They left him alone on the sidewalk. The smart thing to

do would be to just get in the car and drive away. But when it came to Ro, he wasn't too smart. The problem was he really liked her. And on some level, he knew she liked him. If he told her about JD's indiscretions, she'd break up with him in a heartbeat. But she'd also wind up hating him for ratting JD out.

Some math theorems took a lifetime to prove. Some took centuries. Others were still unsolved, waiting for some young mind to make a name for future generations. One thing math taught him was patience.

All good things come to geeks who wait.

CHAPTER 21

WHEN SHE GOT in the car, Ro knew that Vicks would be angry. After she quickly packed an overnight bag, she took time to make up her face and look as nice as possible. But once on the road, she was also aware that Ben had things on his mind other than her beauty. Thinking about the abducted girl not only made her nervous, it made her incredibly sad.

During Gretchen's treatment, Ro, along with Griffen, had been strongly encouraged to attend sibling support groups. Griffen had always found the members meddlesome and the group useless. Occasionally, Ro found the sessions helpful since no one at home was talking. Other times all the intense talk and sharing made her incredibly anxious. Though she would never admit it to anyone, especially her parents, she was happy to escape New York and go somewhere where she'd be anonymous.

Like her mother, she had wanted to get away from death. Now it was hitting her in the face. Her heart was beating and her breath quickened. She wanted Ben to calm her down, but he was so focused on his own thoughts, she knew he would be useless. Truly she didn't know what she was going to say to the Doogans. Perhaps the smartest thing was to say nothing.

Through the windshield, she peered at an evening that was cloudless and cold, a million stars gazing down from an inky sky. The road had poor lighting and Vicks was driving quickly, as if he'd done it a thousand times. They drove for a while until they passed the turnoff for the Cochiti pueblo.

About three weeks ago—it was on a Saturday—to get their minds off of murder, she and Vicks had taken a trip into Santa Fe. They walked through the plaza and under the portico of the Palace of the Governors—a seventeenth-century building—where Indians from the pueblos sold their crafts and jewelry. Dozens of artisans—mostly silversmiths and jewelry makers but also potters—had spread out their wares on blankets. Tourists gazed down on the items, scrutinizing each piece while the Indians sat placidly, reading, eating, talking with one another, and trying to make a living with their creative output. Vicks had bought her a Cochiti storyteller—a group of ceramic Indian ladies molded in one piece. They all had their mouths open. It was a spontaneous gift and it touched her deeply. Not that it was all that expensive, but he saw her staring at it and purchased it when she wasn't looking. She kept it on her nightstand and said goodnight to each gal before she switched off the light.

Vicks had turned on music. Aside from the satellite radio, the ride had been silent. She began to bite her nails. Ben gently laid a hand over hers to stop the compulsion. He seemed to have read what was on her mind. "They're nice people. Don't worry."

Ro said, "Like, what do we do?"

"We don't do anything," Ben said. "We just wait."

"How long, do you think?"

"No idea." He blew out air. "I told my grandparents that you might be staying over."

"What do you prefer? I mean, I can go home with Shanks."

"He'll probably be there the better part of the night." A beat. "It depends if you can miss school or not."

"If I'm going to write a college essay about this, I suppose I want the total experience." Tears formed in her eyes. "You know I'm not gonna do it, right?"

"I know."

"This is horrible."

"I hope it's Katie," Ben said. "It would be nice if the Doogans could give their daughter a proper burial." Another pause. "You wouldn't think that it was a big deal. Dead is dead. And we knew that Ellen was gone way before we found her. But it *is* a big deal. Not just for my parents, but for me. To have a place to visit, to honor my sister's memory. To lay flowers at her grave. To talk to her."

The car fell silent.

"How often do you visit?" Ro asked.

"We've been going on her birthday, the anniversary of her burial, and on Christmas. Sometimes I go by myself. What about you?"

"On the anniversary of her death and on her birthday. Not on Christmas, although we should. It's so pathetic in our house now. Mom makes this huge dinner on Christmas Eve—

that no one eats—because she's so depressed. This year, I don't know what we'll do. It'll be pretty bad. Want to come over, Vicks?"

"Before or after I visit my own sister?"

"Either, both. I can go with you to the grave." She took a swipe at her eyes. "The only thing this year that'll save the day from being a total washout will be the winter dance."

"Yeah, that's right. It's the night of Christmas Day."

"Are you coming?"

"No. But the kids would probably like it. Why don't you take them? Griff is your brother."

"Well, if you're definitely not coming, I'll take them." Silence. Then Ro said, "I worry about you. No one can remain on fire without burning up. I know you think that I'm a slave to having friends and having fun and being popular. And there's truth in that. But if I don't take my mind off what happened, it just eats at me like psychological cancer. Then my mother loses two daughters instead of one."

They passed the turnoff for the Santo Domingo pueblo.

Ben said, "Ro, I'm glad that you've found a healthy way to adjust. It's just not me."

"The thing is, Vicks, when it first happened, I didn't want to do anything either. I forced myself. And it worked out okay. Maybe you should force yourself as well."

"I'm not interested in school dances."

"You could go to the movies once in a while."

"Not with your friends."

"So maybe instead of looking at murder files, we'll go to the movies. Just the two of us."

"Thanks for trying, Ro, but your tenacity is misdirected. Don't let me bring you down."

Ro didn't answer him. "What were you like before Ellen died?"

"Wow." He paused. "Let me think. My life has really been divided into before and after. I used to go skating. I used to go snowboarding. I was pretty good at one point."

"What about now?"

"Haven't gone since it happened." He thought a moment. "I was different before it happened, Ro. You would have hated me. I was a real prick. I thought I knew everything. I was belligerent, I was impulsive, and I was really sarcastic. I drove my parents crazy. I argued with everything they said. I thought they were incredibly stupid. I found Haley to be a real pain in the ass. Lilly and she bugged me constantly. I wasn't very patient with them. More than once I slammed the door in their faces."

He paused.

"I liked Ellen." His eyes moistened. "She was such a nice person. It wasn't that she was the most popular girl in school. But she was well liked. More than that, she was respected. At her funeral, there wasn't a dry eye in the house." He smiled. "JD and Weekly bawling like babies."

Ro looked at him. "JD came to the funeral?"

"Of course he came. His whole family came. The entire community showed up." He wiped his eyes with his shirtsleeve. "How can I explain this to you? I'm not really friends with those guys. But I know that if I needed something, I could go to JD or Salinez or Martinez or Weekly or any of the others and say, 'Hey, I need your car or some money or to crash at your house for a couple of days.' And they'd give me whatever I needed. And I'd do the same for them."

"You'd do that for Weekly?"

"Of course. We're not mortal enemies just because we punched each other. That's just guys, Ro. When we were in grade school, we were always beating on each other. Mainly because school was so fucking boring. High school used to be a joke. Then a group of parents including my own started raising money to improve the school. It's still boring but at least we've got some dedicated teachers and a few classes that don't put me to sleep."

Ro was cold. She turned up the heater in the car. They passed the San Felipe turnoff. Ben said, "Before I forget, could you do me a favor?"

"Anything."

"Go into my backpack and put the gun and ammo in the glove compartment. It's not loaded."

"Sure." She retrieved the backpack, and took out the weapon and the box of bullets. "It feels really weird to hold it. My parents are so antigun. They'd freak if they knew you had one."

"You didn't mind it when we heard that bear."

"They'd freak if they knew I went hiking in the vicinity of bears."

"If you hike in the backcountry long enough, you're going to come into contact with critters."

"Ben, I grew up in Scarsdale, which is a wealthy suburb of New York. My parents are liberals through and through. They are politically correct, antigun, pro-choice, and most of all, staunchly against anything Republican."

"Then it's good you came to Santa Fe. It's called the City Different for a reason. We're a refuge city—not only for illegals, but also for old hippies, dropouts, and slackers. Which is fine. I'm socially liberal. But I am a law-and-order conservative."

"Why am I not surprised?"

"If I ever find the guy responsible for Ellen's death, I'm going to push the needle into his veins myself."

"Ugh!"

"Not ugh. Right on! If I could torture him before I killed him, I would."

"No comment. Then again, my sister wasn't killed, so I'm not going to judge."

"Ellen wasn't killed, Ro, she was murdered. Killed implies a car accident or falling from a roof. Murder means some bastard knowingly and willingly and probably with sexual pleasure snapped her neck. And when I find him, he is going to die!"

"I hear you." She almost brought her thumbnail to her mouth but thought better of it. "What happens if a cop pulls you over and you have a gun in your car?"

"I tell him it's in the glove compartment and my dad has permits. This is my dad's car. It's considered an extension of his house. If it was in your car, it would be illegal. That's why I hid it."

They passed the turnoff for Sandia.

Ben said, "It's a few more miles of freeway, then we'll have to travel the streets. We've got about another half hour."

"Okay." Ro was really nervous about meeting the Doogan family. "If I act like a jerk, just nudge me."

"Why would you act like a jerk?"

"Sometimes I hide my anxiety with perkiness."

"Why'd you come?" Ben asked her. "It's not a trick question. I really want to know why you're putting yourself through this."

"Honestly, I came to be with you. I didn't want you to endure this alone."

Ben smiled. "No matter what happens in the future, Doro-thy, I don't think I've ever had a better friend."

"Thank you." A pause. "So maybe you'll consider staying in school full-time next semester. It's like five more months of high school. What's the rush to become an adult?"

"I've already signed up for UNM. I've already signed the internship papers for Circuitchip. But I will miss seeing your beautiful face even from afar."

"You think I'm beautiful?"

"Of course you're beautiful. JD is right when he says you're the hottest girl on the planet."

"My charms aren't working very well on you." Ben said nothing. She said, "Come to the winter dance."

"I can't, Ro. I made plans." A pause. "I'm only telling you this in case I die or something, so you'll know the truth. I promised my mother I wouldn't lie again, but I can't tell her the truth. I don't want either of my parents to know."

"Now I am intrigued. What's going on?"

"I told my parents that I was going to visit my friend—the one I told you about. Grant Statler. He's at home with his family in L.A. for winter break—and I *might* go visit him. But my objective is to go to the Bay Area in California."

She didn't speak right away. "Does this have to do with Julia Rehnquist? Like I have to ask."

"I've been in contact with the family for two months. They've agreed to talk to me. I've got this chance. I'm not go-ing to blow it."

"Vicks, I understand your obsession with Katie Doogan. You know the family. It happened on the heels of your sister. Julia Rehnquist was abducted over nine hundred miles from your sister."

"Don't waste your breath."

"God, it's like you go from one death to another to another."

"And another and another until I find him! You said yourself that he's going to repeat it. What should I do? Wait until he comes back here?"

"No, you should go to Shanks, not gallivant all over the country."

"I'm going to Shanks. This week, like I promised. I also promised Ortiz. I'm giving them my stuff."

"I'll believe it when I see it. Are you going to meet with the detective on the Rehnquist case?"

"Derek Whitecliffe. Maybe." He paused. "I made plans to meet with the Rehnquists months ago, FYI."

"Yeah, well, things change, Vicks, and so should you." She held up her hand to stop him from answering her. "But that's not going to happen. Instead I will wish you luck."

"Thank you. Very nice to wish me luck instead of saying I'm an obsessive weirdo."

"I didn't say that."

"You thought it, right?"

"I can barely control my mouth. But my thoughts are my own, Vicks. And if that pisses you off, too damn bad."

CHAPTER 22

THERE WERE BARRIERS about a hundred yards from the trail-head. A black-uniformed police officer stopped them, pantomiming to them to turn around. Ben rolled down the window. "I'm with Detective Samuel Shanks from the River Remez PD. Can you check with him, please?"

"Can't leave the post. You have to turn around."

As if on cue, Shanks materialized. This time Ben pressed the electric button and the passenger glass disappeared. He yelled out, "Sam."

Shanks turned around and jogged over to the car. To the uniform, he said, "It's okay. He's with me." He turned to the kid. "You'll have to park down the road. You can't block any access for the equipment."

"Got it." Ben found a place about a quarter mile away and as dark as death. Ro clung to his arm as they carefully stepped over earth and roots until the reflected beams of the klieg lights pointed to a spot down the mountainside.

Sam was waiting near the trailhead. He said, "You brought a friend?"

"Dorothy Majors, Detective Shanks. She found the area where the police are now digging."

Shanks said, "Congrats, Ben. You finally found someone to feed your obsession."

"I'm not feeding it," Ro protested. "I'm trying to stop it. But like any good therapist, first I've got to establish rapport."

Shanks smiled. "Are you okay, honey?"

Immediately her eyes watered. Ben put his arm around her shoulder and she nestled into his chest. "If you need to talk to us, we'll be spending the night at my grandparents'."

Shanks said, "How are they all doing?"

"My grandparents? They're fine, and that's from firsthand knowledge. I just saw the clan this past Thursday for Thanksgiving."

"How many showed up this year?"

"Sixty-eight."

"Is your grandpa still building rockets?"

"A man needs a passion." Ben turned to Ro. "My grandpa worked in Huntsville when he was young."

"I have no idea where that is."

"Alabama. Marshall Space Flight Center. It's part of NASA. He's always worked for the government, but I think that time down south was his favorite. The space program is still in his blood."

"Is this the Vicksburg grandparent?"

"No, this is the Weil. The Vicksburg side was originally from Mississippi."

"That makes total sense." She hit her head. "Duh."

Ben stuck his hands in his pockets. He shifted from foot to foot. "Are Margot and Alan here?"

"Farther down the mountain. Ortiz called them . . . didn't want them to hear it on the news. He has the dental records. All we need is a body." Shanks rubbed his gloved hands together. "One part of me really hopes it's her. I can't stand the idea of making them go through all this without any results."

"Where is Detective Ortiz?"

"With the Doogans." Shanks rocked on his feet. "I told them you might be coming."

"Do they want to see me? It seems that everyone is looking at me with a wary eye."

"They know you by now. No one is seriously thinking of you as a suspect. Not even Ortiz. I saw the videotape." He looked at Ben with squinty eyes. "Which means I know what you've been doing in your spare time and I'm really pissed at you. How long have you been sitting on piles of data?"

"Awhile."

"How long's awhile? One year?" Silence. "Two years?"

"Whatever."

"Don't give me that bullshit. Why didn't you come to me?"

"I told him he should show everything to you," Ro piped in. "He's got a lot of stuff."

Shanks turned his eyes to her. "You knew about this?"

"Don't blame me, sir. You can lead a horse to water, et cetera."

Shanks shook his head. "I want to see what you have now, Ben. Come in Wednesday after school. Not a request, an order. No excuses, no bullshit."

"I'll give you everything I have." A pause. "What about Ortiz? I prefer to keep it between us."

"Not going to happen, especially if this turns out to be Katie Doogan." He stared into space. "How many cases have you, in your mind, tied to Ellen's case?"

"Maybe a couple of others."

"One, two, three?"

Ro said, "At least two. I promise he'll be there Wednesday."

"Good to see someone is on my side." Shanks exhaled swiftly. "Three P.M. sharp! Now let's go see Margot and Alan."

THERE WAS A path of footlights to follow, adding just enough illumination to see one foot in front of the other. Wet detritus had been tamped down by the unexpected foot traffic. It took them twenty minutes to hike to the spot. The area had been roped off with yellow tape and there were personnel all over the place. About a half dozen officials were digging by hand. From what Ben saw, it appeared as if they had barely scratched the surface.

Ro was shivering, rubbing her shoulders and arms. Ben went into his backpack and pulled out a box of hand and toe warmers. "Put these in your boots and these in your gloves. They'll keep you toasty."

She placed them in her gloves. "I've used these for skiing." She started to unlace her boots. "Thanks."

He dropped packets in his boots, and within five minutes, his feet went from frigid to hot. The Doogans were standing as close to the crime scene as they were allowed. Margot was wearing a thick down-filled coat. Alan had on a leather bomber. They were holding hands. Ben didn't see Bryan but he saw Kevin. The kid was a little bit older than Haley. Katie had been the only daughter.

"Let's get this done."

Margot saw the kids coming and dropped Alan's hand. "Ben!" She gave him a tight bear hug. "Oh my!" She sniffed back tears and pulled away. A quick glance to Ro, then back at Ben. "I suppose I should say thank you."

"Maybe we should wait for that one. This is my friend Ro." When Margot gave her a cool appraisal, Ben said, "We were hiking together, looking for anything, and she was the one who actually found the spot. We bonded because she lost a sister from cancer at the same time I lost Ellen."

Margot hugged Ro. "Thank you for coming."

"I'm so sorry, Mrs. Doogan."

"Margot, please." Her wild red hair was tamed under a knitted cap.

Ben shook hands with Alan and his son. "How's it going, Kev? Are you driving yet?"

"He's only fifteen," Margot said. "Please don't rush things. As if I don't have enough anxiety."

"It's a part of life." Alan was wearing a cap. For the most part, the man was bald except for a gray ponytail hanging down from the nape of his neck.

"Got a car in mind yet?" Ben asked Kevin.

"I like Beemers."

"Dream on," Margot said.

"Can you talk to my parents for me?"

"I'm not your best advocate. I still don't have my own wheels. I'm borrowing a jalopy from my grandparents to get back and forth to Albuquerque."

"What are you doing down here?" Margot asked.

"Taking some classes at UNM. I'm also going to be interning at Circuitchip."

"That's great, Ben," Alan said. "Good for you."

Ben asked, "How's Bryan?"

Alan said, "He wanted to come down. We told him to wait. They've been digging for two hours. They haven't gotten too far. They're trying to be careful."

"To the point of ridiculousness." Margot walked away for a moment and then came back. "I'm a wreck."

"I'm sorry you have to go through this," Ben said. No one spoke for the next ten minutes. About fifteen feet away, Ortiz and Shanks were deep in conversation, occasionally glancing in their direction.

Ben said, "Excuse me for a moment."

Ro followed. They walked over to the cops. Ortiz said, "So we're all meeting this Wednesday?"

"That's a fact."

To Ro, Ortiz said, "You too?"

"No, not me. I'm done playing Nancy Drew."

"Can you convince Ben to follow your lead?" Shanks asked.

"I can't convince him to go to a lousy school dance," she said.

Ortiz said, "And you're going to bring all of your files, right?"

"I'll bring you everything I have." Ben slowly backed away. "See you then."

When they were alone, Ro said, "You seemed a little . . . apprehensive about divulging your info."

Ben shrugged. "I'll certainly give them my Demon files."

"And Julia Rehnquist?"

"Yes . . . and Jamey Moore." A shrug. "Looks like I'm done."

"So why are you going to Berkeley? Let the police handle it now."

Ben sighed. "Nora's expecting me, Ro. Please don't tell Shanks. If I find something, I'll let him know."

Nora being Nora Rehnquist, Julia's mother. Ro turned away and focused her attention on the action below. "They've been working for a while."

"It's a deep hole."

A half hour passed. Then an hour went by. At eighteen minutes after ten, one of the techs jumped up and told everyone to stop digging. "I think I found something."

Margot's voice: "I need to sit down."

As Alan and Kevin eased her to the ground, the tech said, "I definitely got something."

Alan was walking in circles. Margot started to sob. Kevin sat down next to her and slung his arm around his mother's shoulders. Ro turned her head away from the action, tears streaming down her face. "I can't look."

"Sit, hon." Ben helped her down. "Do you want to leave?"

"It's okay." She was rocking back and forth. "I'm okay."

He shouldn't have brought her here. But just as she couldn't control him, he couldn't control her. He walked away, alone, hands in his pockets, eyes on the grave, as minutes passed one by one by one until they coalesced into an hour, watching the techs pull up bits, analyzing the hints and secrets that the ground had yielded.

CHAPTER 23

NO NEED TO wait for all the details. They left knowing that the grave contained human remains along with clothing and other items. Identification wouldn't take place until tomorrow afternoon at the earliest. It was time to get to shelter. Ro was growing paler by the hour. She needed heat and a bed.

Grandma Pauline was up waiting; Grandpa Ed had retired hours earlier. Once Ben and Ro were settled in separate rooms, Ben slept the slumber of the dead. He woke up at seven, famished, and without remembering any dreams.

Ro was still sleeping, but his grandma and grandpa were having coffee, watching the sun come up. The dining room was compact but had a nice view of their property. A small kiva fireplace was built into a corner, the fire flickering light but not a lot of heat.

The old folks were vital people with straight spines and

wide smiles. Pauline was slender and had very long, gray hair—the style set a long time ago by the Indians and made superfashionable by Georgia O'Keeffe. Grandpa was shorter than her by an inch and very broad across the chest. His head was a cue ball.

Their typical breakfast was flour tortillas and dips along with juice and coffee. Grandma Pauline said, "I can make you eggs if you want, Ben."

"This is fine. I'll certainly take some coffee."

Pauline poured a cup and sat back down. "I've been thinking, Ben, about redecorating the kids' dormitory. You're a little big for a twin."

"Well, don't redecorate for my sake." He tore off a piece of tortilla and dipped it in the salsa—way stronger than picante, but the heat cleared his head. "I'll be studying at the library a lot."

"I told you it was fine," Ed chimed in.

"Maybe he'd like to sleep on a bigger mattress. All of the grandchildren are getting older, so it can't hurt." Pauline smiled. "Tell me about the girl."

"She has a boyfriend, Grandma. We're just friends."

The smile retreated. "Well, she seems like a fine young lady."

"She is a fine young lady. She's just going with someone else."

Ed said, "You want to see what I've been working on?"

Pauline said, "For goodness' sakes, it's seven fifteen in the morning."

"Grandpa, we'll have lots of time to work together after the first of the year. I'll be here all the time."

"Yes, I suppose." Ed stood up. "I'm gonna get the paper." He left the room.

Ben said, "I believe that my presence is changing the family dynamics."

"Oh, he's always like that. He lives in his head."

"Sounds familiar."

"You are a lot like him." She leaned over. "It took him over a year to ask me out on a date. I was dating someone else and almost gave up." She pointed to the bedroom where Ro was still sleeping. "I've seen the way she looks at you. She likes you."

"Yes, she does. She also likes her boyfriend."

"Who in this world is better than you? The answer is no one."

Ben kissed her cheek. "Thank you for putting us up." His phone vibrated. He looked at the message, then stowed the cell back in his pocket. "I'm going to wake up Sleeping Beauty. School and all that jazz."

"I'm going to redecorate the room whether you give me input or not, Ben. You might as well speak up."

"What colors were you thinking about?"

"Something warm—yellows, golds, and oranges. What do you think?"

"I like it. Knock yourself out, Grandma." He tore off a final bit of tortilla and scooped up a healthy dose of salsa. "Wow, that's good but really strong. What's in there? Essence of newt and ghost chili peppers?"

"I'll wrap some up to go for you."

"Just put it in the gas tank of my car. With that as fuel, we'll just jet-propel ourselves back to River Remez."

AT THAT HOUR the streets were quiet, although Ben was assiduously avoiding congested areas like the university. UNM had several locations but the main one was in Albuquerque, located on historic Route 66. Unlike Los Angeles and Chicago, the cities of New Mexico still retained old-style motels and diners and even a couple of drive-in theaters. Things moved slowly in the Land of Enchantment. To Ben, New Mexico was the bomb. To everyone else, it was the home of the bomb.

The sun was washing over the peaks of the mountains, bathing the crests in gold light: blinding reflections that hid the mysteries within. It was almost eight, rush hour on the highway. By nine, most of it would be almost over. He said to Ro, "You want to stop and get some breakfast?"

"I wouldn't mind some coffee." She turned to him. "Have you eaten?"

"Just a little salsa. I'd love another cup of coffee. I don't want to make you late for school but we're going to hit traffic if we leave now. How about Larry's? It's open twenty-four hours."

"Do they serve lattes or is it swill from an urn?"

"It isn't girlie coffee but it isn't swill either. It's actually pretty good."

"Larry's it is."

He turned the car around and pulled into a coffee shop that had obviously once been an IHOP. For the last ten years, it had been Larry's, but it still had the same blue booths and the same bronze-and-black insulated coffeepots. The waitress was around seventy, had dark, dyed hair tied up in a net, and wore a frilly white apron. She handed them menus and mugs.

"Coffee?"

"Yes, that would be great," Ben said. She came back with a coffeepot and a pad and pencil. He ordered French toast. Ro ordered the egg-white omelet. After the waitress left, Ben said, "Sorry to put you through this."

"I wanted to come, Vicks." She sipped her coffee. "Might not have been the best decision, but it was my decision. Did they find out anything yet?"

"I got a text from Shanks this morning. They're going over the dental records this afternoon."

"They found a jaw?"

"They found . . . do you really want to hear this?"

"Yes, I really want to hear this."

He exhaled. "Both of the jaws were broken. The maxilla— the upper jaw—was in pieces, but the mandible was for the most part intact."

"She was beaten."

"Or it's natural weathering. The upper jawbone is much more fragile than the lower jawbone."

"It was definitely a girl?"

"Yeah. We'll learn more this afternoon."

"Shanks will tell you?"

"He won't tell me everything, but he'll tell me enough." The waitress brought their food and the check. "It's important to me to know as much as I can. If it's Katie and if it's similar to Ellen, it tells me that I've been on the right track. Otherwise I'm back to square one."

"I thought you were going to leave the detection to the experts." She took his hand. "It's time to join the human race, Vicks." Her touch was warm and delicate. Even so, he slid his hand away. She went back to eating her omelet. "Are you sure you won't reconsider the winter dance?"

"I have nonrefundable plane tickets."

"I could probably get the tickets moved to the next day. I'm good over the phone with a sob story."

"Don't bother. Especially after last night. My heart's not there, okay?"

She put down her fork. "I understand. I'll take the girls and Griff and Ezra."

"Thank you. We're a good team." When she didn't answer, he said, "I also know that Haley scored some tickets for Milquetoast. I promised I'd take her and Lilly. Griff and Ezra can come if they can get tickets. Be happy to take them all."

"I'll let the boys know. When is it?"

"Middle of February. It's on a Saturday night. I'll drive them to Albuquerque and they can sleep at my grandparents'. I'll take them home the next day."

"I can pick them up if you want."

"Nah, I'll drive them back on Sunday. Have to be back in Remez High on Monday anyway." He pointed at her with a forkful of French toast. "We've got a tutoring date on Sunday, remember?"

"Of course." Her smile was sad. "I'll miss you at school, Vicks."

"You hardly ever saw me."

"I know." Ro looked away. "My bad."

IT MADE THE papers by Tuesday. The *Albuquerque Journal* and the *Trib*, of course, but also all the state papers: the *Alamogordo News*, the *Carlsbad Current*, the *Las Cruces Sun-News*, the *Roswell Record*, the *Los Alamos Monitor*, the *Santa Fe New Mexican*, and the *Journal of Santa Fe*—which was really the *Albuquerque Journal* with a Santa Fe pullout.

Katie Doogan's remains had been positively identified by dental records. The memorial service and the funeral for the slain teen were scheduled for Saturday at eleven. Most of the remains were still with the coroner, but something of Katie's would be laid to rest. The Doogans would have a permanent place to visit their daughter.

There were scant details of the crime scene, but stories did manage to rehash at great length the unsolved case of Ellen Vicksburg, sending Laura into a tailspin of depression. Ben's father reacted by working longer hours that day. Neither of their children went to school on Monday or Tuesday. Haley remained holed up in her room refusing to take calls from anyone but Lilly. Not even Griffen made the cut.

Ben was the communication center for the family, thanking people for their kind words. But unlike when Ellen was abducted, he only had to deal with the hoopla for a day or two. By Wednesday, things had returned to a semblance of normalcy. He and Haley went back to school. Haley adapted like Haley, and Ben remained alone by choice.

By the afternoon, he was glad to leave school early. Ro caught up with him as he was unlocking his bike. "Hey."

He didn't bother looking up. "Hi." A pause. "Are you okay?"

"I guess. At least no one mentioned us by name."

"The anonymous hikers."

She fidgeted. "Are you okay? I mean, that spread—"

"Yeah, it was pretty bad."

"I'm sorry, Ben."

"So am I." He stood up and stored the lock in his backpack, regarding her objectively—smart and with personality to spare. She wore a midnight-blue cashmere V-neck that showed off not only her eyes, but also her swanlike neck. Her jeans gave her hips that wonderful feminine curve. Her boots emphasized her long, graceful legs. He said, "Services for Katie are on Saturday. I'll be spending the weekend in Albuquerque and I probably won't be back until Sunday evening."

She said, "I'm going to the services, Vicks. It's something I want and need to do."

He nodded. "Um, you want to go down together? Don't want you getting lost."

"We're not going in the mountains and I have navigation. I'll be fine."

"Ro, I'd like you to come with me." A hint of surprise on her face. "Unless you'd rather be alone."

"No, I'd much rather come with you, Vicks, but there's a hitch. I have to cheerlead at a state game Friday night in Silver City. I can't leave until Saturday morning. I'm sure you were planning to go down on Friday afternoon."

"We'll leave early Saturday. Not a problem."

"Thank you."

On impulse, he leaned over and kissed her cheek. "See you then."

He hopped on his bike and pedaled away. One day they'd get together: not to hunt bodies, not to look at murder files, not to go to funerals or police stations or even for tutoring or hiking. One day they'd get together just because.

CHAPTER 24

SHANKS HAD SET up in an interview room instead of using his office. It turned out to be a good idea because with the table, Ben could spread out his files. The kid was dressed in a bomber jacket, gray T-shirt and jeans, and high-tops. There were bags under his eyes. He looked way too tired for his years.

"It'll be just the two of us," Shanks said.

"Where's Detective Ortiz?"

"Between the Demon and the Doogan cases, he's swamped. He's waiting to see what you have. If anyone could use help right now, it's him."

"I'm off the suspect list for Katie Doogan?"

"You were never seriously on." Shanks raised his eyebrows. "Show me what you got. Then get some coffee."

"Last time that happened, I wound up making a pot for the

entire office." Ben took several rubber bands off the case folders and began to spread them out. "If I'm gonna do a service,
I should get paid."

"You're paid in caffeine." Shanks shoved two mugs into his
hands. "Go."

Kicking him out allowed Shanks to look at what the kid
had amassed. It was organized, it was neat, and it was thorough. It took Ben ten minutes to return, and by that time
Shanks had already started reading the Katie Doogan file. He
was so absorbed in the material that he didn't look up when
Ben came in, just grabbed the handle of his mug, sipped, and
kept reading. After he gave the file a first pass, he flipped back
and forth between the pages. Finally, he put it down.

"Pretty accurate in your predictions."

"I was just using Ellen's case as my reference point."

"The spots where you chose to search were close to where
you found the grave." Shanks looked in the kid's eyes. "The
Sandias encompass a lot of area. Why'd you search where you
did?"

"It all goes back to my theories."

"What are your theories?"

"What they've always been. I must have told you a zillion
times."

"Well, I'm paying attention now. Talk to me."

Ben sipped coffee for a minute, organizing his thoughts.

"This isn't someone local. Instead it's someone who's familiar with New Mexico, someone who's been here, maybe
even stayed here for a few months, but doesn't make his home
in the state. He's confident enough to stalk girls, he's confident enough to snatch them off the street, he's confident

enough to rape and murder them, and he's confident enough to bury them in a deep grave that he no doubt dug even before he committed the crime. This was premeditated.

"But he's not confident enough to go deep into the national forest and get himself back out without help. You know how thick and dense the forest can be in summertime. That's when Ellen was abducted. Katie was abducted in the spring, but it was warmer down in Albuquerque than it was in River Remez. In the forest, everything looks the same. It's all trees and brush, all greens and browns. And it's dense, with filtered sunlight at best. Without a compass, you get mixed up because the trees throw off lots of shadows. Sometimes it's even hard to tell east from west. Unless you're a very experienced hiker who can read a compass and unless you know the area very well, you're going to get lost. Especially at night. In the dark, there are other things to worry about. Bears are out there, mountain lions are out there, maybe even jaguars. And there are always coyotes. You're not going to chance going deep into the interior. My sister was strangled. She wasn't shot. My take on this dude is he's not all that familiar with firearms. He gets his kicks out of killing up close and personal.

"Sam, this is a guy who needs to be near roads. But he has to go into the forest to get rid of the body. So, once he's in the forest, he needs to orient himself. He needs to be near some kind of natural landmark. It's not going to be a tree or a boulder. It's going to be something that he can rely on. It can't be small rias or creeks because in the spring, with all the winds, they dry up and usually don't become wet again until the monsoons start up in late July and August. That means he's going to need something larger, like a big creek or a stream, something that's always running. The banks of the waterway also provide a natural guide. The water itself provides sound for orientation and for privacy. The soil is different. It gives underneath your feet. It's softer, easier to dig a grave in. The smell along riverbanks is different. Mustier, filled with decomposed material that's moldy because of the constant moisture. A riverbank provides just enough of a difference from the rest of the forest to give him a little direction, so he knows where he's going.

"Last, he needs relatively easy access from the road to the burial spot and back. He has to be out of the way to do his dirty work. But the pathway has to be easy enough for him to climb down lugging a dead body and then it's got to be easy enough to climb back up. Both Katie and Ellen were buried directly into the ground. It's a lot easier to lug something in a suitcase or garbage bag. But he prefers to carry dead bodies. He probably gets some kind of kick out of it. I don't know what his motivation is by burying them as he did, and I don't care. I'm just interested in frying the guy."

Ben sat back and folded his arms across his chest. Then he sat up and took a sip of coffee. "This is lukewarm. Can I get myself a refill?"

"Go ahead."

"How about for you?"

Wordlessly, Shanks handed him the mug. As soon as the kid was gone, the detective started skimming through his other files. Katie Doogan's was the only file that Ben had connected to Ellen Vicksburg's murder. He knew there had to be more files that Ben didn't bring.

The kid just wouldn't let go.

That was the nature of police work. It bred obsessive personality disorder. When the teen came back, Shanks said,

"You want to explain your system of filing? The colored dots? These orange-dotted folders look like Demon victims."

"They are."

"When did you put all these cases together?"

"A year or two ago."

"You linked together these women with Billy Ray Barnes way before he was arrested."

Ben nodded.

"Okay. I'm impressed." Shanks sorted through the six orange-dotted files. "You got two women who haven't been positively identified as victims of the Demon. This one—Christine Hernandez—I know that APD is waiting on DNA for her. However, this one from Teasdale, Oklahoma . . . Bristol Carrington." Shanks held up the file. "She's not on the radar. How'd you find her?"

"Teasdale PD homicide reward. Then once I saw the place, I worked backward. Teasdale is a small town; the closest bigger town is Norman, Oklahoma. If you look at a map, Norman is a straight shot through Amarillo to Albuquerque. And Bristol's profile seemed to fit with the rest of the Demon victims."

"Okay." Shanks stood up. "I'm calling up Ortiz right now. I'm going to borrow this file. It's going to take a while." And it did. By the time Shanks had related all the information and faxed the papers, forty minutes had gone by. When he returned, Ben had fallen asleep. The detective gently shook the boy's shoulders.

Ben lifted his head and rubbed his eyes. "I think I need more coffee."

"How about we go get some dinner? No shoptalk for at least a half hour."

"I won't object." He stood up and started to pile the folders atop one another.

Shanks said, "You know you're going to have to leave these with me."

"They're yours. I already made copies." He handed the pile to the detective.

"I have this sneaking suspicion that these aren't all of your files, right?" When Ben didn't answer, Shanks repeated, "Right?"

"I have a few more at home."

"Ben, I'm losing patience." Shanks pointed to the chair and the teen sat back down. "What are you holding back? Wait. Don't tell me. Let me guess. Because I can be a detective too. You have files that are related to Ellen's murder. But for some reason only known to you, you left those at home." When the kid looked at the ceiling, Shanks said, "Why are you keeping those from me? Is it because you don't trust me or is it because you think I'm incompetent?"

"No and no." Ben looked down. "I didn't want to get you involved until I knew more."

"I'm already involved, Ben."

"You're involved but I'm committed—"

"Stop that, Ben."

"Sam, it's like that joke about eggs and bacon. The chicken is involved; the pig is committed."

"Ben, what other cases do you have that are similar to Ellen's? And no bullshit. I'm tired."

"Jeez, Sam, don't get so angry."

Shanks took in a deep breath and let it out. "I'm not angry." Of course he was. He forced himself to smile, kept his pen poised on his notebook. "How about if we start with names, Ben."

"Julia Rehnquist and Jamey Moore."

"Spell them." When Ben did, Shanks said, "Tell me about the first one—Julia Rehnquist."

"Happened a year and a half after Ellen, December nineteenth. She was sixteen, abducted from Berkeley, and found in Mount Diablo State Park in California."

"How long have you known about her?"

"The body was discovered this past summer . . . like right before school started. That's when I found out."

"So, tell me what you know about it."

Ben sipped his coffee. "Just what I can pull up from the computer. I tried to see if there was any physical evidence like a print or a DNA profile, but the newspapers were sketchy. I checked on the homicide bulletins . . . nothing much came up. But I do know where she was found. I just wanted to find out a little more before I told you about it. I didn't want to look like an idiot or a crazy person."

"Idiot no, crazy person a little more likely." A pause. "Tell me about the second girl, Jamey Moore."

"I just found out about her two weeks ago. That's when I knew I had to come in to talk to you."

"So why didn't you do it then?"

"I wanted to give Katie Doogan one more shot before I concentrated on anyone else."

"Well, you succeeded. Tell me about Jamey Moore."

"She was from Knoxville. She disappeared on September twenty-first. Her body was found in the Smoky Mountains two weeks ago, near Cosby, Tennessee."

"So, you've known about it for two weeks."

"Yes. She's a little different, Sam. She wasn't an innocent. She had a history of being a runaway. I'm interested in her because the date of her abduction is close to the autumnal equinox. She may be part of the pattern."

"You have pictures of them? The girls?"

"In my files. Just what I printed from the local papers."

Shanks looked at his watch. "It's getting dark. Did you bike here?"

"Yeah."

"Okay. This is what you're going to do. Are you listening, Ben?"

"I'm right here."

"You are going to call up your mother and tell her that I'm taking you out to dinner. After we eat, I'll stow your bike in my van, I'll take you home, and I'll pick up the files, and then you're finished doing snoop work. Do you have any problem with any of that?"

"No."

"Good." Shanks focused on the boy's eyes. "I suppose you have a host of reasons why those cases are similar to Ellen's case."

"The age, the physical appearance, the circumstances, where they were buried, and now the date of the abductions." Ben fidgeted. "Since I told you about the files, could you call up the primary detective on the Rehnquist case and get some details?"

"Blimey, young lad, I never thought about that." The kid looked abashed. Shanks shook his head. "I'll call as soon as I look up the case so I know what I'm talking about."

"When are you going to do that?"

"I'm planning on doing it right now unless you want to eat at four fifteen."

"So . . . like what do I do while you look up the cases?"

"You can call your mother and tell her that I'm taking you out to dinner."

"Can I come with you to look at the cases? I promise I won't read over your shoulder."

Without answering, Shanks got up and Ben followed. After Shanks shut the door to his office, he said, "Sit down and be quiet. If I have any questions, I'll ask you."

"Can I call my mother?"

"Yeah, go ahead." Shanks entered "Julia Rehnquist" into the search program on the computer. The information was basic: sixteen-year-old girl found buried in a rectangular grave in Mount Diablo in Contra Costa, California, near Danville. She was last seen out for a jog on December nineteenth of last year. She appeared to have been abducted in broad daylight. Anyone with information should call the Berkeley PD at the following number and ask for Derek Whitecliffe or the Danville PD. Shanks wrote down the digits and the name of the primary. There was also a picture of the girl. Shanks did notice physical similarities to Ellen and Katie—not sisters, but maybe they could have been cousins.

Next was Jamey Moore. She was seventeen, a runaway, and went missing on September 21 of this year. The body was found buried in a rectangular three-foot-by-four-foot-by-four-foot grave. Anyone with information, etc. He took down the number and the name of the primary detective—Jack Bonet. He also printed out the picture. She appeared a little older and a little harder, but she was definitely from the same mold.

Shanks turned off the computer. Ben said, "Any luck?"

"Got the names of the primary detectives."

"Derek Whitecliffe in Berkeley. I don't know about the other one."

"Jack Bonet in Knoxville."

"Are you going to call them?"

"Yes. I do think you're onto something." Ben's grin was immediate. Shanks said, "I shouldn't be telling you this, but I will anyway. Albuquerque retrieved some biological evidence from Katie Doogan. It will take a while to process. It might be smart to wait until we have something concrete like a DNA match between Katie Doogan and Ellen. Once we get a connection, we can start thinking about a serial killer. And once we have a serial killer, we can start linking up the dates. The more information we have, the easier it will be to get other police agencies to cooperate and be excited."

"So, you're not going to call them?"

"Of course I'm going to call them. But first, let me do my homework, Vicks."

"I hear you, Sam. But what if there's already DNA from Julia Rehnquist? Since you have DNA from Ellen, can't we just see if there's a match? Like what about CODIS?"

"That's for matching DNA to known perps."

"Surely there is some file where you can match DNA to DNA."

"Of course you can match DNA to DNA. But there is no way I can push the New Mexico state lab to make a match between someone in Berkeley and someone in River Remez. Right now, the lab is tied up with the Demon and now with Katie Doogan."

Ben took out his computer. A few keystrokes later he said, "There are crime labs in Berkeley, Oakland, Contra Costa County—"

"Okay, you're right. Maybe they'll want to do some DNA matching. Great. But I repeat. Let me do my homework first."

Shanks started doing math. "Okay. Here we go. From Ellen's murder to Katie's murder was nine months. From Katie to Julia was nine months, and from Julia to Jamey was nine months."

"Three years, four girls, four seasons. Ro and I—" Ben stopped himself.

"What? Don't go mute on me now."

"We were thinking that the guy completed the cycle—all four seasons. Maybe that's what he had in mind to do. Four murders, and because he completed a cycle, maybe he'd just stop."

"If it's a true serial killer, he isn't going to stop," Shanks said. "But four murders in three years that are almost to the day nine months apart: that's pretty meticulous. He also buries his victims in neat, rectangular graves. He inters them deep beneath the ground. He's very, very organized."

"Exactly. That's why I think he's going to repeat the cycle, this time being precise with the dates."

"If you are correct, then we should add nine months to Jamey and that would put us at the summer solstice of next year."

"Right where he started with Ellen."

"Of course, he could accelerate the process. Winter solstice is around the corner."

"I thought about that," Ben told him. "But like you said, this guy is meticulous. Maybe he needs a full nine months to plan things out."

"Do you have any idea why he picked these cities?" Shanks opened his computer again. "After all, you've been sitting on this longer than I have."

"I don't know why he chose the places he did." Shanks

didn't respond and was busy clicking on his keyboard. Ben said, "Can I see what you're doing?"

"Just sit tight and keep your own computer open. I might have a few questions for you to look up." Then Shanks noticed the grin on the kid's face. He said, "I'm feeding your addiction. I am an enabler."

Ben laughed. "What are you looking up?"

"Transcontinental highways," Shanks said. "Three major ones: Interstate 90 and Interstate 80 go north of here. Interstate 40 goes through Albuquerque." A few more clicks. "Here we are. Forty also goes through Nashville, Knoxville, and Memphis, Tennessee. Albuquerque and Knoxville are linked by the highway. River Remez is a straight shot north on the 25, only a little over an hour away. What about Berkeley? Where does Interstate 40 start in California?"

"Barstow," Ben said.

"How far is Barstow from Berkeley?"

"There are two Barstows in California. One is in San Bernardino, the other is in Fresno. The one in San Bernardino is three hundred and forty-eight miles from Berkeley as the crow flies. The one in Fresno is only one hundred and forty-seven miles."

"I'm looking at the one near the Mojave Desert."

"That's the one in San Bernardino—farther from Berkeley."

Shanks turned off his computer first. "Okay. So, three out of the four cities make sense. The other is off the pattern."

"Let me do some poking around on my computer," Ben said.

"No," Shanks told him. "As helpful as you've been, you've got to stop playing cop and start living your life."

"I am living my life. I'm perfectly capable of living my life and looking into my sister's death. They are orthogonal events."

Shanks said, "I'm picking up all your files tonight. Every single one of them. I'm sure they will keep me busy for days. If you keep sleuthing on your own, you'll piss me off. I'll confiscate your computer."

"I don't believe you."

"Don't test me." Shanks tried to make a stern face, but fell short. "I'll tell you what. I'll be the first one to tell you if we get a DNA match between Ellen and anyone. In the meantime, you stay out of it."

"Are you going to call Berkeley?"

"I'm going to run Ellen's DNA through CODIS tomorrow, just to make sure I didn't miss something. If nothing pops up, I'll think about calling up Berkeley. I still might wait until we see what happens with Katie Doogan."

Ben's face was the picture of impatience. "What if Katie Doogan doesn't match my sister? Will you still call up Berkeley?"

"One way or the other, I'll call up Berkeley. You could be wrong about Katie but still right about Julia. But if you're right about Katie, I will go to Berkeley with a lot more confidence. Let's go grab some dinner."

"So you're still speaking to me?" Ben asked.

"Of course I'm speaking to you. I like you . . . sometimes." Shanks stood up. "Let's go to Rani's. They have a dinner buffet. Do you like Indian Indian?"

"I do like Indian Indian. And I love buffets."

"Never know it by looking at you." Shanks stuffed the files that Ben gave him into his desk. He locked the drawers. "Your pants are falling off. Must be all that hiking and biking."

"And being seventeen."

"Yeah, that too. Don't rub it in."

CHAPTER 25

THE RIDE TO the memorial service for Katie Doogan was silent. Once there, Ben and Ro were swallowed up in a crowd of over five hundred community members showing their support, among them his family, somewhere. Ben knew that murderers often come to these gatherings for a sick thrill, but it was impossible to pick anyone out—from the service to the funeral and then to the house to pay final respects. On the ride home, Ben had dozens of thoughts racing through his head. Radio provided background noise and that was good. A half hour before the off-ramp to River Remez, Ro spoke up.

"How'd the session go with Shanks?"

"He told me to stop."

"Are you going to listen?"

"I haven't decided. I asked him to call up Berkeley to get information about Julia Rehnquist. But I think he wants to wait until he's got something like DNA linking up Katie Doogan with my sister."

"Makes sense. He needs time to absorb everything you've given him. It's a lot of information."

"I think he's on board with me. But he wants me out."

"Maybe he doesn't want you involved because you might be getting close."

"But I'm not close. I don't have a name and I don't have the next city. All I have is maybe a pattern."

"Why don't you step back for a little bit? Get some perspective."

"I'm sure you're right." When Ro seemed nervous, Ben said, "What's on your mind?"

She fidgeted. "I think I'm gonna break up with JD."

It took a moment to absorb her words. It was so out of place—trivial given all that they had gone through. But maybe it was the gravity of what happened that had given her the impetus to change.

"Okay." A beat. "Can I ask why?"

"It's been a while coming."

"Okay." Another pause. "You know I'm still going to UNM—"

"I know. It has nothing to do with you staying at Remez. It's what I need to do. The only thing that makes me hesitate is the winter dance. But I know that's not a reason to stick around. And just maybe I still have some feelings for him."

Ben licked his lips. "Do you love him?"

"No, I don't *love* him. But I do like him. And I don't want to leave him stranded and without a date. He's actually been pretty nice to me."

"If you want to break up, don't worry about the winter dance. He's probably got a list of girls waiting in the wings."

She twisted her head around to look at him. "Why do you say that?"

Oops. "Because JD's the bomb. You know that." She was quiet. "I know you really want to go to the dance. You bought your dress and everything."

"So I shouldn't break up with him?"

"You should do what you really want to do."

"Like you said, Vicks, a dress is not a reason to stay with someone." She thought a moment. "I mean, I could break up with him after the winter dance." Ro looked at him with those baby blues. "What do you think I should do?"

"I can't answer that." Ro tapped her foot and waited. He said, "You like him enough to go to the winter dance with him, right?"

"Yeah, I do want to go to the dance," she said. "But I sure as hell don't want to go to the after party."

"Then go to the dance but not the after party."

"But if I go to the dance with him, I'll have to go to the after party."

"What's wrong with the after party?"

"It's different from the regular parties, Vicks. It's at a motel. He'll expect me to do things."

"Oh . . ." Ben's face went hot. "Don't do anything you don't want to do." She was dry-eyed, tense. He said, "This isn't my forte. This is something you should discuss with Shannon or Chelsea."

She looked out the window and shook her head. "I threw myself into school. I had no choice. It was either do that or just cry all the time. I didn't want to come here. I'm so angry that my parents did this to me. I should have finished up in New York. But then Griff would have to deal with my mom without me. I couldn't do it to him."

"I know. It really sucks."

"Sometimes it really does. But then I think it happened for the best. Especially meeting you . . ." She looked at him. "It's brought out this flood of emotions that I've held back for the last three years. It feels so good to finally have someone who I can talk to."

Disappointed didn't begin to describe how Ben felt. He'd gone from friend to therapist. "Right."

"I can't go to the winter dance without going to the after party, Vicks. And I don't want to go to the after party."

"You have a decision to make."

"Yes, I do." She paused. "I'll drop you off at home. Or rather since you're driving my car, you can drop yourself off at your home and I'll go talk to him."

"No, no, no. That's not what we agreed on. I'm going with you."

"Vicks, stop it. I can handle this on my own."

"Humor me, please."

"All right, you can come. But stay in the background. Because I still might change my mind. I'm still on the fence about this."

"If you're still on the fence, why go talk to him now?" Silence. "Ro, you had a real hard day. Real emotional and long. Why don't you just sleep on it and see how you feel in the morning?"

"Because if I see how I feel in the morning, I'm going to change my mind. I'm going to go to school and get sucked

into all that social crap because I'm pathetic. I can't stand being disliked."

"It's really not so bad once you get used to it."

"You're not disliked, okay? Weird, yes. Eccentric, yes.
Vaguely disconcerting, yes. But no one dislikes you. I'm going to go talk to JD and I'm going to do it now. So either point
the car in that direction or get out and walk home."

"This isn't going to end well."

"Just let me handle it."

BEN PULLED UP to the curb at JD's house at three in the afternoon. JD was the oldest of five and his parents lived in a
sprawling two-story adobe, modern in style, with soaring
ceilings and lots of points and angles. Ro said, "Wait here."

"No." Ben spoke with authority. "We're going in together."

"Whatever." She got out and slammed the door.

It was cold outside. Heavy gray clouds hung low in the
skies. The winds were fierce. The air smelled like rain and electricity. Ro rang the bell, one of those deep gongs. A moment
later Weekly answered the door, dressed in a dirty T-shirt and
torn jeans. He was barefoot, his blond hair hanging over his
eyes. His breath hinted of pot and alcohol. Obviously, there
were no adults around.

Wordlessly, Ro breezed past him into the living room,
where JD was playing the Hari-katchi-something-killer-
fighter game on his giant flat screen. At the moment Ro
looked pretty killer-fighter herself. JD turned around, took
in her face. Then he saw Ben, standing ten paces behind her.
He went back to playing his video game.

Ro said, "Can I talk to you alone?"

He didn't answer. JD was dressed in a wifebeater and jeans.

The guy had it all—built and good-looking with a square chin and wide, white smile. He was popular, he was charming, he was funny, and he was really smart. But Ben knew he had a dark side, having been on the receiving end of it. Then again, JD knew what Ben was capable of. That made them even.

Ro said, "It won't take too long, JD."

JD continued to play. Without looking at her, he said, "Anything you want to say to me, you can say in front of my friends."

There were six of them. She said, "I'd really prefer to talk to you alone."

"And I don't really care what you'd really prefer." He turned around and gave her a sneer masquerading as a smile. "Your preference isn't important."

His posse booed. Weekly said, "Ooooh . . . dis."

"I know why you're here," JD said. "If you want to go out with the geek, go out with the geek. I'm out the door in six months, so I really don't give a solitary shit."

"It has nothing to do with Vicks, JD. Can you just give me a minute alone?"

"No. Go fuck yourself. And go fuck Vicks. He's a virgin. He can use it a lot more than me."

"It has nothing to do with Vicks," she repeated. "We're just friends."

"We're just friends," JD imitated.

"It's the truth," Ro insisted. "I've been totally true to you."

"Unlike me, is that what you're saying?" Abruptly, JD threw the joystick at the TV. It crashed into the flat screen and shattered it, bits of black glass flying all over the room. JD said, "Did he give you all the deets, Do-ro-thy?"

Ben felt his heart beating hard. "Shut up, JD!"

"Did he give you a play-by-play of what he saw?"

"JD, shut *up*!"

"What are you *talking* about?" Ro's eyes flitted between JD and Ben. "Play-by-play of what?"

"Ro, let's get out of here," Ben said.

"Wait a minute, wait a minute." A pause. "What play-by-play?" Another pause. "What deets?"

It was JD's turn to be confused. He turned to Ben. "You didn't—"

"Just shut the fuck up!" Ben took Ro's hand, but she pulled away. "We need to go."

"Absolutely not!" She stared at JD. "Details of what?" When he didn't answer, she said, "What did you see, Vicks?" He was silent and so was the room. And then it dawned on her. "You've been *cheating* on me?"

No one spoke.

"I'm in my prime, toots." JD's voice went down a notch. "A guy's gotta do what a guy's gotta do."

"You actually *cheated* on me?" Ro was stunned. "With who?"

"Why don't you ask Vicks? He was there."

Ben was irate. "You are such an asshole!"

She turned her anger on Ben. "You knew about this and didn't tell me?" Her eyes darted between the boys. The blue orbs welled up with tears and she ran out of the room. Ben was on her tail.

"Ro, stop—"

She turned, her face filled with fury. "What was that all about, Vicks?" She shoved him in the chest. "Some kind of bro code?" She pushed him again. "You knew he was cheating on me and you never said a word?" When he didn't answer, she said. "You know what? He's despicable, but you're a real douchebag. Give me the keys to my car!"

"I don't think you should be driving—"

"Give me the goddamn . . ." She stuck her hand in his pocket and pulled them out. "Go to hell!" She ran to her Explorer and peeled away.

Ben sighed, staring at the empty curb, trying to figure out what had just gone wrong. A moment later JD came out, hands in his pockets. "Cold outside. Why don't you come in?"

"I'm going to pass."

JD said, "Are you banging her?"

"No, I'm not banging her." Ben bit his lip. "She's been totally true to you."

"Misplaced loyalty." JD sighed. "I'm really in the shits right now. I just lost my girl and I broke the flat screen." He sighed again. "Need a ride home, Vicks?"

"No . . . I'll walk."

"It's looking pretty nasty outside."

"'S'right." His jaw was working a mile a minute. "I'll walk."

"Suit yourself." JD returned to the warmth of his house and his friends.

Ben put his head down, stuck his hands in his pockets, and braced himself against a bitter wind.

CHAPTER 26

WALKING WAS A bad decision. Within minutes, it started to rain. It wasn't the gentle rain of spring. It wasn't even the warm downpour of a monsoon. It was a cold rain with big fat droplets, pelting him in the frost of late autumn. It was a sharp rain that came with pinpoints of ice, the weather definitely heralding winter. He kept a poncho in his backpack. River Remez was unpredictable at this time of year. Unfortunately, his knapsack was in Ro's car.

It soon became the rainstorm from hell: lightning bolts so close they almost buzzed his head and blinded him. Thunder crackled with anger and vengeance. He should have taken off running, but after the past week, he had no reserves of energy to draw on. Walking and shivering, soaked to the skin. The blare of a horn made him jump. The Explorer slowed and Ro rolled down the window and threw out his knapsack. It fell into a rain puddle with a thud. Then she took off again.

As he bent down to get it, she put the SUV in reverse and gunned the engine. She passed him a second time going in reverse, splashing him head to foot. The she put the car back into drive, pulled up alongside him, and rolled down the window. "Get in."

"No."

"Stop being an idiot. Get in!"

"I don't want to talk to you right now. Go away."

"It's dangerous outside. Get in or I'll call the cops!"

Ben picked up the dripping backpack and stepped into the passenger seat. Ro floored the gas and the SUV took off, the wheels screeching in a giant skid headed for the cliff. Ben grabbed the wheel and hooked left, falling on top of Ro to steer into the turn and ride out the skid. As soon as he could manage to get a foot on the brake, he pulled over to the side of the road. Pulling the key from the ignition, he fell back in the passenger seat, trying to catch his breath.

"Are you fucking crazy? You almost killed both of us."

"Who?" When he didn't answer, she said, "Who was JD screwing?"

"Lisa Holloway." He bent forward and turned up the heat. There wasn't an inch of dry space on his clothing. He wiped a wet hand on a wet shirt. "I'd leave this minute except I'm worried that if you drive, you'll kill yourself. Move over and I'll drive you home."

She didn't budge. "How'd you find out?"

"Move."

"No. Not until you tell me how you found out."

"You don't want to hear this."

"Yes, I fucking do want to hear it. How?"

"They were in the supply room. I walked in on them."

"God, what a total asshole! And she's a total whore!" She glared at him. "How long have you known?"

"A couple of months."

"And you never thought to tell me?" Silence. "The guy was playing me for an idiot and it never dawned on you to tell me?"

"I didn't want to make you unhappy."

"Do I look happy now?" She brushed tears away from her eyes. "How would you feel if it was the reverse?"

"That's different. I'm always miserable. To have a girl cheat on me would feel ego-syntonic."

"Ego . . . where do you come up with these words?" She pulled off her jacket and tossed it into the backseat. She was staring out the windshield. "Don't call me anymore. I don't want to see you again either."

"Fine. Don't see me again. But you know that's not fair. He was the asshole, not me. I was just trying to spare your feelings. And if that was a mistake, that's all it was. A mistake."

She didn't answer. Then she said, "I'll take you home."

"I'm not driving with you."

"Fine. Then walk."

He started to get out, but she held his arm. "You can drive to your house. But then I drive myself home."

"Okay. So move over."

She didn't move. "Anything else I should know about? Like are you doing it with one of my friends? Because that would upset me . . . not that you were doing it, but that you didn't tell me."

"Are you fucking *blind*? Everyone in the entire school knows that I'm thoroughly besotted with you. I hang around you like a dog waiting for table scraps."

"When you're not acting like a weirdo and a ghoul and going through murder files."

"Now you're getting personal. Either let me drive home or I'm leaving."

Ro's lip quivered. "How could he *cheat* on me?"

"Because he's a prick. You should have known that from the beginning."

"What's wrong with the guys in this school?"

"It's not the school, Ro, it's guys. God knows how I might have been had Ellen not died. I told you, before it happened I was an asshole. Sometimes I'm still an asshole. Now kindly move your butt so we can get going."

"Are you really besotted with me?"

"Totally. Can we go now?"

Her eyes misted. "I don't know if I'm ready for a new boyfriend."

"That's okay. You don't have to be my girlfriend." For the first time in a long time, he felt a genuine smile coming on. "But at least you're not someone else's girlfriend."

"Vicks, you have to be honest with me. No more keeping secrets. No more holding back. Is there anything else you want to tell me?"

"No. Now how about if I drive home, put on some dry clothes, and think about your question without freezing my ass off?"

"Will you go to the winter dance with me?"

Ben groaned out loud. "You've got to be kidding."

"If you really were besotted, you'd do it for me."

"I can't. You know that. I'll be in San Francisco. I've already booked my ticket and it's not refundable."

"You'd rather go on some wild-goose chase where you

don't belong, hunting down some lost cause rather than take me to the winter dance?"

"You want me to be honest with you, right? The answer is yes. And it's not a wild-goose chase and you know it." Her face was dejected. He said, "I went to homecoming for you."

"But not *with* me."

"Because you had another date." He hit his forehead in frustration. "I'm crazy about you, Ro, but I am not going to the winter dance. I have to go to San Francisco and I'm leaving on Christmas. I only have a short time to talk to the family and get them on board."

"Why don't you let Shanks handle it? He said he'd call up the detective after he was prepared. Why do you have to be involved?"

"Committed," he muttered. "I don't know. I tilt at windmills. I'm going, okay."

"You'll be doing this forever until you find him."

"Probably."

"Give me the keys. I can drive now." When he hesitated, she said, "Give me the keys."

"I promise I'll take you to prom if we're still okay with each other." She didn't answer. Ben said, "At least your dress won't go to waste."

"I'll have to get a totally different dress for prom, so it *will* go to waste."

"Well . . . then I'm sorry."

"You won't take me to the winter dance?"

"Okay already!" Ben was shouting. "Okay, I'll take you. I'll change my ticket and everything. I'm totally whipped, okay. But going to the dance is a mistake. JD is going to make my life miserable, but that's okay. I've known the guy forever and I'm used to his shit. But he's going to make your life a misery. But if you want to go, I'll transfer my ticket and take you."

"Forget it," Ro said. "You're right. I am being ridiculous." A pause. "It's nice of you to offer. Sometimes it's just the thought that counts." She held out her palm and he gave her the keys.

Five minutes later she pulled up in front of Ben's house. He said, "Do you want to come in?"

"Yeah, why not?"

He bounded out in the rain to open the car door for her. They ran to the front portal. Once they were inside, he could finally relax. No one was home and the house was warm and felt as comforting as a flannel blanket.

"Can I get you anything?" He rubbed his arms. "Hot chocolate, maybe?"

"What are you? Twelve?"

"Beer? Vodka?"

"You're getting warmer."

"Just let me change, okay. I'll be right out."

He was about to close the door to his room when she charged in, throwing her arms around his neck and pressing her lips against his, holding him in a tight embrace while her fingers raked through his hair. Within moments, they were kissing hard and passionately. Ben felt dizzy and woozy. He was cold and shivering and burning with desire.

The front door slammed. "Anyone home? Ben?"

"Oh God, it's Haley." He broke away, grabbed some dry clothes, and locked himself in the bathroom, breathing hard, trying to put the brakes on his arousal. He could hear Haley in his bedroom.

"Oh, hi, Ro. Where's Ben?"

He couldn't hear what she said. He changed quickly, getting himself reasonably under control. It took a few minutes. When he went back out, he had a smile on his face. Haley and Lilly were staring at him with weird expressions. He said, "Where's Ro?"

Haley said, "She left."

"She *left*?"

"Yeah." Haley looked at him. "Did you guys have a fight or something?"

"No . . . maybe." He was panicked and confused. "I need privacy. Like right now!"

"Well, excuse me!"

Ben locked the door and called Ro's cell. When she didn't answer, he called again. And again. She picked up on the fourth try. He said, "Why'd you leave?"

"Why do you think?"

"Honestly, I have no idea."

"Vicks, I'm sorry I attacked you—"

"Oh please, please, please don't apologize for kissing me. It was the best thing that ever happened to me in my entire life! Come back!" She was silent. "Hello?"

"I'm still here."

"Come back, Ro. Please?"

"Ben, you pushed me away!"

"I didn't push you away. My sister came home. It would have been impolitic for her to see me in my obviously aroused state." He heard her break into laughter over the phone. "Where are you?"

"I just pulled up into my driveway."

"Come back."

"I don't want to. It's pouring outside and I don't want to drive."

"Okay. I'll come to your house."

"Do you have a car?"

"I have a poncho and a bike."

"It's pouring outside, Vicks. Don't be ridiculous. Besides, I don't want to see you right now."

"Why not?"

"Because I need to think, okay?"

"Ro, come back. If you don't, I really will bike out to see you."

"I don't want to see you, Ben. I don't want to see anyone right now, okay? I want to be by myself. I need space. I mean, you need space all the time. So how about giving me the same consideration that I give you?" When he didn't answer, she said, "It's not that easy, is it?"

"Okay. You need space." He was pacing the floor. "When can I see you?"

"I'll call you. And don't come here or I'll get really mad. Respect my wishes like I respect your wishes." She hung up and Ben threw the phone across the room and onto his bed. "Shit! Shit, shit, shit!" There was a knock on the door. He swung it open and glared at Lilly.

She swallowed hard. "We're baking chocolate chip cookies. Wanna help?"

"You need my help in baking? Seriously?" When Lilly was silent, he said, "I'll be out in a minute. Do you know where my mom is, by any chance?"

"I think she said something about a board meeting."

"That's right." Meaning he'd be without a car for at least the next two hours. "Give me a minute, okay?"

"Take your time, Ben." She closed the door gently.

He leaned against the wall. Life was sincerely fucked, but it made no sense to take it out on the girls.

Go bake cookies. Distraction was the name of the game.

CHAPTER 27

WHEN HE CAME out, the girls were wearing oversized flowered aprons. Haley was reading the back of the chocolate chip package and Lilly had a bowl and a wooden spoon. The house was a typical open floor plan. The kitchen looked out to the living space and was separated from it by a breakfast bar. He pulled up a stool on the living room side. "Hey."

Haley was mixing something yellow and gooey in a bowl. "Why is Ro upset?"

"She broke up with JD."

"What?" both girls whispered. Haley said, "What happened?"

"He cheated on her."

"Oh my God!" Haley said. "What an asshole."

"Seems to be the general consensus."

The doorbell rang. Ben looked at the entry hall and grew hopeful. Maybe Ro had changed her mind.

It was JD.

"She's not here." He tried to close the door in his face, but JD stepped forward and caught the edge with his hand. "Where is she?"

"Home."

Outside, it was raining sheets of water. Lightning strikes were illuminating JD as if he were Thor himself. He said, "Could I talk to you?"

Ben waited.

"Can I come inside? Little cold out here."

Ben paused and then stepped aside. JD took off his muddy boots. When he took off his jacket, Ben said, "Give it to me."

"It's soaked."

"I'll hang it up in the shower. Come in."

Haley and Lilly were looking at JD with their mouths open. He said, "Hi, girls."

"Hi," Lilly whispered. Haley waved and JD winked at her. Ben caught it, but it didn't bother him. There was something uniquely smarmy about Weekly. But JD was just being JD. He had changed from his wifebeater into a long-sleeved black polo shirt that was stretching across his chest. He said, "Girls, could you hold off on the baking for a little bit?"

Lilly took Haley's hand. "Let's go play Angry Birds."

"Could you hang this up for me?" Ben gave Haley JD's sodden jacket. When he heard the door close, he said, "What do you want?"

JD looked around the house as if it were foreign territory. Ben didn't know why. Nothing had changed since he had last been here. He said, "Vicks, I got no problem with you."

"Why would you have a problem with me?"

"True enough. I haven't spoken more than ten words to you in the last three years. I'm just curious. Did you tell her?"

"No. But once you opened your big mouth, I told her what I saw and who with."

"Then she really didn't know until . . ."

"No, of course she didn't know. Do you really think I'd rat you out?"

"Fuck!" JD punched the wall.

"Easy there, Conor McGregor," Ben said. "You're beating on someone else's house."

"I'm a fucking idiot!" He looked at Ben. "You gotta help me get her back, dude."

"Are you on something? I've been waiting an entire semester for her to toss your sorry ass over the cliff. Why on earth would I throw you a rope?"

"Can I sit down?"

"Go ahead."

JD was quiet. "Okay, Vicks, this is the deal. You're gone all next semester. If Ro and I break up, who do you think is going to suffer? Her status comes from me. With her knocked out of the top position, I go back to Shannon. So Weekly's out his girl and that's gonna piss him off. And if he takes it out on anyone, it's gonna be Ro. And even if I decided not to torture her, which I really need to do because she dumped me, Shannon will do it for me. Shannon is real jealous of her. She hates her."

"How do you know that Shannon hates Ro?" When JD averted his eyes, Ben got it. "You're banging Shannon?"

"We just kinda never stopped."

"She's your best friend's girl!"

"She was my girlfriend first."

"That's why she's called an ex-girlfriend. What do you do? Booty-call her when you're not banging Lisa?"

"I'm a dog." He drummed his fingers along the breakfast bar. "What does it matter? In six months I'm at Duke, Ro's back east, and you're still here, doing what you're doing. We're talking like five months, Vicks. Can you picture Ro sitting by herself, getting tormented by Shannon and Chelsea? She's going to wither."

Ben didn't say anything.

"You know I'm right about this," JD said. "Listen, dude. I know Ro likes you better than she likes me. I can live with that. But I still want her because she's hot. Why should I take second best?"

"Maybe she wants a boyfriend who doesn't cheat on her."

"You just don't understand." He shook his head. "It's not your fault. You're in arrested development because of what happened—"

"JD, I'm this close to kicking your ass out of here."

"Once you've had it, you can't go back." He stood up and began to pace. "You really can't. That's just the way pussy works."

"Keep your voice down!" Ben pointed to Haley's room.

"Sorry." JD sat back down. "I've got a proposition for you."

Ben threw up his hands. "What?"

"You are going to UNM in Albuquerque next semester, right?"

"Yes."

"And you're going to be working at Circuitchip, right?"

"Yes."

"That's good stuff, Vicks. Congratulations."

"Thank you for your kind words. Can you get on with it?"

"Okay. That means you're not in school anymore—"

"I'll be at school on Mondays."

"But basically, you're gone, right?" JD said. "Just listen before you say no. This is the proposition. I'll take Ro from Monday through Friday night and you can have her on the weekends when you're here in River Remez."

Ben let out a forced laugh. "Are you out of your fucking mind?"

"I want her for arm candy, okay. I want her so I don't have to go back to Shannon. I don't want to be Shannon's boyfriend. I like banging her, but she's dumb and she talks too much."

"JD, what is *wrong* with you?"

"You know what I want, dude?" JD said. "I want to be a college student. I want to play football, get drunk, bang women, and as an aside, get into law school. So I can be a lawyer and get drunk and bang women and look at old football tapes of my glory days."

Ben couldn't help it. He stifled a smile.

JD began pacing. "Vicks, I need Ro to keep Shannon and Lisa off my back. I don't need Ro for sex. I would take Ro for sex. If I was banging her, I probably wouldn't be banging Shannon or Lisa. But she ain't gonna give me play, so what's the point? You can have her. She's more your speed anyway. I'm a practical man."

Ben shook his head. "I really don't know what to say to you."

"You can say that I'm right. You know that Ro's going to shrivel up unless she's the center of the universe. Do you really want her to be miserable for the next five months when I've hit upon a really easy solution?"

In a very strange way, JD was making sense. "You know, even if I were to agree to something so crack-ass, she'd never agree to it."

"One day without my protection and with you gone, she'll agree to it. Dude, if you know her like I know her, you know I'm right. Besides, you hate all that school shit. I'll take her to the winter dance—"

"Not the after party. You are *not* going to a motel with her."

"I won't take her to the after party. We can say that . . ." He snapped his fingers. "I'll tell everyone we're working it out. That'll get her out of the after party. I'll take Lisa to the after party. She'll be thrilled and it'll make Shannon jealous." When he saw Ben staring at him, he said, "It's like football, Vicks. You plan several moves in advance. I'll take Ro to the winter dance. Seriously, you don't want to go to the winter dance."

"Seriously."

JD gave him a knowing grin. "It's the perfect solution. I'll take her to the winter dance, I'll take her to the spring fling, I'll take her to prom—"

"No, I'm taking her to prom."

"You want to go to prom?"

"I promised her. I'm taking her."

"Vicks, I have to take her to prom. If I lose out to you on that, it'll ruin my rep."

"I don't give a rat's ass about your rep. I'm taking her to prom. And if that's a deal breaker, then we are done talking."

The doorbell rang.

"Jeez, what now!" Ben got up and looked through the

peephole. It was Ro. When he opened the door, she said, "We can talk now."

Ben raised his eyebrows. "JD's here."

She took a step backward. "You let him in your *house*?"

"Come in."

"I'm not coming in with that asshole here. Get rid of him."

"Come in, Ro. He wants to apologize."

"I'm sorry," JD shouted from inside.

Ro stormed into the house, pushing Ben out of the way. "You're a real asshole," she said to JD.

"I never denied it."

"How could you *do* that to me?" She was teary-eyed again. "*Why* did you do that to me?"

"Rosers, I truly think you are the most beautiful girl in the world—"

"Answer the damn question!"

"I am answering the damn question. I want you, but I also want sex. I'm a dog."

"You're a dog and an asshole. I'm never speaking to you again. Get out of here!"

"You never really *liked* me, okay?" JD snapped back. "I mean, you liked who I was and what I could bring to the table, but you never really liked *me*!"

Ro was quiet.

Ben broke the silence. "Anyone want coffee?" When they both glared at him, he said, "You two can continue on with your evil-eye staring contest. I need caffeine."

Ro said, "I liked you. I don't like you now, but I did like you."

"And my sisters like me too," JD said. "But I don't want a sister for a girlfriend."

Silence again. Ben got out the coffee and poured the water into the machine. They all listened to Mr. Coffee burble.

JD said, "I'm sorry I cheated on you. You like to hang with Vicks, hang with him. He's a good guy. I don't see what you see in him when you can have me, but there's no accounting for bad taste."

"I'm smarter than you," Ben said.

"Agreed. But in everything else . . . seriously."

When he took out a mug, Ro said, "I'll take a cup."

"JD?"

"Yeah, why not."

Ben served them coffee. Between Shanks and this, he'd always have a job as a barista. "Are you going to say anything, JD, or do I have to say it?"

"It'd be better if you said it."

"Say what?" Ro asked.

"You have to promise that you're not going to slap me and walk out, okay." Ben sipped coffee and pointed to JD. "This is his idea."

"But you agree with it," JD said.

"I haven't agreed to anything. I'm only reporting, so don't kill the messenger." Ro waited. "JD still wants you for his 'official' girlfriend." Ben made air quotes. "You'd be like a beard for him so he can pretend that you didn't dump him. And you'd still have the hottest guy in the school."

She stared at Ben. "I guess this is the part where I slap you."

"Ro, if you do dump him, he'll make your life miserable. I've known this boy for a long time. Like I told you in the car, he's an asshole and a prick."

"All true," JD said.

"I won't be there to protect you. I can't stand the thought of your being unhappy."

Her eyes flitted between Ben and JD. "You both are lunatics. I don't want to have anything to do with either one of you."

Ben took her hand but she pulled it away. "Dorothy, you know how I feel about you."

"And that's why you're willing to share me?"

"No, no," JD said. "It's not that we're sharing you. That's the wrong way of looking at it." He sipped coffee. "Rosers, think of it like that vampire chick flick from like years ago. You know the one." He made his voice high. "I want the vampire, I want the zombie, I want the vampire, I want the zombie."

"Werewolf," Ro said.

"Who wins out?" Ben asked. "The vampire or the zombie?"

"Werewolf."

"The werewolf wins out?"

"No, the vampire."

Ben said, "Okay, I'm the vampire, JD. You're the zombie."

"No, no, no," JD said. "I'm the vampire, you're the zombie—"

"Werewolf!" Ro shouted. "There is no zombie. And you know what both of you really are? You're both idiots!"

"Ro, you're missing the meta-message here," Ben said. "We're fighting over you, hon."

JD said, "It's like this, Rosers. It's not a choice between the vampire and the zombie—"

"Werewolf! There is no zombie! Jeez, don't you listen?"

"This is the choice. You can have superman. Me: tall, athletic, good-looking, socially adept, and really smart . . . who will probably have my own sports agency and be a multimillionaire before the age of forty. Or you can have this moody, reclusive geek . . . who has a good chance of becoming the next Bill Gates or Mark Zuckerberg and will be a billionaire before the age of thirty."

Ben couldn't help it. He doubled over in laughter.

"So pleased with yourselves!" Ro said. "You both are douchebags."

JD said, "Dorothy, you are the prettiest, smartest, and wittiest girl in the entire school. And I daresay you're probably the prettiest, smartest, and wittiest girl in any high school across the country."

"Stow it, JD. I am not going back to you. You made a fool out of me."

"I'll publicly apologize. I'll eat shit. I'll make it appear that you're holding all the cards."

"While you're doing Lisa, right?"

"He's also doing Shannon." Ben avoided JD's shocked stare. "To make an informed decision, she's got to know everything."

"You're doing *Shannon*?" Ro was incredulous. Then she said, "Is Weekly doing her too?"

"Sure is, Mama."

"God!" She shook her head. "And I thought Scarsdale was bad."

"It probably is," JD said. "You just never made it into twelfth grade. Ro, no one gives a shit about school anymore. We're all like freaky-deaky. That means you can spend the next five months under my protection, or you can sit by yourself and be miserable."

No one spoke.

JD said, "You know how this guy feels about school dances

and all that hoopla." He was pointing to Ben. "I'll take you to the winter dance, I'll take you to the spring fling, I'll take you to prom."

"No, I'm taking her to prom," Ben said.

"Hells no," JD said.

"Hells yes," Ben said.

"Will you two idiots please shut up?" Ro folded her arms across her chest. "You can both take me to the prom. Queen Elizabeth I had her retinue." She pointed to JD. "You can be Leicester." Then to Ben: "And you can be Essex."

"I'll be Leicester," Ben said.

"Why?" JD asked. "What's so good about Leicester?"

"He lives out his natural life. Essex gets his head chopped off, but he is young, good-looking, and the queen's favorite. It's kind of a trade-off."

"I'll be Essex." JD stood and stretched. "So . . . we're all okay on this?"

"No, we're not okay on this! But this is what I'll agree to," Ro said. "You can take me to the winter dance. But not to the after party."

"Agreed."

"And that's as far as I'll go right now," Ro told him. "You'd better start eating shit on Monday, JD. And you'd better be really good at it or else all bets are off. I don't want people snickering behind my back. Now go away. I want to talk to Vicks in private. That is why I came over. Not to deal with you!"

JD was trying to hide a smirk, but it wasn't quite working. Ro said, "Get out of here!"

"I need my jacket."

"I'll get it." When Ben came back, he said, "You take care

of her, JD. If you don't, I'll kill you. I've studied enough murders that I truly believe I could do it and get away with it."

"You are so weird." JD put on his jacket. "A little menacing, dude. I'll admit that, but you're still very bizarre."

As soon as the front door closed, the two girls came out from hiding. Ro said, "Did you hear anything?"

"Everything," Haley said. "I agree with you, Ro. They both are real idiots."

Lilly said, "On the other hand, it's so romantic to have two guys fighting over you."

"I don't have two guys," Ro said. "I have two cretins." She spoke to Ben. "You two are enough to make me turn gay."

"Lucky girls," Ben told her.

Despite herself, Ro smiled. "I need to talk to Ben in private."

Lilly pulled Haley's arm. "C'mon, best friend, we're back in quarantine."

"You can stay here," Ro said. "We'll go to his room. Don't you dare listen in. I mean that, Haley."

"You were yelling," Haley said.

"Not really," Lilly said. "We were just eavesdropping."

Ro took Ben's hand. "I've got *plenty* to say to you."

"Any of it good?"

"Dream on."

CHAPTER 28

AFTER RO CLOSED and locked the door to the bedroom, she leaned against the wall with her arms crossed over her chest. Her voice was low and filled with anger. "This was going to be the 'let's get together' talk. After what happened, the most you can hope for is rapprochement." She shook her head. "I don't even know why I'm talking to you at all. Do I mean that little to you that you're willing to blow me off?"

"Just the opposite." Ben exhaled. "Your happiness is paramount. Even if it makes me miserable."

"Didn't sound like it out there. Sounded like you and JD were having a great time. If you love someone, you don't share the person with someone else."

"Of course I don't want to *share* you." Ben looked out the window of the bedroom. The lightning and thunder had abated, but it was still gray, wet, and dreary. The wind was raging. "Okay, Dorothy, you win. I'll drop my plans and stay here until we graduate."

Ro stared at him. "You'd do that for me?"

"I'd do anything for you." He softened his voice. "Anything."

She was silent for a moment. "No, don't do that. Even I'm not that self-centered."

Ben said, "Ro, you're stuck here. You can either spend the time you have left as the queen bee or you can be a drone. I vote queen bee—not for me but for you. What does it matter anyway? In six months you'll fly away and won't look back."

"Sadly, I suppose there's some truth in that." She cleared her throat. "Did you know he was doing Shannon too?"

"No. He just told me."

"I don't know how he managed juggling me and them. I know he's eighteen, but still that takes a lot of stamina . . . not that I did all that much with him."

"I don't need to hear this."

She said, "He's right, you know. I really did start off liking him . . . a lot. It just died."

"What happened?"

"I guess I just started thinking about serious things: my sister, your sister, Katie Doogan, Julia Rehnquist, death and murder. JD suddenly seemed so . . . frivolous."

"Sorry for dragging you into my neurosis."

"No, Vicks, you can't repress forever." Another shrug. "At least I get to go to the winter dance in my supercool dress." She sat down on his bed and patted the mattress. "Sit down next to me."

"Gladly." She put her head on his shoulder and he kissed her cheek. "I really do love you."

She lay down on the bed and drew him on top of her. Reaching up, she tucked an errant piece of hair behind his ear. "I love you too."

"You don't have to say it if you don't mean it."

"I do mean it, and that's the problem." She blinked back tears. "I love you and I don't want to love you." She wrapped a lock of his hair around a finger then pulled the finger out. Did it again until it was a ringlet. "Because if you love someone and you have to leave that someone, it's very painful."

"I know. Ellen's death was a total game changer. I live in the present. And the present is I'm madly in love with you."

Ro stroked his cheek. "Tell me something, Ben. If you had a choice between being with me forever just like we are at this moment . . . or finding your sister's killer, what would you do?"

Ben knew what she wanted. But he couldn't give it to her and he hated himself for it. "That's not a fair question. Why can't I love you *and* find my sister's killer?"

"I asked you to make a choice and you made it." Ro pushed him away and sat up. "Now I want to know why."

He stood up and paced. "Why do you think?"

"Because you're obsessed, single-minded, and mulish . . . not to mention depressed and anhedonic?"

"Because he could *murder* again, Ro. He *will* murder again and again and again. And I'd rather lose my one chance at happiness than make some other family so profoundly un-happy."

She wouldn't look at him. "Give me your flight and hotel information for Berkeley or Mount Diablo or whatever."

"You hate me."

"I admire you. I don't know if I like you right now. Doesn't matter. Give me your information."

"Why?"

"You're not telling your parents, and if you crash, at least someone should know where you are."

He didn't trust her one whit. Still, he went to his computer to retrieve the data. "It's going to take a minute. I'd encoded everything so my mother can't access my information."

"She snooped on your computer?"

"Yes, she did. I'm still mad at her for that."

"It sounds like something my mother would do. She probably has." She stared out the window. "Vicks, why are you going? You gave it all to Shanks. He's on it. Let him handle it."

"I told you. The family agreed to meet with me. I'd look like an idiot if I canceled."

"Yeah, okay." When Ben looked up, she said, "I do have some understanding of the situation. When are you meeting with them?"

"The twenty-eighth at two in the afternoon."

"So why are you leaving on Christmas Day?"

"Cheaper flight."

"You'll lose it all in the hotel costs."

"Motel, not hotel. You know crazy, mulish, anhedonic me, Ro. I want to walk the area where she was found. I want to see if I'm missing something. And yes, if I do discover anything, I'll tell Shanks." He tapped a key and the printer sprang to life. He retrieved the papers. "Here you go."

She read the itinerary. "Okay. Here's the deal. Sit down." When he sat in his desk chair, she said, "No, sit next to me on the bed."

"My pleasure." He kissed her cheek again. "I do love you."

"You're not going to like what I have to say." Ben's smile faded. Ro was quiet for a moment. "I've reached an epiphany."

"What?"

"I'm either going to have to accept who you are or I'm just going to have to stop seeing you." She faced him. "You make out like you'd rather see me happy than anything, and in reality, you do whatever you want, when you want, and exactly how you want."

"That's not fair. I came to homecoming just for you. You know how I hate that stuff."

"Which is why you're thrilled to have JD take me off your hands. We're not all that different." She stood up. "Because when it comes to doing what you're doing and doing what *I* want to do, it isn't close. You truly are a self-contained unit."

Ben got off the bed and began to pace. "Exactly how much do you want me to suffer, Dorothy?" His eyes teared up. "Haven't we both suffered enough?"

"Move on!"

"I *can't*!" he cried out. "I *promised* her. I swore that I'd either find him or die trying!"

And what could she possibly say to that.

"It's like JD said, I'm in arrested development," Ben said. "I'm sorry I can't be what you want. Maybe one day when the case is finally solved, you'll like me better."

"I like you fine, Vicks. You don't like you."

"Maybe I don't like me, but I certainly like you." A pause. "Look. I've been doing what I'm doing for almost three years. You've been with another guy since you got here. You barely talk to me at school. No one changes overnight. Maybe you should develop a little fucking patience."

"Maybe I should." She tapped her foot. Then she let out a small laugh. "I must admit there is something . . . perversely amusing about dangling JD over the precipice. So, this is what

I'm going to do. I'm going to the winter dance. I'm going to wear my cool, sexy dress. I'm going to hold my head up high, and if anyone gets in my way or tries to put me down, I am going to give him or her the wrath of God."

"Good for you." Ben meant it.

"Wait until you hear me out before you give me kudos." She gave a forced smile. "Then I'm going to meet you in Berkeley and we'll do whatever you do—together. And unless you say within seconds, 'Great, Ro. I really appreciate that,' I'm going to walk out that door and don't bother talking to me ever again."

"Great, Ro. I really appreciate that."

"Eureka!" She patted his cheek. "You can be taught."

"Can I say one thing?"

"Not if it's negative."

"It's one thing for me to lie to my parents. It's another thing for you to lie to yours."

"Who is going to lie? I will tell them that we're going together so we can look at colleges in Berkeley and Stanford. We'll already be in Berkeley. No problem taking a quick detour to Stanford. And I'll have the pictures on my phone to prove it. I'll just tell them that you got a head start."

"They'll allow you to travel with me?"

"Ben, they're New York liberals. They don't care who I sleep with. Well, maybe you, they'd care."

"I know. I'm weird."

"Oh please. They don't think you're weird because of your obsessions. My dad thinks you're crazy because you could probably waltz into Princeton and you're not even applying. That really offends his sensibilities."

Ben walked over to her, held her face, and kissed her softly.

"I would love for you to come with me." He kissed her again, this time a little longer. "As much as you want to be with me, that's how much I want to be with you." A third time and then a fourth. "And if it appears that I wasn't fighting for you with JD, I will gladly punch his face until he's pulp."

"Nah, don't do that." This time she kissed him. "Then who'll take me to the spring fling?" She threw her arms around his neck. The kisses were long and passionate. "You're pretty good at this." She pressed against his groin. "Not so bad in more ways than one." Her phone rang. "Oh God!" She checked her watch. "I've got to go."

"Don't go," he begged. "We're just getting started!"

Her smile was brilliant. "I need to pick up Griff."

"I'll come with you."

"No. Don't." Pause. "I need to be alone. And you need some time to think too. See? I know you by now. But I'm still coming with you to California. I figure if we can survive with each other twenty-four/seven in a dingy motel room—"

"It's not dingy," Ben said. "It got pretty good reviews on Orbitz and Travelocity."

"Does it have two twins or a queen?"

"It's a queen."

"Change it to singles." She kissed him again. "If we make it through the week and we both feel the same way afterward . . . then I suppose I'll just resign myself to who you are and that's pretty strange."

He grabbed her and kissed her until they were both lost in the moment, feeling things long buried . . . love, passion, and sexual desire. For the first time in years, he was glad to be alive.

Her phone beeped again.

She pulled away. "I've really got to go." She bumped into his bed. "I'll bring my hiking boots to California. I'll need them, right? That was real, real good, by the way." She bumped into his desk. "Real good."

"I don't think you should be driving."

"Is that your geeky way of saying you want to be with me?"

"No, I really mean you shouldn't be driving. But I absolutely do want to be with you."

"Okay." She tossed him the keys. "Let's go."

His face turned hot. He knew he was blushing. "I need to wait a few moments. The girls are out there."

She looked at his pants and laughed. "You're okay, you know that?"

"Surprised?"

"No, but it's just that you're shorter than J . . . forget it. It's not nice."

This time his laughter was unrestrained. "That's the nicest thing anyone ever told me."

"Just hurry up. I'm already late. Think of homecoming or something."

A minute passed. Ben said, "Let's go."

"You sure you're okay?"

"If you don't touch me. I'm a little quick on the trigger right now."

"You know what, Vicks? I'm happy."

"I'm happy too." He stopped at the door, turned around, and took a step toward her, holding her face in his hands, concentrating on her eyes, the black dilated pupils surrounded by pure blue. Within moments, they moistened, water overflowing onto her cheeks. He took his thumbs and swept them along her lower lids. "Seems like I've been waiting a lifetime to do that."

"Do what?"

"Wipe away your tears."

He broke away and opened the door. Haley and Lilly looked up with apprehension. Lilly held out a plate. "Cookies?"

"Sure." He swiped two. "I'm starving."

Ro hung up her cell. "I'm about to pick up Griff and Ezra. How about we all go out to an early dinner? I haven't eaten all day. I'm famished. It'll mean you'll have to squish in the backseat, but something tells me that's okay."

"It's four thirty," Haley said. "What's even open?"

"Pantry." Ben took another cookie. "I could use a burger. I'll drive." He put on a jacket and opened the front door. The storm had picked up again. Rain was coming down in torrents. "Wait here, guys. Let me warm up the car. It's freezing outside."

Haley touched her brother's arm. She whispered. "Everything okay?"

Ben grinned as he pointed outside. "As right as rain."

Sometimes there is a happily ever after.

THEY DARTED OUTSIDE, *headed toward a white Explorer: a boy and the three girls, each female looking yummier than the last.*

Not that he planned on doing anything. Those days were over. He'd done it and no one was the wiser and he knew he had to stop before someone put the pieces together.

He was only in New Mexico for a short time. He didn't even have to be here. He chose to be here. He chose to come and to drive out of the way just to stare, just to imagine, just to wish he had the opportunity—

No, no, no. No more opportunity, no more, no more, no more.

Take a deep breath and settle down.

There were other things in life.

Maybe.

Settle down, settle down, settle down.

Deep breath. Deep, deep breath.

Minutes passed.

Okay, he convinced himself, no more.

This was just a whim, a passing fancy.

To come here and relive.

And relive and relive and relive and relive and relive . . .

PROLOGUE

THE THOUGHT KEPT pulsating through his brain—an arterial beat with synapses jumping one after the other and the other and the other until he wanted to scream.

One more time, one more time, one more time, one more time.

He had sworn that if he did manage to complete a cycle without detection, he would stop. He wanted to stop. Truly and sincerely, he wanted to quit. He had an astronomically high IQ. Men like him didn't self-destruct. Internal immolation was for the mentally ill, those with flawed frontal lobes who couldn't contain their impulses. He was no psychopath. He had fear. He had a conscience. He had empathy and sympathy and all those things that were necessary to live in a social world.

Except, once in a while, things got to him.

Hence the repetitive thought.

He didn't fear the obsession. As long as he kept it inside his brain, he was fine. But from past experience, his obsession—a disorder of thought—often led to a compulsion—a disorder of action. That's what he was fighting against: acting on his obsession. He didn't want to do it anymore. Because once he started with the first one, he'd have to go through another cycle. And now he was older and much wiser, and the task in front of him just seemed so onerous.

But the thought was making him anxious. Interrupting his sleep and giving him panic attacks. He was too young for that. He was too smart and too savvy and he had to do something to quell the obsession even if it was a temporary fix.

He decided to meet it halfway . . . obsession leading to partial compulsion.

He'd dig a grave.

He hoped that the act of bringing shovel to dirt would stanch some of the nervous energy. There was physicality in breaking ground, in pushing a spade into hard-packed dirt, hoisting the soil over his shoulder until it became a mound of clotted mud. Surely that would deter him . . . all the force needed to shape the precise dimensions. All the cunning required to pick the spot and hide it from the dozens of trackers and hikers who crisscrossed the area (although very few came once the ground froze over).

The solution was in front of his face: just dig the damn grave. Even if he decided not to fill it, it would make him feel warm and fuzzy knowing it was there.

Just in case.

CHAPTER 1

WINTER CAME ON like a beast.

By late December, northern New Mexico howled with cold winds, freezing rain, and harsh temperatures. Out came the boxes packed with winter wear: the boots and gloves and parkas and waterproof jackets that Ro was sure she wouldn't need when the family moved to the Southwest. But Santa Fe was high desert and that meant occasional blizzards with bitter nighttime temperatures. It was weird for her to see cacti covered in snow.

School was out for the holidays, allowing normal families the opportunity to vacation in hospitable climates. Of course, *her* family chose to stay put, because why tan in Hawaii when you could be a paleface with chapped lips in the zero humidity of the mountains? It had been ages since her family had gone anywhere fun. Her parents existed, but they didn't do a lot of living.

Her mother threw herself into redoing the house with Christmas cheer. There were wreaths of holly on every door; dozens of red, pink, and white poinsettia plants placed at strategic locations; and garlands of juniper and gold tinsel around the staircase banister and the second-story railings. In the center of the living room sat a ginormous Christmas tree dripping with tinsel and ornaments both old and new. There was white fluff under the tree and gaily wrapped presents. But the scene, instead of coming across as jolly, looked more like a funeral parlor. That's what happens when decorating is less an act of joy and more like a compulsion to stave off depression.

Their temporary house was a modern take on a traditional adobe home. Instead of fluid, undulating walls and rounded corners, it was all sharp angles and lines with tall windows and baronial doors. Vicks had told her that it was typical of a house built by part-timers—some rich Texan or Californian erecting a visible paean to a sizable ego. But Ro loved living in something modern. Their place in Scarsdale was as traditional as the mores of the suburb.

Her dad, trying to add some brightness into dreary lives, had hired a worker to string multicolored Christmas lights instead of the traditional New Mexican farolitos—paper bags filled with sand and lit by tea candles. No one used real farolitos on their roofs anymore—can you say "fire hazard"?—but they did use pretty good plastic replicas. Even so, in the black nights of the poorly lit street, Ro thought her house stood out like a garish beacon.

By Christmas Eve, the night had turned savage with temperatures in the teens. The aftermath of the noontime rains had turned to sheets of ice as the skies cleared and the mercury dipped below freezing. Had there been any moisture left in the sky, it would have been a white Christmas. Instead, it was all chill and no atmosphere.

At least the house smelled like the holidays. Her mom was a fantastic cook and she'd been going at it for two days. Yesterday was all the desserts—cookies and cakes and pies and the aroma of winter spices. Today was the meats and side dishes: turkey and ham and potatoes and candied yams and string beans and salad.

At six thirty, the Majors sat down for dinner. Mom had chosen a red satin dress and black pumps. She had diamonds on her earlobes and pearls around her neck. Dad had on the requisite black suit and Griff looked like a thinner, shorter version of Dad. He had slicked back his unruly hair and looked preternaturally stiff. Ro had donned black—a symbol of mourning for her former life back east. The food was phenomenal; the conversation not so much. It didn't exactly flow but it wasn't as stilted as it had been in Christmases past. By eight, they were finished with the main meal. Ro wasn't ready for dessert, but tradition was tradition, as feeble as it was, and she knew she had no choice but to consume copious quantities of sugar and fat.

The knock on the door was unexpected. Griffen was up and out of his chair before she could look up.

Jane Majors looked at her daughter. "Who on earth?"

"It's probably Vicks."

"You invited him here on Christmas Eve?"

"No, I didn't invite him. I just said if it's anyone it's probably him . . . and the girls."

"They don't believe in Christmas dinner?"

"Mom, I don't know. I'll go see who it is."

Her dad said, "Tell him he's welcome to stay for dessert."

Ro turned to her mother. "Is that okay?"

"Of course." Her tone was more reserved than welcoming.

Ro hadn't seen Vicks in over a week. She had agreed to go with his family to his sister's grave tomorrow, and now she was having second thoughts. She wasn't creeped out at going to a cemetery—she had visited her sister's grave often enough—it's just that she felt like a ghoulish intruder. But he insisted it was okay.

Griff was deep in conversation with Vicks and the girls. They were dressed appropriately for the weather in jackets, boots, and scarves. Ro was not. "Hey."

Ben's eyes did a quick up-and-down. "You look nice."

"Thanks, Vicks." She rubbed her arms. Secretly she was glad that someone saw her looking so hot. "It's freezing out here. My mother has invited all of you for dessert."

"They're going to a carnival," Griffen said. "They invited us to come."

"Carnival?"

"The Canyon Road walk," Ben said. "It's a Santa Fe tradition on Christmas Eve."

"Where all the art galleries are?"

"Yep. The street is closed off to cars and overrun with people."

"Like, everyone in Santa Fe is there," Haley said.

Lilly said, "It's totally wholesome. There is lots of off-key caroling and dogs dressed up as reindeer. It sounds corny but it's actually a lot of fun."

Ben said, "I haven't gone since . . . in a while. Come. It'll be fun."

"Thanks, but my mom will be upset if we leave."

Griffen made a point of giving a disgusted sigh. "It's like a tomb in there."

Ro opened the front door. "Come in and say hello."

The five of them went inside the house.

"Merry Christmas," Ben said. "We're just stopping by. Sorry to interrupt."

"No interruption." Mom's eyes swept over their casual dress. "We were just finishing up. Would you like to stay for dessert?"

"Uh, thank you." Ben said. "That's very nice of you."

Griffen said, "They're on their way to a carnival, Mom. They're just being polite."

"Carnival?" Dad said. "On Christmas Eve?"

"No, it's not a carnival," Ben said. "It's a tradition in Santa Fe to do a walk up Canyon Road. Lots of the galleries are open and they serve coffee and hot cider and hot chocolate. There are bonfires and lots of caroling."

"Bad caroling," Lilly said. "And bad brass bands."

"I'm stuffed, Mom," Griffen said. "Maybe, like, we can go and come back for dessert?"

Dad looked at Ben. "How long does it take?"

"About an hour. But if you have other plans—"

"We don't," Griffen said. "I should change, right?"

Vicks's eyes darted between Ro and her parents. He was barely on their good side so he was hesitant. "I don't want to interrupt any traditions you have."

"Traditions we have? Seriously, dude?"

"Griffen, be polite," Dad warned him.

"C'mon," Griffen cajoled. "It's okay, right?"

"Everyone can come," Ben said.

"I'm not going anywhere," Dad said. "It must be ten degrees outside."

"It's pretty cold," Ben said.

"Let them go, Jane." Dad loosened his tie. "I'm stuffed." He looked at Ben. "Be back in an hour plus fifteen for dessert. I'll probably enjoy it better myself." He stood up. "I'm going to go change into something warm and comfortable. Merry Christmas."

Mom paused, then began gathering up dirty plates. "Well, I suppose the decision has been made."

"I'll stay home with you," Ro offered. "I don't want you cleaning up this mess by yourself."

"Why don't we go and we'll clean up everything when we come back?" Vicks suggested. "Least I can do for interrupting your dinner."

"That's an idea." Ro smiled. "Go relax, Mom. We'll take care of everything later."

Dad had returned in sweats. "Make sure you do. Go. To tell you the truth, I would like to be alone with Mom. It's a rare thing."

Mom cracked a smile. "Thank you. That was a very nice thing to say."

Dad put his arm around Mom and kissed her cheek. "Heartfelt." To the kids: "Clean up everything when you come back. Mom worked hard enough."

TWENTY MINUTES LATER, with everyone dressed and sweating in the car's heat, Vicks pulled into the line of vehicles on Paseo de Peralta, waiting to get into one of the parking lots across from the mouth of Canyon Road. His mom's SUV inched across the asphalt until they were finally allowed in. Cars were everywhere. People were everywhere. Old snow had turned to blocks of ice. The parking lot was one big skating rink with frozen water crunching under tires and refreezing as soon as it hit the frigid air. Ben found a parking space. As soon as they got out of the car, Ro took a couple of steps and her feet slid out. Vicks caught her by the arm. Then his gloved hand took hers and the crew walked to the beginning of Canyon Road.

Griff and the girls disappeared almost immediately in the swell of humanity. Vicks got two cups of cider, gave one to Ro, and surveyed the scene. He pointed to an open gallery. "Want to go inside?"

"What's inside?" Ro asked him.

"Dunno, but it's probably warm."

"Enough motivation for me."

Inside was jewelry, cases of gold and silver crafted with a native flair. The pieces were studded with semiprecious stones, mostly turquoise, but also coral and opal and accented with diamonds. The shapes were fluid and modern. Ro studied each item with an assiduousness that was usually reserved for SAT exams. Maybe that was her problem. There was no jewelry section on the test.

"Pretty, pretty." She slipped her arm around Ben's waist. "You'd better get me out of here or it'll cost you."

"Wallet's pretty empty but I do have my parents' CC."

She punched his shoulder. "Let's go have some fun."

They started up the incline and through the throng of people. It was hard not to get into the holiday spirit because it slapped you in the face. The narrow road was packed with families and pets and there were twinkly Christmas lights everywhere. Couples were linked arm in arm, toddlers sat on parents' shoulders, red-nosed kids ran up and down and weaved between people. There were men dressed up as Santa and dogs dressed up as reindeer, and bonfires burned at strategic locations, places to thaw frozen fingers.

There were stalls set up to serve hot cider, cocoa, and cof-fee, needed more as hand warmers than thirst quenchers. Some booths were also selling cookies and kettle corn.

When they got to the top of the road, Ro looked down at the crowds. She realized she was genuinely happy. "This is incredibly corny." She kissed his cheek. "But it's fun, and to tell the truth, it was great to get out of the house. It was glum in there."

"I hear you. My father doesn't care about the holidays any-more, and my mom cares too much. The thought of going to the grave tomorrow always puts her in a deep funk on Christ-mas Eve."

"Why does she do it?"

"Her way of celebrating Christmas with Ellen, I guess. I really don't know." Vicks rubbed his hands together. "You're still determined to make this trip with me to California? You can back out if you want."

"Why would I? California, at the very least, is warm."

"Actually San Francisco is scheduled for rain."

"I own an umbrella. I won't get in your way." Ro looked at him. "As long as whatever you find out, you'll take to Shanks."

He shrugged. "Let's not talk about that now."

"Okay. What do you want to talk about?"

"How gorgeous you are."

"That's always a good topic." She threw her arms around his neck and gave him a passionate kiss.

"Oh God," Vicks said. "Now I can't walk. How am I going to share a room with you, Dorothy?"

"Did you get separate beds?"

"Yes, I did, but it won't help. Your aura will waft across the divide."

"We'll have to wait and see what happens." She stood on her tiptoes and kissed his nose. "Let's go find the others."

They were sitting on a bench in front of a bonfire, Griffen positioned between his two ladies. Lilly had on a makeshift wreath around her neck and Haley was drinking something hot from a paper cup. Griff was staring, transfixed by the flames.

Vicks interrupted his reverie. "We need to get back."

Three heads lifted up. Lilly stood before the others. "What'd you think about the walk, Ro?"

"Fabulous." Lilly's eyes went to Ro's and Ben's clasped gloves. Her smile was as gracious as it was sad. Poor kid. Ro said, "I'm going to take you guys and Ezra to the winter dance tomorrow. This guy is crapping out on you."

Haley said, "What are you wearing to the dance, Ro?"

"It's a surprise." She felt something tickle her nose and brushed it off. "We should be heading back." Again something landed on her nose, light and wet. She looked up, and as if on cue, millions of snowflakes were dancing in the sky. God had found a saltshaker. She linked her arm with Ben's as they all walked down the rest of the incline. "This is incredibly beautiful."

He brushed snow off her face and gently kissed her lips. "How did I get so lucky?"

"You didn't." Ro laughed. "You have to do the dishes, remember?"

"I'd do a zillion dishes for this moment. It's probably the finest of my life."

"You're a cheap date."

"I love you."

"I love you too." She put her head against his shoulder as

they ambled back to the car, her face wet with hundreds of snowflakes. She had lived with snow all her life, but . . . the evening, the setting, the boy. It all came together. It was magical. "I don't want this to ever end."

"I know. I feel the same way."

But Ro knew that it was going to end. It always did. When you've experienced loss, happiness was always slightly tainted, like waiting for the other shoe to drop.

CHAPTER 2

AT ONE IN the morning, with the rest of the house asleep, Ben could finally concentrate. Being in love threw him off balance. It was a joyous feeling but unsettling—like being stoned or drunk. He was so used to being in control, it was hard to let go even for something so wonderful and arousing.

Arousing was an understatement.

Since Ro had come into his life, it was not surprising that desire had decided to wake up and party. Now it was impossible to get to sleep without intervention. He was just starting to settle down although his mind kept racing and racing.

The good news was the winter solstice had come and gone with nothing in River Remez to show for it. Ben kept expecting an ominous beep on his computer, but so far, it hadn't materialized. The future was out there, but he couldn't think about it. Instead, he did what he did best. He autopsied the past.

On his monitor was the Julia Rehnquist murder case—as much as he could find out without looking at the actual police file. In a few days, he'd be in Berkeley, talking to the family, gleaning as much information from them as social convention would allow. Shanks was still dithering about making the call to the Berkeley PD. Perhaps he wasn't the only one who didn't want to look stupid. Sam couched it in caution, waiting until Katie Doogan's biological evidence had been processed.

Dredging up the past for the Rehnquist family would be painful. Ben hoped the information would be worth the agony. He needed data: times, places, hobbies, friends, boyfriends, likes, dislikes, where she hung out, and what she did. His questions seemed without limit. He'd have to narrow his focus because he couldn't overwhelm them.

There was a small knock on his door. Someone had noticed his light was on. He got up and put on a robe. His room was like ice because he'd been airing out the smell of teenage boy. He closed the window and opened his door. Lilly was dressed in flannel pajamas and a robe and slippers. Ben asked, "Are you okay?"

She nodded, her face surrounded by a mane of black hair. Her hands were holding a small package. In the dim light, Ben couldn't see all that much, but her black eyes were twinkling.

"Merry Christmas, Ben." She handed him a wrapped package.

He saw the excitement in her eyes. "Why, thank you." He took the box. "Don't we usually do this on Christmas Day?"

"How about you open mine tonight and I'll open yours tomorrow?"

Clearly, she didn't want to wait and clearly, she wanted to do this with just the two of them. He said, "Okay. You got me curious." He pulled off the paper. Inside the box was an engraved silver belt buckle festooned with turquoise. The piece had taken lots of hours to make and lots of attention to detail. "Let me get a little light on this." He turned on the overhead fixture. "This is absolutely gorgeous."

"See the wolf in the middle?"

"Yes, I do. That's me. Benjamin the wolf . . . the lone wolf. Man, you really are a pro. This is incredibly well done."

She smiled shyly.

"The engraving is beautiful. You've done the eagle feathers and these wavy lines are the water, right?"

She nodded.

"So, what are these bolts—lightning, thunder, or rattlesnakes?"

"Lightning. A million volts of electricity. That's you. All energy."

"And most of it entropy," Ben said. "It is by far the most beautiful present that someone has ever given me." He kissed her cheek. "Thank you very much."

"Will you wear it?"

"Of course I'll wear it, but only on special occasions."

Lilly brought out another box. "This is for Ro."

"For Ro? Why didn't you give it to her when you saw her?"

"I'd rather you give it to her." She looked down. "It's a ring."

"That's so nice of you, Lilly. I'm sure she'll love it."

"She's a keeper, Ben. Ro is."

"You think so?"

Lilly nodded. "A real keeper." Then her eyes watered.

For as long as he remembered, Lilly had had a crush on him. Ben had always thought it silly. Seeing her ache at this moment put it in a different perspective. There was no age limit on pain. Lilly hid her face behind her hands. "I gotta go."

"C'mere, honey." Ben took her in his arms as she wept. "It's okay, sweetie. You'll be okay."

"I'm so infantile."

"Not at all." He pulled her off his chest and held her shoulders. "Don't you worry, hon. I guarantee you that someday your prince will come."

"I don't think so, Ben."

"You've got to trust me on this one, Lilly. And whoever it is will be a very lucky guy."

She wiped her eyes and quickly changed the subject. "I hope you like it . . . the buckle. I thought about making a cuff but you're not the cuff type."

"No, I'm not a cuff man at all." He smiled at her. "I will cherish the buckle forever, Lilly. Again, thank you. I owe you one, girl."

She sighed. "We'll miss you in school. It was nice having a senior in our corner."

"You still have Ro," Ben said.

"She's Griffen's senior, not our senior."

"I'll be back every weekend. If anyone gives you a hard time, just let me know. I have a gun and I know how to use it."

She smiled again. "Anyway . . . Merry Christmas."

"Thank you and I hope you like my present a fraction as much as I like yours. Do you need me to turn on some lights so you don't trip over the furniture?"

"Not necessary. Indians are good trackers. Besides, I think I know this house pretty well."

"Yeah, I guess you do."

"Good night." She faded into the darkness. He closed the

door to his room and shut down his computer. He turned off the lights and then slid into bed.

He had closed the window but had forgotten to pull the drapes. He was glad for the oversight. Nature was putting on quite a show: flakes dancing in the outdoor lights.

A gentle snow. A good omen.

THE HEADSTONE WAS marble and simple. The inscription even more:

ELLEN VICKSBURG

BELOVED DAUGHTER AND CHERISHED SISTER

Two dates signifying her truncated life. Ro hadn't wanted to cry in front of Ben's family. It was like co-opting their pain, which was something she hated when it was done to her. Maybe it was the bleak weather or maybe it was just the time of year, but she felt a lone tear escaping and spilling over her lower lashes. She stood a few paces behind the family to give them privacy. And just like in her family, it seemed as if Ben's father took it the hardest. It was terrible to see a grown man weep.

The family held hands and said a prayer. Then Ben's mother knelt down and brushed snow off the headstone and Haley placed a pink rose on the grave. And that was that. Haley and her parents walked toward the car, but Vicks was walking toward her.

"You okay?" Ro grimaced. "Of course you're not okay, but I'm at a loss for words. I'm usually on the other side."

"I'm fine."

"You're not ready to go. I can feel it."

"I need a few more minutes. Do you mind waiting for me?"

"I'll meet you at my car. Not too long, Vicks. It's cold."

Colder for Ellen, Ben thought. "See you in a few minutes."

WHEN HE GOT to the grave, he sat down on a hard pile of snow that was quickly turning to ice. The sky was a pale blue with white streaks of clouds. The temperature was dropping.

"Well, here I am again." A pause. "Been an interesting year, El. I'm basically done with high school and I guess it's time to move on . . . move away.

"You know how hard that is for me. I'm not good at change. But I'm trying. I'm taking almost a full load at UNM next semester. I've also got an internship at Circuitchip. I think the hardest part is going to be living with Grandma and Grandpa. They're great folks, but you know them. They have a different concept of privacy."

Ben laughed softly.

"They'll probably drive me nuts. I was never as patient as you were . . . but I am getting better. You wouldn't believe how much more tolerant I've become. I've taken your lead, El.

"I know you're out there somewhere watching me, so you know about Ro. You like everyone, so I'm sure you'd like her, but she's not exactly your type . . . she's not my type, for that matter . . . not that I know what my type is. I think you'd approve, though. It's weird having a girlfriend . . . if that's what it is. I guess that's what it is. I just wish you were here to give me some guidance. To give Haley guidance also . . . sister to sister. I know she misses you.

"I hear you talking in my brain, but it's always what I think you're gonna say . . . which may be completely off base. When we used to talk, if there was complaining to be done, it was usually me to you. But I try hard not to complain too much anymore. I try to remember my blessings.

"I also try really, really hard to remember you. Sometimes I have to look at pictures. Sometimes it's hard to do that. But like I've said before, I promise to actively try to remember you."

He looked down then at the headstone.

"I haven't forgotten about my other promise either. I think this year will be a good one for that. I just feel it, Ellen. I'm coming closer. And now that Shanks is on board, I feel it's gonna happen. Maybe I'm being overly optimistic, but sometimes freaky feelings turn out to be true.

"Anyway . . . as always, wherever you are, put in a good word for me, okay? Because your pesky little brother still loves you a whole lot and wishes you were here."

He got up, brushed off his pants, wiped his eyes, and headed toward the car.

CHAPTER 3

THE PLANE TOUCHED down at three in the afternoon under blue skies and a bright sun. Though the mountains were majestic, Ro felt the infinity of the ocean. The sea was the stuff of legends, the coastline a step away from freedom and adventure, not to mention tanning on the white sands, catching the sun's rays.

As soon as she exited the Jetway, she realized that she was feeling a bit too positive. The temperature outside was a crisp fifty degrees. Not exactly tanning weather, but it was cool enough to enjoy cashmere. Not that she needed to dress up. When Vicks was in work mode, he was all business.

Ben was waiting for her at the baggage claim. He had taken the time to dress nicely—jeans, a white shirt, and a brown leather jacket. He had his hands stuffed in his pockets, eyes intense, his hair grazing his shoulders. He took her carry-on and kissed her cheek. "Is that it?"

"You said to travel lightly. I obey commands." She took his hand. "I'm really glad to see you."

He sounded tired. "I'm glad to see you too."

"You went hiking today?"

"Yeah."

"Similar to the others?"

"The area was less wilderness and more like a state park, but where Julia was buried was remote."

"Near water?"

"Yeah, although the creek was dry in the summer. Now, with all the recent rains, it's pretty full."

"Are you okay?"

"Now that you're here, I feel better. Nora Rehnquist e-mailed me. She wants to meet tomorrow. A few days early. I'm nervous. It was different with Margot and Alan. I was with them from the start. With Nora . . . I don't know. I feel kind of creepy."

"Is she hesitant to talk with you?"

"Just the opposite. I think she's anxious. Her daughter's case has stalled just like Ellen's. I think she's hoping to kick-start the investigation." He stopped walking. "I just don't want to offend her with my questions."

"I've seen you in action, Ben. Just be real."

"Thanks, Dorothy. I'm happy you're here. Are you hungry?"

"I'll want dinner."

"The room I got . . . it's less than cheerful."

"It's a dump?"

"Kinda. I'll switch it out if you want."

"Is it clean?"

"Yes, but it smells of disinfectant."

"Charming."

"There's an Italian restaurant a few blocks away that's not too bad."

"Whatever, Vicks. I'm not picky. Well, I am picky. Just not tonight. When are you meeting with Nora Rehnquist?"

"One o'clock tomorrow. They live near Cal. I figured we can take in the campus tomorrow morning and do Stanford the next day. How was the dance?"

"I got to wear my dress and everyone oohed and aahed."

"Did JD behave himself?"

"He was Prince Charming. I don't trust him at all."

"That's a good thing. JD's always had a fluid sense of honesty." He looked away. "Was he nice to you when you two were going together?"

"Actually, he was. Even sweet at times."

"Well, then . . . I like him better for it."

They walked to the rental car. The body was rusted and full of pockmarks, but it did have wheels and a windshield. When Vicks put the key in the ignition, it started up—a good sign.

"Do you want to go to a movie before dinner?" he said. "I think the less time we spend in the motel, the better. I'm embarrassed by it. You deserve better."

"Thanks, Vicks. That's very nice of you to say." She patted his knee. "Don't worry about it. I like my material trappings, but I'm flexible." In Ro's limited experience with men, she had always found that guys respond well to flexibility.

THEY FINALLY SETTLED in around eleven in the evening, both of them eating light and avoiding the garlic and bean dip. Ro had never shared a room other than a camp bunk where she had ruled as queen. She had always had her own personal space, decorated with her things.

This space was another planet. The motel room had stark white walls and a utilitarian dresser. Two double beds were separated by a nightstand with drawers. The bathroom wasn't much bigger than the closet. The towels were tortilla thin and smelled of bleach. It did host a flat screen, but neither one of them wanted to watch TV.

She took the bed on the right, he took the one on the left.

After brushing her teeth with bottled water and using copious amounts of mouthwash, she put on a nightgown. It wasn't a sexy baby doll or anything like that, but it was sleeveless and fell a few inches above the knees. When she came out, Vicks looked for just a moment. He had changed into a wifebeater and board shorts. After a quick glance, he went back to his book, which had something to do with the creation of the universe. Her book was about a pseudo-sadomasochistic affair. She was skimming it on an electronic reader—a good idea so Vicks wouldn't know how lowbrow she was. Around midnight, she was losing interest. She said, "I'm a little tired."

"Sure." Vicks reached over and turned off the light.

They lay in silence and in darkness. Outside, the weather had turned cruel. The winds had picked up and whistled through the trees. Rain splattered on the rooftop. The blinds were drawn, but Ro could see the bright halogen lights from the parking lot seeping through the windows. She pulled the thin sheets to her chin. Vicks was restless; she could hear him moving. "You okay?"

"I'm hot." He threw the covers off his body. "I'm boiling."

"You're hot, I'm freezing. So what else is new?"

"I think my nerves are getting to me."

She could smell his sweat. She got out of the bed, shivering in the diaphanous nighty, and sat at his bedside. She felt his forehead. "You are hot. Maybe you're getting sick."

"No, it's anxiety about tomorrow. I'll be okay." His profile was backlit by the light filtering in through the blinds. He said, "You're shivering."

"I'm cold."

The pause was longer than it should have been, but eventually he opened his covers. She slid inside and snuggled next to him. His sheets were damp and musty. Immediately, Ro felt electricity between her legs. Within moments she was warm and they were kissing. His arms were around her waist, his fingers running down her back although he was avoiding all of the R- and X-rated areas.

She shoved her groin into his. He was hard and embarrassed by it. He tried to give himself a little space, but she threw her leg over his and pushed him closer. She lifted her nightgown and pulled it over her head. His gasp was audible. She said, "I showed you mine, now you show me yours."

"I didn't bring any protect—"

"I'm on birth control." She tugged at his board shorts and slid them down over his knees. He took them off, then the wifebeater. She told him by action that she was more than willing.

Ro closed her eyes. The boy could kiss. Each one of them was sweeter than the last. She could make a meal on them. She dug nails into his back, she bit his shoulder. If he felt any pain, he didn't show it. The sex was just something to get over with. But the kisses . . . the way he took her face in his hands and kissed her all over . . . the way he whispered that he loved her. She wanted all of that to last forever.

His breathing quickened along with his rhythm. When it was over, he lay on top for a moment, her hand clasped around his sweaty waist. Eventually he rolled off and they lay on their backs, his eyes wide open staring at the ceiling. His breathing was still audible.

She knew Vicks well enough to know he wasn't a talker, so she helped him out. "Would you mind getting me a wash-cloth?"

"Yeah, of course. Anything." He got up and stubbed his toe. She reached over and turned on the light and saw that he was embarrassed by his nakedness. When he tried to cover up, he looked down and then jumped back. His groin was coated in blood. He wiped himself off on his sheet. "Why didn't you tell me you had your period?"

"Because I don't have my period." His head jerked up, staring with wide eyes. Ro smiled. "Surprise, surprise."

He covered his mouth. He was frozen on the spot.

"Vicks, the washcloth?"

"Right." He disappeared into the bathroom and came out a minute later. He had taken the time to wet it with warm water, and also brought her a dry towel. He crawled back under the sheets. His face was white. "I'm . . . sorry."

"Why? You didn't like it?"

"No, of course I liked it . . . I loved it. I'm . . . are you okay?"

"I'm fine." She rubbed the washcloth between her legs. The warmth soothed the burning inside. "I mean, it hurt, but it didn't take all that long."

He turned red and covered his face with his hands. "Oh God!"

She kissed his shoulder. "Ben, it's fine. We'll learn together."

He finally screwed up the courage to look at her. "God, I love you."

"I love you too."

"Are you really okay?"

"Psychologically I'm fine. Physically a little sore but that's to be expected. How are you?"

"Okay . . . I think." He paused. "I'm glad you told me afterward. Otherwise I would have been even more terrified. I thought at least one of us knew what we were doing."

She laughed. "It doesn't take a lot of conscious thought."

He laughed back. "You're right about that." He paused again. "Why are you on birth control if . . . ?"

"Reasonable question," Ro said. "I had a boyfriend back home . . . kind of a clone of JD."

"Football player?"

"Yeah, a BMOC—tall, good-looking, smart. Anyway, I always thought that we'd be doing it senior year. You know . . . get it out of the way before I went to college. I can't think of a worse experience than having your first time be with a hookup. But then my considerate parents decided to uproot the family. He wanted to do it before I left."

"Naturally."

"Yeah, naturally. But at that point, I decided I didn't like him enough. Then we went to New Mexico and I met JD right away. I thought, well, he'll be the one. So I kept taking birth-control pills. But then that didn't happen . . . and we got together." She patted his head. "Looks like you won the lottery."

"Better than the lottery." He kissed her again. "Waaaay better than the lottery." He raised his eyebrows. "Wanna do it again?"

"Aren't you the randy one?"

He fell on top of her. "Talk about randy. I saw what you have on your iPad."

"You peeked at my personal junk?"

"You left it on when you went to the bathroom, and yes, I admit that I'm extremely nosy." Ben kissed her nose. "I must say I blushed when I read the prose. However . . ." He lifted up a finger. "If you have anything specific you'd like me to do, I'm very open-minded."

She played with his curls, rolling them around her finger and watching them bounce when she removed it. "How about . . ." Bouncy, bouncy. "How about if you just kiss me . . . and we'll let nature take its course."

THEY GOT UP early. Actually, they never went to sleep. Ro donned a pink cable-knit sweater and some skinny jeans that she tucked into knee-high boots. The pants felt too tight around her sore crotch, but some things couldn't be helped. Vicks had put on a sweatshirt and jeans. With her heels, Ro's height was lips level with Ben's and that was all that mattered.

Breakfast was juice and toast, and then they went out to greet the day. The Bay Area, which was customarily shrouded in mist, was stunning in the daylight. It was around nine in the morning when they climbed through the Berkeley Hills, pausing to take in the panoramic view of the town and the ocean below. They saw the orange color of the Golden Gate Bridge spanning across the water, the bay throwing off a million diamonds in the sunlight. It was enough to convince her to apply to colleges in California. How wonderful to wake up and breathe the brine in the air.

They walked hand in hand, wending a pathway through the hills until they hit the Cal campus. Ro had expected to be out of breath, trudging up the incline, but her lungs felt full with each inhale. When she remarked upon it, Ben said, "You're at sea level."

She punched his shoulder. "What a smart guy."

They walked up Telegraph Avenue, where dozens of vendors were setting up shop on the sidewalks—selling everything from vintage vinyl records to bumper stickers that extolled the virtues of anarchy. The street was lined with alternative retail stores: head shops, metaphysical bookstores, places selling comic books and anime, and tables with heaps of used clothing. Message T-shirts were everywhere: in stores, in stalls, and being sold by random people from the trunks of their cars.

And they say that reading was dead.

Ben's expression was one of awe, taking in the sights, the lens of his eye snapping pictures like a camera. Ro tugged at his hands to hurry him along. They hadn't even gone onto the campus proper.

"Do you believe this?" he told her.

"In what way? Good, bad, indifferent?"

"Just in the sheer number of people here."

"You really are a country boy."

"Metro area of Albuquerque is like eight hundred thousand."

"Spread out over a big space. How many people live in New Mexico?"

"Around two million."

"California has like forty million people. It's a country. Let's go."

But he continued staring at the stalls. He stopped in front of a leather artisan. The man was in his fifties with a gray ponytail and a gray rabbi beard. Ben said, "Lilly made me this beautiful silver buckle for Christmas. I should get a belt."

"Shit!" Ro said. "I meant to call Lilly and thank her for the ring. It's really gorgeous."

The old ponytailed man looked up at them. "You want a belt?" His cloudy blue eyes went to Ben's face. "What pants size do you wear?"

"Thirty."

"Yeah, right," Ro said.

"Maybe twenty-eight."

"On a good day."

The old man smiled. To Ben, he said, "Try this one."

Ben looked at a beautifully tooled piece of leather and asked the price. Too expensive. The guy handed him another belt with less tooling. They agreed upon a price, Ben tried it on, and then he bought it. The transaction took about five minutes—typical of the way guys handled purchases. Ben took out his phone. "I have Lilly's number if you want to call her."

"Oh sure." When he started to recite the numbers, she said, "Why don't I call from your phone?"

"Because she would think that I'm calling her. I have to be careful not to give her any ideas."

"Yeah, the poor thing does have it bad for you."

"It's a harmless crush, but I don't want to encourage anything." He gave Ro the number and she placed the call, thanking her for the ring as effusively as she could. She sounded genuinely pleased.

"How's Berkeley?" she asked.

"We're on our way to campus. The area is beautiful."

"That's nice. I envy you. I can't wait until I get to college. Thanks for calling, Ro. I'm thrilled that you like the ring." A pause. "Is Ben there? I'd like to say hi."

"Of course." Ro handed him the phone and mouthed, *She asked.*

He took the cell. "Hey there, kiddo."

"How's it going?" Lilly asked. "Ro says it's beautiful."

"True that."

"What do you think about the Berkeley campus?"

"Haven't been there yet."

"It's got a great math and physics department, you know." Ben smiled. "Are you trying to get rid of me?"

"Just sayin' . . ."

"How's my sister doing?"

"Haven't seen her in a couple of days. I thought I might give her and Griff a little time alone."

"Hmm . . . I don't know if I like that idea."

"Don't worry. She tells me everything."

"Okay, just so long as it's G-rated."

"Maybe PG."

"More on the *G* than on the *P*, Lilly."

"Gotcha. Have a good time. Just keep an open mind about Berkeley, Ben. All the UCs are sister labs to Los Alamos."

"Yes, Ms. Busybody, I'm aware of that. I'll talk to you later." He hung up and handed Ro back the phone. He kissed her. "I love you."

"I love you too." There was something plaintive in his eyes. "What is it?"

"I'm just thinking how much I'll miss you when you leave River Remez."

"You can come with me. You'll certainly get in everywhere I'll apply to." No response. "Just think about it, Ben, okay?"

"Sure." His tone of voice said: Out of the question. "Okay, beautiful. Let's go raid the campus and see what all the fuss is about."

WALKING THROUGH UC Berkeley only confirmed Vicks's notion that he was a stranger in a strange land: the geography, the amount of people, the vastness. The buildings varied in size and style, very different from the eastern campuses he had seen in pictures. Some Beaux arts buildings would have fit in nicely in Harvard, but other structures were done in California stucco, and of course, there were lots of modern square monoliths that looked like giant office buildings. What set the campus apart was the amount of greenery in the dead of winter.

Ro said, "A little bigger than UNM?"

"I think you could fit all of New Mexico in here."

"It's almost January and people are walking around in sweaters and jeans. Trees have leaves on them. The sky is gorgeous and I can already feel a tan on my face." She shrugged. "I think I've found home." She turned to him. "For both of us. I mean what's stopping you?"

"Out-of-state tuition," Vicks said. "I'm sure this is like fifty grand or something per year."

"You could get a merit scholarship, Vicks."

Ben didn't appear to hear her. He kept gawking. "You know this school is one of the birthplaces of modern physics. The math department is renowned. And like Lilly just re-minded me, the Berkeley lab is a sister to Los Alamos."

"The gates are wide open, Vicks."

"It would be competitive. Look at all these people." A stare. "And this is Christmas break."

"They're international students. It's a wonder that Tai-wan or Vietnam still has any population." Ro gasped. "Wait a minute, wait a minute." She grabbed his arm. "Vicks, you're *Native American*. Your grandmother is a full-blooded Santa Clara Indian."

"That's a technicality. I do have enough blood to be a tribe member, but—"

"Oh my God, Vicks, you have URM status."

"What the hell is that?"

"Under-represented minority."

"Are you kidding me?" He looked incredulous. "I'm as much Jewish as I am Indian."

"Don't say you're Jewish. Colleges are filled with smart Jews. That won't get you anywhere."

"That's so racist. I thought you were liberal."

"What? Jews aren't smart?"

He shook his head in disbelief. "Ro, I'm happy where I am. I'm certainly not applying anywhere as a represent—what did you call it?"

"Under-represented minority." She sighed. "I am so ex-asperated. You're not only wasting your grades and scores, you're wasting your minority status. C'mon, Vicks. Haven't Jews and Indians suffered enough?" Ro made scales with her hands. "Think the Holocaust and Wounded Knee." When Ben didn't speak, she said, "Am I making this up?"

"Dorothy, my father's a lawyer, my mother is a teacher. I've got aunts and uncles who have MDs and PhDs. None of us are suffering. I'm not taking minority status away from someone who really needs it."

"What is wrong with you?" Ro said. "It's not like you're cheating or anything. I mean you even speak Indian, don't you?"

"You mean Tewa?"

"Whatever. You speak it, right?"

"No, Ro, I speak English. I'm American."

She put her hand to her chest. "You are killing me!" When he laughed, she hit him, then pulled out a camera. "C'mon, Sitting Bull. Take some pictures of me to show my parents that this trip was really about college."

"Sitting Bull was Sioux—a Plains Indian—totally different culture from Pueblo Indians."

"It was a *joke,* Vicks."

"I know." He grinned. "I'm a deadpan fool."

She shoved the camera in his hand. "Take my good side."

He complied by taking a snapshot of her posing in front of Barrows Hall. She posed here, she posed there, she posed everywhere, making both funny and sultry faces. They took selfies, smiling like idiots. After the photo shoot was done, they took in an early lunch.

Neither ate much. Ro wasn't hungry and Vicks was antsy. As the clock got closer to interview time, he became downright nervous. He had turned from quiet to silent. He checked his phone. He checked his notepad. Finally, he turned to her. "We should be heading over."

"You want to walk? We might get there a little early if we drive."

"I want to factor in getting-lost time."

According to the GPS, the Rehnquists lived five miles away just outside of Berkeley proper. They had passed the house before coming onto campus.

"Sure, let's go back," Ro said.

Conversation ceased. It was hard for Ro to go five minutes without talking, let alone a half hour. She took out her phone and tried to busy herself in texts and calls. Ben drove like an automaton, staring out the windshield, barely moving a muscle beyond the mechanics of driving.

"You okay?" she asked.

"Fine."

"Should I shut up?"

"I'm fine," he repeated.

The tension was horrible, but Ro didn't speak. She had just lost her virginity to a boy whom she barely knew, at least in terms of what made him tick. She knew that Ben loved her. She was sure of that. But as for emotional nurturance, their encounter last night could have been a hookup.

CHAPTER 4

THE WOMAN GREETED them with a wan smile. She was patrician: lean features with dark hair and a fair complexion. She was around fifty, but her eyes said she had lived in pain for a thousand years. Ro had seen those eyes in her own mother's face . . . in Laura Vicksburg's as well. They made her sad and weary.

"Nora Rehnquist." She offered a soft hand to Vicks and then to Ro. "Please come in."

Vicks said, "Thank you so much for seeing us."

"Not a problem." Her voice was formal.

The living room was built at the turn of the century: old dark wooden floors creaked even as they stepped on the Oriental area rug that covered the planks. There was a big fireplace with painted tiles and dark wooden beams on the ceilings. The walls were painted cream, and the furniture was all clean lines, bright colors, and beautifully appointed. Light

poured in from several view windows that showed off greenery from the hills below and the distant bay. Ro took in the
view, looking at the boats in the harbor, and beyond to a mist-
topped Golden Gate Bridge.

Nora was dressed in dark slacks and a soft blue sweater
with silver jewelry. She was around five nine, about three
inches taller than Ro, who was the first to speak up. "Thanks
for your time, Mrs. Rehnquist. This can't be easy for you."

"I'm hoping it's mutually beneficial," she said. "Please sit.
Can I offer you something to drink? Water, soda, coffee?"

Vicks started to say no, but Ro interrupted. "Is the coffee
made?"

She smiled. "I can put on a fresh pot. I'd like a cup myself.
Is it Dorothy?"

"Yes, ma'am."

"Oh please, call me Nora."

"Then please call me Ro." She gave her a half smile. "Lovely
home. The view is spectacular."

"Thank you." Her eyes looked out the window and beyond. "We just finished construction. It became a much longer project because of the interruption."

The interruption—good euphemism. Ro nodded.

Nora said, "My husband wanted to move immediately. I
hesitated—too much disruption for the other children and I
found it hard to let go of whatever I had left of Julia: mainly
her room and her belongings. I don't know if I made the right
decision, but here we are."

Ro said, "It took my mother some time to move after my
sister died. For what it's worth, I think you made a good
decision."

She looked confused. "It was *your* sister who died?"

"My sister died of cancer. Ben's sister, Ellen, was murdered."

"Oh . . ." A pause. "Do you want regular or decaf?"

"Regular."

She turned to Ben. "You want a cup too, right?"

"If you're making it anyway."

"I am." She left them in the living room with the expansive view while she made coffee in the kitchen. Ben smiled at Ro and mouthed *Thanks*. When Nora returned with a tray several minutes later, she placed it on the living room table, but balanced her own cup and saucer on her lap.

She said, "If I may be blunt, Ben, how long have you been looking into your sister's death?" She took a sip. "I assume you've been doing this long before you contacted me."

Talking about the familiar, Ben visibly relaxed. "I started the day she went missing with the usual things: the searches and the plastering of paper on telephone polls, the interviews, the appearance on TV, the candlelight vigils."

"I'm well aware of the drill."

"Yeah, it's pretty much . . . routine." He paused. "I never stopped hoping until we found her, but after a certain time passed, we all knew it was unlikely that she'd be returned to us alive. When we found the body, and it was confirmed— that's when I really got serious. Since then, I don't think a day goes by when I don't think about who did it. I want justice for Ellen, of course. But even more, I just want this not to happen again." He shook his head. "That's the only thing I think about. It can't happen again."

"But you think it did happen again with my daughter."

"Yes." Vicks looked away. "That's what eats me alive."

Nora nodded. "I was taken by your theory of the dates . . .

the solstices and the equinoxes. I spent the last few months online looking at anything that might fit the pattern. Lots of weird things go on at those times."

"It's a big Wiccan day," Ro said. "Other pagan celebrations too."

"You think the girls were the victims of satanic rituals?" Nora asked.

Ben said, "I've given the theory some thought. From what I've read, satanic rituals usually involve props—candles, incense, knives, symbols carved into trees, or stone or flesh. Those murders are bloodbaths. My sister was strangled."

"Julia as well."

Ro was taken aback: Nora was so collected, as if she needed a clear head and a cool demeanor to get the job done.

The woman asked, "What about Katie Doogan?"

"I don't know," Ben answered.

"But you suspect . . ."

"Yes, I suspect it was up close and personal because other things were similar." Vicks bit his lip. "I'm sure the lead detective has some suspicions, but he's not sharing right now. Which, of course, is prudent."

"But you still contacted me. Was that prudent?"

"We'll see."

"Who is the lead detective for Katie Doogan?"

"Milton Ortiz. I know he's working with the lead detective on my sister's case, Sam Shanks."

Nora nodded. "When will they have information about Katie Doogan?"

"The lab is analyzing the biological evidence taken from Katie. Once they generate a profile from Katie, they want to see if it matches my sister's killer."

"If you've taken a profile from evidence off your sister, why hasn't the lead called up Berkeley?"

"Detective Shanks made a judgment call. He just found out about Julia because I just told him." A pause. "I'm careful to a fault. Anyway, since I waited this long, Sam wanted a match with Katie before involving Berkeley. But even if there isn't a match, I know he'll be calling up the BPD regardless."

Silence.

"I think he's trying to be sensitive," Ben told her. "And probably like me, he doesn't want to look like a doofus."

"It's one thing if *you* hold off. You're not a professional. But once you told him . . ." Her face was angry.

Ben said, "I've gotten to know Detective Shanks very well. He's a good guy, Nora. I know he wants to have something concrete before he contacts Berkeley."

Nora said, "You're defending him."

"He's all I have."

"Touché." Nora smiled sadly. "Let me tell you what my detectives have found." She leaned forward. "An unknown DNA male profile and a partial profile from another male. Most of the citizens in Berkeley and the environs offered samples. I would welcome a new profile to test them against."

"*Two* profiles?"

"One profile was taken from material under her fingernails: the killer. The second profile was taken off her clothes. It wasn't blood, it was sweat. My daughter was out jogging. It was a warm day. She could have bumped into another sweaty jogger. We don't know."

"This is different. I'll talk to Shanks."

Nora put down her saucer and picked up a notepad. "I appreciate your detective's sensitivity, but I don't care about being disappointed. I only care about results. If the River Remez PD has a profile, please tell them to get in touch with Berkeley."

"I'll make a call. It would help if you told the Berkeley PD about the latest development. Means much more coming from you than from me."

"I will call Derek Whitecliffe as soon as we're done. From your comments, I found your sister's grave eerily similar to my daughter's—the fact that it was meticulously dug. What about Katie Doogan's grave?"

"The same."

Her exhale was one of frustration. "What is wrong with law enforcement that they can't coordinate?"

Ben answered, sounding more like Shanks than he would care to admit, "I suppose we're just working on our one case and they're working on a lot of them."

"Why? What's the crime rate in River Remez?"

"Practically nothing. But in Santa Fe and especially in Albuquerque where Katie Doogan lived, it's pretty high. New Mexico is home to a lot of bad guys. It's a good refuge for men on the run."

"We're not doing too much better," Nora said. "I think Oakland has one of the highest crime rates in the country." A sigh. "Maybe I should be more patient." She looked at Ben. "I'm not a patient person."

"Ben has enough patience for all of us," Ro told her. "He's prudent, patient, and meticulous."

"A good person to have on our side." Nora's eyes teared up.

Ben looked down. "I'm sorry if this is too personal—"

"Oh please," Nora said. "What's your question?"

"I walked the area yesterday where Julia was found. It's pretty far from here."

"You walked in Mount Diablo?"

"Yes, ma'am. I wanted to see how similar it was to where my sister was found."

"And?"

"It's similar. Wooded area in a national park, very isolated, and in the backcountry, as we call it. The spot was far away from the trail and near running water."

"That's important?"

"In my mind. I think the streams gave the killer a guide to where he had dug his grave."

"Do you think he dug the grave beforehand?"

"He had to have done it beforehand. To be that precise, it was planned." Nora said nothing. Ben said, "The spot is about twenty miles from here."

"He definitely took her to that dreaded 'second location.'"

"I know that on the day she disappeared, she was jogging near here."

Nora looked away. "Would you like me to show you where? It's a bit of a climb."

"We're both excellent walkers." Ro got up. "Thanks for the coffee."

"You're welcome. Hold on a minute."

Nora disappeared, then she came back a moment later with some fresh roses from the garden. "Let's go."

IT WASN'T A sheer vertical drop, but the walk was steep. They seemed to be climbing up hundreds of tiny, moss-covered steps. When they got to the top, even this close to sea level, Ro was winded—unlike Ben, who never seemed to get out of breath. At the top of the stairs was a gravel trail that cut through a woodsy area of pine and brush. Ben's eyes scanned the area like two radar beams, his head swiveling around like a camera panning over a movie scene. Nora, on the other hand, marched forward oblivious to the surroundings. Ro vacillated between the two of them: keeping up with Nora while pulling Ben along. The day held beautiful weather and the path was filled with people—walking, speed walking, and jogging. As Ro tugged at Ben's hand, she had to twist and turn to avoid moving bodies. It was easy to see how people could bump into one another. The path was narrow but lit by sunshine. It certainly wasn't hidden.

Nora suddenly veered off course, leaving the trail and bushwacking her way through brush and trees. The area became darker and spooky with shadows where someone could lie in wait. The ground underneath was soft and giving. There were piles of pine needles. Ro was wearing rubber-soled boots, definitely not hiking shoes. Ben fared much better in his high-tops.

Nora came to an abrupt halt near a pine tree that looked like any other pine tree. Her eyes went wet. "They found one of her sneakers here." She bent down and squatted, gently caressing the ground. "Right . . . here." She placed the roses from her garden at the spot and stood up. "I always say a little prayer when I come."

Nora closed her eyes and then opened them a moment later. She said, "What do you think?"

Ben was quiet, looking over the surroundings. It took a few moments before he spoke. "Where's the nearest road?"

"Spoken like a true detective," Nora said. "It's down about a hundred feet down. He probably knocked her out and dragged her to his car. If there were two of them, it wouldn't be that hard to overcome her."

"Does Detective Whitecliffe really suspect two men? That might redefine my way of thinking."

"You'll have to ask him. I'll tell him to expect your call."

"Thanks." A pause. "Did the detectives find any drag marks in the brush?"

"I don't think so. She may have been walking at this point and just lost her footing and a shoe. Or if there were two of them, they could have carried her down."

Vicks nodded.

"You don't think so?"

"No, it makes sense . . . to let gravity work for you."

"Meaning?"

"It's easier to go down than up. Did you find any other items belonging to your daughter other than the sneaker?"

"No. Nothing. And the police looked."

"Huh." Ben thought a moment. "Can you show me the quickest way down to the road?"

"Of course."

It took a few minutes until they reached an unpaved utility pathway that was camouflaged by trees and brush. Ben said, "Where does this connect to?"

"If you follow it for about three hundred feet, it connects to a paved road. You want to see?"

"Sure . . . in a minute." He looked at her. "Did they find tire tracks?" When Nora didn't answer, Ben said, "If they had a car here, there would have been tire tracks. Look how loose the gravel is."

Nora pulled out her smartphone. "I'll make a note to ask Derek about it."

"Can I see where this leads?" Ben asked.

"Of course."

They walked over the gravel, Ro constantly stopping to empty her shoes of rocks. The pathway ended in a right angle to a busy paved road. Ben folded his arms across his chest. He stared at the traffic. "Is this the main road to Mount Diablo?"

"It leads to a main highway, yes."

"What other roads near here lead to Mount Diablo?"

"You mean the main highway. There is another major thoroughfare on the other side of the jogging trail. The detectives discounted it once they found the sneaker. Besides, the other side of the jogging trail would involve going up instead of going down."

Ben paused. "But the cops did search on the other side of the jogging trail."

"We searched over the entire area trying to find Julia. We thought she might have fallen and seriously hurt herself. That's why we looked down the hill first. And that's where we found the sneaker." A pause. Nora said, "What are you thinking about?"

"I really don't know, Nora. I'm just thinking about him . . . what he was thinking. Doing what he does . . . the guy isn't random. He's very organized. He's been eluding us for at least three years." Vicks gave Ro a quick glance, then he spoke to the ground. "I'm just thinking if you want to be clever and throw someone off track, you might decide to go up instead of down."

"Her shoe was found down the hill."

"Anyone can take off a shoe and throw it down the hill." He looked up. "You know, I can see the jogging path from here. I mean, not well, but I can see the shadows going by even this far down. This particular spot has hiding places—no doubt about that—but it's not as secluded as I'd like for an abduction. One good yelp and you'd get someone's attention."

No one spoke.

"If it's not too much trouble, I would like to see the jogging trail again."

"Let's go."

The climb back up through the woods was arduous and uncomfortably devoid of human speech. They walked along the pathway for roughly another quarter of a mile. Then Vicks abruptly stopped. His eyes were directed upward. "What's that shack about halfway up the hill?"

"What are you looking at?" Nora asked.

"Stand where I am." Ben pointed upward. "See that thing peeping out between the pine and the redwood . . . looks like an outhouse or a gardener's shed."

She squinted. "I have no idea. I don't think I've ever noticed it before."

"Judging from the flies, it's probably an outhouse," Ro said. A fetid breeze passed downward. She made a face. They all did.

Ben said, "Surely someone looked inside when they were searching for Julia."

Nora was upset. "How could I have never noticed it before? I searched the entire area. How did you spot it?"

"Hiding in plain sight," Ben said. "This part of the mountain is pretty dense and that's probably why they built the outhouse up there . . . privacy. Also, who would want to get close to something smelly? Do you mind if I take a look?"

Nora said, "I'll come with you."

Vicks said, "Wanna wait here, Ro?"

The choice was between something gross and being alone in a spot where someone had been abducted. It really wasn't any choice. Ro said, "I'll come with you." The pathway to the outhouse was a rut in the ground. The structure was hard to see even as they approached it, playing peekaboo with the trees. Ro couldn't see it well but she sure could smell it. She held her nose but Vicks didn't seem bothered. He walked up to the shack, which was constructed of old, rotted wood, and stood there, breathing in the stench. The door was ajar, a cloud of buzzing flies and gnats guarding the entrance. Ben swung the door open all the way, stepped back, and stared inside.

Ro was ready to gag. Nora wasn't faring that much better.

Finally, Vicks closed the door. "It's an outhouse, all right."

"I think we came to that conclusion halfway up the path," Ro said.

"Why don't you two go back down and I'll be there in a minute."

"What on earth are you looking for?" Ro asked him. She was breathing through her mouth. She could taste the air and it wasn't good.

"Don't know. I'll meet you down there in fifteen, okay?"

Nora hooked her arm in Ro's. "Let's let the lad do his thing."

Vicks said, "And the other road is straight up the hill?"

"Yes, but you're going to have to climb through all the trees and untended brush to get to the top." Nora paused. "About a quarter mile down, there are steps to the jogging trail. You might be better off going to the top that way. The foliage is dense. It's easy to lose your way."

"No problem." He lowered his backpack and pulled out his smartphone and a compass. "I have high tech and low tech. Either way, I'm covered."

IT TOOK BEN twenty minutes hiking through the brush to find the street above without any GPS. As he approached he couldn't see the asphalt until he was right on top of it, but he could hear cars going by. The road was narrow and there was residential housing on the other side of the lane. Cars were lined up on the parkland side, almost bumper-to-bumper as curb space was at a premium. Anyone could hide from view there, blocked from the windows of the houses by the solid metal wall of vehicles. It wouldn't have been exactly easy to drag the body up and stow it in the trunk of a car, but it could be done quickly if meticulously planned.

Ben wondered if the police had canvassed the area. And if they had, would the residents have noticed anything? No doubt they were used to seeing people who parked their cars across the street and went down to the jogging trail via the steps.

He said to himself out loud, "How did you do it?" If he assumed that the killer took her up instead of down, Ben had to ask himself some questions.

To drag her up, he had to have knocked her out. It was too hard to manage a writhing, screaming girl going uphill on a rocky incline. Julia had been bound and strangled with no blunt-force trauma to the head. If he knocked her out, he had done it chemically.

The outhouse was a perfect place for him to hide. It was off the jogging trail and it wasn't used all that much. If he had staked out the area, all he had to do was wait until he saw his prey approach the shack. That would give him time to look around and make sure things were safe. When she came out, he pounced. Dragged her behind the shed and placed the rag over her nose until she lost consciousness. Then he dragged her up the hill—the killer knew exactly where he parked— popped the trunk, and threw her inside. Once she was taken

care of, how hard would it be to toss her shoe down the hillside to throw people off track? Then he'd go back to the car
and drive to that "dreaded second location," as Nora called it.

It was as likely a scenario as the one that the cops had come
up with: dragging her down the mountain and her losing the
shoe but nothing else.

As he walked down the hill, Ben was still trying to organize his brain because there was a problem with his thinking.
Julia lived close to the trail. Julia was also a runner. Before she
went on her jog, she most likely would have gone to the bathroom. And if the urge hit her, she'd probably have enough
control to wait until she got home and could use a clean bathroom. Why would she go into a filthy outhouse unless it was
an absolute emergency?

And if she was having bladder or bowel problems, would
she have really jogged that day?

As much as he hated the idea, he went back to the outhouse,
held his nose, and opened the door. He tried to put himself in
Julia's mind. Would she *really* have made a pit stop here?

Ugh, as Ro would say.

The wooden walls were rotting and the roof let in daylight.
There was a toilet seat that covered the shit hole in the ground.
He could understand a guy taking a piss in the cavity, but who
in their right mind would sit on such a disgusting toilet seat?
Maybe a guy in desperation but never, ever a girl. His eyes
looked into the brown, mushy gap.

And then he saw his answer.

He felt faint.

Still holding his nose, he left and quickly climbed down
the hillside. He fast-walked along the jogging path, spying
Nora and Ro on a bench, chatting away. It was good that Ro

had come with him. Besides the fact that he loved her, it was also good because she was so adroit socially. He took in a deep breath of fresh air and let it out slowly. Did it again and again and again. He threw his shoulders back and put on his best bland expression. He went over to the bench.

"Hey." They both looked up. "I'm all done."

"Find anything?" Nora asked.

Ben looked down. "I know this is going to sound odd . . ." He took in a breath and let it out. "On the day that Julia was abducted . . . did she by any chance . . . like, have her period?"

Nora turned a ghastly shade of white. She dropped her head to her knees. Immediately Ben and Ro started fussing over her. She batted them away with her forearm. "Stop. I'm all right."

The next few moments passed in awful silence. Finally, Nora lifted her head. Ben had pulled out a water bottle from his backpack. He undid the top. "Here, Nora, take a drink."

"Thank you." Nora took a sip, and then another sip. She exhaled forcefully but her intake of breath was still shallow. "I'm all right, thank you."

More time passed. She drank again. Then she looked at Ben. "Yes, she did have her period and it was unusually heavy." Tears spilled out of her eyes. "I didn't want her to go jogging, but she insisted." More tears. "How'd you know? It wasn't a lucky guess."

Ben rubbed his eyes. God, he felt tired . . . more than tired. He felt as if someone had taken a cudgel and whacked him over the head. "This is just a thought, Nora."

"Go on!" Her voice was stiff and harsh. He didn't take offense.

Ben said, "I don't think the killer was thinking about pulling a random girl off the jogging trail. He's a thinker . . . a planner. I think he was staking out the outhouse. The spot is hidden. Just as important, the killer can hide the victim behind the building for privacy."

"You think he raped her behind an *outhouse*?"

"No, but I think that's where he abducted her from."

When he stopped talking, Nora said, "You're trying to protect me. But the more I know . . . you can be as blunt as you need to be, okay?"

His eyes got moist. "Nora, I think he drugged her chemically . . . a rag to the nose until she passed out. I think he dragged her unconscious body up the hill to the street above. I walked the area. The road is filled with parked cars. It's easy to hide behind them. I think he knew exactly where to park his car. When he got up there, he stowed her in the trunk but not before taking her shoe. And once she was locked up and knocked out, he went back to the trail and threw the shoe down the hill to throw the cops off. Then he went back up to his car and drove away."

Nora waited. "What does that have to do with her period?"

Ben steeled himself. "Why would Julia have used an outhouse when she lived so close? It had to be an emergency, something she needed to do right away, and something that didn't involve sitting on the toilet seat." He felt himself go hot. "Ellen was older than I was, but I remember stuff about her." He exhaled. "Sometimes girls leak and it's embarrassing for them. When I looked down the toilet hole, I saw a few tampons." He wiped his eyes. "She was probably leaking and she didn't want to be embarrassed."

CHAPTER 5

ONCE BACK AT the motel, Ben started stuffing his meager belongings into his duffel. He was panting, his skin red and flushed. "We've got to get out of here!"

"Our plane tickets aren't until tomorrow," Ro told him. "Besides, I haven't seen Stanford."

"I don't give a rat's ass about Stanford, Ro. I need to get out of here. I can't breathe, I can't function, I can't think, I can't talk!" He turned on her. "It's bad enough that I do what I do with my own sister. But to see someone else in misery like that and know I played a part in it . . . Uh-uh, never again!" He zipped up his duffel. "You do what you want. I'm leaving."

Ro stood there in a seedy motel of his choosing, staring at him with her arms crossed over her chest. "Go then." The sound of her voice made him stop. "I'll be fine. I'll take care of the car and the motel bill and whatever else you leave behind in your wake. Unless you need the car to get to the airport. If so, I'll rent something or take an Uber or a taxi."

He continued to look at her with vacant eyes. Eventually, he threw his duffel on one of the beds and plopped onto his back on the mattress. "I'm acting like an idiot."

Ro sat down next to him and took his hand. "I'm sorry you had to go through all that misery, Ben. I saw all the suffering in your eyes. For what it's worth, I liked your theory."

"Doesn't bring me any closer to who he is."

"Who they are?"

"It's only one killer. I'm sure of it." He sat up. "Why do you put up with me? I'm not rich, I'm not a BMOC, I don't play football, I'm not even all that cute."

"You're very cute. And maybe I put up with you because I love you."

"Whatever for?" He spoke more to himself than to her. "I love you too. I love you and thank you very much for doing this for me." He looked at his watch. It was past four. "Let's grab an early dinner and call it a night." He turned to her. "I'd be happy to see Stanford. It would be my pleasure to do something nice for you. We'll stick to the plan."

"What does 'call it a night' mean to you?" Ro asked him.

"What does it mean to you?"

"It means doing something more than eating a greasy meal and reading bad pornography." She smiled. "Maybe it means acting out our own pornography."

His smile was genuine. "I just thought . . . after last night and what happened today . . . that maybe the timing was off . . . what am I saying here?"

"Is that what you want?"

"Not at all. I'm trying to be nice."

"Haven't you ever heard that nice guys finish last?"

"You're not too . . . sore?"

"I'm like shredded beef, but probably most girls are after their first time. Don't worry. It won't last forever."

He stared at her. "You are amazing!"

"I am. My only regret is I should have started with JD and worked my way up." At that, Vicks doubled over in laughter. Then she said, "Actually, I should have started with my old boyfriend in Scarsdale and worked up from him."

He was still laughing. "He was small?"

"Average."

"Uh . . . just how many have you seen?"

She threw her arms around his neck and kissed his mouth. "Enough to know that I hit the jackpot."

THE FOLLOWING DAY was just as beautiful and made even better because they didn't talk about death. Vicks was driving, and Ro was navigating via the GPS on her phone.

"It'll take about an hour either way. One way is to go through San Francisco via the 280. The other way is to go down the 580 through Sunnyvale and Silicon Valley."

"Any advantage or disadvantage in the routes?"

"It's basically one big circle because we're leaving from Oakland International tonight. I say we try both routes. We have enough time." It was half past ten in the morning and they had just checked out of the motel, both working on about five hours of sleep that had been segmented by lots of physical activity. When Ro had showered this morning, she could barely stand. "Let's go through Silicon Valley. I, for one, would like to see Google or Facebook or Adobe or one of the many other Fortune 500 companies in the area."

"They're just buildings, Ro, unless you want a tour or something like that. I never knew you were interested in high tech."

"I'm not. I'm just hoping that some nerdy millionaire will see my booty and have to have me at all costs."

"I'm sure you could find many nerdy millionaires to fight over you. Yeah, even billionaires."

"Probably. I do have an exceptionally fine booty."

Vicks smiled, steeped in a recent memory. "Well, you got the nerd part down with me. Sorry about not fulfilling the millionaire part. But I'll be happy to go with you on a tour."

"No, I'll pass. Whenever guys talk about technology, my eyes glaze over."

"I'll keep that in mind."

"You know, Vicks, you're really not all that nerdy. I mean, you are all math and science, but for one thing, you are really cute. And I'm not the only one who thinks that."

"I know. Lisa Holloway."

"The slut!" Ro began to sulk. "You could probably nail her with a smile and a beckoning finger."

"I have no interest in banging Lisa Holloway."

"How could he *do* that to me!" She was mustering up new-found outrage at JD. "And doing Shannon Stork at the same time? God, what an asshole!"

"Yeah, all true, but JD isn't really a bad dude. He's weak when it comes to sex."

"Why are you being so forgiving of him?"

Vicks grinned. "Because I have you and he doesn't."

She slapped his shoulder, looking at his profile—straight nose, nice chin, lots of gorgeous curls. "There's something about you, Vicks. A long time ago, I suspect you had another life that wasn't nerdy at all."

"Well, I did once have friends."

"Wanna tell me about it?" she asked. "We certainly have time."

"Nope. I'd rather tell you how beautiful you are."

"I already know that." She gave a dismissive wave. "Boring."

"How about we talk about our favorite subject?"

"What's that?"

"You. Tell me all about your life."

"Okay, you asked for it." For Ro, it was always easier to talk about herself than anything else. She talked and talked. And then she talked some more. She talked until they detoured through the main drag of the town of Mountain View, one of the many homes of high tech in Silicon Valley. The street was lined by a slew of restaurants and cafés, and at eleven thirty, the sidewalks were dense with people, almost all of whom seemed to be under thirty. There were lots of seriously skinny guys wearing shorts and T-shirts and hoodies. There were also lots of girls wearing the same uniform. None of them—male or female—looked as if they'd ever done competitive sports or ever thought about fashion. It wasn't that they had bad bodies or faces. With a little effort, some of them could have been cute. But by the way most of them carried themselves, it was clear that they didn't seem to care a whit about how they looked.

"These are definitely not my peeps," Ro said. "Hard to believe that we're the same species. But then again diamonds and carbon graphite have the same molecular composition."

"Good analogy," Ben said. "You're being a snob, by the way."

"No, I'm being superficial. These are your peeps, darlin'. God, with the way you look, you could probably get laid with a different girl every day."

"Thank you, I think, for the compliment. Just think about how well you'd do here."

"I'd be beating them off with a stick."

"You'd need a mace with a steel chain."

Ro grinned. "Well, I'm sure Facebook or Google or Adobe or LinkedIn would hire you in a heartbeat, especially with your experience at Circuitchip."

"I could get a job here, but this isn't really my thing. I'm more physics than high tech."

"What about Stanford? Didn't someone discover the Jason Biggs particle or something like that at Stanford?"

Vicks started laughing. "The Higgs boson particle."

"Whatever . . . I don't even know what all the fuss is about."

"Really simply put, it's the particle responsible for all the matter in the universe. It was discovered at CERN in conjunction with the Fermi Institute in Chicago. But Stanford, like all the other labs, has been working on it for a long time."

"CERN?"

"It's a laboratory in Geneva. It has this huge particle accelerator—a Large Hadron Collider. All accelerators essentially do the same thing. They smash atoms against each other at high speed and see what subatomic particles are released. Some are linear and some are circular. CERN has the largest linear accelerator. It's about seventeen miles long and was built underground. They've known for a while that there had to be a Higgs boson in the universe, but they couldn't find them within the proper accuracy. I think they wanted something like point-zero-zero-zero-five significance so obviously it took a while to find something with that little room for error. Actually, they didn't really prove it was there—the Higgs boson. What they did is prove that it was impossible that it didn't exist." He didn't talk for a moment. "Your eyes are glazing over."

"'S'right. Your voice is lulling me to sleep."

Vicks laughed. "In my own nerdy way, I'm not really high tech. I mean, I like my computer but I'm not obsessed with video games or apps or social networking. I'm much less Facebook and way more Lawrence Liv—" He stopped talking, going silent and pale.

"What is it?"

"Shit!" he whispered. "Shit, I'm an idiot!"

"Ben, you're white. What is it?"

Abruptly, he hung a steep right turn, almost mowing down an Asian girl and a chubby guy. Ro screamed, but he didn't slow down until he found an empty parking spot. He yanked the wheel and pulled over to the curb, cutting off another driver who gave them a decidedly angry series of honks. Ro was trying to catch her breath as Ben muttered obscenities, most of them directed to himself. She gasped, "What is *wrong* with you?"

He ignored the question, and reached over and pulled out his duffel from the back. Immediately, he took out his laptop. "What's wrong? I'm a *moron*, that's what's wrong!" He pressed a key on his computer in rapid succession. "C'mon and connect, you stupid machine! There has to be some Wi-Fi somewhere in the stupid area!" Again, he pushed the key several times in a row.

"You're going to freeze your computer."

He slammed his laptop shut. "Give me your phone."

"How about a please?" When he didn't answer, Ro gave it to him. Her heart was still beating like a machine gun. "You know you almost killed those two pedestrians, Ben."

He still didn't respond because he didn't hear anything. Too busy trying to extract something from the Internet. "How could I have missed it? I'm such a cretin." He showed her a map on the phone. "Just listen, okay." Silence. "Look at this. If you start out in Berkeley and take the 24 through Walnut Creek, you can reach Mount Diablo State Park. Then all you have to do is . . . hold on . . . go back on the 24 South until you hit the 680 South. Then you hit the 580 and you're there."

"Where?"

"Livermore, California." He hit his forehead. "He was headed for Lawrence Livermore, Ro. The guy started out at Berkeley, abducted Julia, raped and killed her, buried her in Mount Diablo, and then went on his way to Lawrence Livermore, which was probably his ultimate destination."

No one spoke.

Ben said, "Dorothy, Lawrence Livermore is not only a sister lab to Berkeley and all the UC campuses, as Lilly so aptly pointed out to me yesterday, it's right next to a satellite lab of Sandia National Laboratories, where Katie Doogan was abducted, and most important, it's a sister to Los Alamos, which is about ten miles from River Remez." His eyes grew wide. "Don't you see it? The murderer is traveling between the national government laboratories!"

She was stunned into silence.

"I'm such an idiot!" Ben reiterated.

"What about Jamey Moore in Tennessee?"

"Oak Ridge National Lab," he said without hesitation. He started playing with the phone again. "Look here, Ro. The killer lands in Knoxville, which is the natural place to land if you're going to Oak Ridge. But instead of going west to Oak Ridge, he abducts and kills Jamey Moore, goes south through

Louisville, then east to the tip of the Smokies in Cosby, Tennessee. He buries her there, and then he turns back and heads for Oak Ridge. Or he kills her on the way back to Knoxville from Oak Ridge." He plopped back in the driver's seat and hit his head. "It's so obvious."

"Okay . . ." Ro was trying to process what he had just told her. "How many other labs are there in the country?"

"God, let me think! There's Fermi in Chicago, Brookhaven in New York, Plasma Lab in Princeton, Lawrence Berkeley on the UC campus, Sandia in New Mexico, which, like I just said, also has a lab in Livermore, California." He paused. "The thing is, there are three national nuclear facilities in the country: Lawrence Livermore, Sandia, and Los Alamos."

"Like they make bombs?"

"They make plutonium pits. Which are the essential component to a nuclear bomb."

"All right," she said. "So exactly what are you thinking?"

"What am I thinking?" Ben stared at her. "We're working with a very prominent scientist if the government is bothering to send him around from lab to lab."

"That's good, Ben. You've narrowed down the killer—"

"No, it's not good! It's not good at all! We're looking at someone with top, top, top security clearance. And because of who he is, he probably keeps a very low profile. He's more like a fly on the wall than a rock star."

"What about scientific conventions at the time of the murders? Maybe we can look those up on the Internet and find out if there was some kind of program which mentions people or—"

"Ro, when scientists get together, it's not like some insurance company playing party games or listening to a motivational speaker. You don't talk about bunker busters, bombs, or computer viruses for hostile nations' nuclear facilities at a convention at a Marriott."

"Okay, okay. I get it." She took his hand. "We'll think of something."

Vicks was growing more morose by the second. "The labs we're talking about, they're impenetrable. We will never find out who he is even if we know what he does!"

"Maybe not. Let's just think logically, Vicks. What's our next step?"

Ben's face was flushed and his eyes were wild. "There is no next step, Dorothy."

"What does that mean?"

"It means I'm fucked, that's what it means!"

CHAPTER 6

IN THE WINTER, Highway 502 cut through snow-covered hillsides, making the road a treacherous mixture of water, ice, and gravel. Before he was even allowed to travel toward Los Alamos National Laboratory, abbreviated to LANL, Ben had been stopped by security, asking him his business on the road. He had been smart enough to bring his snowboard, playing the dumb kid who wanted to do some pop-tarts and ollies in the backcountry around the Caldera, a collapsed cone of a dormant volcano. The vast acreage of grasslands was rented out for cattle grazing in temperate weather. In the frigid air of winter, the unique geography was often below zero at ten thousand feet elevation. His snowboarding story made sense and the fact that he held a New Mexico driver's license helped give credence to his lies. If the guards were suspicious, they didn't let on. They passed him through, and now he was fighting through the elements.

He had taken several tours of Los Alamos when he was younger. Obviously, the standard spiel doesn't say or show much, but he thought it might be a good idea to do it again. As he traveled, Ben took note of those blue signs with white lettering that marked bland one-story white stucco buildings—the various tech areas, each division gated and guarded and behind steel fences. He had been through the roads many times before, but this time everything seemed more menacing. He slowed down to take forbidden pictures, stupid because he didn't even know what he was looking for. At this point, he was just trying to master the lay of the land.

This was your destination—before you left a trail of destruction and misery!

There were enough buildings in these quarters to do something awful, but would the guy be brazen enough to rape and murder in the confines of the lab?

Ben realized he was sweating and turned down the heat. Eventually, the blue signs gave way to the actual town. Los Alamos was a nice place. It had schools, its own police and firemen, and a little outdoor skating rink. It had cafés and parks and an outdoor stadium, a few motels and its own little municipal airport, and more than one museum that gave comprehensive histories of the lab and the technology behind the first A-bomb. It also had streets with names like Oppenheimer Road or Bikini Atoll and even Highway 502, as it passed through the town limits, was known as Trinity Drive. The town wavered between being proud of its heritage and making excuses for it.

Ben drove aimlessly through the streets and roads, passing motels—*did you stay there?*—passing the airport—*did you come in through there?*—passing restaurants—*did you eat there?* His excursion took hours. As the sun started sinking, he turned around and headed home, dejected. As if things weren't bad enough, it started to snow, making visibility a blur, causing him to slow down and take each curve with care. He was fighting depression along with an undeniable urge to speed up and crash into the mountainside.

But then a cooler head prevailed.

He crawled his way back to River Remez.

RO DROVE WHILE Ben sulked, which, except for sex, seemed to be his high-rate behavior. Through the windshield was a white landscape, the sunny sky was an incredibly bright blue that was New Mexico's trademark. But it was deceptive because it was freezing outside. She said, "Do you miss California yet?"

He was still sulking. "I still don't understand why we have to involve Shanks. It's just a stupid theory. It's not going to make a difference in the investigation. He's as hamstrung as we are."

"Just tell him, okay."

"He's totally pissed at me for going to Berkeley behind his back."

"You wounded his pride. Who cares as long as he sent the DNA profile to Berkeley?" Silence. "Did he do it? Send in the profile?"

"Yesterday."

"And?"

"I guess we'll find out," Vicks said.

She pulled into a parking spot at the station. They got out, and slipped on their jackets, entered the adobe building, and took off the jackets. It was blazing inside. The secretary greeted Ben by name and ushered the two of them into an interview room. It was brightly lit. There was a table against a wall, three or four chairs, and nothing else. Sam Shanks came in a moment later, carrying coffee mugs. His chest strained the buttons of his shirt. Wordlessly, he handed them to Ben, who got up and left.

Shanks's eyes hardened as he looked at Ro. "I thought you were on my side. He's got to stop."

"Sir, he was going to Berkeley with or without me and I figured the least I could do is make sure he didn't get himself into trouble."

"How long have you known about his trip to Berkeley?"

"I found out right before Christmas break."

"Why didn't you tell me?"

"Because he didn't want me to tell you. And, for the record, I wish he'd stop too. It isn't leading to a good place."

"If he keeps going, it may lead him into a very dangerous place." Shanks scratched his head. "Why does he keep holding back? Last thing I need is another person riding my tail."

"Did Nora Rehnquist call you?"

"The Berkeley PD called at the behest of Nora Rehnquist, who is no doubt riding their tails."

Vicks came back in with three cups of coffee. He distributed them and sat down. "What did I miss?"

"Nora Rehnquist is riding his ass," Ro told him.

"I said 'tail,'" Shanks said.

Ro smiled. "Yes, you did."

Vicks sipped his coffee. "Nora called you?"

"No, Berkeley called after you called me. They're not happy with you either. It seems you have awoken the sleeping giant in Nora Rehnquist."

"Nora and I are on the same side."

"Vicksburg, we're *all* on the same side."

Ben said, "Did you get a match with my sister and Julia Rehnquist?"

Shanks laughed. "That's Vicks. Cut to the chase."

"Yes or no?"

"Yes, we got a DNA match on one of the profiles Berkeley had pulled off Julia Rehnquist with your sister, Ben."

Vicks clapped his hands. "I *knew* it!"

"You were right and I thank you for your persistence. This is a really good break. If Katie Doogan matches, it'll blow the case wide open. Of course, if you had told me about your theories, I might have done something months ago. And yes, we sent the profile through CODIS again. No hit."

"Damn!" A sigh. "Not that I expected anything." He perked up. "Are you going to contact Knoxville on Jamey Moore's case?"

"I have a call in to them." Shanks gave Ben the full force of his stare. "Vicks, this is what I want right now. I want you to park your tail down and give me every reason you came up with to link these two cases together." Shanks took out a notepad. "Go."

Ben obliged with a half-hour recitation. He went through all the similarities. He went through everything he and Ro had done in California, from walking the pathway to the dump spot at Mount Diablo to his outhouse explorations and his theories about how Julia was abducted. He went through everything in detail, except for one important fact. Ro cleared her throat. Both of the boys looked at her. "Can I have a minute alone with him?"

"What's going on?" Shanks asked.

Her smile was grim. "Just a few minutes, please." Reluctantly, Shanks left. Then she turned angry and hard. "Why do you do that, Ben? Why do you give him *almost* the whole thing? It's like a woman leaving out a crucial element of a family recipe."

"Because even if I told him about the labs, there's nothing he could do about it."

"There's nothing *you* can do about it. I mean, what are your plans? Breaking into a nuclear facility? Maybe that's the real agenda here. Because jail would give you plenty of time for your research."

"C'mon, give me some credit."

"Why are you *withholding* vital information from him?"

"Because—" He suddenly stopped talking. "You're right. I'll tell him."

"Thank you. I'll go get him."

When Shanks returned, his eyes darted between the two teens. "Yes?"

Ro looked at Ben, and reluctantly, as if he were parting with a wad of money, he slowly told the detective about the murders' proximities to the national laboratories—Los Alamos, Sandia, Lawrence Livermore/Berkeley, and Oak Ridge. As Ben spoke, Shanks's complexion grew gray.

Vicks said, "I could be wrong."

Shanks glared at him. "Why didn't you tell me this before?"

"I didn't want to tell you the wrong information—"

"Cut the crap, okay? Just stop *doing* that!" Vicks said nothing. He looked chastened. Shanks was clearly still digesting the information. "A scientist serial killer."

"Possibly," Ben said.

"Okay." Silence. "Okay . . . let me think about how to handle this. I've got to talk to some people."

"What do you want me to do?" Vicks asked.

"What do I want . . ." Shanks's eyes zeroed in on Ben's. "You . . . do . . . *nothing*. As much as I'd love to use your brainpower, you've got to stop right *now*. We're working from theoretical to potentially very dangerous. You don't want to mess around with the government, okay?"

"It's not like I probed into any top security, Sam. I accessed the information on my laptop."

"*Stop* it, Ben!" Shanks pounded the table. "If you interfere, I swear I will lock you up. Is that what you want?" No one spoke. Then Shanks said, "Promise me you will not interfere."

"I promise."

"Say it again."

"I swear to God, I will not interfere with your case."

"With Ellen's case."

"I swear to God, I will not interfere with your investigation into my sister's case."

"Okay." Shanks seemed mollified. "Okay, both of you go home. I've got to think."

Vicks stood up. "Will you keep me posted, at least?"

"Yes." Shanks stood up and gave the kid a bear hug. "I know it's hard for you, Ben. You've taken it as far as you can and you've done a fantastic job. Way better than any of us. Right now, I really need your cooperation to back off completely, okay?"

"Sure." Vicks took Ro's hand and the two of them walked out of the police station. Ro waited until they were in the car. "You're not going to listen to him."

"No. Why should I? Any concrete information came from me."

Ro's eyes started to water. "You're gonna get yourself killed and it's going to devastate all the people who love you. That's very selfish of you." She turned on the motor and pulled the car out of the lot. Tears were running down her cheeks.

"I'm not going to get killed . . . oh, c'mon. Please don't cry. I hate it when you cry."

"It's preparatory mourning."

"I promise I won't do anything beyond looking up stuff on a laptop, okay? I mean, how much trouble could I get into doing that?"

"What if the murderer traces your computer?"

"He's not going to trace my computer."

"How do you know? If he's some hotshot scientist, he probably has all these things at his fingertips that you don't know about." A fresh batch of tears. "Vicks, he knows who you are! He knows that you are the brother of the girl he murdered. But you don't know who he is. And the closer you get, the more he's going to take measures to stop you. And seeing as he knows you but you don't know him, he has a sizable advantage. If you don't stop, I'm going to break up with you."

"Oh, c'mon! That's not fair!"

"Benjamin Vicksburg, this monster kills teenaged girls and I am a teenaged girl. Have you ever thought about that? Why should I risk my life for you?"

Ben was quiet. Then he said, "Okay. Good point. You're right. I won't look stuff up on my computer."

"What does that mean? You'll look stuff up on someone else's computer?"

"There's always the library—"

"Ben!"

"Dorothy, don't do this to me! I promised her!"

And what could she say to that. Ellen was as alive to him as she had been the day she went missing. He couldn't let her go. It was just too damn painful. Ro sighed. "Just be careful, okay?"

Vicks rubbed his chin. "Maybe . . . maybe it would be better if I waited until you were gone."

"Gone?"

"Done with high school and off to college. Out of town." Another pause. "I've told Shanks everything I know. I'm pretty busy anyway. Maybe it would be healthy to take a breather . . . for both of us."

This time, her tears were those of joy. "Do you really *mean* it?"

"I can't compromise your safety. As long as we're together, I can't do this without worrying about you."

"And your sister . . . remember, she's turning fifteen in, like, six months."

"No need to remind me." Awkward silence. "You're right. I'll give it a rest. I'd literally kill myself if something happened to you or Haley. I can't risk that."

"I think that's the nicest thing you've ever said to me."

He sighed. "Okay, I'll stop. But . . . there's one more thing I need to do."

"Vicks—"

"It won't compromise anything. Then I promise I won't do anything while you're here in River Remez. Is that fair enough?"

"What are you going to do?"

"I just want to talk to someone. Then I promise I'm all yours, body and soul."

"Talk to whom?"

"Not important. Do we have a deal?"

"Yes, we have a deal. Shake." Ro looked at his hands to make sure his fingers weren't crossed. They weren't. But since he was wearing boots, she couldn't swear to his toes.

CHAPTER 7

BEN KNOCKED AND Lilly answered the door. Her dachshund came charging at Ben's knee, yapping with excitement. Ben bent down. "Hey, Oliver, whaddup?"

The dog was running around in circles. Lilly was all smiles. "You wanna come in?"

"I do." Ben wiped his boots on the mat, kicking off the snow, and stepped inside the house. It was hot. There were baking smells that were very inviting. He took off his ski hat and his parka. Lilly said, "Haley's not here."

"I know that," Ben said. "I just dropped off Griff and her at the movies. I came to see your dad."

"My dad?"

"You know . . . that fearsome, paternal thing that slinks around the house. Is he around?"

"Oliver, quiet." The dachshund rolled over on his back. Lilly scratched his belly. "He's working in his shop."

"In the garage, right?"

"I'll get him for you. Just make sure Mr. O doesn't pee on the carpet."

"You know, Haley misses you."

"No, she doesn't."

"Yes, she does. In the car, she was complaining to Griff that you don't come with them anymore. She said it wasn't nice to Ezra, but I could tell she was hurt by your absence."

"She's not hurt, and I'm perfectly nice to Ezra. As a matter of fact, he's coming over to play video games and eat leftover Thai that Mom made last night."

Ben broke into a slow smile. "Is he now . . ."

Lilly hit him. "Stop it!" She smiled again. "You want some noodles?"

"No, thank you."

"How about a cookie? Sure you do." She grabbed the biggest one off the baking sheet. "Here you go."

"Thank you, hon." He took a bite and smiled. "Delicious. But I really do need to see your dad."

"Right . . . I'll get him."

George Tafoya lumbered in five minutes later. He was as big and wide as his wife, June, was narrow and petite. He had dark hair, dark eyes, brown skin, a wide nose, and full lips. His hands and face were coated in sawdust. "How's it going, Ben?"

"Okay," Ben answered. "You have a few minutes, George? I need to talk to you."

"Let me wash up."

"We can just go in the garage."

"Nah, let me wash up. Matter of fact, I'm hungry. Let's go out for some pie."

Ben looked at him. "Pie?"

"Yeah, pie. I'm in the mood for pie. What the hell is wrong with pie?"

"Daddy!" Lilly was aghast.

"Nothing," Ben said. "I like pie."

"So, let me wash up and we'll go to the Pie House."

"That's fine, George." Ben scratched his stubbled face. "I was kinda hoping to talk in a little bit more privacy."

"We'll take a back booth." George was already on his way to the bathroom.

When he left, Lilly shook her head. "He really likes you, you know. He's just a gruff guy."

"I know your dad. We're all friends here." The doorbell rang, and a moment later Ezra Rael came in with an armful of games. He spotted Ben. "Are Haley and Griff here?"

"At the movies."

"Oh." The kid stood there, rooted to his spot. Lilly relieved him of the materials. "Wanna cookie, Ez?"

"Sure."

George came out a moment later. He looked at his daughter. "You didn't tell me he was coming over."

The boy blushed. Lilly said, "Yes, I did. You just don't hear me when I talk."

"I can't leave you two here alone—"

"Daddy, *stop* it."

"Your mom will kill me."

"We can talk here, George. There are perfectly good cookies if you need a sugar fix."

The old man shook his head. "We'll bring the pie home." He glared at his daughter. "Won't take more than a half hour." His eyes went to Ezra. "You behave yourself."

"Daddy!"

Ben pulled his arm. "C'mon, George. The quicker we go, the quicker we come home."

"You drive," he told Ben.

"You sure?"

"You can't drive?"

"Of course I can drive. I drove here."

"Then drive to the Pie House," George said. "You know where it is?"

"Yes, George, I've lived here my entire life." Ben took out his car keys. "See you two later."

"No funny business," George reiterated.

GEORGE WAS A big man and he had to push the passenger seat all the way back to get comfortable. After Ben pulled out of the driveway and drove a hundred feet down the road, the old man said, "My house is bugged."

"Huh?" Ben turned to him, and then faced the road. "Did I just hear right?"

"Maybe my garage and car too, although I can't swear to that. You can't tell anyone."

"Sure . . . no, of course not." Ben was trying to think of a way to keep the conversation going. "Is it the government?"

"I sure hope so. Better them than Iran or China or Russia, but even if it was a hostile entity, they wouldn't find out anything. June and I don't sit around talking trade secrets. I suspect the bugging is homegrown and that's fine. Good old Uncle Sam can listen in on me. We work with very sensitive material and I guess after Wen Ho Lee and some of the other major snafus at the lab, they're attempting to be a little more mindful of what's going on. June and I have got nothing to hide, but you look like you have something on your mind. Maybe one day you'll want a government job, and if you're on crack or something, it's none of their business."

"I'm not on crack." Ben turned right, heading for the Pie House. He was flabbergasted. "How did you find out your house is bugged?"

"About two years ago, the dishwasher conked out. We rarely use it and the one time we wanted to use it after a party, we were surprised it didn't work. June called a repairman and made an appointment for two days later. Then an hour later someone shows up."

"An hour later?"

"Yeah, says he was in the neighborhood and just decided to kill two birds with one stone. That kind of service is unheard of for River Remez, right? Everything takes days. No one is in a hurry. Anyway, this guy pulls the dishwasher out and fixes it, and about a half hour later we got a working dishwasher. Fine and dandy except two days later another repairman shows up at the time that June made the original appointment. June tells him they already sent someone out two days ago. The repairman says no one was sent out. June tells him to call his office. Besides, look at the dishwasher. It works. The guy decides to check it out and it does work. But then he looks a little further. He starts pulling out a wire, then another one, then another. Finally, June tells him not to mess with it . . . sticks all the wires back behind the dishwasher . . . and we left it at that. We went out for dinner the next night, and she told me about it. She's working on some top-secret projects, so she put two and two together."

"God, that's weird." Ben pulled into the Pie House and they both got out. George zipped up his jacket and, walking at a clipped pace, entered the establishment. He said, "Pick a pie."

"Apple?"

"How about chocolate cream?"

"That's fine."

"We'll get both."

"George, I'm not even hungry."

"Give it to your mother. You want some coffee? Sure you do." The man bought two pies and two coffees. He also bought two individual pieces of coconut cream pie. They sat in the car with the motor running, and ate pie with plastic forks and drank coffee from paper cups. George stuffed a wad of whipped cream into his mouth. "What's on your mind, Ben?"

"I need your help."

"You want a recommendation for Caltech?"

"What? No. I'm staying here for college."

"Big mistake."

"That's not what I want to talk about. It's about my sister's case." Slowly and in detail, Ben went over everything he had learned and his conclusions about who the killer might be. George stared out the windshield while Ben talked, as if the old man was watching TV, and ate pie, licking his fingers and smacking his lips. When Ben was done, George wiped his lips with a napkin. "Let's go home."

Ben started up the car and waited for George to speak. He didn't have to wait very long.

"Give me the date again."

"For Ellen's abduction or for all the murders?"

"Start with Ellen." After Ben gave him the date, George said, "You ever been inside the complex, Ben?"

"Just the standard tours."

"If you were to come visit me at my office—if they'd let you in—security would put a cassette around your neck and take it back when you leave. Every action inside the hub is recorded or monitored or both: audio, video, my computer, phone calls, e-mails. You can't make a move without someone noticing it. If you're asking me to look up who visited around the time your sister was abducted, I'm going to have to think up something that doesn't get my ass fired, or worse, land me in jail."

"Both of those options are out," Ben said.

"On the other hand, if what you're telling me has any merit, I'll be happy to land my ass in jail to expose someone so evil, especially if it prevents something bad from happening in the future." He turned to Ben. "It'd be helpful if you had something other than your hunch for me to go on."

"I wish I had more, but I don't." Silence. "George, I don't want you to do anything that gets you in trouble. I want to make that clear."

"Then what do you want?"

"I suppose I just want you to keep your eyes and ears open, especially around the upcoming vernal equinox."

George said. "I'll keep my eyes and ears open. Now here's something I want you to do for me."

"I'm not applying to Caltech—"

"I want you to stop probing into this shit, Ben. You did all you could and now leave it up to the experts. If Shanks said he'll talk to people, he'll talk to people. Go out and be seventeen. By your age, I had already knocked up my first wife."

Ben laughed. "That's what I should aspire to?"

"If it's a choice between knocking up a girl or facing down the U.S. government, yeah, that is what you should aspire to."

Ben pulled up in the driveway. "Thanks for your help, George."

"Just remember what I told you. No more." George stared out the window again. "From what you told me, the guy operates every nine months, which would put the date of his operation closer to the summer solstice."

"He could deviate."

"Doesn't sound like it. Sounds like he's on a nine-month schedule."

"That's what I'm afraid of." Ben felt the pie churning in his stomach. "I'm afraid he's coming back to River Remez to start the cycle all over again."

CHAPTER 8

IN THE BOYFRIEND department, Ben got the sex part down pretty quickly. It was the other things in which he needed tutoring. Ro knew who Vicks was. Or rather what he wasn't. He wasn't inconsiderate or rude or harsh or mean. But he was absent. Even when he was around, which wasn't that often given their conflicting schedules, his mind was elsewhere. She knew he loved her, but his brain functioned differently from that of any guy she'd ever met. He rarely texted, he rarely called. She initiated all of the interaction between them. They saw each other on weekends, but the distance and his lack of checking in made it hard to keep a relationship going.

In the beginning of February, on a Sunday, they were alone in her house and in her room. It wasn't particularly girlie, but it was set up just the way she liked. She had an enormous closet and a makeup area in addition to a functional desk. Her bedding was all pastels and whites and filled with soft, downy pillows. But she doubted whether Ben had ever noticed any of her things. His thought process was always thus: her, alone, a bedroom, sex.

But today, she had other things on her mind, and he was aware enough to know that she was peeved. He wore his usual T-shirt and jeans and sneakers. Once in a while she wished he'd put on a regular shirt. He looked good when he dressed up.

He said, "Something bothering you?"

"Good call," Ro said.

"What'd I do?"

"It's what you don't do. You never call me. What's up with that?"

"I don't?"

"No. You don't."

"Okay. I'll call you more. I thought we talked all the time."

"That's because I call you."

"Oh. Okay." He thought a moment. "I can see where that would be annoying. Sorry."

He said it so plainly and so logically. Ro said, "You have a chance to make it up to me next week. It's Valentine's Day. This is what you're going to do, okay?"

"Okay."

"I want roses when I wake up in the morning—a dozen red roses. I'm very conventional. You pick me up later and take me out to a romantic dinner and then top it off with a blingy gift. Is that clear enough?"

He was writing the instructions down in his phone. When he was done, he stowed the phone in his pocket. "Got it." When she sighed, he said, "It'll be perfect. I promise you." He kissed her. "Really. I promise."

"I'll believe it when I see it."

"Can we make love?"

She hit him.

"That's a no?"

"What am I going to do with you?"

"What do you want to do with me?"

Ro shook her head and started unbuttoning her blouse. Sometimes she made love to him because she wanted to and it felt really good. But there were times, like today, when it was just something to do, something to pass the time so she wouldn't get annoyed at him.

VALENTINE'S DAY: NO roses waiting in the morning. Nor was there even a phone call. Ro had checked her cell a dozen times, then the message machine on the landline. She was about to call him, but then she thought better of it.

Fuck it.

By the time she made it to school and opened her locker, she was furious. What did it take to get through to him?

Or maybe he just didn't care.

Her cheeks went wet. She saw JD staring at her. The boy looked real fine and that made her even madder. There was still that spark with him, and with Ben's absence, it was growing stronger. She quickly averted her eyes, but he walked over to her and placed a sympathetic hand on her shoulder.

"You okay?"

"I'm fine." She managed a smile. "Really, I'm okay."

"Okay." He pressed a small wrapped package into her hands. "Happy Valentine's Day, sugar." When he saw the surprise in her eyes, he said, "If I'm supposed to be wooing you back, I have to play the part."

"What is it? A plastic ring?"

His smile was wide. "Why don't you open it and find out?"

She tore open the paper and lifted the lid on the box.

Inside were small gold hoops, each with a tiny yellow diamond. They were gorgeous. She couldn't speak.

"Try them on," JD urged. She did and he nodded. "Beautiful. But it's the girl, not the jewelry." He leaned casually against the locker. "Look, I know that Vicks probably has something planned—"

"Not that I know of," Ro blurted out.

JD was silent. Then he said, "O-kay."

She checked her phone. Still no damn call. "Thank you very much." She kissed his cheek. "I love them."

"Ben isn't taking you out?" JD asked.

"I wouldn't know. He hasn't called." When JD laughed, she hit him. "It's not funny."

"No, it's not ha-ha funny." JD shrugged. "It's just ironic funny. He worked so hard to get you and he doesn't have a clue how to keep you."

"Excuse me? Talk about not being able to keep a girl."

"At least I knew I was fucking up. Vicks is just oblivious. He's not a bad guy, Ro. But his mind doesn't work like yours or mine. Let me take you out for dinner. He obviously forgot."

"No, he didn't. He wrote it down in his phone."

"After you told him what to do, right?"

Ro didn't answer right away. "He loves me."

"I know. What's there not to love?"

"I love him."

"Fine. He loves you and you love him. I get it. If he doesn't call, can I take you out?"

"If he doesn't call by four, you can take me out for coffee."

"Girls go out for coffee, Ro. I go out to eat. Let's go to Kiki's. It's casual enough that it's not a real dinner date but they serve great burgers. Deal?"

"Don't you have practice?"

"Not today. I think Coach has to do something for the missus." The bell rang. "I'll upgrade you to something better than Kiki's, but tell me soon. All the good places will be booked up."

"He's gonna call." She was talking to JD's back. Then she checked her phone again.

Nothing.

By the time lunch ended, Ro decided that she wasn't going to talk to Ben even if he deigned to call. But it turned out to be a moot point. She couldn't find her phone. She checked her purse and her locker. She backtracked to all the classrooms and bathrooms, but it had simply disappeared.

"Want mine?" JD asked.

"No, I want to find mine. I want to see if he called . . ." She was suddenly *furious*! "Actually, I don't care if he called. If he wants to be with me bad enough, he'll show up after school. If he doesn't, I've had it."

"Whatever you want, princess."

"How come you weren't this nice when we were going together?"

"They paved paradise and put up a parking lot." He took her books and walked her to her locker. As she fiddled with her schoolwork, he leaned against the wall. "How about . . . if I take you somewhere really nice?"

"You're not getting any play."

"I'm not asking for play." He grinned. "We can just talk . . . isn't that what you girls like anyway?"

Ro shook her head and rolled her eyes.

"I know I have no credibility, but really, I can control myself. You don't play quarterback like I do without control."

"Maybe he'll show up." Ro didn't believe her own words.

"Look, I'll follow you home. If he's there, I'll just keep driving by. If he's not, we'll make an evening of it. Maybe go to a movie first and then dinner."

"Stop being so nice." When he was silent, she said, "Okay . . . okay, fine. No harm in a movie and dinner, right?"

"No harm at all."

And that's exactly what happened when Ben didn't show up after school or at her house.

But not quite.

The movie was some stupid love story—soppy and romantic, the way Ro liked it. The place JD chose for dinner was much nicer than a coffee shop, but not an elegant restaurant that would have been over-the-top for the evening. The dessert was a special chocolate cake baked in the shape of a heart. It oozed chocolate fudge as soon as she took a bite. She shared it with JD and they laughed as chocolate dripped onto the table. The evening was perfect for what he had proposed and he behaved himself. He saved the kiss for when they were done and Ro didn't feel the least bit guilty about it.

When JD suggested a ride to top off the evening, she was wary. But then she realized how lonely she'd been for male attention. He was the wrong boy and she knew it was wrong, but she didn't care. He took her somewhere up in the hills and they stared at the twinkling lights of Santa Fe. It was cold outside—freezing, to be exact—but the night was clear and the view was spectacular. He pulled something from the backseat. Ro figured it was a joint—JD was a recreational doper—but it turned out to be a bottle of champagne and plastic flutes. She looked at him with suspicious eyes.

He said, "Just thought it would be a nice topper." A pause. "You don't have to."

"One glass."

"That's the girl I know and love."

"Where were you three months ago?"

"With my head in my ass." He poured and they clicked glasses. "For what it's worth, I'm really, really sorry."

Ro didn't answer. When he refilled her glass, she hadn't realized that she had polished off the first. When he poured a third glass, she was feeling it—not enough to be drunk but enough to be happy.

"You know I love you." JD sipped champagne. "You just gotta understand guys. We're dogs. We need training. To train us properly, you need to dole out the treats for good behavior."

Ro hit him. "I gave you plenty of treats."

JD leaned over and kissed her cheek. "With someone as hot as you, it's never enough."

Her head started spinning. She shivered. "You still have that blanket in the back?"

JD grinned. "I do."

"Stop smirking. I'm cold. You turned off the motor. Why did you do that?"

"Because with the motor on, the car is more visible to the cops and we are underage and drinking, my love." He reached over and then tumbled into the backseat. He pulled the blanket from the hatch. "Come here, Ro. I promise I won't assault you."

"I don't believe you."

"Yeah, that's probably smart. I'm a total bullshitter."

Takes one to know one, she thought. When she didn't move, he laughed and leaned over to the front, where she was still sitting. "C'mon!" He grabbed her arm and pulled her over. She tumbled into the back and then they both started laughing.

He was tipsy, but she was soused. "You're gonna take advantage of me, right?"

"I sure hope so." JD kissed her and then kissed her again. His hands started roaming. Not that it bothered Ro. Both JD and his body were familiar territory and it felt nice. It felt good, much better than when they were going together because there was no honor to protect.

He was on top before she could protest, her head orbiting outer space. Kissing her while trying to yank down her panties.

"Stop!" she said.

And he did. "Yes?"

Ro was dizzy. "Nothing."

He started kissing her again. And she kept kissing him because she was cold and he was warming her up, because his kisses felt good and she was drunk. And because she didn't push him away, he tried again. He was inches from starting the act, but he stopped himself. His eyes looked into hers, waiting for permission.

Damn him.

It would have been better if he had forced her. She tried to stall but she wasn't thinking clearly. She slurred out, "Not without a condom."

"Oh . . . right!" He got off, leaned over to the front seat, and opened the glove compartment.

Of course he'd have condoms.

Ro didn't remember what she said to him. But she did remember that he said all the right things. And to be honest, especially in her state, she had become a little curious. Nothing wrong with that. It felt good. But it also felt dirty, and not in a good way. She took back all the evil thoughts she had about Lisa and Shannon. It was bad enough that she let him do it once. But then they did it again. He probably would have done it a third time except the booze was finally wearing off and she told him she needed to get home.

For once he did most of the talking. How much he loved her, how it was going to be different, how he had changed and was a better person because of what happened, blah, blah, blah.

She was listening with half an ear—mad at him but madder at herself. The day was shit, the night was shit, and then, as he approached her house, she knew things were only going to get shittier.

She sat up. "That's Vicks's car. Keep driving!"

"What?"

"Just go around the block!" JD complied and when he was several houses away, she said, "Drop me off here."

"What?"

"Pull over!" Ro yelled.

He stopped the car but took her arm before she could leave. "He's gonna know what happened. Let me come in with you."

"Not a chance!"

"Please, Dorothy." His voice went soft. "C'mon. I love you. What kind of a guy would I be if I didn't come in with you?" He touched her face, wiped away the tears on her cheek. "I'm not about to let you walk in pitch-dark in freezing weather."

"We're two houses away. I need to think."

"I'm going to pull up in front of your house. He's gonna know, so there's no sense in the charade, okay."

"Don't come in with me." As soon as he hit the driveway, she got out of the car. She poked her head back inside. "Go away. I'll see you in school tomorrow."

"You're not acting smart."

"That seems to be my theme song tonight." She slammed the door, dried her face, took a deep breath, and went inside her house. Ben was sitting on the sofa, dressed in a suit and tie, looking more gorgeous than she had ever seen him. She had this overwhelming desire to make love to him, to undo what had been done. But one look at his face and she knew that wasn't going to happen. He had been talking to Griff, but when she came in, Griff got up and walked off to his room and closed the door.

Like they say, the best defense is a good offense. Ro wanted the right tone of coolness and indignation. "Nice of you to call."

He said, "I called around a hundred times. Check your phone."

"I lost my phone."

"Check your purse."

"I lost my phone, Ben."

"Check your purse." His voice was quietly insistent.

And there was her cell. She stared at it like it was an alien object. "How did . . ."

"Did you happen to complain to JD that I wasn't calling you?" When Ro was silent, Ben said, "Thought so. He took it out when you weren't looking."

She scrolled down. There were around twenty missed calls, starting around three in the afternoon.

Ben's contempt made her wither. "You know you can check

your messages even if you don't have your phone." When she didn't answer, he said, "You thought I forgot."

She couldn't talk. Tears started pouring out of her eyes. Not that he'd notice. He wasn't looking at her.

"I wanted to *surprise* you," he said. "Once in a while I'd like to do something that wasn't choreographed by you." He rubbed his eyes. "Well, that certainly backfired." He stood up. "I'm going now."

"No, don't." She was pleading. "Please stay."

"You're kidding me, right?" He waited. "No, Dorothy, I'm not staying. I am definitely not staying! And you know you reek of booze, right?"

She was light-headed, but this time it wasn't from champagne. "Nothing happened."

"Don't tell me that," Ben whispered. "You may not have had sex with him . . . but something definitely *happened*." He reached in his pocket, pulled out a small, wrapped package, and threw it on the couch. "Happy Valentine's Day."

She heard his car start and then the sound faded into nothingness. She sat down, breathing hard and shaking from the cold and guilt. She made a stab at wiping her tears away, but all that did was smear her makeup.

Her brain whirled with rationalizations. It was as much his fault as it was hers. They were both probably better off. What did it matter anyway? He was never around. He agreed to the stupid arrangement with JD. It was just high school. Who cared anyway?

His gift, lying on the couch, was wrapped in silver foil with a red bow. She picked it up and pulled the card out of the envelope. It had a smiling heart on the front. Her eyes were blurry from crying and fatigue, but not blurry enough because she could make out Ben's handwriting.

> *My gorgeous Dorothy,*
> *I had given up on everything. You brought me back*
> *to life.*
> *I love you now and will love you forever and always.*
> *Ben*

Dry-eyed, she slipped the card back in the envelope and opened the gift. It was a white-gold bracelet chain studded with small diamonds. Her hands were shaking too hard to open the clasp, so she forced her fingers through the opening and managed to get it onto her wrist without breaking it. It was beautiful. Left to his own devices, the boy had great taste.

She took off JD's earrings and stared at them. She had wanted bling; she got her bling.

She took the wrapping, the box, and the card and locked herself in her bedroom. There she lay on her bed without bothering to get undressed.

Too numb to cry.

She always knew she was shallow. But until today, she didn't know that she was also terrible.

Clearly the wrong sister had died.

CHAPTER 9

HEY, BEAUTIFUL." JD'S eyes were twinkling. "How's the hottest girl on the planet?"

Ro blinked several times, trying to contain her anger. She had gotten no sleep last night and predictably, she was in a horrible mood. "Did you take my phone out of my purse and then put it back at the end of the evening?" When he was quiet, she whispered, "Don't ever talk to me again."

"Hey!" He grabbed her arm as she walked away. "I'm talking to you."

"Let go of me!"

He dropped her arm. "You can be pissed all you want—"

"I wasn't asking for permission." Again, she started to walk away.

"Don't lay this all on me, Ro," he shouted to her back. "There were two people there."

When she looked over her shoulder, he was in front of his

locker. Missing the combination on the first try, he banged the door so hard he dented it. Everyone turned around. He banged it again and again. At that point, Ro had a choice. She could walk on, nursing her victimhood, or she could admit the truth, which she didn't do too often. That it was her own bad behavior that had led to this debacle.

Sighing, she did an about-face. JD was breathing hard as he slammed the door a final time. It was totally warped.

"You're going to have to pay for that." He didn't say anything, just continued to snort. She whispered, "JD, you got me drunk."

"You weren't drunk. You were tipsy and so was I." He turned to face her. "The only difference is I meant everything I said last night." He lowered his voice. "You know why those crappy teenage Hollywood movies always end with the good-looking jock getting fucked in the ass? Because in real life, the Tom Bradys get the Gisele Bündchens. They're all jealous! Everyone just loves it when I fuck up."

He looked straight into her eyes.

"You dumped me and you did it in front of my friends. It was a little embarrassing."

"I asked if we could talk privately. You told me to talk in front of your friends."

"Because you came with *him* and everyone knew what was gonna happen. I figured if I took it in public, it would be better." A pause. "Why'd you bring Vicks with you? Why didn't you just call me up or something? It wasn't any of his business."

"He insisted on coming. He said you had a temper."

"Like he could protect you if I unloaded?"

"He could shield me so I could run." Her attempt at humor fell flat. "I'm sorry if it embarrassed you."

"He wanted to see me suffer."

"He's not like that. He doesn't hate you. Well, maybe now he does. Now he hates both of us."

"Seriously." He shook his head. "Can we start over? Last night was all I ever wanted."

"That and football."

"What's better than love and football?"

"You mean sex and football."

"You don't understand dudes, Ro. With us, sex is love. If a dude is saying he loves you and isn't trying to jump your bones, he likes Broadway musicals and flower arranging. And let me tell you something about gay dudes. They bang more than anyone."

She placed her hands on his steely chest, and he brought her into a sweet embrace. It felt really good to be loved, but she knew he was the wrong person. "JD, I have to make this right with Vicks."

"Forget it, Ro. Once he writes you off, he's done."

"I have to try anyway." Her eyes became wet. "I love him, JD. I can't help it."

He dropped his arms. "You slept with me. He's not going to forgive you . . . unless you lie."

"If I lied to him, would you tell him the truth?"

He shook his head. "No. I won't blow your cover. He's not a rat, but neither am I." He took her hand and looked at the newest piece of jewelry dangling from her wrist. "He gave this to you?"

"More like he threw it on my couch when he left."

JD's jaw bulged out of his cheek. "Believe it or not, I am capable of guilt. I fucked him over. He doesn't deserve that, not after what he's gone through."

"But you did it anyway."

"And I'd probably do it again. You are so worth it." When she remained quiet, he sighed. "Go figure it out, Ro. But you know you're only prolonging your own misery."

Ro knew he was right. "You know, JD, I've had a boyfriend since I was thirteen. Maybe I need to learn how to live without constant attention from the opposite sex."

"That's not going to happen either. We live to be adored." He shrugged. "You don't need a boyfriend. But it's stupid for you not to have a boyfriend. I love you, baby. Every time I see you, my perfectly conditioned heart goes all aflutter." When she smiled, he said, "You at least like me, right?"

"There's part of me that loves you."

"Okay, that's good. I love you and you love me partly." Silence. "I'll make it right, Ro. Just you and me. I swear."

Ro stroked his face. "I'm going down to Albuquerque tonight, JD. I know Vicks will slam the door in my face, but I need to try."

"Fine. Once he rejects you, can we get back together?"

"JD, I need to think. I need to confront my demons."

"That's a very bad idea. All self-flagellation will do is make you sore."

"I know. But right now, I have to try even if I fall on my face." She paused. "Will you still love me with a crushed nose?"

"I will, but not as much." JD threw up his hands. "You know where to find me."

"I do now that I have my phone again. Whether I call you or not is up for grabs."

RO DITCHED CHEERLEADING and drove straight down to Albuquerque, finally steeling up the courage to listen to the messages that Ben left for her last night. The first few were superexcited—get dressed up, he'll meet her at her house at five. Then those were followed by annoyance in his voice. Then his voice was worried. *Where are you?* Finally, she hit the last one.

"Hi, it's me again. I just talked to Shannon Stork and . . . she said you went out to dinner with JD. So . . . I guess when you didn't hear from me right away . . . you made plans."

Click.

She had messed up royally. It had been pure self-destruction.

She had always been an attention hog. When Gretchen got sick, and everything was rightly focused on her, Ro was smart enough to keep her egotistical needs in check, but in truth, she was resentful. It was Gretchen this and Gretchen that, and it made Ro angry. Just because Gretchen was dying didn't mean Ro wasn't alive.

Stupid, stupid, stupid.

After Gretchen had passed, Griff, being Griff, faded into the background and everyone became focused on her. She was the star again and it felt good even though she knew it shouldn't. She never felt the so-called survivor's guilt.

And then Ben came along. When they started going together, Ro was deliriously happy. Still, there was one little itty-bitty feeling in her mind that Vicks would have liked Gretchen better than her. There wasn't a thieving, cheating, conniving bone in her sister's diseased body. Ro wondered if her outrageous behavior last night was just a clumsy way of admitting defeat to her sister's ghost.

As she drove, the weather picked up. Snow flurries dotted the window and the highway. It wasn't all that cold, but the sky held dark clouds. She wondered what she'd say to Ben's grandparents. They were nice folks but they would hate her if Ben told them what happened. But she doubted he would and she doubted he had. When she arrived at the house, the skies had become obscured by falling snow. Grandma Pauline was welcoming. Ben wasn't home yet, but she invited Ro to come in and wait.

Waiting and waiting and waiting until it became embarrassing. Ro tried calling him. She tried texting him. She tried e-mailing him. No answer. She made excuses, told his grandmother that her phone had died. Could she please call and ask where he was? The old woman couldn't reach him either. She peeked out the window. "I wish he'd get home soon."

"I'm sure he's fine."

"You can't drive home in this weather, Ro."

"I'll sleep over. Don't worry, Pauline. I'll wait up for him. Please go to bed."

She was unconvinced, but retreated into the bedroom. Ro continued to wait up, listening to the howling winds, shivering as the temperature dropped in the house. She wrapped a blanket around her shoulders, took off her shoes, and lay on the couch, hoping it would all just go away.

The door opened at eleven thirty. He wasn't surprised to see her, but he wasn't happy about it. He didn't speak. His hair was a fright, his face was pasty, and his eyes were underlined with big black circles. He looked at his watch. His eyes were somewhere past her face. She said, "Ben, can we please, please talk?"

He looked at his watch again. "No, we can't. It took me forty minutes to get home. I'm dog tired and I've got a big test and a full day of work tomorrow." He glanced at his watch a third time. "You can't go back. It's too late and it's horrible outside. The road conditions are ripe for fatalities. Just wait until morning, okay."

"At least you don't want me to die." She gave him a smile that immediately withered on her face.

He said, "You can have my room. I'll bunk in one of the other rooms. Do you need some pajamas or something?"

"You have sweats?"

"I do. Hold on." He disappeared into his room and she followed. He handed her a T-shirt and some pants. "Is this okay?"

Ro grabbed his arm. "Just give me a few minutes, okay?" When he didn't answer, she said, "Please? I love you." He refused to look at her. "Really. I do love you. Really and truly." When he still didn't answer, she pleaded, "Say something!"

"I'm tired, Ro." He gently extricated his arm from her grip. "Please . . . be considerate, okay?"

"Then I'm going home."

"No, you're not. Stop trying to bully me."

She sighed. "Okay. You're right. Can we talk in the morning?"

"Fine. We'll talk in the morning."

"What time in the morning?"

"I don't know, Dorothy. Let me go to sleep first."

"What time do you usually wake up?"

His eyes were heavy. "Around seven."

"So how about six? I'll wake you up."

"Fine. Good night."

But for her, it was anything but. The weather grew colder and louder. The winds were furious and some kind of tree kept banging against the window, waking her up at ten-minute intervals. Plus, the bed smelled of him. It made her weepy every time she was startled awake. Then the pillow-case got all wet. She finally gave up and turned on the light. It was around two A.M.

She'd have to deliver the best eat-shit speech of her life to pull this off because she certainly wasn't going to make it on looks. There were deep bags under her eyes and her complexion was a gluey mess that even makeup wasn't going to hide. She looked in his closet for something warm to put over the sweats. She found a terry robe, put it on, and glanced around the room, which was as spare as a monk's cell.

There was a bed, a desk, a desk chair and chest of drawers, and a file cabinet that was locked. That was probably where he kept his case notes about Ellen. Atop his desk were two framed pictures—one of Haley and one of Ellen. Once there had been four framed pictures; along with Ben's sisters, there had been one of the two of them and one of Ro alone looking gorgeous.

She picked up Ellen's photo.

Definitely the other girl in the relationship.

She put it down and very quietly began to search the drawers for the missing pictures.

Ben was compulsively neat. The top drawer was underwear and socks; middle one was T-shirts and jeans. The bottom drawer was empty except for two picture frames sans photos. She closed the drawer softly with a pretty good intuition about where the missing pictures were.

The top layer of the trash can was filled with papers scrawled with indecipherable equations. There were also tissues and what looked like Ben's discarded breakfast—a paper cup with coffee still in it, a breakfast bar wrapping, and orange peels.

Ro waded through the junk until she got to the bottom, where she extracted the photo of the two of them with an orange peel stuck on it. She removed the rind, and stared at the picture. It was taken at the Berkeley campus. They looked so happy—they had been happy—and that brought about a new batch of tears. She stowed that one in her purse. She left the solo picture of herself—completely intact—underneath the garbage.

Apparently, she hadn't even inspired enough emotion in him to be ripped to shreds.

WHEN HER CELL phone's alarm went off at five thirty, Ro felt like death warmed over. Shivering, she dressed as quickly as she could, as much for warmth as for anything else. Tiptoeing into the darkened hallway, she didn't hear a sound except some very loud snoring. Ben didn't snore, so it was probably his grandfather. She waited in the living room for him to get up. By six, the house began to stir. His grandmother found her sitting on the couch like an abandoned puppy. Pauline acted the cheerful doddering old lady, but her sharp eyes knew the score. She lit the fireplace and offered Ro breakfast—coffee and orange juice—while she waited for Ben. Running out of options, Ro finally addressed the gorilla in the living room.

"Do you know when Ben gets up?"

Pauline said, "He's usually up by now. Where did he sleep?"

Ro shrugged. "I don't know. I took his room."

Pauline went down the hallway and opened a few doors. Then she went outside. Then she came back for the report. "His car is gone. He must have left for school."

It was quarter to seven. Since Ro hadn't heard him get up, she surmised he left very early to avoid her. She felt her face go hot. "Okay." His grandmother was trying not to look at her with pity. It embarrassed both of them. Ro offered her finest phony smile. "Um . . . I should be heading back as well."

"They haven't plowed the roads yet."

"I've a four-wheel drive. I'm assuming the highway is okay."

"Are you sure you don't want to stay a little longer?"

"I'll be fine. Thanks." Ro hugged the old woman good-bye—trying not to cry—and made a quick exit. Outside, the air was frigid, the sky was deep blue, and the landscape was pure white. Her car was covered in snow, as were all the neighbors' cars. But unlike the other cars, her windshield had been scraped and cleared. She hated that he had done something nice for her. It made her feel even lower, if that were possible.

Sitting in her car, trying to calm down, she texted him. You can't avoid me forever.

Right as she put the car into drive, her phone beeped. She looked at the responding text.

Yes, I can.

CHAPTER 10

DESPITE HER BEST efforts, Ro couldn't find Vicks anywhere in school on Monday. Instead, she found Haley, who was, as always, with Lilly. She asked, "Do you know where your brother is?"

"He's in Albuquerque," Haley said. "He's sick."

"Okay." She couldn't look either little girl in the eye. "We broke up."

"I know." Haley's eyes went cold.

"I would like to talk to him, though. Could you please tell him to call me? I'm a little tired of talking to his voice mail."

No response.

Ro shifted the books in her hands and then left. Fuck it all. She had been forced to come here. *Stop being so self-critical. Have fun. You're only seventeen once.*

Thank God.

As the week dragged on, she became more and more cranky.

It was bad enough that Haley was avoiding her, but she was also avoiding Griff, who in turn became pouty and then just downright rude. Ro, usually the social butterfly, was on the outs with everyone. It was foreign territory and the worst part was she hadn't a clue how to rectify anything.

So she avoided everyone, isolating herself, eating lunch in an empty classroom, trying to pretend she didn't care about anyone or anything. She stopped wearing makeup and dressed in baggy clothes every day. She did wash her hair, which was about the only thing that distinguished her from a homeless person.

On Thursday, about fifteen minutes before the lunch bell was due to ring, Lilly found her reading a book.

"Can I sit down?"

Ro shrugged but didn't object.

"Are you back with JD?" she asked her.

"None of your business," Ro replied coolly.

"Okay." Lilly gave her a weak smile. "Sorry to bother you."

Ro regarded the girl's face. There wasn't an ounce of malice. "I'm sorry, Lilly. I'm edgy."

Lilly said, "Ro, if you really love him, don't give up so easily. He'll come around." She took a deep breath and let it out. "And if you don't really love him, it's for the best, so don't worry about it."

Ro lost it, tears rushing down her cheeks. "I cheated on him."

"I know."

"He *told* you?"

"No."

"Is JD shooting off his mouth?" She wiped her tears with the back of her hand.

"No, not at all." Lilly made a face. "It's not that hard to guess what happened. You made Ben happier than I've ever seen him. Conversely, now he's overtly miserable." A pause. "And JD's looking a lot happier."

"Oh God!" Ro buried her face in her hands. "Lilly, I feel horrible. I'd get down on my knees and beg if I thought it would do any good. He won't talk to me. He won't answer any of my pleading e-mails or texts. I don't expect him to forgive me. All I want is a chance to tell him how truly sorry I am—face-to-face. I just want to talk to him."

"If you know Ben at all, you know he's not much for conversation. His mind doesn't work like that. Don't *say* something to him, Ro. *Do* something for him."

Ro stared at her. "Like what?"

"You should know what's important to him." She got up. "I'm not saying it'll be easy. But that's what you do when you truly love someone, Ro. You do something . . . even if it hurts."

DO SOMETHING FOR *him. Even if it hurts.*

Ro doubted that Lilly meant B&D.

She had two choices. She could wallow in self-pity—something that she had mastered at a very young age—or she could follow some sage advice. Wallowing hadn't done her any good. Might as well try option two.

As soon as she got home from school, Ro went to her bedroom, locked the door, and turned off her phone—which, truth be told, hadn't been all that busy lately. She flipped open her laptop. In the Google search box, she typed "scientific conventions, Los Alamos" and the date of Ellen Vicksburg's abduction.

There was a lot on Ellen Vicksburg, lots on Los Alamos,

but nothing on scientific conventions. Then she typed in "scientist, physicist, chemist conventions," and the date of Ellen Vicksburg's abduction.

Nothing.

Ro tried other combinations: conventions before Ellen's abduction date, conventions after she was abducted. When that proved fruitless, she tried again but this time she used Katie Doogan's information. Then she tried Julia Rehnquist and Jamey Moore. She kept at it, passing on dinner and neglecting her homework. At twelve thirty, she gave up, bone-tired and nursing a massive headache from not eating. Eventually, she dropped into a deep and disturbing sleep.

THANK GOD IT was Friday and the friggin' week was almost over. Once again she ate lunch by herself. This time it was JD who found her. Ro really didn't want to talk to him or anyone else, but since he and Lilly were about the only two people who acknowledged her, she couldn't afford to be picky. JD looked good. As always, he had a killer body. But now that football had ended, he'd decided to grow out his sandy hair for baseball season. It softened his rock-jawed face.

"Can I sit?"

"Sure. Why the hell not?"

"Have you given any thought to what we talked about?"

"What did we talk about, JD?" He pointed to her then to himself. "Oh that."

"Yes that."

"I'm still working it out."

"What the fuck does that mean?"

"You told me to work it out," she sulked. "No need to get nasty."

"Ro, we've got like . . . what . . . four months left. It's not like you were engaged to the guy or anything." He was looking soulful. "How can I get you back with me? I'll do anything you want. I've already ditched Lisa and Shannon. I'm just waiting for you to come to your senses. I'm sure Vicks moved on as soon as he dumped you."

"I wouldn't know. He doesn't speak to me."

He softened his tone. "Look, Rosers, I know you like him. Vicks has a lot to like. But I know him way better than you do, and believe me when I tell you he isn't ever gonna come around. You can continue waiting for Godot or you could actually have a little fun." He leaned in. "Remember fun? Laughing, smiling . . . that kind of thing."

She shrugged.

JD said, "What can I do for you, Dorothy? You want to be cheerleading captain of the squad, I can make that happen. I can get Shannon to step down. Turn on a little charm and she'd do it. She'd do anything I want her to do. You want me to make that happen?"

"Thank you, JD, but I'm fine where I am."

"Well, how about we go out for dinner and a movie? I'll take you anywhere you want. We can even see those crappy teen movies where the jock always gets fucked in the ass."

"The jocks always do get fucked, don't they?"

"Always."

"Jocks and the snotty, pretty, popular girl . . . she gets fucked up too."

"And the obnoxious rich guy . . . which I hope to be one day."

She laughed. There was something so endearing about him, she almost caved. But for once she decided on integrity.

"Thanks for the invitation, but I'm going to pass. I still need thinking time."

He continued to stare at her. "I shoulda been like this when we were going together."

"Yeah, you shoulda."

"See, they're right. Jocks are fuckups."

"So are snotty, pretty, popular girls."

"Can we fuck up together?"

She stood and kissed his forehead. "I like you. You're a good guy. Keep trying. Even if it doesn't get you anywhere, begging is good for the soul."

AFTER SCHOOL, RO found Shannon. For the last ten days, she had turned ice cold. Everyone knew that Vicks and she were done, so the logical thing for Ro to do was to go back to JD. But when she hadn't hooked up with him, Shannon became furious. She wanted JD but couldn't have him. Ro could have him, but she didn't want him.

Ain't life just a bitch!

Shannon looked pert and fit. In a terse voice meant to instill fear, she said, "Practice. Four o'clock, sharp. We've got a game on Sunday."

"I'm not coming," Ro said.

Her eyes narrowed. "You know the rules, Ro. You miss practice three times, you're out."

"Make it two and we have a deal." A pause. Ro said, "Shannon, I'm quitting."

"You're *quitting*?"

"Yes, I am *quitting*."

Shannon got superhuffy. "You can't do that."

"Well, then how about this? I'll miss three times and then you'll throw me off the squad."

"You can't do that!"

"Uh, yes I can." Ro sighed. "Besides, cheering for baseball is boring."

"Who are we going to get for the game?"

"Have someone from JV move up. God, you must have a zillion people to take my place."

"Ro, the game is in two days!"

"That's not my problem, Shannon. Besides, you're the last person on earth I'd do a favor for. You told Vicks that I went out with JD. You're such a bitch!"

"He called me. He was frantic! He was gonna call the police! I felt bad for him . . . more than you did, obviously!" Tears welled up in Shannon's eyes. "And who the hell are you to be Miss Self-righteous? Playing with one guy while you're screwing the other?"

"You're one to talk about screwing someone else's boyfriend," Ro snapped back.

"He was my boyfriend first. I loved him. I still do. You don't give a damn about him."

"On the contrary, I do give a damn . . . a little damn, but I still care—"

"I hate you!" She stamped her foot. "You're selfish, egotistical, horrible, and a lousy cheerleader—"

"Now, that one really hurts!"

"Fuck you!" She marched off.

Ro wanted to laugh, but just couldn't. Thinking about her words . . .

He was frantic! I felt bad for him.

She put on sunglasses and, holding her head up high, she walked to her car. There was only so much self-loathing a person could take without cracking. She was at the tipping point, but wasn't yet ready to fall over the edge.

TGIF. AS USUAL, Griff refused to talk to her. They walked inside the house and he went straight to his room, making a point of slamming the door. Mom was on the couch crocheting and jumped at the sound. "What is wrong with him?"

Ro shrugged innocently. "I quit cheerleading."

"You did?" Mom put her hook down. Her face registered shock. "Why?"

"Because it's silly. Because I don't want to do it anymore."

"Ro, what's going on? Why is Griffen so moody?"

"Nothing's going on. It's the same old, same old. Life sucks." Ro kissed her mother's cheek. "Don't worry about it. It'll all work out. And if it doesn't, so what?" Her mother's eyes were moist. "Mom, let's wake up early and have breakfast together tomorrow. Just the two of us."

"Is there something you need to tell me?" She took her daughter's hand. "If you need to say something to me, don't be afraid."

"I'm not pregnant. I just want to spend some time with you." The woman was visibly relieved. God, even her mom thought her a skank. "Tomorrow morning, we've got a date. Mark it down."

Ro went to her room and closed the door. She opened her laptop and began looking for any scientific conventions around the time of Ellen Vicksburg's abduction, no matter where they were. After thirty minutes of finding basically nothing, she stopped trying.

She was now out of Vicks's life. Which meant he was probably at his computer continuing where he had left off, mining the same fields that she was. Anyone could type in names and dates and occupations and try to find a link. This guy—this monster—was crafty. Vicks had called him a fly on the wall—a sneaky bastard who had gotten away with at least three murders, probably four.

If Ro was going to make any headway, she needed to do some divergent thinking.

Her dad worked for the government all his life. And he traveled a lot. He was a suit-and-tie guy, a prominent man, and his hotel of choice—or rather, what the government would pay for—was usually some kind of business establishment like a Marriott or Hilton.

If a scientist was traveling on the government's dime, Ro figured that maybe his place would be a step below a Marriott. One of those Executive Inn–type chains, but even those varied from city to city.

She turned back to her laptop. Ten minutes later, she had printed out a list of motels and hotels in the area, opting for places with two and a half stars or better, with room service, and within ten miles of the labs.

Then she picked up her cell and began to punch in numbers. When someone at the desk answered, Ro said, "Hi, this is Wanda Crumb. I'm calling for Dr. Kesley's lab in Berkeley, California. He's coming to the area and he was wondering if you give a professional discount to scientists who work at Los Alamos . . . no? . . . thank you very much."

Cross one off the list.

"Hi, this is Belinda Littlebee. I'm calling on behalf of Dr. Marina's lab in Oak Ridge, Tennessee. She's coming into the area and she was wondering if you give a professional discount to scientists working at Los Alamos . . . okay, thank you."

Number two was nixed.

So were three through six and then seven and then eight. That took care of all those Executive Inn types of motels. Her next decision was whether to go up or down in price. Up was easier because those places were more accessible. She tried the Marriott.

"Hi, this is Samantha Dooling. I'm calling for Dr. Outbottle's laboratory in Brookhaven, New York. He's coming into the area and he was wondering if you give a professional discount to scientists working at Los Ala—okay, thank you."

She crossed off the Marriott, then the Hyatt, and then the Hilton, which left Ro with the big tourist hotels that the government wouldn't pay for, and small inns that were out of the way. After she eliminated all of those, there was nothing left except seedy motels on a high-crime strip and one independent hotel called the Jackson Lodge. It was outside River Remez, about fifteen miles from Los Alamos, but freeway close. In a last-ditch effort, she called up the front desk.

"Hi, this is Nambia Allenson. I'm calling for Dr. Tony Beetle's lab in Chicago at the Fermi Institute. Dr. Beetle was invited to speak at Los Alamos and he's wondering if you give any professional discounts to scientist—oh, you do?" Ro was shocked. "Uh, great. How much? Thirty percent . . . great. Thank you . . . no, I can't make a reservation until I run this by my boss. Have to get clearance by the brass and all that kind of stuff, you know. So I'll have to get back to you."

She hung up, her heart beating out of her chest. Now what?

Eighteen was the magic age for so many things. Unfortunately, her birthday was still three weeks away. And there wasn't a whole lot of time left. Each day was crucial. She sat on her bed and thought for a long time. She wasn't proud of her solution, but it *was* a solution.

After Gretchen died, her room, like Ellen Vicksburg's room, had become a shrine: completely untouched, from the junk in her desk drawer to the out-of-date fashions in her closet. When the family was uprooted to New Mexico, Ro didn't want to leave Gretchen behind. So she took pieces of her—a birth certificate, a Social Security card, a picture student ID, a library card—stuff she knew her mother wouldn't miss, because after Gretchen's death their mom never went into her room. Often, Ro had looked at her sister's ID. When she did, it was as if Gretchen was talking to her.

Yes, at one time I did exist.

Ro put the birth certificate, the Social Security card, and the picture ID in her purse. Their stats were basically the same—blond hair, blue eyes, five six, and around a hundred and twenty pounds. Although Ro was prettier, they did resemble each other. Her friends used to joke that Gretchen looked like Ro on a bad day.

After she died, they didn't joke anymore.

She took off her ratty pajamas and donned a soft, gray sweater with a deep V in the front. She wiggled into a black pencil skirt. Out came her four-inch heels. She took time with her makeup and appraised herself in the mirror.

Not bad at all. She grabbed her coat, a scarf, and a hat. It was freezing outside.

In the hallway, her mother was attempting to talk to Griff. Mom cornered her. This time she wouldn't take no for an answer. "What's going on with him, Dorothy?"

"Griff's mad at me because Ben and I had a falling-out and he likes Ben."

"Oh dear. Do you want me to call up Laura?"

"No, Mom, don't get involved. It'll work out."

"Why is there always so much conflict?"

"I don't know, but unlike the world's situation, ours will resolve." She kissed her mom's cheek and checked her watch. "I gotta go. Don't wait up."

She hurried out the door. Her first stop was a rush to the DMV before it closed. That little bit of bureaucracy took well over an hour, but when she got out, she had now become Gretchen Majors.

According to her new driver's license, she was four months shy of twenty.

Not the best solution, but a solution.

She couldn't order a drink.

But she could get a job.

CHAPTER 11

THE JACKSON LODGE fell somewhere between a motel and a hotel—definitely not a dive like the motel Ro had stayed in at Berkeley, but modest compared to the hotels on the Plaza. Like almost all of Santa Fe, it was adobe style with vigas and latillas on the ceiling and Saltillo tiles covered with knockoff Navajo rugs on the floor. The front desk was sided in wood with turquoise diamond inserts. Behind the counter, next to the official certificates of hotel ratings, there were several wide-angle photographs of the Sangres along with a rack of flyers advertising what to do in Santa Fe, Taos, and Albuquerque—things that Ro had heard about but never got around to doing. There was the Sandia tram and casino, Camel Rock Casino, Buffalo Thunder, the floating staircase at the Loretto, Taos Pueblo, and rafting on the Rio Grande, which probably wasn't too big of an activity right now seeing as it was around fifteen degrees outside.

The desk was manned by a brown-uniformed girl who looked just a few years older than Ro. She was dark complexioned with a round face and big brown eyes. Her name was Pearl.

Ro put on her friendliest smile. "Hello."

"Hi, how can I help you?"

"I'm actually looking for a job."

She stared at Ro. "Uh . . . did you see an ad or something?"

"No, actually, I'm just doing it the hard way. Pounding the pavement." Ro smiled again. "I mean, I'm sure you get busy and could use some extra hands."

Pearl looked around. There wasn't a person in sight. "Uh, it's been pretty quiet."

Ro sighed. "Do you have an application that I could fill out?"

"Uh, maybe I should get the manager."

"Sure."

She disappeared behind a wall. A few minutes later she returned with a guy—also in a brown uniform—in tow. He was older, midtwenties, and his name tag said he was Tomas. He had a long face and acne on his cheeks. His brown eyes gave Ro the quick once-over. This was a very good sign.

"Hi," she told him. "I'm looking for work."

"Uh . . . I don't think we have any jobs right now. Sorry."

"C'mon," she told him. "I need money."

"Sorry. Unless you're interested in housekeeping."

"You mean a maid?"

"We call it housekeeping. I don't think we need anyone, but if we do, that's your best option."

Ro took the application and looked around. There was an open café with a bar that held around ten empty tables. The place was devoid of patrons as well as staff. "How about a waitress?" She pointed to the café. "I don't see anyone on the floor."

"There aren't any customers."

"Surely you have an occasional person wanting a cup of coffee . . . or a drink?"

"The bartender handles that."

"I don't see a bartender."

"He's in the back."

"You have an answer for everything, Tomas." She leaned over the desk, showing him cleavage. "Why don't we do this? It's a Friday night. It's bound to get a little busy. Let me waitress for tonight. I'll just work for tips. See what happens."

"I can't hire you. I'm not in a position to do that."

"You're not hiring me. You're giving me a break." She locked eyes with him. "Please?"

His eyes went to the right place then back to her face. "I suppose if it's okay with Salvador, it's okay with me." He was mystified. "You know we don't get a lot of bar business, especially at this time of year."

"You have clients in the hotel?"

"Yeah."

"Male clients?"

"Yeah, mostly."

She gave him a dazzling smile. "I can get you bar business."

Tomas blushed. "Maybe. You have to be nineteen to serve liquor, you know."

Out popped her brand-new temporary ID card. She grinned and said, "Thank you for giving me a chance." A pause. "Salvador's the bartender, not the country, right?"

"That's El Salvador."

"Just checking to see if you were listening." She went over to the café. The man she assumed to be Salvador was puttering behind the counter. She explained the situation to him.

"Less work for you," she told him.

He stared at her boobs. "Yeah . . ."

"So it's okay?"

His eyes finally lifted from the spot. "Uh, do you see anyone here?"

"No. But it's only five o'clock."

"The point is . . . what's your name?"

"Ro—Gretchen." She stuck out her hand. "Gretchen Majors."

He took her hand. His was sweaty. "I don't make a lot of money. Tips are like all I get when I get something . . . you sense me?"

"I do. How much do you get in tips per night?"

His mind started whirring. "Like a hundred bucks."

"Salvador, let's be reasonable."

"Fifty."

"I said *reasonable*."

"Fifty bucks."

"You probably get a third that much, but I'll assume you get half. Twenty-five, say, even thirty a night. I'll give you the first thirty dollars I make and anything after that is mine."

"No way. Those tips are mine." He was still staring at her. "Unless you pay me in another way."

"Dream on, handsome. We'll split it fifty-fifty. That's the most I'm going to do. Believe me, you'll be happy you agreed to it. I'm a lot sexier than you are."

"That's true."

"Fifty-fifty."

"And I get the first thirty dollars up front?"

"Yes. That's probably more money in tips than you've ever made. Deal?"

"Sure."

"You won't regret it. I'll make it worth it . . . monetarily. That means moneywise."

"I know what 'monetarily' means. I'm not dumb."

"Of course. I'm a little tense. I need this job."

"Fine. I mean, it's only one night. Then you're out."

"You don't really mean that, do you?"

"Maybe I'll give you a couple of nights because you're cute."

"Thank you. Do you have a tray I can carry so people can tell I'm a cocktail waitress?"

"No."

"Do you have a menu? Food and drink go together, you know."

He pointed to the bar countertop. Behind a plastic sandwich-board easel was a list of ready-made sandwiches and snacks—peanuts, packaged cheese and crackers, potato chips, corn chips, corn snacks, M&M's, Oreos, and a jar of pickles that were an unnatural shade of emerald green. Together with the olives and pearl onions for the martinis, the wedges of lemons, limes, and oranges, plus a jar of maraschino cherries, that was it for the grub in the area. "I think your bar food could use a little updating."

"Tell it to the boss."

"Do the guests get any kind of edibles for free?"

"Ice."

"How much are the peanuts?"

"A dollar each."

Ro checked her purse. "Give me twenty packets. Also, give me twenty shot glasses." Salvador looked at her. "Trust me. I know what I'm doing."

He handed her the plastic bags of peanuts. She distributed half of them in the shot glasses, put one glass on each of the ten tables, then put three on the bar top. She kept the rest behind the bar for refills. "Give me some of the martini olives."

He was skeptical.

"I'll only put them on the bar, okay?"

He raised his eyebrows. "If the boss sees me doing this, I'm dead."

"Who's the boss?"

"Elaine. She's not here."

"How often does she come around?"

"Not often." He paused, then gave her the tub of martini olives. "Do what you want."

"You're a believer." She put a few of them in shot glasses on the bar counter. It was five in the afternoon. "Now leave the rest to me, okay?" As three men came off the elevator, Ro said to Salvador, "Watch and learn, amigo.

"Hey, guys, where are you going?" They turned to Ro, clearly baffled. She said, "It's cold outside. C'mon. Have a seat. Keep it in-house, you know." She smiled. "Please?"

"We're going to dinner," one of them said. "Do you serve dinner?"

"No, but I serve happy hour. Have a cocktail first. That and my gorgeous face will put you all in a good mood."

They smiled, shrugged, and sat down. One of them started popping peanuts into his mouth. Salt was good for business. They ordered a whiskey straight up, a glass of red wine, and a martini with an olive. Ro took the order by memory and related it to Sal. "I'm going to need a pad and pencil."

He handed her what she had asked for. The next two men started toward the door, but when they saw the trio already sitting at a table, they stopped and discussed. Ro gave them her most blinding smile, which clinched the deal. She showed them to a table and immediatcly took their order before they could change their minds. "Any snacks before dinner?"

"What do you have?" asked a suit.

"Not much, I'm afraid. How about if I buy you some olives and you buy the martinis."

The suit laughed. "Sure."

Ro gave the second order of the night to Sal. This time he was smiling. Within an hour, five tables were filled, the guests drinking and snacking. Then it went dry for a couple of hours. When dinnertime was over, around eight, the suits started re-turning. Ro went to work again—smiling and wiggling. By nine, it was packed. Her only problem was she had never heard of half the drinks.

She went up to Sal. "I need a whiskey sour and a—God, I'll feel like I'm saying something racist—a Negro something." She looked at him pleadingly. "Help me out, soldier."

"A negroni?"

"Yeah, that's it."

"You don't know a lot about drinks, do you."

"No, I do not."

"I figured you for a boozer. Figured that's why you wanted to work at a bar. Freebies."

"Good guess, but wrong. I'm not a boozer. It does strange things to my judgment and it's too many calories."

"Pot?"

"Only on occasion. Basically, my downfall is hubris. But that's for another day. I also need another order of olives and nuts."

"We're running out."

She grinned. "Told you."

Sal handed her the drinks. "This one's the sour, the pink one is the negroni. The color comes from Campari. That's an Italian liqueur."

"Sal, you are not only knowledgeable, you are a savior. Thank you."

By the end of the evening, Salvador was begging Tomas to hire her on. They each had fifty-six dollars in their pockets and would have had more if the bar hadn't run out of snacks. He said, "We did twenty times the usual business, Tom. It's a no-brainer."

"I need to check with Elaine."

"If you don't hire me tonight, I'm moving on," Ro told him. "I need money and I need job security."

Tomas was still suspicious. But peer pressure prevailed and he handed her an application. "This all depends on what Elaine says."

"Fine. Talk to Elaine." She filled out all the boxes as she talked. "Tell her I'm not only good for business, but I'll be good for repeat business." She smiled. "And I'm happy to help out wherever I'm needed—like if you guys need a few minutes to go to the bathroom or talk to your girlfriend or something. I'll be happy to do desk duty for you."

"You ever work hotel management?" Tomas asked.

"In New York," she lied. "How about this?" She leaned over and looked sincerely into Tomas's eyes. "I'll come in early tomorrow and you can give me a tutorial on the computer . . . how your hotel works. I pick things up very quickly."

"Only if Elaine says okay."

"Tell her I'll work minimum wage and for tips." She handed him back the application. "Good night."

She left without looking back, walking straight to her car parked in a very dark lot. When Salvador spoke, she jumped.

"Sorry to scare you."

"No prob. Thanks for helping me out. I really appreciate it. I need the money."

He stared at her. "You know you could do way better somewhere else."

"I could." He was not as dumb as she thought. "Honestly, I want to work behind the desk. That's the goal. And I thought this was a good place to start. It's close to home."

"Okay." His eyes cased her body. "I think there's more to your story, but I'll buy it. Want to go out for a drink at a real bar? My treat."

"You saw my ID. I'm nineteen."

"I'll drink, you can have soda."

"I'm zonked. I've got some studying to do. I'm going home to bed."

"JC?"

"Pardon?"

"Junior college."

"Yeah, junior college. Of course I go to junior college." She gave his arm a light punch. "I'm nineteen. And my mom's waiting up for me. I really gotta go."

"You live at home?"

"Yes, I do, Salvador."

"So do I. I live with my mom. My old man split like ten years ago."

"The louse."

"Yeah, he's a real son of a bitch. But he does send me money when I ask."

"Everyone has a bit of redemption."

"C'mon. Let's grab a cup of coffee. I think you know this already, but you're really cute."

"Thank you for the compliment. And you're a cute guy, Salvador. But right now, I'm a little heavy in the boy department." He looked confused and rightly so. "I have two boy-friends. A third would be a little ridiculous."

"Two boyfriends?"

"Yes. One is currently talking to me and the other is not."

"Oh . . . what happened?"

"I started with boyfriend number one. Then I dumped him for boyfriend number two. I like the second one a lot better than the first. But then I cheated on two with one and now two isn't talking to me."

"You cheated on your second boyfriend with your ex?"

"Yes." The man was able to follow a rather circuitous train of thought. "Exactly."

"Cheating with your ex doesn't count."

"Now, that's a very enlightened attitude, Salvador. Unfor-tunately, boyfriend two didn't see it that way."

"So really you have only one boyfriend . . . number one."

"Sort of. We're not going together anymore."

"So, you really don't have any boyfriend. Why won't you go out with me?"

"Because boyfriend one really wants me back and I'm just too damn lazy to cultivate yet another personality."

"Are they big guys?" Salvador flexed his muscles. "Could I take them down?"

"Number two is thin and wiry." She thought of Ben picking up Weekly and tossing him in the trash cans. "When he gets riled, he's pretty strong. Number one is a big, big guy. He plays football. He's kind of a take-no-prisoners guy."

"He was in prison?"

She patted Salvador's cheek. "I'll see you tomorrow night. Thanks for your help."

"We could make beautiful music together, Gretchen."

She winced at the sound of her sister's name. "I don't know about music, Salvador. For the here and now, let's just settle on making some decent tips."

CHAPTER 12

THE NEXT DAY, Ro not only got the job, she got the tutorial. How to check people in, how to check them out, how to assign them a room, how to move them if they're unhappy in their rooms, the smoking and nonsmoking rooms, adjoining rooms, discounts for repeat customers, corporate discounts, and on and on.

"Do you get a lot of repeat customers?"

"Most of them are repeats," Tomas said. "We give good discounts."

"Yeah, right." Her heart started racing. "Like if one of the repeats wants a certain room, do you have a way to access the back files to see what room they had?"

"Absolutely."

"How do you do that?"

Tomas looked at his watch. "We've been at this for a while. We'll do it another time. If you ever get to work the desk."

"I can dream," Ro said. "How far do the files go back?"

"Since they were computerized—probably twenty-five, thirty years ago."

"Okay. That means you have a lot of names in the computer." Tomas looked at her and laughed. She laughed too. "Dumb question." She saw a suit who'd patronized the bar yesterday looking for her. "I'd better run."

"Congrats on getting the job."

"With your help, Tomas."

"I did put in a good word for you."

"I appreciate it." She winked at him.

He winked back, but he didn't have the gesture quite down. It came off like a tic. It was going to be a long haul, but she was in for the long haul.

WORKING HARD AND late, Ro now understood sleep. The job got her home around eleven thirty. With homework and unwinding time, she went to bed around one and woke up at seven to go to school. She became chronically sleep-deprived and that meant she dozed whenever she had a spare moment. More than once, someone shook her shoulder in calculus class. When her teachers asked, she told them she was fine, although everyone knew she was lying.

Her biggest nap was during lunch. She rarely ate because snoozing was much more satisfying. As a result, she lost a few pounds, which allowed her to indulge in cookies and potato chips from the Jackson stash. Her complexion went to seed but that's why makeup was invented. She took catnaps seriously, so she tried not to be annoyed when JD woke her up one lunch period.

"Hey, babe."

She picked her head up and rubbed her eyes. "What time is it?"

"We've got ten minutes more of lunch until the bell rings. It took me a while to find you. Mind if I eat my lunch?"

"No, go ahead." She reached into her knapsack and pulled out a tuna fish on soggy rye, then put it back in the paper bag without eating it. "How are you?"

"I'd be a lot better if you wouldn't avoid me."

JD's bites were bigger than her head. He had two sandwiches, which he was wolfing down in record time. "I'm not avoiding you, JD. I'm just tired."

"Yeah, about that. Why are you so tired?"

"I got a job. I work late."

He stared at me. "You got a *job*?"

"Yep."

"Why?"

"Why not?"

"How about because you don't need one." He regarded her face. "What kind of a job?"

"Something low level and minimum wage that is commensurate with my skill level."

"You're punishing yourself, right?" She didn't answer. "You know that you and Vicks wouldn't have lasted more than a few months anyway. It was doomed from the start."

She was too tired to argue Vicks's merits. They were getting harder for her to remember. "Whatever."

JD said, "Quit the job and come back to your former life."

"Well, it's this way, JD." She yawned. "As popular as I was last semester, that's as unpopular as I am this semester."

"That's ridiculous. Go back on the cheerleading squad. I miss you."

"Not going to happen. Shannon hates me. She thought that once we broke up, she'd be your girl again. It was bad enough to lose you to me. But now that we're not even dating and you're still not coming around, she's really furious. And of course, that's all my fault. And where Shannon goes, so do Chelsea and Lisa. So now *they* hate me. And Weekly hates me because secretly he'd like to bang me. But he's too scared to stand up to you, so he devotes his life to making my life miserable. And Mark Salinez . . . he doesn't take no for an answer."

"I'll beat him up."

"JD, you can't just beat people up because they're pushy. Leave Mark alone. He's harmless."

"Whatever you want, baby. I'm here to protect and serve."

"Since I'm not Miss Popular anymore, I thought at least I could sit with my brother at lunch. But Haley hates me right now. So, by extension, Griff is totally pissed off and hates me. Worse still, Haley is being a bitch to him. And Vicks, of course, won't even answer my phone calls. You are the only one who's still nice to me. You and Lilly. I swear that girl is from a different planet."

"Ro, let me take you out to dinner. We could both use a little R and R."

"I'm working, JD."

"What are you doing? Like a counter girl at DQ?"

"O ye of little faith!"

"I'm just saying that for anything decent you have to be over eighteen."

"And so says my driver's license."

"You got a fake ID?"

"What's the dif?" She smiled "You're not going to rat me out, so I'm safe for the moment."

"Just quit!"

"Ah, you care." She kissed his lips gently. "I do appreciate this little tête-à-tête. If I wasn't so tired, I'd be happy to go out to dinner with you. But between sleep and food, food doesn't stand a chance."

JD sat back in his chair. "This is *killing* me! I mean, all this time we could be together before graduation. I know you don't worship me, but c'mon. We had a lot of fun together."

"We did have fun." She rubbed her eyes. "Give me a little more time. Maybe by then I'll be free of my obligations and we can resume where we left off."

"What *obligations*?"

"You wouldn't understand." She stood up. "It's something I need to do."

IT WAS THE first weekend in nearly three weeks that Ben had decided to come home. It was good to be missed. His mother was happy to see him and although he saw his father in Albuquerque at least once a week, his dad seemed in a particularly jovial mood. Even Haley seemed to welcome his presence. She and Lilly chatted away about the vagaries and vicissitudes of Remez High: who was popular, who was not, who was going with whom, what movies they saw, what TV shows they were watching. Ben noticed that Griffen Majors wasn't mentioned at all. He didn't comment on it, but he filed it away. By eleven in the evening, he was zonked. He slept the sleep of the dead and woke up a little before seven in the morning. The house was quiet and he was alone.

Early morning was his favorite time of day. Everything was new and fresh and filled with promise that rarely was realized.

But hope counted for something and so did coffee. He started a pot, turned off the alarm, and went out to the front yard to grab the *Journal* and the *New Mexican*. He peeled off the Santa Fe section from the *Journal* and read the Albuquerque news first. It was almost as if New Mexico's most populated city was becoming his new home base.

It was a small paper and reading it cover to cover took all of ten minutes.

He moved on to the local news in the Santa Fe section and grimaced as he read the headlines. Then he looked at the *New Mexican*, where he reread the same story. Both papers showed a picture. Some idiot had graffitied the Palace of the Governors. The place had been constructed in the seventeenth century and was the oldest government building in the country still in use. It was not only a historical landmark, but an American Treasure. And some asshole decided it would be fun to spray-paint black bull's-eyes all over the dun adobe walls. There was going to be a community pancake breakfast starting at eight for anyone who was willing to volunteer their time to cover up the desecration.

Ben checked his watch. It was seven thirty. He got up from the breakfast bar just as his father came out. His dad greeted him. "God bless you. You made coffee."

"Help yourself."

"Where are you going?"

"Getting dressed. Might as well do something productive." Ben showed his father the article.

The old man made a face. "That's terrible. I can maybe come for a couple of hours. But then I have stuff to do."

"Don't bother. I'm sure it'll be a big turnout. Especially with free pancakes."

"Stupid kids." He poured himself a cup of coffee. "Probably teenaged boys with inadequate penile size."

Ben laughed. "Since when have you become Freudian?"

"The Austrian does have a time and place." His dad smiled. "Good to see you doing something productive."

"You mean, good to see you not moping around." Ben kissed the top of his father's head. "Thanks, Dad, for not throwing in the towel . . . on me, I mean."

"Why in the world would I do that?" He went back to his paper. "Ruin my favorite source of recreation."

"Which is?"

"Embarrassing you and your sister. I just love to watch you young'uns squirm."

PAINT CANS WERE spread out on Palace, the street closed off between Washington and Grant. The back wall of the portico of the Palace of the Governors—where the Indians set up to display their wares—was pocked with black spray-painted bull's-eyes, as was the second story of the building. The asshole had had a busy night.

Stations were set up in the blocked-off street while volunteers served piles of pancakes and syrup, orange juice, and lots and lots of coffee. The Palace abutted the grassy plains of the plaza, which hummed with people ready, willing, and able to make amends for some tagger's indiscretions. A crowd of around fifty ate while awaiting assignments. Ladders were being set up against the building. There was a sign-up sheet, a disclaimer sheet, and loads of aprons along with water buckets and paintbrushes. The tagging was all over the building, but within an hour a lot of the damage was masked by adobe-colored hues.

Ben was concentrating on his area when he heard a familiar voice say hello.

"How's it going?" Shanks asked. "Haven't seen you for a while." When the boy shrugged, he said, "Problems?"

"No problems," Ben said. "There would be problems if she was still around, but she's no longer in the picture."

"The pretty blonde?"

"Yep," Ben said. "The pretty blonde."

"I'm sorry."

"So am I," Ben said. "You recognize the tag, Sam?"

"No, I don't. It's not associated with any of the local gangs."

"I can believe that. Most of the locals, including the gangs, have more respect for their heritage. Asshole kid."

"Kid or kids?"

"I think it was done by a single hand. Look at the paint. Each one is identical in shape and size . . . like a signature, like he's trying real hard to preserve his identity because he's lost it somewhere. Precise little booger."

"Studying psychology in school?"

"Armchair psychology."

"Sounds pretty good to me. Are you sure you don't want to join the academy?"

Ben smiled and kept painting.

Shanks said, "We got a final on Katie Doogan's DNA." Ben immediately stopped painting and looked at him with anticipation. "It took a long time because there wasn't very much biological evidence that we could test. Fraction of a fraction, but we did get a profile back, Ben. You were right. It's a match for your sister."

Ben froze, couldn't talk.

Shanks went on. "I found out late last night. I've been

spending the last few hours trying to figure out a way to tell you and your parents. Then I saw you here." He looked down. "Sorry to spring this on you, son. I guess I should have been more diplomatic."

"It's fine, Sam. It's . . . there's no easy way." He turned to Shanks. "What about Jamey Moore?"

"Now that we have three matches—Ellen, Julia Rehnquist, and Katie Doogan—Tennessee will go through with the request for DNA comparison. Ortiz and I are on it. This is the break we've all been waiting for. We can coordinate—several departments looking at the same thing."

"How are we going to find him?"

"You mean how are the police going to find him?" When Ben didn't respond, Shanks said, "The police are doing everything they can—every legal maneuver and then some. Serial killers are big news. We've got manpower now. We're going to find the son of a bitch, Ben. I promise you."

Shanks put a hand on the kid's shoulder.

"Ben, I'll call you when I have something to report. I promise."

"Thanks, Sam. Thanks for . . ." Ben didn't finish.

Shanks said, "You're one of a kind, Ben. Don't ever change. You just got to find work that makes the best of your . . . unique personality."

"I think that's a compliment."

"It is." Shanks looked at the building, covered with tags and splotches of paint. "I've got to get back to the station house. Feel free to drop in anytime. And I'm sure you'll take me up on that one."

"Most likely I will."

After Sam left, Ben kept painting. Almost all the desecration had been covered up, but there were a few tags left at the top of the building. Ben stared at a tag, squinting into the sun, his forehead suddenly furrowing.

It was like a figure-ground puzzle. Once he had seen it, it was amazing that he had missed it in the first place.

The tags weren't bull's-eyes. The tags were initials.

It was as clear as a bell: an *M* on top of a *G*.

CHAPTER 13

WHEN RO OPENED the door, Ben didn't bother to hide his anger. He was seething, but it wasn't directed at her.

He stepped over the threshold. "I need to see Griffen."

"He's in his room—"

"Thanks." Ben moved past her and knocked on Griffen's door. When the boy opened up, Ben walked inside and closed the door in Ro's face. He locked the door. The kid was fair-complexioned. Anything embarrassing set him off. This time the blush spread across his cheeks like a runaway paint spill.

"What's up?" Griffen said.

Without answering, Ben started searching through the kid's closet. Griffen tried to muster up anger. But it came across as something else. He was wide-eyed . . . scared. "What are you doing?"

"Looking for spray-paint cans." Ben started moving coats

to the side to get to some hidden shelving. "If I'm wrong, a thousand apologies. Okay if I hunt around?"

"No, it's not okay. Get out."

The kid wasn't even smart enough to throw away the cans he didn't use. Ben held up one of them and turned on him. "I just spent one of my few free mornings painting a national landmark that some asshole had the temerity to tag. And that pissed me off."

Griffen batted the can away from Ben. "Get the fuck *out* of here!"

"Aren't you a hotshot? Doing stuff in the dead of night where no one can see you. You want to be a criminal, at least have the balls to do it in daylight."

"You're talking to me about balls? You're a fucking wimp who can't even keep a girlfriend. Get the *fuck* out of my life!"

"Fine, Griff. This wimp will be happy to get the fuck out of your life when you man up and tell the police what you did. Because if you don't, this wimp is going to haul your ass down to the police."

Griffen charged at him. Ben easily deflected the snorting little bull and took him down in a headlock. He said, "Now that was stupid!"

"Let go of me!" Griffen screamed while writhing in his grip. "Let *go* of me!"

Ro was knocking hard on the door. "What's going on!"

"Nothing," Ben said. "We're fine."

Ro started banging. "Let me in! Ben, open the door!" When neither of them moved to help her out, she said, "If you don't open the door right now, I'm going to call the police."

Ben shouted out, "So call the police! That's what we both want, right, Griff?"

Griff shouted out. "Go away, Ro!"

"Griffen!" She banged again. "Open *up*!"

"Go away and leave me the fuck alone, Ro. I hate you!"

The knocking stopped. Ben still had him in a hold. The kid was clawing his arm. He was drawing blood. "Want to know how to get out of it?"

"Let *go* of me!" Griffen's eyes were wet. "You're *choking* me."

"If you're able to talk, you're not choking. And stop pawing me. It hurts!" Griff was still struggling. "Will you relax? This wimp is going to teach you something!" Ben shifted the boy's position until he had him in a side headlock. "It's a different move if it's from behind and that involves poking my eyes. I don't trust you right now!"

"Fuck off!"

"I'll teach you how to get out of this hold if you promise you won't take my head off." The boy was still struggling. "Relax, Griff. I'm not going to let go. Right now, I'm still stronger than you."

"You're a fucking bully."

"And you're a coward! That's what taggers are. They're cowards!"

Griffen went silent. Ben saw the moisture in the boy's eyes but he kept on going. "You spray-painted a registered American Treasure. Now you've got a choice, Griff. You can learn something or you can go to the police. And, buddy, this wimp has no problem taking you down."

Finally, Griff stopped struggling. It was probably the first time the kid had ever been in hand-to-hand combat. They made them soft in the burbs.

Ben said, "Okay. This is what you do. Are you listening?" When he didn't get an answer, he repeated, "Are you listening?"

"Yes, I'm fucking listening."

"Will you please cool it with the profanity? It's lost its potency."

Ro was back at the door. "What's going on?" She knocked harder. "I'm going to call the police."

Griffen said, "Just go away, Ro. We're fine!"

"Open the door!"

Ben let Griff go and opened the door. "See? He's still alive."

Ro was in tears. "What *happened*?"

"Nothing!" Griff slammed the door in her face.

"That wasn't nice."

"I hate her," the kid muttered.

"She's your only sibling. Stop talking like that."

"She ruined *everything*!"

Ben shrugged. "She's your sister and she'll be in your life long after I've left it. She's family and I'm not."

"Haley hates me."

"I figured she must be giving you a hard time. When we talked last night, your name didn't come up." When Griffen didn't answer, Ben said, "I'll talk to her."

"Don't."

"You're right. I don't have to fight your battles. But she doesn't need to fight mine either." No one spoke. Ben finally said, "How about if I take you and Haley and Lilly out to dinner tonight? We can even include Ezra, although I don't know how much Lilly likes being fixed up with him."

"Ezra really likes her." Griff sat on the bed. "He's pissed at me too."

"Why?"

"Because now that Haley isn't talking to me, everything just kinda fell apart."

"There are other girls in the school, you know. You're a good-looking guy."

Griffen shrugged. "I know."

"I'm one to talk about a love life. Stand up." When he did, Ben grabbed him in a headlock. "You ready to learn something?" When Griffen didn't answer, he said, "You hurt me, you're dead."

"I'm not going to hurt you."

"Okay." Ben secured his balance. "First off, twist your body to the side so that your chin is in my ribs. That'll clear your jugular and you're less likely to pass out from the pressure, okay?"

"How?"

"Just twist your body and the head will follow."

"Which way?"

"Counterclockwise." After Griffen turned, Ben said, "Good. Okay. Now, what you're supposed to do forcefully, you're going to do gently, okay? I got dirt on you. Don't take advantage of my good nature."

"Fuck you!"

But he said it in a conversational tone of voice.

Ben said, "I'm gonna move my leg. And when I do, take your right hand, cross over your body, and push your hand in back of my right knee. If you press it hard enough, my leg will buckle. Don't do it hard or I'll take your head down with me."

"Okay."

Ben held his breath and Griffen placed his hand behind his knee. Ben said, "Press it gently . . . see how you're pushing into my leg. If you did it fast and hard, I'd go under immediately. Now, while you're pressing the back of my knee, take your left arm or hand and bring it across my throat." Ben helped him place it across his throat. "Okay, now you're perfect. You press under my knee with your right hand and hit my Adam's apple with your left hand and twist."

He did it gently. Ben said, "Bring your left hand back a little more . . . stretch . . . okay . . . twist . . ." The kid popped out of the hold. "There you go."

Griffen didn't say anything. Ben said, "You put me in a headlock and I'll show you what it feels like to do it quickly." Griff did, and within a moment, Ben was free.

"That was cool," Griff said. "Can I try again?"

"Sure. The key is to relax to get a better extension. The more relaxed you are, the more strength you have."

He did it again. Ben was impressed. "You're a natural."

Griff lowered his head and smiled.

"I'm still pissed at you," Ben said. "But I'm giving you a pass this time. Don't you dare do it again." A pause. "Why, Griff?"

Griffen shrugged.

Ben blew out air. "Like I said before, I'm taking Haley and Lilly out for dinner tonight. I want you to come. It's your chance to redeem yourself. Don't disappoint me."

"You gotta ask Haley about that. I'm not her favorite person right now."

"Then she's being stupid. We're all going and that's that." Ben rolled his shoulders. "There's a chance that I'm going snowboarding tomorrow if I can find a good spot. Weather has been up and down, which breeds avalanches, but even if the backcountry bowls aren't suitable, the ski basin is still making snow. If you want to come with me, be at my house by seven. Be on time. I'm not going to wait around. Got it?"

Griffen nodded.

Ben walked out of his room.

Ro was gone. But he noticed the door to her room was ajar. He knocked on the frame.

"It's open." Ro was in her bathroom. She had changed from sweats to a sweater and a skirt. She was staring in the mirror and putting on eye makeup.

His Valentine's Day gift dangled from her wrist. He wondered if she put it on just for him. But then he remembered she was wearing it when she answered the door. "Sorry if I scared you."

She continued to look in the mirror. She started to talk, but flapped her hands instead and tried to brush away tears without smearing her makeup. She steadied her voice. "What happened?"

Ben looked down and then up again. "Ask Griffen."

"He doesn't talk to me," Ro muttered. "He hates me."

"He doesn't hate you—"

"Oh yes, he really does. But . . ." She put on some mascara. "I suppose he won't hate me forever." She examined her eyes and moved on to her blush. Then she turned to him. "Would you like some water or coffee?"

"No, thank you." He licked his lips. "I'm taking the kids out for dinner."

"That's really nice. I know Griff will really appreciate it. He's been alone since . . . for a while. Thanks for doing it."

Ben tapped his toe. "I'd invite you along, but it looks like you've already got some plans."

Her eyes got wet. "Damn." She blotted away the moisture. "I got a job, Vicks. I'm going to work."

"You got a *job*?"

"Yes, I did indeed."

"Doing what?"

"Not important. Thanks for the invitation. Maybe some other time?"

Ben didn't answer. Seeing her so upset . . . it was difficult to hold on to his anger. "I'm taking him snowboarding . . . Griff . . . tomorrow . . . if he wants to come."

"I'm sure he'd love it." She turned to face him. "When was the last time you snowboarded?"

"Over three years ago." He rubbed his head. "I suspect it's like driving a car. A little rusty at first, but I'm sure I'll do okay enough to teach him something. At one time I was pretty good."

"I ski, but I've never tried snowboarding."

"You can come."

"I'd love to, but I'm working tomorrow as well."

"I repeat: Doing what?"

"It varies."

"Can you get more specific?"

"Like I said, it doesn't matter." She pulled out a lipstick and examined the color. "Too dark." She looked at him. "Are you coming to school on Monday?"

"Probably." Ben sighed. "Good luck with whatever you're doing." He gave her a dismissive wave, the kind she used to give him when they first met. He made sure when he left that he didn't slam the door.

CHAPTER 14

THE POLICY WAS thus: during the day and evening up until ten, there were always two people so Ro wasn't needed and she couldn't sneak around. The graveyard shift from ten to six had been manned by Gary the Ghoul forever. It seemed he didn't take time off because he didn't want to. He loved the dead of night and he loved being by himself.

Opportunity knocked on a perfect pre-spring day in early March. The sun was out in full force, the big New Mexican sky was colored that unreal blue, and temperatures hovered in the sixties. It was a day when no one wanted to be indoors, let alone working. Pearl had decided to call in "sick"—something Ro would have done—but Tomas was a good soul, steady and dedicated. Ro was thinking of ways to sabotage his industriousness.

She wangled another tutorial on the computer. The basics weren't that complicated, but to do what she wanted, she needed diligence and enough facility that Tomas would trust her alone at the front desk. She squinted at the monitor. "So if we've got a returning client and he wants the same room, I press insert here . . ."

"Right."

"And then I type in the name."

"Right."

"And type in *repeat*."

"Right."

"And that will give me a list of all the dates that the client has stayed with us."

"Yes."

"How do I get a log of the previous rooms?"

"Type in *repeat*, the client's name, the date you want. Then, in the request box, type in the room number."

"Okay." She followed his instructions and sure enough, there was a complete client history. "What does this little star after the room number mean?"

"That means a corporate discount."

Her heart started beating. "Like what kind of corporate discount? What corporations do we have in Santa Fe?"

"Not for corporations we have, for corporations coming into the city. Mostly we get tours coming in that book with us. Like if we go back to Christmas . . ." He clicked some keys. "Here we go . . . all these rooms have a star after them. This was booked out by some corporation."

"Do you know which corporation?"

"I can look it up, but I have to go to another window."

"Out of curiosity, which corporation was this one?"

He turned to her. "Why?"

"I'm a curious person."

He was puzzled, but he took her at her word. He clicked
a few more keys, closed a window, and opened another window. "Okay . . . this was done by the Peyton Museum in Dallas." He pointed to the monitor. "See in this aside . . . they
booked a Christmas art tour."

"You have the asides so you know what it was about."

"Most of the time, yeah."

Ro was dying to ask about Los Alamos discounts, but of
course she didn't. Her head was buzzing. First thing on the
agenda was flattery. "This is really complicated."

He smiled. "Not so much once you know it."

"How long did it take you to learn all of this?"

"Six months. Now it's just kinda boring. There are lots of
details and it's easy to screw up, especially doing it hour after
hour."

"So why don't you take a break?"

"Uh, do you see anyone else at the desk?"

Ro pointed to herself. "It's a gorgeous day outside."

"I'm sure Pearl's enjoying it."

She homed in on him with her baby blues. "Tomas, you
did me a favor. Let me do one for you. Take an hour off. I can
handle the desk."

"No, no, no—"

"Yes, yes, yes." Her smile was brilliant. "You need a lunch
hour anyway."

"I have my brown bag in the back."

"Take your lunch outside and breathe some fresh air. I'm
not doing anything anyway. I'm happy to help you out."

He was clearly suspicious. "Are you trying to worm your
way into my job?"

She was offended—for real. "Not at all. I'm a full-time stu-

dent, remember. I couldn't work your job even if it was offered to me. Besides, no one is as good at it as you are."

"You're definitely up to something."

"Forget it." She acted hurt and, of course, it worked. He
was a guy and she was gorgeous.

"You really think you can handle the desk?"

"Tomas, it's after the official checkout time and an hour
away from check-in time. It's called a lull. Go to Fort Marcy.
It's like five minutes away. Take your cell. If I have a problem,
I promise to call you."

"O-kay." He went into the back room and retrieved his
sack lunch. "I'll be at Fort Marcy." He gave her a weak smile.
"Why do I think you're after something?"

"Because you're dedicated and you don't want me to screw
up and get you busted. I won't. Go." She practically had to
push him out the door. She waited five minutes before she
went to work.

She punched in the date of Ellen Vicksburg's abduction
and the monitor shot back a list of thirty names. She printed
them out. Then she started going backward and forward—a
week before Ellen was abducted, a week after it happened.
She printed out those lists. Then she went a full month before
the abduction, figuring if he had dug a grave in the mountains, he would have had to have been in town before he'd
done what he did. No repeat names immediately popped out,
but she couldn't print out the forms and investigate at the
same time.

People came up to the desk. One wanted a wake-up call.
One wanted to know a good place for dinner. Another asked
if a fax had come through. Another paid for a card to use the
computer at the business center. But even with the interrup-

tions, she had almost used up a ream of paper, printing out names and dates. When she looked at the clock, almost forty-five minutes had passed, but she had barely scratched the surface when Tomas walked through the door. Panicked, she tried to return the computer to the home screen, but she must have pressed the wrong button. She tried again, then again, and the computer froze.

Then she froze.

Turning her back to the monitor, she picked up the phone and pressed one of the lines just as Tomas walked through the gate to the front desk.

"Line three for you. You can take it in the back."

"Sure." He walked into the back room. Again, she frantically pressed the home button while Tomas was talking to a dead line in the back room. She pressed the button again, and finally, all her spy work was suddenly offscreen and she was left with the floating home icon. There was still a pile of paper in the printer and a lot of explaining to do if he saw it. Ro gathered up the paper and wrapped her coat around the sheaves. Tomas came back out.

"No one was on the line," he told her.

"Strange." She picked up her crumpled coat and swung the gate open, liberating her from the front desk. "Be right back."

Before he could ask any questions, she ran to the bathroom. Once inside, she straightened the papers into a neat pile. Looking back out the door, she peeked at the desk and saw that Tomas was involved with a guest. Taking the opportunity, she ran out and dumped everything in her SUV. Tomas was on the phone when she went into the back room and opened up a new ream of paper, replacing what she had taken. It wasn't right to steal, even for a noble purpose. She'd buy some replacement paper tomorrow at OfficeMax. When Tomas got off the phone, she gave him a dazzling smile. "Enjoy yourself?"

"Yes, actually I did. Thanks, Gretchen. Any problems?"

"No, everything went swimmingly. Uh, Mr. Graydon in three-twenty wants a six o'clock wake-up call. I don't know how to program it."

He was relaxed and happy. That made him cooperative. "I can show you that."

"Please."

He did and she made a point of checking her watch. "I think I'll take a little breather before I start my shift."

"Sure. Thanks again."

"I'm happy to help. Even if Pearl is here, I'll pitch in. I know you guys can get very busy. And people get impatient—"

"You ain't kidding." Tomas looked at her with wonderment. "You're so pretty. Surely you have a life. I know you have a boyfriend."

"You've been talking to Salvador?"

"It seems like a complicated situation. We could talk about it over dinner sometime . . . just as friends."

"If we can ever find a few moments, sure."

"He's very lucky, your boyfriend."

"He is, but truly he doesn't know it." She left, knowing Tomas was looking at her ass. And that was okay. Keep them guessing. It keeps them interested.

RO'S DAYS WERE filled with monotony: get up, go to school, go to work, fit in homework, drop off to sleep. Repeat. Although Ro wasn't quite sure what she was accomplishing, she knew it was something, because within a few days the hatch of her car was filled with two boxes of paper. She didn't know how to decipher what she had, but at least she had it. Pearl and Tomas were more than happy to have help. Then, out of nowhere, it appeared, as if Ellen were guiding with a celestial hand: Gary the Ghoul needed a few days off for his grandfather's funeral back east. Tomas proudly presented Ro as a competent substitute to Elaine—a woman in her thirties, short, squat, with a round face, dark eyes, and short dark hair. The boss was confused.

"Tomas . . ." Her voice was stern. "You have to be trained to work the desk."

Tomas squirmed. Ro stepped in. "So Tomas will train me."

"It takes a while."

"Look, Elaine, I don't know how to use your specific programs," Ro said, "but I've done this thousands of times at other hotels. I'm sure Tomas can give me a quick tutorial and I'll pick it up. And I get off at eleven anyway. I mean, why not?"

"Because you don't know what you're doing and you could mess things up."

"It's for two nights. Give me a little credit." Ro shifted her weight from one hip to the other. "I know you're shorthanded on the weekends. I'd like you to see how competent I am. That way, maybe you'll consider hiring me as a part-time weekend person."

"I need you at the lounge." She looked Ro up and down. "You've done a good job there."

"Because I'm smart." Ro was bordering on begging. "No one wants to work the graveyard. Give me a chance. I'm already on the payroll."

Tomas said, "She's smart. She'll pick it up. And it's only two days."

Elaine relented. "One day at a time. If you make it through the first night to my satisfaction, I'll let you do the second night."

She was appreciative but not overly so. "Great."

AFTER WORKING SIX hours in the lounge, Ro changed into an official Jackson Lodge uniform and slipped behind the front desk, relieving Pearl of her duties. "Busy?"

"Surprisingly so," Pearl said. "I'm sure at two in the morning it'll be dead. You know we have a bell, so you don't have to stand behind the desk the whole time."

"Uh, yeah, that's right. Thanks. I think I'll be visible for a while. In the meantime, do you have any work you want me to do?"

"Uh, thanks. If you could type in today's reservations, it would help me a lot. And you know how to program wake-up calls?"

"Yes."

"Gary usually does follow-ups fifteen minutes later."

"I can do that."

"You have one at four thirty, and two at five, two at six, and one at seven thirty."

"Not a problem."

She eyed Ro with suspicion. "I don't know why . . . I keep thinking you're after something."

"How about money?"

"Fair enough." Pearl gathered up her bag. Then she wrote down some numbers. "Call if you need anything. It's better to ask than to mess up. Then I have to spend time redoing everything."

"I understand. Don't worry. I can do this, Pearl."

"I have a feeling you can do lots of things."

Ro nodded. "I do have my strong points."

THE NEED FOR sleep was overwhelming, but she had to muscle through it. It was the chance of a lifetime—being alone and uninterrupted. Her parents called constantly. She had lied and told them that her job had always been a desk assignment. They didn't like her working, but put up with it to avoid drama. But with this new assignment—overnight in a hotel—Ro was pushing it. Even after she told them it was temporary, her dad wanted to come down. Eventually she got them to back off, but both of them were rightly concerned. When they called her, Ro made a point to be chipper even though she was dying to get off the phone and hack into files.

They stopped calling by two. By then, the place was a tomb.

The first order of business was her homework. Her brain was groggy but she managed to get through it. After homework, she moved on to inputting the day's reservations for Pearl. She had to do the job well to get the staff on her side.

An hour later she had finished up the reservations. It was just her and the computer and the back room for privacy. Although Tomas had showed her how to bring up the various convention identifications, it did involve several steps and several windows. Mistakes could be tolerated. But she couldn't afford to crash the system. If only Vicks were there to help her. He could have done it in a snap.

It took a while of playing with keystroke combinations. After a lot of trial and error, she was finally able to figure out how to bring up conventions and match them to groups. Tomas was right. Many tours booked in the city, mostly in the summer and a few around Christmas and New Year's. The hotel did a lot of business with travel agents and art museums. During opera and chamber-music season in the summer, it booked musical tours. The companies may have gotten a discount, but there were lots of them to make up the difference in cost.

She experimented with the data, printing out lists of names. Around four thirty in the morning, after dealing with lists upon lists of names, she finally struck gold, finding the code for a group of clients associated with Los Alamos National Laboratory. The date was a year after Ellen's abduction.

She almost cried. She now had names—people she could look up and cross-reference. Her phone alarm went off. She jumped in her seat. She had a wake-up call reminder to get out.

She dutifully called the room: Harold Beitman in 204. "Hi, this is Gretchen from the front desk. I just wanted to make sure you got your wake-up call."

"I got it. Where's the guy who's usually here?"

"Mr. Jenkins will be back in two days."

"He can stay away as far as I'm concerned. You're a hell of a lot nicer to hear at four thirty in the morning. Are you the same Gretchen who waited on me in the lounge last night?"

"Yes, I am."

"Ah . . . Gretchen. You can call me anytime."

"Have a good morning, Mr. Beitman. We look forward to seeing you again at the Jackson."

"Ditto."

She hung up and smiled. It was too bad courtesans were no longer in fashion. Ro knew she had certainly missed her calling.

CHAPTER 15

IT WAS A cold peace but at least Ben could look at her without his stomach churning. She'd wave, he'd wave. And since it was only once a week, he could deal. She looked terrible. There were dark circles under her eyes. She was bony with a pasty complexion. He felt bad for her. Then he'd feel bad for himself. Then he got angry: at her, at JD, who was definitely avoiding him, and finally at himself for letting a stupid, idiotic fling get to him. Of course, no one wanted to feel like a jackass and she definitely had made a jackass out of him.

So, Ben did what he did best: isolated himself. Whenever there was a break, he sequestered himself in an empty room, reading, doing homework, or playing on his computer. He tried to pick the most out-of-the-way space where no one would look—not that anyone was bothering—but the school simply wasn't big enough to get lost in.

Ben knew JD was in the room without even looking up. The guy had that kind of discernible gait.

"Hey."

The sound of his voice made Ben's blood boil. His brain was having an internal dialogue.

Easy, guy. You're a civilized human being. Let him talk and let it pass.

"Uh, could I talk to you for just a minute?"

Just let it pass.

JD said, "Um . . . look . . . this is the situation. It isn't about me. It's about Ro. I'm really concerned about her. She's been a wreck for the last month . . . since it happened, you know."

Silence.

"Vicks, I don't know if you've noticed, but she's like totally . . . retreated. She quit cheerleading. She doesn't talk to anyone, she stays by herself. She took some kind of stupid job and she leaves as soon as school's over. Even her parents aren't sure what she does. Only that she's exhausted all the time and doesn't talk to anyone. She works weekends. She looks terrible. I know you hate her . . . maybe not hate her, but I know you hate me. But this isn't about me."

Ben looked up and then down. JD was sweating. The room temperature was around sixty. *Steady, boy.*

A big exhale. "Her birthday's this weekend. I'm having a little party for her Friday at my house . . . small . . . just the guys and a few girls." Another exhale. "Initially I wanted it to be like a surprise. But then . . . well, you know Shannon. She can't keep a secret."

Silence.

"But I did get Ro to agree to come. And like I said, this isn't about me or anything. Ben, I know it would be something special to her if you'd show up. I mean, you don't have to stay . . . just make an appearance. Honestly, I'm real concerned about her health. And you certainly don't need any more ghosts to haunt you."

With that, Ben's brain gave up. He gathered up his schoolwork and stuffed it into his backpack. "No."

"C'mon, Vicks." JD grabbed his arm. "Think about someone other than yourself for once."

The pop came so fast that the poor bastard didn't even have a second to deflect it: a perfect uppercut on the chin. Ben felt the punch clear down to his wrist. JD's face registered utter shock although it shouldn't have. When they were younger, they had scrapped all the time. "In case that wasn't clear enough, the answer is still no."

Ben ambled out of the room, slipping his backpack over one shoulder. Juvenile. But it felt so damn good. He went to his locker, working hard to get the numbers right while shaking out his hand. He could feel Ro's presence over his shoulder, heard her say, "How's your hand?"

"Probably better than JD's jaw." He shook out his hand again and turned to face her. "It hurts."

"Thanks for inviting me out to dinner the other night."

"You caught me in a weak moment."

His repressed anger slapped Ro in the face. She sighed. It was better to get it all out because he already hated her. It couldn't get any worse. "I slept with him that night . . . with JD . . . on Valentine's—"

"I get it, okay." He glared at her with open hostility. "What would you like me to say to that?"

"I dunno. I'm sure if you think hard enough, something will come to you." His eyes were far away. He was retreating into his brain, which was usually a dark place. "He got me drunk, but no excuses. I'm way beyond excuses. I'm just telling you this because I want to totally come clean before I ask a favor of you." Silence. "Vicks?"

"I hear you."

"Okay." She swallowed hard. "Here goes nothing. It's my birthday this weekend . . . on Monday, actually—"

"I know."

"You know? Oh, that's right. JD told you about the party."

"No, I knew before that. My memory is still intact."

"Okay. You know." A pause. "Everyone is asking me what I want. Do I want clothes or money or jewelry or a trip for spring break or whatever. All those things are fine. I mean, who doesn't love a good diamond? But that's not what I really want." She took in a deep breath and let it out. "What I really, really want for my birthday is for you to forgive me."

When he didn't respond, she pressed on.

"I mean, you don't have to like me . . . obviously you don't. But if you could forgive me, that would be a great present for me."

He remained silent.

"I know it's selfish. But selfishly, I'm tired of feeling like a terrible person—"

"I forgive you." Vicks looked up and gave her a forced smile. "Done."

"Okay." A pause. "On the heels of that pithy comment, is there anything you'd like to add?"

"That's it. I forgive you. Happy birthday."

"Okay." She shrugged. "I got what I wanted . . . I guess. Thanks." When she started to leave, she felt his finger gently tap her arm. She turned around. "Yes?"

He dropped his hand. "Dorothy, you are *not* a terrible person. You're a good person who . . ." A sigh. "Who, in my opinion, made a terrible decision that broke my heart. But one terrible decision does not . . . take away all the nice things you've done for me. I'd like to hate you, but I don't. And that's about as good as it's gonna get right now."

She bit her lip hard. "Thanks for saying that." A tear escaped. "Seriously."

Vicks pulled something out of his locker. "I was gonna give this to Griff to give to you. But as long as you're here and we're talking . . . kind of . . ." He offered her a small wrapped package. "Like I said, my memory is still intact. Happy birthday."

She stared at the gift through blurry, wet eyes. "You bought me a present?"

"I did. Open it."

She ripped off the paper and ribbon, and then opened the box. It was the same bracelet that he had bought her for Valentine's Day, except it was in yellow gold. She couldn't speak.

Ben said, "I saw that you wear the one I gave you. So I went to the same store. And the woman at the jewelry shop told me that the two different golds look pretty together . . ." He laughed. "I'm just not very creative at these kinds of things."

Ro laughed as water rolled down her cheeks. Her hands were shaking. "I could use a little help."

Vicks latched the bracelet onto her wrist. "Actually, they do look pretty together." He held her arm as he inspected the jewelry. "It's kind of like our relationship. The white gold is flashy, sparkly, the flames blistering hot white. Yellow flames are less hot, not as intense but more mellow. Less expectation but there's still something burning, and that will never go away." He kissed her cheek. "Happy birthday, Ro. Enjoy your party with JD."

"Vicks?"

"No, I will not go to your birthday party. Even if I was interested in going, which I'm not, after my encounter with JD, I think he's disinclined to invite me again."

"Can I take you out to dinner? Just the two of us?"

"You take *me* out for *your* birthday?"

"Ordinarily, it would be the other way around, but I figure I owe you one . . . or two or three." She waited, but as usual he didn't say anything. "I'm leaving in what—four months. Let's go to Geronimo. I can't leave Santa Fe without going to Geronimo, right?"

His eyes turned far away. Then he shrugged. "Okay, let's go to Geronimo. Let me check my very busy schedule." A second passed. "What about Saturday night?"

"That's the party. But I'll cancel it if that's the only time you can make it."

"No, no, we can do Sunday. Around seven?"

"Has to be later. Around eight thirty?"

"Yeah, your job. What's that all about? What do you do?"

"If you must know, I work at the Jackson Lodge doing whatever they need me to do, which is mostly glorified wait-ressing. But I do have a name tag and a uniform."

"You're a waitress?"

"A cocktail waitress, to be exact. But sometimes, if I'm a real good girl, they let me work behind the desk."

"A *cocktail* waitress? Uh, don't you have to be nineteen to do that?"

"That's the least of the issues, Vicks. I'm a little tired of getting pinched in the butt, but I make great tips. And I have a tremendous business-card collection from horny men hoping I do the nasty on the side. I've kept them all. Never know when you might want to blackmail someone."

"That sounds awful."

"I'm making it out to be worse than it is. Mostly it's boring. You are the first person who actually knows what I do. Please don't tell anyone. And please, please don't come see me there. I'd die of embarrassment. Let's do eight thirty, this Sunday night. I'll meet you there."

"Fine."

"You know I still love you," she told him. "Say the word, Ben, and I'm groveling at your feet."

Vicks shook his head. "No, no, no. We're not traveling down that road again."

"No problem. Let's take a different road." When he didn't respond, she said, "You need time. I understand."

He closed the locker and turned to her. "It's not gonna happen, hon. I've got my pride but that could be whittled away . . . I really miss you."

"I miss you too." Her eyes were wet again.

"Dorothy, this has nothing to do with what happened between us." He blew out air. "This is the deal. When we stopped being a couple, I went back to researching my sister's case. And I ain't stopping for anything or anyone."

It was always about Ellen. Ro said, "I can accept that."

"No, Ro, you don't understand. We can't be a couple anymore. Like you told me, he knows who I am. I don't know if he's watching me, but if he is, it's too dangerous for you."

"What about Haley?"

"I can watch over her. But I can't watch you and her at the same time." He shrugged. "She's my sister. She comes first."

He looked around. "I know this obsession can't go on like this forever. Eventually there will be other people in my life. But, at this moment, I'm seventeen and unattached and intend to stay that way until I get this monster off the streets." He rubbed his eyes. "Go back to JD, hon. As a matter of fact, I'd like you to be his girl again. He can protect you in a way that I can't. You'd be doing me a favor." When Ro didn't answer, Ben said, "Still want to have dinner with me?"

"Of course." But Ro was less excited. She tried to muster up some pride. "During dinner, how about if you catch me up on what you're doing with the case."

"That'll take about a minute because I'm nowhere. But I'd love your input." Ben smiled but it looked more like a gesture of pain. "I'll see you on Sunday, Majors."

She watched him leave. All those horrible hours of standing on her feet just so she could work the desk to find information, doing all that crap *and* pretending to be her deceased sister, and he was dumping her anyway.

That's what you do when you love someone. You do something for him, even if it hurts.

It really, really hurt. But she'd do it again in a heartbeat.

CHAPTER 16

RO HADN'T BEEN to Canyon Road since the Christmas Eve walk. Geronimo was at the top of the hill, an adobe structure done in territorial-style architecture with a patio that was empty in the bright cold night. The inside was elegant—high ceilings, whitewashed walls, a fireplace with candles, and a horn chandelier. Booths held colorful pillows and graceful table service.

She was ten minutes late when the host led her to a corner table where Vicks was waiting. He stood up when he saw her. He was dressed in a black, wide-wale corduroy jacket, a white shirt, a red tie, and black jeans. He looked older in the dim light, definitely more masculine. She approved. She was wearing a black shearling coat that Vicks helped her take off.

The host said, "May I take that for you?"

"Yes, thank you." She had chosen her outfit with great care—a deep purple sweater dress with a V-neck from which peeked a little cleavage. Her new suede black boots that were a gift from her mom. And of course, Ben's bracelets. She wanted to showcase them.

The host pulled out her chair and both Ben and Ro sat down.

"I was getting nervous," Vicks said.

"Thought I'd bailed?"

"It was a possibility . . . especially after seeing these prices."

She smiled. It wasn't a genuine expression of happiness but she tried to make it lovely. "What's good here?"

"THANK YOU." SHE regarded his face. "When did you start growing a beard?"

He rubbed the stubble on his chin. "I used to shave every other day when I was in school. Now I shave once a week Sunday night and that's only because facial hair isn't allowed at school. I'm really lazy."

"You shaved when we were in San Francisco?"

"I didn't want to appear sloppy."

"I like it. Makes you look very dark and mysterious."

The waiter came over with an ice bucket, two glasses, and a bottle of champagne. He was in his thirties and slightly balding. His name was Yves. "From the gentlemen over there." Ro looked in the direction he pointed, toward four middle-aged businessmen who raised their glasses to her in a toast. She smiled and nodded back.

"I'm sorry, ma'am," the waiter said, "but I'll need to see your ID before I pour."

She beckoned him close with a finger. "Listen, Yves. I work as a cocktail waitress at a local hotel, so those guys probably assumed I am twenty-one. I'm not. Knowing New Mexico law, I wouldn't dream of getting you in trouble. This is what I want you to do. Take the bottle back and bring us two diet 7 Ups with a couple drops of cranberry juice in champagne flutes. It *is* pink champagne, correct?"

"Yes, ma'am."

"I don't want to insult them. I'm going to take out my ID now. Look at it and nod. And then take the bottle in the back." She pulled out a Gucci wallet and showed him the Gretchen Majors ID. He took the bottle back with him.

Vicks said, "Admirers from the Jackson?"

"Making friends wherever I go."

When the waiter returned with the flutes, Ro turned to her patrons and nodded, holding up the crystal container of colored 7 Up. Then she hid her face with a menu. "How've you been?"

"All right." An awkward pause. "I know you didn't want jewelry for your birthday but someone gave you a nice set of ear candy."

"I didn't say I didn't want jewelry. What I said is I wanted your forgiveness more than jewelry. To have both is fine with me. I'm surprised you noticed."

"Hard not to."

"A gift from my grandparents. Someone still loves me."

"Everyone loves you. What did your parents buy you? The necklace?"

"Yep. Cartier. Mom has excellent taste."

"Did JD get you anything?"

"But of course: a Tiffany silver heart pendant."

"Where's a Tiffany around here?"

"There's this new invention called online shopping."

"Ah."

"I am blinged out to the max." The suits were walking her way. She gave them a demure smile. "Thank you very much."

The man who spoke was in his forties. He was graying, slightly stooped, and slightly pudgy. "A mere token for brightening our week, Miss Gretchen." He kissed her hand then looked at Vicks. "And who is the lucky fellow?"

"This is my boyfriend, Ben," she told him. Vicks shook his hand.

The man said, "Ah, to be your age again." He turned back to Ro. "We're leaving tomorrow morning—early. You shall be missed."

"Thank you for the champagne and your generosity. Have a good trip back to Springfield."

The suit knew he was being dismissed. "Thank you." They all said their good-byes. She turned to Vicks. "Sorry about calling you my boyfriend. I had to discourage any sort of hope."

"*Gretchen?*"

She turned bright red. "You have to be nineteen in New Mexico to work in a cocktail lounge."

"Your sister's ID?"

"Correct."

"I hope it's worth it."

"Twenty-buck tip for a twelve ninety-nine cocktail, yeah, it's worth it." Her grin was the real thing. "We are no longer an item, so really, it's none of your business. Besides, I occasionally do the desk. Even then I get a lot of leering, but it's nice having a barrier between me and them."

"Why are you *doing* this? It's not like you need the money."

"It's an honest living. Stop being a snob."

"I'm not a snob. It just seems like . . . a poor fit." He

shrugged. "Why would you want to work in a place where sleazy guys are checking out your ass?"

"It's a nice ass."

"It's a terrific ass but that's not the point."

"Let's move on, Vicks. We can talk about other things. What are you thinking about ordering?"

"If you're trying to be contrite, you have an odd way of showing it." Actually, he liked her better for it. Perusing the menu, he said, "Chicken sounds good."

"You don't have to get the cheapest entrée on the menu. How about we start with some caviar?"

"Caviar, Ro? Really?"

"I'm having some. If you don't like it, start with whatever you do like."

"Are you paying for this or is this going on your dad's credit card?"

"I'll disregard the dis. I am paying. I'm a working girl."

"I'm working too. Let's split it."

"How much do you get paid for your part-time internship? Like a thousand a year?"

"Twenty-five hundred."

"Friday night I made a little under two hundred in tips and that's after splitting it with the bartender. I am definitely taking you out. Sure you don't want caviar?"

"I've never had it."

"It's fishy, but really good. We'll order a half ounce. You want a salad? I'm having one . . . golden beets, arugula, and artisan goat cheese. How about if you take the sliders and we'll split?"

"Whatever you want."

"That's what I want. What are you having for your entrée?"

"Chicken."

"Ugh. Get the sirloin."

"I don't want steak. Is that okay with you?"

She grinned. "I'm sorry. If you really want chicken, get chicken."

"Actually, I like salmon."

"Then get salmon. I'm getting sirloin." She put down the menu. "How's that for a switch? The guy eating fish and the girl eating meat. How's UNM, college boy?"

"I wound up taking three upper-division math courses and a physics course."

"And Circuitchip?"

"A little lightweight but I'm learning stuff." A pause. "Heard from any colleges?"

"Most of the acceptances won't come out until April. I did get into St. John's. Rolling admissions."

"Oh . . . I didn't know you applied to St. John's."

"At one point, I thought about staying here." She looked pointedly at him. "That's changed. I take it you got into St. John's as well?"

"Yep."

"So if I don't get in anywhere else, we'll be classmates."

"You'll get into a ton of places."

"Could be. I raised my math score thanks to some help." Yves came back. She batted long, mascaraed lashes. She suspected he was gay, but even gay guys like attention from pretty girls. "We'll start with the half ounce of Osetrova caviar. I'll have the beet, goat cheese, and arugula salad and the sirloin . . . you know, make it the T-bone. Medium rare." She handed him the menu.

He looked at Ben, who said, "Angus sliders and the salmon."

"And how would you like the salmon prepared? The chef recommends medium rare."

"Medium rare?" Ben said. "For fish?"

Ro said, "Do medium."

Yves nodded somewhat less than approvingly. When he left, Ben said, "What is medium rare for fish?"

"It's slightly raw on the inside."

"That sounds terrible."

"If the fish is good quality, it's actually delicious. You've never had sushi?"

"Not hot sushi. But I'll take your word for it, Miss Sophisticate. How's my sister doing? You probably see her more than I do."

"She seems fine. She and Lilly and Ezra and Griff have reunited. They are once again a tight little quadrangle."

Ben was quiet. Then he said, "How's JD?"

"Saw him last night at the party. First time in a long time we actually spent more than a minute talking. That's when he gave me the Tiffany necklace."

"He likes you a lot."

"He loves me, actually." She looked straight into his eyes. "First time he told me was right before we did it. Didn't think too much of it because I knew he was sweet-talking me. I was also pretty plastered, so maybe I didn't hear right. But I did make him wear a condom both times. I guess I wasn't totally blitzed." He was clearly uncomfortable. "I'm really, really sorry, for what it's worth. It was the stupidest thing I've ever done."

"I'm okay. And even if I'm not, like you said, let's move on."

"At least it taught me something." She studied her red-lacquered nails. "I mean, JD certainly didn't force himself on me, but he did take advantage of me. Boys and alcohol don't mix. Good lesson to learn before college. I should have listened to my mother."

Vicks's smile was genuine. "You have this way . . . of turning bad stuff into good stuff."

"I appreciate the compliment." She couldn't stop looking at his face. There was so much depth in his eyes. "Do you still love me?"

"Unfortunately, I do. That's never going to change."

"If you want to be more than friends, now's the time to speak up." When he didn't say anything, she said, "Okay. Got my answer."

"Dorothy, I thought I made this clear—"

"I can take care of myself."

"I'm being selfish. If something happens to you, I don't want it on my conscience."

"I absolve you, my son."

"We're not starting up again." He shook his head. "Besides, you'd just cheat on me again."

She had nothing to feel self-righteous about. Still, his words wounded deeply.

"Ro, I'm *boring*!" He exhaled. "I mean, I don't think I'm boring. Inside my head are all sorts of ideas. But you're not a mind reader, and even if you did read my mind, you'd probably find my thoughts tedious. In the back of my brain, I actually understand what you did. I'm good company for an hour and then . . . I dunno . . . my mind starts to wander. I start thinking about a physics problem or a math problem or how the hell am I gonna get past those gates at Los Alamos. It's gonna take a very unusual girl to put up with me. You, on the other hand, are . . . social and graceful and—"

"What I am is a wit like Dorothy Parker. Actually, I was named after her by my grandmother. Or was it Dorothy Kilgallen."

"Who was she?"

"Also a wit. If you're named Dorothy, you're either a forties socialite wit or someone from Kansas."

"You *are* a wit," he told her. "I'm a loner. We're *terrible* together."

"Not everything was terrible."

Vicks raised his eyebrows. The first honest smile turned his lips upward. "Was he good?"

"No!"

"You're ly-ing."

"I am not!"

"Ro, what you need to say is he was good, but I was way better."

"Of course you were way better. For one thing, I love you. And just for pure practicality, I actually remember sex with you. With him, I don't remember anything."

"Except you made him wear condoms. Why'd you do that?"

"I dunno . . . I was stalling. I really didn't want to do it."

"Then why *did* you?"

"I don't know. It was stupid." It was her turn to squirm. "You don't hate me?"

"No, I don't hate you."

"What about JD?"

"Don't hate him since I punched him. The best part was he didn't punch back." He patted her hand. "Are you two officially back together?"

"Nope. I tell him, 'Do whoever you want. Say whatever you want. You're not getting play from me.'" She threw up her hands. "What is it with you guys? You never want what you have and you always want what you don't have."

"Hon, we're all confused. Girls mystify us. I grew up with sisters and I still don't have a clue."

"Fair enough." The caviar came. She prepared a bite for him, adding shredded egg and onion to the fish roe and the cracker. "Try it."

Before he could object, she stuffed it in his mouth. He chewed. "It's good."

"Have more." She offered him another cracker. "How's your research coming?"

Vicks took the cracker. "I'm totally stumped on how to move forward. Shanks won't do anything concrete with the labs because my ideas are based on intuition and a map. And even if I did have evidence, it's doubtful if a guy like Shanks could penetrate a classified lab. I'm just that stupid hamster spinning in the wheel . . . all this exertion and going nowhere." His face registered defeat. "This city is crazy. It can nab a visiting scientist shooting prairie dogs, but a serial killer? They're helpless."

They polished off the caviar. Ro said, "You really are discouraged, aren't you."

"Been some rough days lately."

The salad and the sliders came. She took a slider and bit into it. "This is really, really dope."

Vicks took the second slider. "Wow." Another bite. "This is *sick*."

"Not to bring up the past, Vicks, but out of curiosity, where were you going to take me on Valentine's Day?"

"Here."

"Here?"

"Yep. I had it planned for a month . . . roses on the table and everything."

"Roses?"

"Yep. A dozen long-stemmed coral roses. I thought red was a cliché."

"I *love* coral roses." She stared at him. "Why didn't you tell me? I could have chosen another place."

"You wanted to go here for your birthday. You're entitled." He gave a small smile. "You know it cost me fifty bucks to reserve a table on Valentine's Day."

"You lost *fifty* dollars?"

"I had to give them my credit card because they were packed."

"That's awful. God, I'd be pissed for that alone. I'll pay you back."

"You can pay for this. That's enough."

The entrées came a few minutes later. Ro said, "How's your salmon?"

"Phenomenal. Do you want a bite?"

"Of course." He fed her and she cut off half the steak and put it on the bread plate. "Try this. You'll die."

"Whoa . . . this is good."

"I didn't know places like this existed beyond NYC."

"Snob."

"And proud of it."

"I really wish you'd quit your job. You've got like three more months of high school. You should be enjoying yourself. I mean, isn't the spring fling coming up?"

"First week in April."

"You should be shopping for a dress, not putting up with the creepy men ogling your butt."

"Maybe I'll ask for the night off. JD has already offered to take me."

"Then do it. Why should you be miserable?"

"Okay." She pushed her plate away. "I'll go to the spring fling with JD." And that was that. "Dessert?"

"I not only ate my food, I ate your steak. I'm stuffed."

"So . . . what you're really saying is we should look at the dessert menu."

"I suppose we can share something."

"Not on your life," Ro told him. "Are you coming to school tomorrow?"

"Yep, I'll be there."

"Okay. This is what I'm going to do. I'm going to start sitting with JD again . . . you know I haven't been sitting at his table. Because I work nights, I like to sleep whenever I can."

"Will you please quit?"

"No. I like the attention. I like the money." Yves came and Ro ordered the cheese soufflé with Grand Marnier and the strawberry crêpes. "I want to sit with you tomorrow. Where do you eat lunch?"

"Gomez's office."

"Fine. I'll meet you there. The rest of the time I'll sit with JD." She looked down. "Not to be a downer, but the vernal equinox is right around the corner."

"I'm well aware of that. I'm taking the day off to watch Haley . . . Haley and Lilly actually. Where one goes, so does the other."

"You don't have to do that. I can watch them at school. And I don't have to be at work until five thirty. I'll make sure they're home and are going to stay there before I leave."

"I don't want them walking anywhere."

"I know. I got it."

"If you take care of them at school, I can probably make it home by four," Ben said. "Then I can relieve you. Is that okay?"

"Whatever you want. I'll be vigilant."

"The other thing is, when do *you* get off work?"

"Me? Late. Doesn't matter. I'm not his type. Too old."

"I'm serious, Ro."

"I'll be in a public place. Stop worrying."

"Just answer the question, please. What time do you get off?"

"Aw, you care. Around eleven, eleven thirty."

"On the equinox, I'll wait for you at the hotel, walk you to your car, and see you home."

"You can't be serious."

"Of course I'm serious." The desserts came. The waiter made a big show of punching down the soufflé to add the Grand Marnier sauce. She smiled until he left, then said, "I don't want you waiting for me at the hotel. It's embarrassing."

"Ro, I promise not to come into the lobby as long as you promise to call me when you're done. That's the deal. If not, I'll come in and snicker at you in your ridiculous uniform. Yes or no?"

"Just *don't* come inside the hotel."

"If you keep your end of the bargain, we won't have a problem." Vicks got up. "I'll be right back."

"Where're you going?"

"Can't you guess?"

A few minutes passed, then a few minutes more. Maybe he wasn't used to rich food, although anyone who could eat fire-laced salsa like he did must be cast iron down there. When he came back, he said, "Let's go."

"I've got to pay."

"I took care of it."

"What!" Her voice came out louder than expected and people turned around. "Just kidding." She spoke softer. "Ben, why did you *do* that?"

He pulled out her chair and helped her up. "I guess my mom raised me right."

He took her hand and they walked out to the parking lot and waited for the valet. Without asking, Ro threw her arms around his neck and planted a kiss on his lips. The next one was more passionate, but less passionate than the one that followed.

"Oh dear Lord!" He kissed her again. "I can't take this." Another kiss. "I really can't!"

"One more time for my birthday, Ben," she whispered. "Then I'm back with JD and you're out of luck. And we're not even cheating because I'm not officially with him yet."

"This is crazy!"

"And that's what makes it fun."

He looked dazed. "My parents are probably still awake. I know Haley is. My house is out."

"My parents are definitely awake." They kissed again.

"I don't want to do it in a car," he said. "You deserve more . . . especially on your birthday."

"My birthday is tomorrow . . . but the car is out of the question." She dropped her hands and kissed his nose. "Lucky for us I know a hotel where the staff gets discount rates."

CHAPTER 17

AS SOON AS Ro heard the click of the lock, something came over her. She had always liked boys, she liked being physical with them, but this was the first time she'd ever felt lust: hard-driving, come-give-it-to-me lust. She had had sex with only two guys, but they were as different in love as they were in life. JD was a warrior, an in-your-face guy who did anything and everything with his eyes wide open. He matched his appearance: steely, strong, and dominating—direct with no hesitation.

Ben was all stealth, quiet and cerebral, utterly mysterious. The force of his eyes made her nervous and excited all at the same time. He rarely spoke with words, but his actions screamed volumes and this time he had the confidence that only comes when two people have been together. It was certainly not their first time, but it was the way she had always imagined her first time would be—a deep craving rather than something to be done. It was no longer an option. It was a need. It took all of thirty seconds before they were disrobed and on top of the bed and on each other.

She could hear his breath quicken. "Oh God, don't you dare come." She hit him. "Don't . . . stop!"

"I don't know how much longer."

She raked his back. She could feel her nails break skin. "Don't you dare!"

"Oh jeez . . ." He flipped her on top. His face sheened with sweat. "You do all the moving. If I move, I'm a goner."

She reached across the bed and grabbed his red tie. He was still wearing his shirt but it was unbuttoned. "Wanna tie me up?"

He winced. "No!"

A rather strong reaction. But then Ben probably associated bound women with dead girls. Ro said, "You want me to tie you up?"

"Don't want that either, but . . ." He sat up and took the red tie. Still inside of her, he knotted it around her neck and pulled it up, first tight, then he loosened it so that the knot fell below her Adam's apple, the tie dangling between her breasts. He took off his shirt and dressed her in it, rolling up the sleeves. Then, he plopped back down on the pillow and stared as she sat upright and nude in his open white shirt and tie. His eyes held such intensity that Ro almost blushed.

"God, you are smokin' hot! Just killer dope! You're fantasyland: a wicked, walking wet dream sitting on top of me! I'm gonna *die*!"

Stealing a glance in the mirror, she thought she did look

hot in a retro way . . . like those centerfolds from seventies girlie magazines. All that was missing was the pouty look and the top hat. "Sort of old-school."

"*I* am old-school," Ben said. "I'm a boy eating a TV dinner on a tray, watching *Ed Sullivan* on a black-and-white TV, thinking that the Beatles are groovy. I'm slavering over Marilyn Monroe and Brigitte Bardot with their big tits and their fantastic asses. I'm stoned to the gills, lying on my bed, staring at my lava lamp and listening to 'In-A-Gadda-Da-Vida.' I'm trick-or-treating in a Batman costume, only to me, Batman is Adam West with Burt Ward as Robin. What the fuck happened to Robin in the movies, can you tell me that?"

"Robin was in the last one."

"As a frickin' afterthought." He yanked her down with his tie until they were face-to-face. *"Kiss me!"*

She kissed him hard and then flipped him around until he was on top of her. It felt better . . . much, much better. It not only felt better, it felt very, very good!

"Do it harder." When he complied, she said, "Not that hard! Do it a little harder and faster! Way faster!"

"God, I'm gonna come!"

"No, you're not!" Again, she raked his back. "Keep going."

"I can't help it!"

She bit his shoulder hard. "Keep going . . . keep . . . going."

And he did—with all the passion and hunger and unfettered desire that she wanted and needed. He kept at it until the intensity started to build inside, something familiar that she had previously felt only when she did it herself.

"Keep . . . going . . . going . . . going." On the verge . . . on the edge . . . she was tipping over. Still digging her nails into his back. "Not yet . . . not yet."

"Tell me!"

"Not . . . yet! . . . Okay . . . okay . . . yyeeesssss! . . . Now!"

"Now?"

"Now!"

A moment later he obliged, the two of them squeezing each other like they were holding a life raft in the middle of frigid waters. Still coupled, they kept kissing, milking every last drop until complete exhaustion overtook them.

She glanced at the red numbers on the bed-stand clock: straight-up twelve. She thought to herself: *Happy birthday to me.*

VICKS'S RINGTONE. THEY'D been dozing on and off for the last hour. As she lay in his arms, his fingers absently stroking her hair, he looked to see who was calling. At one in the morning, it had to be either his mom or his dad.

"I'm fine, Dad," he whispered. "I'm with Ro. We're talking."

His dad was shouting, "You can talk at the house. You still have school tomorrow."

"Dad, I've been on my own for the last three months. I stay out late all the time, only you don't know about it and Grandma and Grandpa don't care. Stop worrying."

"Well, when are you coming home?" his dad asked.

"I'll be home in an hour." Ro hit his chest and gave him the V-sign. "Two hours maybe. I'm fine. Go to bed . . . no, I'm not going to wake you . . . I love you too." He hung up and went back to playing with Ro's hair.

"Wowzers," she told him. "Are you okay?"

"Never been better."

"How's your back?" When he turned over, Ro grimaced. The skin was streaked with red lines, some of it bleeding, some of it swollen. "It's pretty nasty. Sorry."

"Next time I'll wear Kevlar."

"Will there be a next time?"

"Well, we're both here and we're both up. Wanna do it again?"

"I do . . . especially now that I finally understand what the big deal is."

"You are . . . phenomenal. Kiss me."

"Not to ruin the moment, but I probably have bad breath."

"Then your bad breath will kiss my bad breath." Ben sighed. "I don't want the night to end and it's going to end. And then I'll be empty."

"It doesn't have to be that way, Ben." When he didn't answer, Ro tried to cover her tracks. "Maybe we should just end it on a high note because I'm sure we can never repeat this."

"Probably not but I'd like to try a couple more times. It ain't morning yet."

"Maybe I should go back to JD and cheat on him with you. That would be kinda sexy, huh?"

"Really sexy." He shifted to his side and looked at her. "Unfortunately, I don't operate that way."

"You're a throwback to when it was cool to be a nice guy."

"Nah, nice was never cool. Even then they had Marlon Brandos and James Deans. It's just biology, Dorothy. Girls get off on bad boys and boys get off on sluts."

"Am I a slut?"

He smiled. "Only in the best sort of way."

She hit him. "Vicks, if I go back to JD, the physical stuff stops here. As much as I love you, I am not good at juggling two guys."

"Yeah, I always knew that JD's sharing idea was crack-ass."

"Why'd you agree to it?"

"I dunno really. Since we were little, JD was always able to talk me into doing stupid stuff."

"You were friendly with him once?"

"I told you we grew up together. I was a dumb ass and he was persuasive." He turned to her. "You've got like three months here before you're gone. I want you to have fun and we both know JD's a fun guy. Go back to him and be a princess again."

Ro sulked. "You just want me out of your hair."

"No, I want you out of harm's way. If you're with him, I won't be worrying about you."

"And we can stay friends?" She propped herself up on her pillow. "No jealousy?"

"Of course I'll be jealous," Vicks told her. "Every time I see you two together, I'll be enraged. I'll curse him, but I'll curse myself more." A pause. "Maybe that's what I need . . . to feel mean again. Anything's better than depression." He lifted her chin and kissed her hard on the mouth. "I want you. Like now!"

She hopped out of bed and searched the shelf on top of the minibar. "Aha." She held up a toothbrush kit. "No need for either of us to suffer. I'm going first." She made her mouth minty fresh and passed the brush on to him. Afterward, they both hopped back into bed. She said, "Guess what I found?" She showed him a condom.

His face registered panic. "I thought you said you're on birth—"

"Calm down. I'm still on the pill, okay. This is for your protection, not mine. I owe you one, Vicks. I want to give you something that I'll never, ever give JD or probably anyone else . . . well, maybe my husband." She got down on all fours and looked over her shoulder. "Unless you aren't interested."

"Oh!" His eyes went wide and wild. "I'm interested." A pause. "Wow. Are you sure?"

"No, I'm not sure. We've never done it. But for you, I'm willing to try. I trust you, Vicks."

"That may be a mistake." He pulled her upright until they were both on their knees. "Kiss me first, Dorothy. I just love it when you kiss me."

They kissed and then they kissed again, making love every which way until the sun came up.

CHAPTER 18

OFF SHIFT AT eleven, Ro was about to call Vicks when Pearl came up with a panicked look. "I have an emergency. My mother's in the hospital."

"God, I'm so sorry," Ro said. "What happened?"

"She passed out behind the wheel and hit a tree. The airbag like blew up, so she's okay, but she's banged up." Tears started streaming down Pearl's cheeks. "She drinks, Gretchen. Sometimes way too much. I don't know whether to kill her or hug her."

"Hug her," Ro told her. "Go, I'll be fine."

"Gretchen, you are a doll."

"Oh please. It's nothing. I just need to make a quick pit stop."

"Yeah, sure."

Five minutes later, she was behind the desk. Pearl's problems had morphed into her good luck. But first, a quick call to

Vicks. "I'm going to be an hour late. The girl behind the desk had an emergency. I have to wait for the night guy, Gary the Ghoul."

"When does he come in?"

"Midnight. Are you outside?"

"Yep."

"Then go home, Vicks."

"You know I'm not going to do that." A pause. "Can I come in? It's cold."

"Absolutely not!"

"Dorothy—"

"No. Go to Kiki's if you want to pass the time. Just don't come in. I'll be out at twelve." She hung up the phone. In actuality, she didn't care if Vicks saw her, but she didn't want him to know what she was doing. After dealing with Pearl's odds and ends, she was finally able to steal a few minutes alone and in the back room.

She had managed to download and print out the entire guest list for the last five years, but had yet to go through it because it was so extensive. There was one more thing she needed to do before saying good-bye to the Jackson Lodge.

She picked up the phone. A moment later a perky woman was on the other end of the line.

"Jackson Lodge, Albuquerque. This is Belinda speaking."

"Hi, Belinda, this is Gretchen from the Jackson, Santa Fe. I'm doing some paperwork and I'm looking up a specific tour that probably went through Albuquerque around three years ago. I need to cross-reference them with some names. I was wondering if I could give you a date and you could tell me whether or not the tour booked and who the guests were."

"You're new, huh?"

"Not so new but I'm only part-time."

"There's a way to access Albuquerque's files remotely. Want me to walk you through it?"

Amazed by her luck, she said, "That would be terrific." It involved closing windows, opening windows, and a password. A minute later she had total access to Jackson Lodge, Albuquerque. "I'm in. Thank you. This way I won't be bothering you."

"No bother. Bye." She hung up.

She quickly entered the date of Katie Doogan's disappearance and printed out that list. Went forward, went backward. Printed out those lists. She skimmed the tours, looking for the magic asterisk that indicated what group booked what and for what purpose. Within twenty minutes, she found the code for Sandia National Laboratory.

She thought to herself, *Belinda, you're the bomb.*

BEN KNEW THAT Ro was okay: she was in a public place. But it was late and he was tired and he still had to drive back to Albuquerque.

He called her cell again.

Ro answered on the third ring. "I'll be out in a few minutes."

"It's past twelve. Is the guy there yet?"

"Yeah, he came in five minutes ago."

"Then leave."

"I'm just finishing up some paperwork. Just go home. I'm fine!"

"I waited this long. I'm not going to crap out now."

"Where are you?"

"By my car in the parking lot."

"Just stay there. I'll be out in a second."

"What's taking so long?"

"Right now, it's talking to you." She hung up.

That's it, Ben told himself. He was going inside, approaching the front door just as his phone rang.

"I see you, Vicksburg. Go back to your car. I'll be out very, very soon."

"If you're not out in five minutes, I'm coming in."

But she had already hung up. Ben was antsy. He whipped around and knocked into a body. "Sorry."

The man jumped, obviously surprised by another person crashing into him—especially at this late hour—but then he quickly averted his eyes, fast-walking to the entrance of the Jackson. He turned around and gave Ben another glance before ducking inside the hotel. He was around six feet but doughy . . . soft around the middle. And he was acting odd although Ben knew he had startled the guy. Ro came out a minute later. She waved and he jogged up to her and squeezed her tightly.

"That was nice." She kissed his cheek. "It is officially the day after the vernal equinox. You can go home now."

"I'm going to follow you home."

"Fine. Follow me home. I'm done arguing with you."

"Did you know that guy who just walked into the hotel?"

"What guy?"

"I bumped into him in the parking lot. He scurried into the hotel."

"Scurried?"

"Yeah . . . scurried. What's he doing out this late?"

"Businessmen work late. I didn't see anyone. Your imagination is getting the better of you."

"No, he was a real guy. He just came into the hotel."

"Maybe I was in the back room. Do you want me to go back in and find out who he was?"

"No." Vicks shook his head. "Can you do it tomorrow?"

"Sure. We get clicks every time a room door opens and closes. I'm beat. Shall we go?"

Ben walked her to her car and waited until she pulled out. Then he got into his car, following behind her until she was home. When she pulled into her driveway, she parked and got out. She opened the front door and gave him a friendly wave good-bye.

He waved back.

He made it to Albuquerque in forty-five minutes.

He was speeding, going way too fast. But not as fast as his racing heart.

AFTER THE EQUINOX passed, Ro could finally relax. She would never admit it to Vicks, but she was happy to be looked after. It meant he cared, but more important, she was a tad nervous. She hadn't signed up for espionage when she moved to New Mexico, but some part of it was exciting—there was a little thrill when she cracked open a surreptitious file.

But just as Vicks had to let go, it was time for her to say good-bye to sleuthing. After April Fools' Day on the Saturday evening of the spring fling, she showed up at Vicks's house, ostensibly to drop off Griff and Ezra so they could go to the dance with the little girls. But she had other plans besides carpooling. She had dressed in a tight pink sweater set and a black pencil skirt, patent leather pumps on her feet.

Ben's mom said, "Thanks for dropping off the kids."

"Not a problem. Are you sure you don't mind doing cab duty? I'd be happy to pitch in."

"If not me, Ben will do it." His mom gave her a forced smile. "Ro, I know you two aren't together anymore, but you know everyone. Maybe you could find a date for him next time . . . you know, fix him up?"

"Laura, I could make some phone calls and fix him up with at least three really cute girls within five minutes. It's him. He's beyond fix-up-able."

"What is wrong with him?"

"He has his own tempo that only he can dance to."

"You know he wasn't always like this. Once he was much more social than Ellen." Her eyes moistened. "Sometimes I feel like I lost them both."

Ro gave her a hug. "This is my opinion . . . and it's only my opinion, but here it is for what it's worth. Ben is obsessive. We see it as a problem, but it's not. It's who he is. His brain was just designed to figure out the great mysteries of life. If it wasn't Ellen, it would be something else."

Laura nodded. "He's like my father. And I never really got him either."

"There you go." Ro smiled. "Is he in his room? I'd like to say hi."

"Sure, go ahead."

She knocked on the door. A few moments later he stuck his head out, then stepped into the hallway and closed the door behind him. "Hi."

Their romantic encounter two weeks ago was still fresh in her mind. It was weird to be with JD and to be thinking about Vicks. By the look in Ben's eyes, it was on his mind as well. He said, "Wow! You look nice."

"Thanks, Vicks. You're taking the kids to the dance, right?"

"Yep."

"Just get them home before eleven or my mother will call the cops."

"No problem." A pause. "How's JD?"

"This is our first official date."

"Have fun."

"Yeah, JD is a lot of fun." She mussed up his hair. "Better than you, Mr. Dour."

"Yeah, but can he figure out murder cases?"

"No."

"Neither can I." His smile was sad. "Have a great time."

"Oh, I will. You don't look this good and not have a great time." Ro flashed him white teeth. "I need your help, Vicks. I have some heavy boxes in my car. Could you carry them in for me?"

"Boxes?" But she was already outside, opening the hatch to her Explorer. She pointed to two boxes tied together with ribbon.

Vicks hoisted them out of the trunk. "These are heavy. What's inside?"

"Lots of paper." Ro opened the front door so he could bring the boxes inside. "This, Vicks, is your birthday present."

"You bought me paper for my birthday?"

"Kind of. Take the boxes to your room."

"Yes, ma'am." He did and put them down with a thud. "My birthday's not until the end of July."

"I know, but I might not be here. I'm giving you your gift early."

"Where are you planning to be on my birthday?"

"In New York, where I belong."

He nodded. "I'll miss you."

"Well, for the time being, I'm still here and you have yet to give me a call except when you're worried about my safety."

Ben said, "I just don't want to bother you."

"Oh please. You're too busy. It's okay. You're not my problem anymore. I've got to go."

"Should I open the boxes now or save them until the date."

"No sense being a stickler. Open them after I leave. You'll love it. It's your favorite thing."

"What's that?"

She smiled and winked. "Data."

UNTYING THE RIBBON, he opened the first box. There was a birthday card, which he put aside. He'd read it later. He lifted out a handful of paper, noticing that the pages weren't numbered. If there was an order to the material, he had to be careful to keep things in place. His eyes began to scan the contents.

There were lists of names: hundreds of them, and not in alphabetical order. The majority of the names were single men but there were some couples and a smattering of single women. Along with the names were street addresses, cities, states, and phone numbers. Beside each name and personal information were dates and numbers.

The lists were in chronological order starting with yesterday's date. The numbers beside the dates kept repeating themselves but in no discernible order. And then it hit him.

Ro had given him these boxes. She worked the desk at the Jackson Lodge.

Okay.

What she had given him was a massive printout of the hotel's registry: from yesterday's guests to God only knew how far back. The next obvious question was why.

Maybe it was time to read the card.

He picked it up and opened it.

Look at the groups circled in red. Didn't have time to check much but it's a start. Will talk to you later.

He started leafing through the pages until he hit the first circled group. In Ro's handwriting, he read:

Received the discount rate for Los Alamos. Group from MIT.

Ben's heart started pounding as his head flooded with thoughts. He frantically paged through the papers until he found the next circled group.

Discount rate for Los Alamos: Fermi Lab.

He clamped his hand over his mouth to prevent himself from panting, turning one page after another as his vision blurred. Her handwriting continued:

Discount rate for Los Alamos: Lawrence Livermore Lab.
Discount rate for Los Alamos: Berkeley Lab.
Discount rate for Los Alamos: Princeton Lab.
Discount rate for Los Alamos: Oak Ridge Lab.
Discount rate for Los Alamos: Brookhaven Lab.
Discount rate for Los Alamos: Lawrence Livermore.

And on and on: circling science conferences in red ink, not only for the Jackson in Santa Fe, but also for its sister hotel in Albuquerque near Sandia NL. At this point, his heart was pounding out of his chest.

Haley knocked on his door. "Ben? Are you ready to go?"

"Give me a few minutes!"

He went through name after name until his head started spinning, until he came upon another circle in red ink:

Date of Katie Doogan's abduction.

Immediately he paged back in time until he saw what he was looking for: the date of his sister's abduction and the lists of names from weeks before and weeks after.

"Ben?"

"I *said* just a few minutes."

"It's been ten minutes. We're late."

"Hold *on*!"

His eyes couldn't focus. He could barely breathe. He felt nausea and elation. He was euphoric and dizzy.

Because he knew that somewhere—among those pages and pages of personal information—was the name of his sister's murderer.

It was the reason why Ro took the job.

And she did it for him.

CHAPTER 19

H E BOUNDED OUT of his room, shirtless and sweaty. Haley and Lilly were dressed in twin poodle skirts. Griffen and Ezra were garbed in cuffed jeans, black T-shirts, and leather jackets. They were all staring at him.

"What are you *doing*?" Haley asked. "We've got to go."

"I'll be ready in a sec." More loudly, he shouted, "Dad?" He turned to Haley. "Is Dad home?" He didn't wait for an answer. He yelled out for his mother and found her in the kitchen. "Is Dad home?"

"Not yet." She stared at him. "What's going on?"

Ben said, "Does he have a black turtleneck I can borrow?"

Haley came into the kitchen. "Mom, can you take us? We're real late."

Laura said, "Why do you need a turtleneck?"

Ben looked at Haley. "The theme is fifties, right?"

"You're *going* to the spring fling?"

"Yeah. Give me five minutes."

"*Why?*"

"Because I want to go. Any other questions?"

"Jeez Louise, I'm just curious. You never go . . ." But Haley was talking to air. Lilly materialized. Haley said, "God, how rude. What is wrong with him?"

Lilly said, "Did you see Ro wearing that tight skirt? That's what's wrong with him."

"It has to be more than that."

"I don't think so, girlfriend."

Ben came out a few minutes later wearing his father's turtleneck, which was two sizes too big and his mother's black beret.

Laura laughed. "Where'd you find that old thing?"

Haley said, "You look ridiculous."

"What's ridiculous? The theme is fifties and I'm going as a beatnik."

Lilly said, "It's supposed to be a sock hop, Ben, not a poetry slam."

"Do you think I should pencil in a little mustache?"

Lilly said, "I think you should lose the beret. You look like a French movie director of questionable sexuality."

"Can we go already?" Haley said.

They piled into the car and arrived at the gym fifteen minutes later. Immediately the kids went inside, having prepurchased tickets, leaving Ben behind. Lisa Holloway was selling tickets at the door. Her black eyes were made up somewhere between ghoul and Goth. Her hair was in a ponytail. She wore a tight black sweater and had painted her lips ruby red. She said, "I don't believe my *eyes.*"

"How's it going, Lisa?"

"Okay. Not that you care. What in the world are you wearing on your head, Vicks?"

"My fifties costume. Do I have to buy a ticket? I'm only gonna be a few minutes." When she didn't answer, he smiled boyishly. "Please? I promise I'll be right back."

"You need a ticket."

His face fell. "Fine. How much?"

"Thirty bucks."

"*Thirty* bucks?" It was clear that Ben hadn't been to a dance in a very long time.

"There's a big spread in there."

"I promise I won't eat."

"Vicks, it's thirty dollars. Them's the rules."

He pulled out his wallet. "I've got twenty-three dollars and . . ." He reached into his pocket. "And twelve cents. I need gas money. Do you take credit cards?"

"Really, Vicks? Credit cards at a school dance?"

"How about a beginner's discount?"

"Give me three bucks and take me to a movie and we'll call it even."

He was still looking for hidden cash in his wallet. "I can make that happen."

"Try not to sound too thrilled."

At the hurt in her voice, Ben looked up. "Any movie you want, Lisa."

Her smile was wide. She gave him a ticket. "Nice to see you somewhat normal again, Vicks."

"'Somewhat' is a loaded word." He winked at her and barreled into the crowd, his eyes taking in the room with a few sweeps. Ro was sitting on JD's lap. Once again, she had taken up her position as rightful queen with her minions glomming on to her every word and action. And she did look happy, as did JD. The two of them were a natural couple. They radiated popular.

Ben wended his way through the crowd, through the ribbons and decorations and bunting and the multicolored strobe lights and the loud, off-key doo-wop fifties music pumped out by the local school band, Onionfeather. There was a spread, and a big one, but the real party would be afterward at Weekly's house. Ro would probably get drunk or stoned and she and JD would probably wind up in bed. He had no one but himself to blame.

He felt blood rushing to his head. Despite his jealousy, he enjoyed the emotion—the righteous indignation and the martyrdom. He broke into the tight circle and took Ro's arm. "I need just a minute alone with her, JD." A statement, not a question. "Maybe two minutes."

"What's going on?" JD asked.

"Nothing." Ben dragged her through the crowd until he found a relatively unpopulated spot in the corner. He put his hands on her shoulders. "Thank you." He looked into her soulful and somewhat moist blue eyes. "Thank you, thank you, thank you, thank you."

"I take it you liked my gift."

"It was the most perfect thing ever. I don't know what else to say except thank you."

"Think for a moment. It should come to you."

"I love you."

"Got it on the first try."

"No, I really, really love you."

"I know you do." She stroked his cheek. "And I love you too. That will never, ever change." Her eyes leaked tears. "I'd better get back to my date. You look ridiculous in a beret." She took it off his head and fluffed out his curls. "Much better."

His hands were still on her shoulders after Onionfeather announced they were taking a break. When the PA music started up, Ben recognized the song. It was one of his grandmother's favorites, sung by one of her favorite singers: Buddy Holly, "True Love Ways."

Ben grinned. "Dorothy Majors, before I leave this stately event, would you please honor me with this dance?"

Her smile lit up her face. "Yes, I will honor you with this one dance. But no hip grinding."

"Damn, you're onto me." He placed one hand around her waist and took her right hand in his left. He started with a slow box step and she immediately stepped on his foot.

"Sorry."

"Not a problem."

"How come all you boys know how to dance?" Ro leaned her head into his chest. "I mean, like, real dancing?"

"Because when we were all twelve, our mothers got together and tried to civilize us with real dance lessons." Ben smiled. "We didn't mind. It was a cheap way to get close to the girls. You're fighting me, by the way. Just relax and let me lead."

"That's what JD always says. I'm not used to real dancing."

"You mean you're not used to letting someone else lead." He tightened his grip around her waist and brought her close to him. "Simple box step. Back, side, forward, side. Just close your eyes and follow me. I won't let you fall."

"This is nice." She snuggled into his arms. "Really nice."

"Yeah, you're feeling it now."

"I certainly am."

Ben felt himself go hot. "Stop that!"

"I meant the dance." She smiled. "You always think I have dirty thoughts on my mind." A pause. "I do, of course. What can I say? Some of us are just randy."

"I wouldn't have it any other way . . ." He smiled. "Whether or not I'm the recipient."

"You made your decision, Vicks. Sleep alone in your own bed of your own making."

"Touché," Ben told her.

At the end of the song, Ben was planning on a chaste peck. Instead he took her mouth and gave her a passionate, movie-worthy kiss. He felt the heat of the spotlight on them. In the background, he heard collective oohs and aahs until Mr. Gomez came up and pulled them apart. "You know the rules." He could barely keep the smile off his face. "Next time it's detention."

Ben grinned. "I need to go outside for some air . . . before I faint."

"Can I join you?" Ro asked.

"You're the problem." He stroked her cheek. "Go back to your date." Ben walked through the gymnasium, beret in hand, and into the night, under a black sky filled with a thousand stars—a thousand wishes. His head was buzzing with music and lust.

"Hey, Vicks!" Ben turned around just as JD landed a solid punch on his jaw. "That's for making an ass out of me in front of everyone." Ben touched his bloody lip and glared at JD, who said, "You don't belong here, Vicksburg. Get the hell out." He turned around, heading back to the gym.

Something deep inside welled up. Without conscious thought, Ben charged, almost sacking the quarterback. JD was solid steel with a solid center of gravity, but Ben knocked the wind out of him.

"You motherfucker!" Ben screamed as he landed a punch on his face. "You screwed my girlfriend."

JD took a blow to the jaw, reached up, and used his height to get Ben in a headlock. He screamed back, "She was my girlfriend before she was your girlfriend." He tightened his arm around Ben's neck. "I should have screwed her first."

Ben grabbed JD's arm and clawed at it with his nails. He slammed his foot on JD's instep as he wheezed out, "I not only screwed her before you did, I screwed her before anyone did!"

Suddenly the pressure eased from his neck and Ben pushed JD off, stumbling over his feet, holding his throat and coughing. JD had a weird look in his eyes.

"She was *cherry*?" Silence. "No, no, Vicks. That's an old trick. It was probably her period."

"Fine, JD." Ben was breathing hard. He touched his split lip, which was still bleeding. "Have it your way . . . whatever."

JD suddenly turned bright red and charged him, tackling him to the ground. His hands encircled Ben's throat, squeezing as Ben tried to break the hold. Pinpoints of light were flashing through Ben's brain but he wasn't going to go down without a fight. He freed his right hand and punched straight up at JD's nose. Red, fresh blood spewed from JD's nostrils, covering Ben's face. He felt the pressure ease from his airway. He heard a lot of screaming in the background as he rolled over and held his own throat, coughing as hard as he could. His breathing was labored, his head still woozy.

He heard the principal's voice.

"What the *hell* is going on?" The man sounded angry. "Are

you both out of your freakin' *minds*?" Weekly helped Ben up. He was still having fits of coughing. JD's entire face was a bloody mess.

The principal said, "I can't believe what I'm seeing! My valedictorian and salutatorian acting like kindergarten thugs!"

"Which one's which?" JD asked.

"Shut the hell up, JD. With a single phone call, I can not only take away your football scholarship, I can revoke your admission to Duke."

"Noooo . . ." Ben choked out. "Don't do that." He broke into another fit of coughing. "We're cool."

JD had turned ashen. He said, "Yeah . . . we're . . . totally cool." Blood was dripping from his nose and onto the ground. He and Ben looked at each other and fist-bumped. Then Ben went back to coughing.

"I'm going to pretend I didn't see this. Both of you . . . get the hell out of here!" The principal stalked away.

The boys stared at each other as they nursed their wounds. Ro was passing out Kleenex from a box. "What the hell just happened?"

"Nothing." JD turned to Ro and grabbed a wad of tissues. "Nothing."

"Nothing?" She was incredulous. "I've lived in New York my entire life. I've been to the city innumerable times. I've never come close to seeing as many fistfights as I've seen here in ten months. What is wrong with you guys? Didn't your mothers ever teach you to use your *words*?"

JD was still mopping up his bloody nose. "Wanna grab some dinner?"

"Not the way you look, bud," Ro told him. "Right now, I want to go home."

"Fine, I'll take you home."

"You know, JD, right now, I don't want to be in the same car as you."

He turned to her with fierce eyes. "You're my date, you kiss him in front of everyone, and you're pissed at me?"

"I'm not pissed at you, JD. I just don't want your blood and snot on my new sweater."

"Fine. Do whatever the hell you want." JD looked at his posse. "Meet up at Kiki's?"

Weekly said, "I'm there."

Mark Salincz said, "Fine with me."

JD glared at Ben. Then he sighed. "You're invited."

"I'm going home."

JD said, "I said you're invited!"

"I've got to take my sister and her group home from the dance, JD," Ben said.

"I've got the perfect solution," Ro said. "Give me your car keys, Vicks. *I'll* take them home."

"I thought you wanted to leave," JD said.

"I changed my mind. I mean, why go home and be cozy and comfy when you can stay at the dance with no date, listening to Onionfeather massacre Roy Orbison." She turned to Ben. "You can pick up your car at my house. I'll leave the keys in the glove compartment."

"I don't want to put you out," Ben said.

"A little late for that, don't you think? So unless you want me to walk, give me your damn car keys." Reluctantly Ben handed them to her. She said, "And don't ring the doorbell to thank me because I don't want to talk to you."

Ben and JD exchanged glances. It could have been unspent adrenaline. It could have been something else. But they suddenly started laughing. Small chuckles at first, until they doubled over into big guffaws.

Ro said, "I swear you two are enough to make a girl join a convent."

JD was still laughing. "You'd make a very cute nun."

Ben tried to stifle the laughter but it didn't work. "Yeah, you've always looked terrific in black."

Ro gave them incredulous looks. "Okay, boys, just go back to your bromance and don't mind me. I'll just hate you both." She marched away.

They both started laughing again. It hurt Ben's throat, it hurt his head, it hurt to smile. But it also felt good. Sometimes you have to be cruel to be kind.

CHAPTER 20

THE RIDE IN the car was silent. When JD pulled up at the coffee shop, he said, "You okay?"

"Fine." A pause. "Nice set of wheels, JD. When did you get this?"

"A year ago."

"Okay. I guess I've been a little out of touch."

"Y'think?" JD paused. "Sure you're okay?"

"I'm fine. You just caught me off guard."

"Yeah, right." He snickered. "Otherwise you woulda busted my ass."

"I didn't say I could bust your ass. But there was a time I could give you a run for your money." He rolled his shoulders. "I'm just a little out of shape."

"Like three years out of shape."

"You weren't talking this way when you were hanging out the window of the Peterson law office."

"That was five years ago, Vicks. And the only reason you got that far was because you punched me in the stomach when I had the flu."

"Give me a break. You had a stuffy nose. And the only reason I punched you in the stomach was that you tried to choke me. Which means nothing has changed!" Ben got out of the car but waited for JD. They walked into Kiki's together.

A sixty-year-old crane-built waitress with a gray bouffant hairdo stared at the boys. "Vicks?"

"You still here, Heidi?"

"Where else should I be?" She looked him up and down. "I haven't seen you in a month of Sundays. When did you grow up?"

"Hi, Heidi," JD said.

"What the hell happened to you?" She looked at Ben again. "What happened to your lip?"

"It wasn't pretty," Weekly said.

"I finally decided to put some character in that pretty-boy face," Ben told her.

"JD almost strangled him," Weekly told her.

"That is utter horseshit," Ben said. "Can we sit down before JD bleeds out?" He followed the guys to their usual booth.

JD said, "You want to talk about bleeding, remember when I bashed your head open with a pool cue?"

"Yes I do. I recall that was after I took out your knees with a baseball bat."

The boys sat down. Weekly said, "Yeah, when was that? Like sixth grade. What was that all about?"

Ben and JD exchanged glances. JD said, "Don't remember." When Ben smiled, JD said, "What? I really don't remember."

"It had to do with pictures of Shannon Stork with her top au naturel that you showed me."

"Yeah, yeah!" JD clapped. "That's right! You told her about the pictures after you promised me you wouldn't."

Ben said, "I did it because you showed her a picture of a one-inch dick and told her it was mine."

"She told you that?"

"How else would I know? I was really insulted. Like what was that? Like a lemur's?"

"Some kind of monkey."

Ben sat back and grinned. "You know I had to show her that it wasn't true. She was real impressed."

"Yeah right." JD said. "What? You didn't. You did? You *did*?"

Ben burst into laughter. "No I didn't. Man, she was pissed at me. But she was way more pissed at you."

"She got over it."

"I never saw the pictures," Weekly said.

"That's because he never showed them to you," Ben told him. "Shannon made him delete them off his phone. He told her he was using Snapchat but he wasn't. He actually downloaded them to his computer." He turned to JD. "Where *are* those pictures?"

"Somewhere in electronic space," JD said.

"Never seen the pictures," Weekly said. "Just the real boobs."

"Nice boobs," JD said.

Ben said, "Shut up, JD, that's his girlfriend."

"I don't mind," Weekly said. "They *are* nice boobs."

"Nothing better than a good set of knockers." JD grinned knowingly at Ben.

Ben wagged a finger. "Don't you dare go there."

"What? Ro?" Weekly perked up. "You got pictures on your phone?"

"No." JD was still smiling. "No, really. I don't have pictures."

"C'mon, you must have something on your phone."

Weekly turned to Ben, who said, "Don't look at me."

Salinez downed his glass of water. "Yeah, you two used to get into it all the time."

"Not all the time," Ben said. "Just when he was being obnoxious."

"Which was all the time," Salinez said.

JD said, "That's because you were throwing things in my face, which was all the time."

"Like what?"

"Like snowboarding," JD said.

"It was the only sport I could beat you at."

"That's only because you practiced and I didn't."

"That could be, but I was still better than you."

"Probably not now."

"For sure I could whup your ass," Ben said. "I'll go to the backcountry with you tomorrow and prove it."

"Except all the snow has melted."

"Not everywhere."

"Next year," Weekly said.

"I won't be here next year." JD looked at Ben. "You shouldn't be here either."

Heidi came over with four hamburgers, fries, and Cokes before Ben could protest. The boys dug in and ate in silence. It was amazing how quickly Ben had slipped into old habits.

Weekly farted out loud. The other boys groaned.

Weekly said, "Hey, remember the time when we were like ten and JD made that toilet-paper bonfire on Halloween?"

"How could I forget?" Ben said. "It burned up two sumacs in my front yard."

"Boy, was your mom pissed," Salinez said. "She was screaming at us."

"I've never seen your mom so angry," Weekly said.

Salinez said, "Wasn't Peewee Thomas with us?"

JD said, "Yeah, you're right. He pissed his pants he was so scared."

"Yeah!" Weekly said. "He said it was sweat. After that, we started calling him Peewee Weewee."

"Whatever happened to Peewee?"

"We drove him off to Texas," Salinez said.

"We drove a lot of people off," Weekly said.

Salinez said, "Man, your mom was mad, Vicks."

"What'd she do?" JD asked. "Like ground you for a year?"

"Almost." He pushed his plate away and grew serious. "Ellen was always a good defense lawyer. Got my sentence reduced with time served."

The table grew quiet.

Weekly said, "Did I ever tell you I had a crush on your sister?"

"I had a crush on your sister," JD said. "Did I ever tell you that Shanks brought me into the station house and questioned me?"

"He did that to me too," Weekly said.

"Times three," Salinez said.

"I was really offended." JD was quiet for a second. "I really liked Ellen. She was one of the few older girls that talked to us. It was pretty amazing because we were so obnoxious."

"Yeah," Weekly said. "Every time we came in."

All four of them said in unison, "Hello, boys."

Ben had known about the interviews because he had read them in his sister's homicide folder. Over time, it had become strange, in his head hearing their voices as younger boys, frozen in time—a tunnel into what he once was.

"You shouldn't have taken it personally," Ben said. "Shanks questioned everyone who knew her, including me. He was grasping at straws." A pause. "He still is."

JD said, "Whatever happened to that older kid . . . Timmy Sanchez."

"He's at Missoula."

"You kept in contact with him?"

"More like I kept track of him."

"You still suspect him?"

"Nah, he didn't have anything to do with it. All that heat made his life miserable for a couple of years. So the family took off." Ben looked at his watch.

JD said, "You want to go?"

"I'm tired." He blew out air. "Got a headache from having some guy's fist in my mouth."

"Tell me about it. I think you broke my nose."

The bill came to sixty-two fifty. They each chipped in twenty bucks and told Heidi to keep the change.

That left Ben with twelve cents before he got his allowance for the week on Monday morning. His car was just about dry, so it looked like he wasn't going anywhere tomorrow. Lucky for him, at home the coffee was free and so was the Wi-Fi.

THE RIDE TO Ro's house was silent. A block away, JD pulled the car over and shut off the motor. He sat back and stared out the windshield as he talked. "You know, three years ago, I had a best friend and tonight I remembered why. What the hell happened to you, Vicks? And don't get all pissy on me. You know how I mean it."

"I hear you."

JD lit a joint, inhaled deeply, and then offered up a hit. Ben started to shake his head, but then thought better of it. He took a long drag. "I dunno. Maybe it was Ellen. Maybe it was just two dudes going their separate ways."

"That's horseshit." JD wiped his nose, which was still leaking blood. "Look. I don't pretend to know what you went through. What you're still going through. But you didn't have to blow me off."

"I didn't blow you off."

"You blew everyone off, Vicks. You became your own clique of one except for maybe that Doogan guy you became so chummy with."

"Bryan?" Ben said. "We were looking for his sister's body, JD. It wasn't exactly good times."

"And I don't have a pair of eyes? I came to every single search for Ellen. I came to look for her, sure, but I also came to support you."

"I knew you were there."

"Right."

"You know, James David, whenever I did call, you were busy with some sport."

"That's horseshit too. I always called you back immediately. Then you'd call me back but not quite as quick. Then I'd call you, and back and forth, always missing each other's calls until you stopped calling altogether."

It was true. Ben shrugged. "I was preoccupied."

"And not with good stuff. You shoulda tried out for the team. You could have made it."

Ben turned to JD. "My sister was murdered and you're wondering why I didn't want to play football? Are we really having this conversation?"

"It would have been healthy—"

"Oh, fuck that! You didn't give a damn about my health. You were just pissed you lost your sidekick and it took you a while to regroup!"

Silence. Then JD blew out air. "I shouldn't have said anything. Forget it. It's ancient history."

"Yes, it is." Ben shook his head.

"You want another hit?"

"Sure." He inhaled and handed the joint back.

JD said, "Don't get pissed at me, because I'm telling you this as a friend . . . or an ex-friend . . . or whatever . . . Vicks, you've got to get out of here."

"Aw, c'mon! Not you too."

"Ben, New Mexico isn't going anywhere. Go back east to MIT or Harvard or Princeton. Isn't Ro's father an alum from Princeton?" Another toke. "Go activate your brain, Vicks. At the very least, follow Ro. I know she loves you. Always has. Man, that girl went after you like a drug dog sniffing pot. Lord only knows why."

Ben said, "She lost a sister."

"Huh?" JD whipped his head around. "What?"

"Ro lost her older sister to cancer around three years ago. You're not supposed to know."

"Ah . . ." JD took another toke and gave the joint to Ben. "Now it all makes sense."

Ben gave him back the joint. "No more. I'm already floating."

"That's the point." JD took another toke. "So that's the bond? Dead siblings?"

"That's the bond and you don't want any part of that." Ben checked his watch. "I really need to get back. I can walk from here."

"You're still pissed at me for Ro," JD said.

"Of course I'm pissed at you."

"'S'right. I've been pissed at you for years."

Ben turned to him. "JD, you and I have been competing since we were two. Banging her while we were dating was just one more matchup, so don't blame me for your poor behavior. That's plain cowardly."

Silence. JD's jaw was working overtime.

Finally, he said, "It was a rotten thing to do. Sorry."

"'S'right." A shrug. "It's better this way. She was a distraction from my research when we were together. I mean, she helped me, for sure . . ." He thought about her gift. "She really put herself out there. But it's time for me to go it alone."

"Have you ever thought of asking me for help?"

"And when would you fit it in, James David? Between your baseball games and your two-hour-a-day workout schedule? Or maybe you could squeeze it in when you're not memorizing the playbook for Duke for next fall? Or how about you do it when you're not running track or running the school or screwing all those girlfriends of yours."

JD extinguished the joint with his fingertips. He threw up his hands. "I tried."

"I've changed. We both have changed. Something that monumental makes you change. But that doesn't mean I don't remember what things were like, that I don't mourn my past."

No one spoke.

"Whatever," JD said. "Are we cool?"

"Yeah, whatever."

"For the record, I'm not fucking around on her anymore."

"Good for you."

"She likes you better than me."

"I know," Ben said. "But you're better for her than me."

"I know." JD looked down. "God, was she really cherry?"

"That's what she told me." There was a small smile on his lips. "Maybe it was her period."

JD didn't speak. Then he started laughing. "You dog!"

Ben laughed as well. "Gotcha, motherfucker."

"Fuck you!" JD punched his arm. "Okay. If you're cool, I'm cool."

"I'm cool." Ben went silent, considering how much to say and how to say it. "Just . . . keep an eye out for her, okay? Keep her safe."

"Safe?" JD wiped his swollen nose. "Is something going on I should know about?"

Ben sat back. "Put it this way. The monster who murdered Ellen hasn't been caught."

A long silence. JD said, "What are you saying?" When Ben didn't answer, he said, "You think he's coming back? *Here*?"

"Maybe." There was a long pause. "I believe my sister was murdered by a serial killer."

JD looked horrified. "A serial killer?"

Ben nodded.

"Jesus . . . how do you know? Shanks told you?"

"No, I told Shanks." Ben looked at him. "This is what I've been doing for the last three years . . . holed up in my room, looking for some answers."

"Christ!" A pause. "Any ideas?"

"Some ideas, but no name." *Not yet.* "The thing is, I may be getting closer, and that's the problem. The killer might know who I am even if I don't know who he is. Which is why I don't want Ro associated with me anymore. Do you still own a gun?"

JD was still digesting the information that had been thrown at him. "Yeah, of course."

"If you're alone with Ro in the car, have it on you, okay?"

"This is totally weirding me out."

"Sorry to lay this on you—"

"No, no, it's all good, I can take care of her, for sure." A pause. "Do *you* carry a gun?"

"In the glove compartment of my dad's car." Ben forced a smile. "Maybe now you can understand why I'm so protective of Haley. Just be vigilant, okay?"

"Right." A beat. "Although after tonight, I don't know if Ro will talk to either one of us again."

"Maybe that would be a good thing."

"Does she know about this? I mean the serial-killer thing?"

"She does."

"Wow." JD made a face. "Should I be worried about my sisters?"

"I don't know for sure, but I think it's me he's after although I don't know why."

"It's good you told me. I'm a good shot. If anyone comes close, I'll blow his fucking head off."

"You'll have to wait in line," Ben said. "How's your nose?"

"Hurts. How's your lip?"

"Hurts."

"We're cool?"

This time Ben's smile was real. "We *are* cool." He turned to

JD. "We're so cool that we don't need the cold war anymore. It's officially over."

"Good to be talking again."

"I don't remember that we ever stopped talking except recently." Ben shrugged. "You cheated on her, she cheated on me, I embarrassed you, big deal. It's *high school*. I mean, like *WTF*."

"I really like her, Vicks."

"She's smart, she's witty, and she's stone gorgeous. But it's not like you two are forever. Once you get to Duke, you'll have to beat girls off you just to take a piss. Especially when they see you come alive on the field. Like, how many colleges and universities tried to recruit you before you decided on Duke? Like a billion?"

"Twenty-six."

"Stop talking like a moonstruck little girl."

JD let out a laugh. "Yeah, you're right." A pause. "It's all coming back. Why we were friends."

"As long as you were number one, we did just fine."

"Yeah, that's true. I'm an egomaniac." JD started the car. As soon as they pulled up in front of Ro's house, Ben opened the door, but JD took his arm. "I want you to do me a favor, Vicks. For old times' sake. For the last three years, I've been listening to the same shit from those morons day after day after day. I don't mind being told I'm God, but occasionally, I'd like another opinion, if only to shoot it down. You're at Remez, what—one day a week? Would it hurt your ass to sit at my table during lunch when you're there?"

"Fine with me. You'll have to ask Ro."

"If you sit with me, she'll sit with you." A pause. "I know

it doesn't matter to you, but it matters to me. I like a posse. It's all image, you know?"

"That's the JD I remember and loathe." Ben shook his head. "How does that work? Do I sit next to Ro or is there like hierarchy?"

"I'll be on her right, you sit on her left. Give her something to tell her grandchildren about." He made his voice high. "'These two boys came *to blows* over me.'" Ben laughed and JD smiled. "That's what she's all about anyway. Attention." He grinned. "So we're really cool again?"

"Yeah, yeah . . . as long as you agree that we're both taking her to prom."

"Yeah, the vampire and the zombie."

"I think it's the vampire and the werewolf."

"I don't know anything about vampires or werewolves, but I do know a thing or two about zombies," JD said. "Get your head out of the dead, Vicks. Come back and join the living."

PROLOGUE

HE DIDN'T START out this way. He didn't wake up one morning and decide to be a sadistic sexual killer. It was gradual . . . very gradual.

It didn't have anything to do with the family (a "good" one) or being bullied in school (no one paid attention to him) or even the voices that he heard (he had learned to disregard them). It did have something to do with the screwed-up circuits of his brain. And opportunity.

He had always liked to watch. He began looking through windows in his early teens. Binoculars allowed him to see details up close, and for the longest time, he was content just to watch. Until one day when he saw her stagger home completely smashed out of her mind from some kind of early Christmas party. It wasn't even rape because she didn't know what was happening—only that she was on the ground, her eyes rolling *to the back of her head until she coughed up vomit and eventually passed out. He finished up while she was out cold.*

She was fourteen, and why should he feel guilty? Where the hell were her parents?

He left her there sleeping it off, unnerved by what he had done, but also exhilarated by it. It had happened on the winter solstice, and since he knew that he couldn't routinely go around doing what he did, he decided to limit his obsession to those four days of the year—the solstices and equinoxes. There was something nice about breaking in the seasons.

The next one was also young, but not drunk. She had cut through the woods on her way somewhere. He saw her as he was driving, just as she ducked into a forested area rich with fall foliage. He wasn't all that familiar with the neighborhood, but he salivated at the idea of tailing her. So he pulled over, parked the car, and followed her deep into the woods. She had fought him, but since she was young, he quickly overpowered her, tied her up, and gagged her. He fucked her. The whole thing took around ten minutes. And then he left her there, squirming in her own vomit and his semen while he ran back to the car and took off to the airport.

He had learned a good lesson, though. It was easier to do it when they were knocked out.

So the next time, in summer, he took a rag soaked in chloroform equivalent and threw it over her nose. After she went limp, he raped her and got the hell out.

And so it went from season to season to season until the inevitable happened. They weren't supposed to die, but he got a little rough, so it wasn't that surprising. But, still, those girls weren't supposed to die. And it was getting out of hand. He had to be more organized.

And so the one in River Remez was his first planned attack. He spent hours digging the precise dimensions of the grave. He was meticulous, exacting, a little compulsive, and a very hard worker. He never shirked any assignment. He was the go-to guy if you really wanted something done, which made him very successful.

When he was finished burying her, he was careful to cam-ouflage what he had done with leaves and detritus, and he even put some animal droppings on top of the site. The night was inky black, and if it hadn't been for the river, he probably would have been hopelessly lost. But he stepped lightly and covered his tracks—literally—and eventually found his way back to civilization.

He left the area the next day by car, dropping off the rental in Dallas and eventually going home, if you could call where he lived home. Home was always the same—an extended-stay motel—but it varied from city to city, depending on his whims.

And he had a lot of whims. Whims were fun. They were the spice of life.

CHAPTER 1

THEY'D COME FULL circle: starting out as a team, becoming a couple, then two individuals, and now they were a team again. It required some adjustment, but Ben remained focused even with the occasional wisps of sadness. There was still a chill in the air, so Ro had dressed in layers—a long pink sweater over black leggings and black Uggs on her feet. She blew on her hands. It was always freezing in Vicks's room.

"The cold keeps my senses sharp and my brain firing," he explained. Papers were spread out all over the floor. He was at his desk while Ro was sitting on his bed, going through one of the many lists of names they had culled from the reams of data she had given him two weeks ago. Years upon years of hotel guests, thousands of entries, but they had narrowed it down to a couple hundred names. From that point, their work involved checking and rechecking and making sure they didn't miss anything.

"Who's this guy?" Ben asked.

"What guy?" Ro was distracted, clicking on her keyboard.

"Meryl Horton. Did we check him out yet?"

"I think Meryl is a woman's name. Hold on." She clicked away. "Yep, Meryl Horton is a woman. A senior scientist at Bell Labs." She looked up. "That doesn't sound like a national lab."

"Wrong lab, wrong sex." Another name bit the dust. He crossed it off. If they found candidates that they liked, they studied their profiles and face images from the files they had created using Ro's purloined information as well as the all-powerful Internet—and maybe a few files that Ben had hacked into. The names they were currently looking at involved a group that had come to Los Alamos around the time of the summer solstice about a year before Ellen's murder.

The next one was Kevin Barnes. Ben talked out loud to himself as well as to Ro. "It would help if these guys had more unusual names. There are a zillion Kevin Barneses."

"Who's the first one that comes up?"

"A singer . . . then a cornerback for the Lions and the Redskins. None of them seem to be scientists but there are a couple of engineers." He pulled up images and put them in the file. As he sorted through the pile, he considered a Kevin Barnes who was a lawyer. He'd gone to Brown University and Columbia Law School. He was forty-four. For some odd reason—they were looking for scientists, not lawyers—he downloaded Barnes's information and pulled up a grainy picture on image search. The guy's eyes were downcast, which gave him a slightly shifty look. Ben kept staring at his face. "I might be crazy but I think I've seen this guy before."

Ro stopped. "Who?"

"This guy, Kevin Barnes. He's a lawyer."

"Why are you looking at lawyers?"

"I don't really know, but he looks familiar." Ben showed her the picture.

She studied it long enough not to dismiss it out of hand. "Maybe." A pause. "If he's a lawyer, why is he getting a Los Alamos discount?"

"You tell me."

Ro bit her bottom lip. "Maybe the coding got messed up. What else do you have on him?"

Ben delved further. There wasn't much on Barnes the lawyer besides his schooling. Not even his specialty. "He's kind of a cipher and that makes him interesting. I'll start a file." A pause. "Where have I seen him, dammit?"

"If you relax, it'll come to you."

She was right. He picked out another candidate. Jason Fillmore. "This guy's a security analyst."

"A stockbroker?"

"No, security as in 'security guards.'"

Ro stopped typing. "Like, as in safeguarding national labs?"

"I don't know where he works, but if he did work for the national labs, he'd be doing a lot of traveling between them." He checked deeper into his personal information. "He's forty-nine and he's worked for the Chicago and Detroit police departments. Which means he knows how to handle a gun."

"The victims were strangled."

"But he could have used a gun to abduct them." Ben read further. "He started his own company—Universal Analysis and Security—eight years ago, providing consulting and systems integration for big corporations. At least, that's what it says in his bio. I looked him up on Facebook. Nothing personal but there's a Facebook page for the company. It was profession-ally done. It says that his company has provided systems and has consulted for numerous government agencies."

"Anything about national labs?" Ro asked.

"It doesn't specify." Ben thought for a moment. "Would a national lab farm out its security to somebody private? I'd think that the government would want to keep that kind of stuff in-house."

"He has a Los Alamos discount."

"That he does." Ben pulled up an image. "He's African American."

Ro looked up. "And that's relevant because . . . ?"

"The conventional wisdom is that serial killers murder within their own race, though that's because it's easier to find and stalk victims in their own neighborhoods. But I suppose if the guy traveled, he'd abduct whoever was convenient."

"Does he look familiar to you?"

"No, I've never seen him. You?"

"He does not look familiar," Ro said.

"He'd be pretty noticeable in this area. Not a lot of blacks." Ben hit the print button. "I'll start a file on him."

"You've started about twenty files. I thought we're nar-rowing this down."

"One step forward and two steps back."

"You know you're picking out every profession except sci-entists."

"I'm not being biased. I'm just selecting guys whose job assignments might include traveling."

"A lawyer?"

"Santa Fe is the capital of New Mexico. Maybe Kevin

Barnes does government business here. We know he isn't local. Otherwise he wouldn't be staying at the Jackson."

"But he could have an office here."

"Good point. I'll see if he has a local address." Ben pulled up an e–phone book with addresses. "Blank." He continued searching the enigmatic Kevin Barnes with Yahoo! and Bing and DuckDuckGo. He tried deep search engines but still came away empty. Kevin Barnes, the lawyer, had assiduously avoided attention. Ben took his picture and clipped it to his information file. Maybe George Tafoya could help him out.

Ben went down to the next name: Martin Feldman. "This guy has been to the area four times in the last three years." He did a Google search. "And he's a scientist: a radiation physicist from Boston with Mass General . . . oops. He's seventy-two." A beat. "Although I suppose that retirement could mean more free time to do damage."

"If he started with your sister, he would have been around sixty-nine. We're going to have to do some probability assessment. I'd put him low down on the list."

"He could have started murdering before my sister—"

"Vicks, the guy digs graves . . . deep graves. It's hard physical labor."

"You're right. I'm just thinking . . . about six years back, before my sister was murdered, prairie dogs were being shot and killed. It turned out it was a retired scientist who had worked at Los Alamos."

"That is creepy. Why was he shooting prairie dogs?"

"God only knows." Ben shrugged. "I know I'm going to have to narrow down the field, but I'm terrified of missing someone."

"Now you know how Shanks must feel."

"You're right about that. I used to think if only the police would be more thorough, pay more attention to detail, more crimes would get solved. And now I have all this information and I can't even place a familiar face. If Shanks had this information, he could do more than we ever could. But since you acquired it illegally, we're stuck."

"There has to be a way where we can turn it over to him and not get me into trouble."

"When you think of one, let me know." Ben started an image search on the next name: Lewis Grady. "I don't think prison blues are your style."

"On the contrary, they'd match my gorgeous eyes." She flung her hair off her face. "How about we give him the list anonymously?"

"He can't use the information, Ro. It's fruit from a poisoned tree. And you would be in *serious* trouble. So I'd have to take the fall for you."

She smiled. "You'd take the fall for me?"

"Absolutely. Everyone would think it was me anyway. Hacking isn't something that fits your carefully crafted image."

"Aw, you care, Vicks."

He sure as hell cared about her. He was sneaking glances at her when she wasn't looking: her lithe body, her soft tawny hair that fell below her shoulders, her luminescent blue eyes. Just thinking about her naked sent an electric jolt through him. God help him if she noticed.

They had been working for more than two hours—all business—when Ben heard the distinct rumble of an SUV pulling into the driveway. It idled for a few minutes, and then the motor shut off. Ro looked at her watch.

"Wow. Where'd the time go?" Her eyes scanned the mess. "You want help cleaning this up?"

"Nah, I'm gonna keep at it for a while." Frustration was beginning to take hold. He needed a break. He got up and stretched. "So where are you and lover boy off to?"

"Movies. Wanna come?"

"No." When Ro laughed, he said, "What's so funny?"

"We're back at the beginning. You being a hermit and me being the envy of everyone in school. I like being queen of the hill but I'm not so sure that you're in a better place."

"I'm not a hermit. I sit with you at lunch."

"Only occasionally, and you never talk."

"But I pretend to listen. And that's pretty good because I'd much rather be investigating homicidal scientists."

She threw a pillow at him. When the doorbell rang, she said, "Tell lover boy that I'm freshening myself up and will be out in a minute."

Ben opened the front door and JD came inside. He had on a leather bomber jacket that made his extra-wide chest extra extra wide. Ben managed a half-assed smile. "She'll be out in a minute."

"Right."

They stared at each other, each one hoping the other would make the situation less tense. "Anything new?" JD finally asked.

"Nope."

When Ro finally materialized, JD put a protective arm around her, squeezing her with a little too much enthusiasm. But she didn't protest. "We're off to the movies," he said. "Wanna come with us?"

"I already asked," Ro said.

"Thanks, but I'm fine." Another strained smile. "See you guys tomorrow."

JD said, "Give me a minute with him, Ro." He gave her the keys to his car. "Warm yourself up."

"Good idea. It's freezing in here." She broke away from JD and left.

JD said, "She's right. Why do you keep the house so cold?"

"I'm hot-blooded. Have a good time."

"Lisa's gonna be there."

Ever since they'd begun talking again, JD was constantly trying to pair Ben with Lisa. He'd known her since third grade. At one point, they had had mutual crushes on one another. He actually liked Lisa. She—like him—had experienced her portion of *shit happens*. But just because they had shared time and space didn't mean they were a couple in this universe. "Say hi for me."

"I told her you were coming."

"But I'm not coming."

"She said you took her to the movies. She said you had a great time."

"I took her to the movies because she let me into the spring fling on a discount ticket. It was some stupid romantic comedy with magic elves. Does that sound like a good time to you?"

"We're seeing *Pantheon*. It's supposed to be a great movie."

"You can give me a summary on Monday."

"It's two hours, Vicks—"

"I'm not coming—"

"Just bang her. She's *dying* for it."

"I'm not interested in banging her. I saw you banging her. It's weird."

"The girl's not entitled to more than one bang in her lifetime?"

"She's entitled to bang whomever she wants, just like I'm entitled to bang whomever I want. And I'm not interested in Lisa, okay?"

"What is *wrong* with you?"

This was going to go on forever unless he put a stop to it. Ben said, "I'm seeing someone."

JD studied him. "That's bullshit."

"You know, I do go to a major university that's around fifty percent women. And I do work at a major company that employs about fifty percent women. I'm kinda cute in that boyish way. So why is it bullshit?"

JD still didn't believe him, but he played along. "Tell me about this phantom girl."

"She's not a phantom girl." Ben kept it believable. "She works at Circuitchip. Her name is Katy Lu. She's nineteen. Don't tell Ro. She'll interrogate me and I'm not interested in answering questions."

"She's Asian?"

"Yeah, she's Asian. What's wrong with Asians?"

"Nothing. I like Asian women. Except they have small racks. How's her rack?"

"She's Asian. It's small."

"Yeah, you can't get it all, right? Sure you don't want to come? Lisa has a big rack." He punched Ben's shoulder a little too hard. "It'll be a nice change of pace."

Ben pointed to the door. "You can leave now."

"When do I get to meet Katy Lu who probably doesn't exist?"

"When I trust you to not fuck my girlfriends." Again Ben pointed to the door. "Go."

But JD still didn't go. He said, "It's cool that we're, like, talking again."

That was JD. One minute he was choking you to death, the next minute he was sloppily sentimental. "Yes, JD, we're buds. Now could you please leave?"

Reluctantly, JD closed the door behind him. Out the window, Ben watched him strut his stuff down the sidewalk. He hated that Ro was with him, but he was glad to be alone. In the kitchen, he was pouring himself a glass of orange juice, trying to figure out his next move, when he heard a throat clear. He looked around. It took him a couple of seconds to spot the source.

Lilly had tucked herself into the corner of the living room, curled up in a ball on his dad's chair. Her laptop was open and there were papers at her feet.

Ben gave her a look. "You've been eavesdropping on me?"

"I wasn't eavesdropping, I was sitting here the whole time." She wore a pout. "It's not my fault that no one noticed."

There was anger in her voice. He knew why. "Lilly, it's just the way guys talk."

"You mean guys talk racist?"

"What if I said that all Asian girls were smart, which is just as much a stereotype as their having small chests? Would that have been racist?"

"No, that would have been a generalization. Racism implies something negative, and by the way you two were talking, having a small rack was definitely something negative . . . like biology is under one's control!"

Her lip was trembling. Ben knew she was deeply hurt. "You're right. I'm sorry, Lilly."

She didn't answer.

"Where's Haley?"

"She and Griffen went out to a movie."

"You didn't want to go?"

"Obviously not. I'm studying for the state math test and I'm tired of being a third wheel or fifth wheel or whatever." Her eyes were pure smoke. "I can go home if my presence bothers you—"

"Lilly—"

"God forbid I should eavesdrop."

"Stop it already. I apologized. Stop milking it." He softened his tone. "It's not true, by the way. I don't have a girlfriend. I made her up to get JD off my back."

"Why are you telling me?" She lifted up her chin in an act of defiance and glowered at him with wet eyes. "It's not any of my business. And either you're lying to JD or you're lying to me. So either way, you're still a liar."

Ben knew she was mad—she had every reason to be mad—but he just wasn't in the mood to hear it. "Stay as long as you want. You know you're always welcome here." He went to his room and closed the door. But instead of going back to the computer and an infinite list of names, Ben stretched out on his bed, trying to figure out the best way to deal with an ensuing headache. As expected, Lilly knocked a few minutes later. "It's open."

Her face was still angry. She muttered, "I'm sorry."

"No apology necessary. I am a liar. You are correct in your assessment."

She pulled out his desk chair and sat down, her steaming black eyes looking somewhere beyond his face. "I'm not offended by you guys saying that Asians have small racks. I mean, maybe a little, but it's true. In general, Asians do have small racks. But why do *you* have to talk like he does?"

"Who's he? JD?"

"Yes, of course, JD. Why do you bring yourself down to his idiotic level? Why do you even hang around him? You never did before."

"Things change."

"Well, *you* shouldn't change."

"Lilly, I lost three years of my life that I'm never getting back. JD and I have known each other forever. We're not tight like before, but it's nice to have a friend."

"But you're not like that."

"Or maybe I am like that and you never noticed."

There were tears in her eyes. "I've got to go."

"I'll walk you home. It's cold and windy. I wouldn't want you to blow away."

"I will not blow away and I have a warm jacket, thank you very much. And I'd rather be alone."

She stormed out. Ben got up, grabbed his parka, and waited until she gathered up her material and stuffed everything into her backpack. He took the heavy load from her hands. "It's good for me to get some air."

She didn't answer, just marched out of the house. Ben locked the door and caught up with her a half block away. "Are you hungry?" He dug his hands into his pockets. "We can grab a bite somewhere."

"Ben, I'm fine." Her walk was brisk considering the g-forces on their faces. The wind was blowing her black mane straight back—like she was a filly on a racetrack. "Just do whatever you want to do."

"What I want is to feed you and walk you home. That's what big brothers do."

"You're not my brother."

He chuckled. He sounded like a sad clown. "You know what, Lilly? Very soon you'll be all grown up and be this gorgeous woman—"

"Oh *please,* don't."

"Let me finish," Ben said. "You'll be this gorgeous girl with a ton of guys drooling after you. And at some point, you'll discover the truth . . . that I'm not the guy you think I am. And you'll be sorely disillusioned. And that'll be upsetting to you. But I have a feeling it'll be worse for me."

"I have no idea what you're talking about." She broke away and walked six paces in front of him.

I think you do, he said to himself.

He was sad at his own thoughts. It was nice to be adored.

CHAPTER 2

THE KID WAS the brother of the first one. He hadn't exactly grown up, but he was taller. Still thin with intense eyes and girlie curls, but now the face was on a budding man's body. He had wiry arms and a keen determination. All those years that he'd spent going in and out of the police department—it had to be for more than inquiries. It made him wonder just what the kid knew.

Was the kid onto something? Probably.

Was he onto him? Possibly.

The thought terrified and thrilled him at the same time.

The teen had a routine but was not exactly predictable. He went to UNM; he worked at Circuitchip. But he still went to high school. Sometimes he was with the girl, sometimes the other guy was with the girl. Most of the time he was alone.

The kid hadn't reacted suspiciously that night.

Was it a ruse? Probably not.

Was his identity still secure? Most likely.

Maybe it had been a coincidence, bumping into him in the dead of night after he had come back from River Remez. He hadn't been sure if he had wanted to fill the grave with a new one or not, but it had felt good having dug the spot just in case. Because if he was going to do another one, with the kid hunting around, it would have to be well planned, which, of course, made the whole thing even more exciting.

Sometimes the planning was even better than the actual event, with the anticipation turning him on until he had to do something about it. He thought about the four girls constantly. Sometimes it was Julia, sometimes it was Jamey, sometimes it was Katie. But mostly it was Ellen. Being the first in his "official" cycle, she owned a special place in his heart.

Still, there were others to distract him.

The girl behind the desk at the hotel—he had had his eye on her from the beginning. He knew her as the cocktail waitress named Gretchen. She was gorgeous, young, nubile, lithe, everything a beautiful girl should be. All the girls he hunted had been young and nubile—those he had taken, those he had not taken, those he had taken but had released for God only knew what reason. All of them had drawn him into an altered state of consciousness. Gretchen was his current fantasy and she was made doubly delicious because she was also part of the kid's life.

Except he knew her name wasn't Gretchen.

It was Dorothy.

Which was even better.

I'll get you, my pretty . . .

And your little dog too.

BY EIGHT IN the evening, Ben was done for the day. He had narrowed down his search to fifty men that could be candidates for "the one." The investigation had come to the point where even he knew he was out of his league. But since he often felt more machine than human, he plugged along, hoping to figure out something before the arrival of the summer solstice. If he couldn't succeed at doing that, maybe at least he could find a way to give the information to Shanks without landing Ro in jail.

He tried to slink out of his room and out of the house with his backpack, but his mother was right there. She had several frequent expressions and this one was angry-eyes mom. Her curly hair framed her face like a halo. She resembled some kind of avenging angel.

"You weren't even going to say good-bye?" Her arms were crossed over her chest.

"I'm not leaving for Albuquerque until tomorrow. I'm just going out."

"Where?"

"Just hanging."

"With your backpack?"

He put his arm around her. "Why are you giving me the third degree? You never did before."

She pulled away. "Just because I leave you alone doesn't mean I don't care. Once in a blue moon, it would be nice to see you."

"So you're seeing me right now."

"Ben, stop it! You've been holed up in your room for the last ten hours. You didn't even make it to dinner. I know what you're doing and I know I can't stop you. I know you made this insane promise to Ellen, but what about your family that's still alive? Don't you think it's a little rude?"

"Point well taken." He gave her a brief smile but it wasn't returned. "What would you like from me?"

"A simple salutation would be nice. Like 'Hi, Mom, how are you?' Surely, that won't tax you too much."

"No need for the sarcasm."

Her eyes watered. "When you were with Ro, *she* talked to us, so *you* talked to us. I got a little spoiled."

She was hurting, but that was nothing new. Ben sighed. "You know how I deal with crap, Mom. I retreat."

"But things must have resolved between you two. You're seeing her again."

"Not as an item. We're just . . ." *Working together,* he had wanted to tell her. "Whatever. Doesn't matter. I apologize if I seem indifferent."

"You *are* indifferent, Ben, but especially to me and your father. I know you're a wonderful grandson. You talk to your grandparents a lot. I know because they tell me things about your life that I don't know about. How do you think that makes me feel?" She pointed to herself. "Don't I count?"

Ben didn't answer right away. "I need to clear my head, Mom. I'll be home in an hour or so. We'll catch up then."

"And it's not just me, Ben. It's Haley too."

"She's complaining to you?"

"No, but since you're not around, she and Griffen have become a very intense twosome."

"So she has a boyfriend. Don't blame that on me."

It was her turn to sigh. "I like Griff, but I don't know how healthy it is, just the two of them *all the time.* And poor Lilly must be so resentful. I never see her anymore. Not that it's your job to fix things, but sometimes it's better coming from a sibling than from a parent."

"I'm aware that Lilly is a bit put out." Ben exhaled. "Haley's not going to listen to me. But maybe Griff will."

"I'm not saying they shouldn't be together, but both of them should have some interests other than each other."

"I agree. Where is Haley now?"

"She and Griff are at the mall. I'm going to pick them up now."

"I'll do it. It'll show I'm still part of her life."

"What about you clearing your head?"

His mom's voice dripped with sarcasm. Ben kissed his mother's cheek. "See you later."

They weren't that different, his mother and him. Both retreated inward when the stress got to be too much. The problem was, she and Ben were stressed out at different times and for different reasons. One of them was always emotionally unavailable. Their happy paths didn't cross that often.

He would make it his business to talk to his parents tonight.

The living before the dead.

CHAPTER 3

APRIL WAS ENVELOPED in the winds of spring, and before Ben blinked, it was almost gone. His classmates were getting acceptances and rejections from colleges and universities, and once again he sat on the sidelines as other people seemed to move forward. JD was going to Duke, and Ro had gotten into Penn, but was wait-listed for Brown and Harvard. Weekly was going to Colorado State, Lisa had her eye on Texas, and the rest of the crew was making do with New Mexico State or UNM. Ben had disconnected from Remez High, but JD found it hard to let go of his reign. He was adamant that Ben take up his former position of second in command. But too much time had passed and too much had changed, and Ben was absent more than he was present.

What really interested him was Haley and Griff and their own little clique taking over the roles of king and queen. With Griff by her side, Haley had developed an air of confidence.

She smiled a lot. She gesticulated a lot. She was constantly surrounded by friends. Unfortunately, Lilly wasn't among her acolytes. It had been a while since Ben had seen her. One day when she was absent from the lunchroom, he went searching and it didn't take long for him to find her, working in an empty classroom. Her hair was covering her face, her lunch laid out neatly on the desk to her right. He watched her for a minute, hearing her pencil scratch against paper, seeing her tuck her hair behind her ear, her mouth chewing on the eraser.

"Hey." She looked up and Ben walked over to her. "You okay?"

She smiled but it was forced. "Just working on a practice math sheet for the state final."

"When is that?"

"In three weeks, I think."

"And you have to work on it during lunch?" She shrugged and went back to her problem. Ben said, "You're pulling a Vicksburg." She looked up. "Doing a disappearing act and using math for an excuse."

"It's not an excuse. My mom's heavily invested in my performance."

"Are you invested in your performance?"

"No." She sighed. "But since I'm practically an only child, what do I know? And you know *Asian* mothers—"

"I already apologized for that crack." Ben sat down. "I'm a good guy. Don't be a brat."

"I'm not a brat. Well, maybe a little bit of a brat." She waved her hand in the air. "As long as you're here, maybe you can make yourself useful." She showed him a problem. "I have to find the area underneath the curve as it expands at the rate of the function of time."

"Just integrate."

"I'm not allowed to integrate. I have to do it with simple geometry at any given point."

"Oh."

"Yeah. *Oh.*"

Ben smiled. She had fight in her and that was good. He picked up the pencil and started dividing the figure into workable polygons. It took sixteen divisions. "This should do it."

She looked at the work. "Maybe you should enter the contest instead of me."

"Maybe you should just tell your mom you don't want to do it."

"Maybe you should just leave me alone." She was muttering under her breath but loud enough so he could hear it. "Can't a girl get a little solitude?"

"Lilly, I know my sister and Griff are wrapped up in one another and she's probably being a little inconsiderate. But she isn't going anywhere and neither is your friendship."

Lilly shrugged. "I don't care, Ben. And what's wrong with being alone, Mr. Asocial extraordinaire? Or should I call you Mr. Popular now?"

"That's a very interesting point. Because now that I'm with the in-crowd, I'm still a fish with a bicycle. It's weird sitting with Ro now that she's back with JD."

"So just get back with Ro," she blurted out. "You obviously still love her. She obviously still loves you. You should try a little forgiveness."

"This is none of your business, but I'm gonna tell you anyway." Ben waited until he got her attention. She finally put her pencil down. "Ro and I are magnets. If the proper poles are aligned, it's instant attraction. But if you align them the wrong way, the poles repel and no amount of forcing them together will change the physics." He erased his sectioning of the math problem and pointed to the smudged paper. "Let me see you solve this without integration."

Her dark eyes shifted from Ben's to the paper in front of her. She stared at the figure in front of her, at first copying his erased lines and arcs, but then she slowly started improving on the solution, her brainpower clicking in as she chewed on the eraser of the pencil, her hair once again hiding her face. Gently, he tucked an errant tress behind her ear. It was an intimate gesture for a guy to do to a fourteen—well, almost fifteen-year-old girl. She looked up and blushed.

He pointed to the paper. "Go on."

She straightened up and cleared her throat. She was a beautiful girl and would be an even more beautiful woman. She glowed, especially when she did something that engaged her. Looking at her was like seeing a memory of his lost innocence.

When Ben was thirteen, he vaguely remembered "liking" Lisa Holloway. And she "liked him back." And that's what it was for the better part of a year: shy smiles and awkward conversations. And he had some kind of recollection of planning a movie date with her. But then Ellen went missing and around the same time Lisa's parents got divorced. The date never materialized, and shortly afterward, Lisa became enamored of the dark side of everything. She went through a slew of older boyfriends, became truant, and was almost kicked out of high school. But then some unseen force reeled her back in during their senior year, although she still dressed in silly costumes. Ben wondered how it would have been if they had gotten together. Would she have cheated on him like Ro did?

Possibly . . . probably. Once bitten, twice shy.

Ben looked over Lilly's shoulder. She had produced an elegant solution. "Very good. Way better than mine."

"You started me off in the right direction."

"Then I'll take the credit." He stood up. "I'm going back to Albuquerque. You have my e-mail. If you need any more help, don't be afraid to use it."

"Thanks." This time her smile was real. "I'm not mad at you, Ben. I could never be mad at you."

"How about Haley?"

"I love Haley. She's my sister and best friend all rolled into one. It's my problem, not anything she and Griff are doing . . . other than being in love. I'll deal." She shrugged. "Honestly, I don't mind the solitude. I do need to study for state finals. I have a fighting chance of winning, but I'll get wiped out in regionals. I can't compete against all those Texas private schools. My mom will be disappointed but she'll get over it. She's working on other things besides math competitions to get me into the Ivies."

"You know you're a lock for the Ivies. You're half Indian and I found out from Ro that it means that you have underrepresented minority status. Plus, you come from a state that's underrepresented in the Ivies. And you are a master silversmith, judging from my recent Christmas gift. And as an aside, you happen to be brilliant."

Her face was filled with electricity. She closed her workbook, got up, stuffed her pages into her backpack, and slung it over her shoulder. "Maybe I'll go say hi to Haley."

"Maybe you should."

She smiled and left, skipping down the hallway.

CHAPTER 4

AS THE TIME *approached, he was getting nervous. Not nervous excitement, but actually nervous, and that gave him pause. He had a wife. He had a child. He had a life beyond this and he certainly wasn't getting any younger. Maybe . . . just maybe it was time to quit.*

Each time he had done something, he'd sworn it was the last time. If he kept going, he'd eventually get caught. Something would trip him up and he knew the police had his DNA. If he kept his nose clean, he'd be fine, and that wasn't a hard thing to do because when he wasn't abducting, raping, and murdering girls, he was living a fairly conventional life. When he didn't travel, he worked regular hours. Kara wasn't a churchgoer, but she was civic-minded. She was involved with the school, volunteered at the library, and ran its book club. She did Pilates with her friends. She spent too much on ridiculous things: designer clothes and handbags, tennis lessons, and absurdly expensive shoes for their son. Not to mention the cost of private school tuition. It seemed that the school was raising its fees every six months. And if he even mentioned putting Ivan in public school, she'd chew his head off. No wonder he was tense.

No wonder he took out his frustration on others.

He hated to admit it but he was more like his dad than he thought. And Kara was more like his mother than he wanted to believe. Not that his parents had been abusive, but his mother was demanding.

Dad had been an engineer. He provided for the family and never raised his voice in anger. As far as he knew, Dad had never been unfaithful because Dad never had a friend. Nor did he seem to care about having friends. He also never cared about material possessions. He drove an old Buick and dressed every day in short-sleeved white shirts, black slacks, and a clip-on tie. Dad had lived life as a loner, sequestering himself behind a locked door whenever his wife started to nag. But even when he was physically around, it was as if he wasn't there. He read a lot—biographies and nonfiction. If they talked at all, it was always about a book. So maybe Dad did teach him something—the importance of being well read and well educated.

School had been his solace. It wasn't the best school, but he was the best. It afforded him the luxury of going to a top university on someone else's dime. But at least his education hadn't gone to waste. He used it, he plied it, he availed himself of all the perks it gave him.

And there were perks. Free travel, free rentals, and lots of open roads. He had always loved to drive. It calmed him down, it gave him perspective, and in the end, it gave him the greatest thing of all—not freedom, although that was important.

What the open road gave him was access to prey.

JUNE ANSWERED THE door. Her hair was pulled back in a tight ponytail, yanking on her temples, giving her a temporary facelift. Not that she needed it. Her skin was smooth, with high cheekbones and dark eyes that always looked suspicious and a bit angry. "Yes?"

She wasn't even bothering with the bare minimum of civility. It wasn't her fault. Math heads were different. Ben said, "Hi, June, I was wondering if George was around."

"Why do you want to see George?"

"I've got a couple of questions for him." He zipped up his parka.

June realized it was cold outside. "Come in."

"Thank you."

June closed the door. "You want some tea, Ben? You look cold."

"No, I'm fine, thank you."

"Suit yourself." She disappeared and the house went silent. Ben suspected that Lilly was in her room and didn't feel like talking. Okay by him. He didn't feel like facing another emotional female. June could be very cool, but it wasn't because she was mean. She was a controlled person and probably somewhat controlling. She didn't come across as a tiger mom, but from Lilly, he knew that she had expectations. And that wasn't a bad thing. Without pressure, a tire went flat.

He thought about Haley, slipping into adolescence, replete with boyfriend and social status. Lilly was becoming more and more withdrawn, and he was helpless to stop it.

But she would blossom eventually. Lilly had always had an inner strength.

George came out. "Hey, Ben."

"Feel like having some pie?" Ben asked.

June made a face. "Pie? What pie? You already ate."

"There's always room for pie," George said.

"You had two pieces of cake, George. If you eat any more desserts, you'll go into a diabetic coma."

"My insulin is fine, thank you very much, and don't look at me like that. You made the cake."

"That doesn't mean you have to eat it all." June hit his belly. "You're getting fat."

Instead of being angry, George just laughed. "You need me to pick up anything while I'm out, June?"

"I can't believe you're really going out for pie."

"Yes, I am really going out for pie."

"Then pick me up a piece of anything sugarless." Again she patted his stomach. "Some of us have self-control. Others just succumb." She shook her head and disappeared from view.

George was still smiling. "I take it you want to drive?"

"Absolutely."

They were three blocks away from George's house when he spoke. "What is it?"

Ben pulled over to the curb and liberated the ten images he'd found through Google from his backpack. "Do you know any of these people?"

George shuffled the faces. "Who are they?"

"They might be associated with the labs."

He continued to study the images. "Vicksburg, just what did you hack into?"

"I didn't hack into anything." George gave him a sour

look. Ben said, "Honest. You can check the hard drive of my computer."

"Hard drives come and hard drives go. How'd you get these names?"

"That's a complicated question."

The old man rubbed his eyes and returned half the stack. "I don't know these." He had handed Ben back images of four scientists and Jason Fillmore, the security analyst. "They may be associated with the labs, but I've never had any dealings with them."

"And the others?"

"I've worked with Percy Sellers, Robert Yin, Kim Dok Park, and Stu Greenberg. I've known Yin and Greenberg for years. They're plasma physicists. Yin is from Fermi, Stu is from Lawrence Livermore."

Ben sat up. "What do you know about Stu Greenberg?"

"He's around sixty. A senior scientist and a brilliant, brilliant guy. June and I had dinner with his wife and him about a year ago when we were in the Bay Area. They're lovely people." He laughed. "I guarantee he isn't who you're looking for."

"You never know what's inside a person's head."

"Stu's head is stuffed with remarkable and ingenious ideas. There's no room for anything else. He also has osteoarthritis and has had several surgeries. I believe he walks with a cane."

Rule *him* out. Ben said, "What about the others?"

"Dr. Park is a biochemist, Sellers's specialty is medical radiology." He pointed to Kevin Barnes. "This guy. He's not a scientist, he's a lawyer."

"I know that." Ben's heart took off and he forced himself to speak slowly. "What kind of a lawyer is he?"

"Immigration. I've dealt with him a few times because he

needed character references from some of the scientists in the labs for visa extensions or permanent residence." George handed him back the remaining stack. "How'd you get these names, Ben?"

"I can't tell you."

"I know you did something illegal. It's going to come back to bite you on the butt. Get rid of your hard drive."

"I didn't do anything illegal, but I can switch drives if you think I should."

"Do it. Now tell me what's going on. Why are you narrowing down your searches to the faces you showed me?"

Ben was prepared for the question and for his answer. "I got these names by looking at scientists who go to a lot of conventions."

"All scientists travel a lot. We present our research. We're always exchanging information with one another. There are hundreds of scientists. How did you narrow it down to these men? And why the lawyer? And stop bullshitting me. It's pissing me off."

Ben cleared his throat. "These particular men have traveled more than once to Los Alamos and over extended periods of time. They've also traveled between the other labs."

"How'd you find that out? I know you don't have the skills to hack into a national laboratory. So you did it in some other way. Are you hacking into the airlines?"

That would have been a good idea, Ben thought. He said, "I can't tell you, George."

"Ben, you have to stop what you're doing right now! I know you didn't get this information from a Google search."

"That is true. But that doesn't mean the feds are coming after me."

George sized him up. "Why the lawyer?"

"He's been to Los Alamos at least six times in the last four years."

"How do you know that?"

"I can't tell you."

"But you didn't do anything illegal." A pause. "Did you pay someone to do something illegal?"

"No, I did not."

George shook his head. "Let's go get some pie."

Ben restarted the motor and put the car into gear. "Tell me about the immigration lawyer, Kevin Barnes. There's not much on him in the search engines. He doesn't have a Facebook or LinkedIn page. He's kind of a cipher."

"Not all of us waste our time being social on the Internet."

"You'd think he'd want some kind of professional page just for business."

"Maybe he has enough clients without going digital."

"Is he a government employee?"

"He works for the labs, but I don't know if he's on the government payroll or he's someone Uncle Sam has outsourced."

"If he works for the government, it would make sense that he wouldn't advertise anything." George didn't comment. "Do you know him?"

"I mind my own business, Ben. I focus on my own work and that's why the lab keeps old guys like me around."

"What are you? Like fifty?"

"None of your damn business." George thought a moment. "Barnes must be doing a good job. He's been around for a while."

"How old is he?"

"In his forties."

"Any personal impressions of the guy?"

George was silent, but he was thinking about the question. "He's weird."

Ben opened and closed his mouth. "He's *weird*?"

"Scientists are not the most social people in the world. We like what we do and what we do requires solitude. I'm always thinking in numbers. So is June. But you don't expect odd behavior from a lawyer. Most of the other lawyers I've met are slick."

"I see you've never met my dad or grandpa." George laughed and then Ben said, "What kind of weird are we talking about?"

"Let me backtrack. If Barnes was a mathematician, I wouldn't have used the adjective 'weird.' It's just you think of a lawyer as being aggressive or forward. From the very few dealings I've had with him, he didn't seem like a lawyerly type. He certainly didn't dress like a lawyer, but that could be because he works around scientists so much he's adopted the dress."

Ben was silent.

George said, "Like I said, he must be competent, otherwise he wouldn't have lasted this long."

"You're defending him."

"I can see you're jumping to conclusions and it's my fault. I stoked the fires. Do me a favor and I won't rat you out to Shanks."

Ben was stunned. If he hadn't been driving, he would have gotten out of the car and slammed the door. "You're thinking of ratting me out?"

"It's my only weapon to get you to stop doing stupid things."

"I *trusted* you."

"Actually, Ben, it had nothing to do with trust. You came to me for *information,* and assumed I wouldn't say anything. And I haven't. But that will change if you keep hacking into systems."

"I haven't hacked into anything." Ben was furious, but George seemed oblivious to his anger. He was in his own world.

Finally, he said, "Let me poke around . . . see what I can dig up." He turned to Ben. "Stop doing what you're doing."

"I'm not doing anything illegal." Ben pulled into a parking space at the Pie House.

"Well, you didn't get these names by picking them out of a hat." George patted his stomach. "All this talking to you isn't good for my waistline. June is right. I'm getting pudgy. Let's go see if we can find something sugarless."

He pulled on the door handle and Ben followed him to the shop. There were quite a few sugarless fruit pies. George chose cherry and Ben went for the sugarless apple.

George said, "You're as skinny as a stork. Why are you buying a sugarless pie?"

Ben said nothing. He didn't know why. Perhaps it was because "sugarless" was an apt description for the better portion of the last three years.

CHAPTER 5

WHOA. FINALLY! I know where I've seen Kevin Barnes."
Ro stopped typing on her computer, looked up, and
waited for Ben to continue. "The night of the equinox . . . while I waited for you to finish up at the
Jackson . . ." He hit the image. "He bumped into my shoulder
in the parking lot."

Ro got up from Ben's bed. "Are you sure?"

"Positive. I even asked you about him. You were going to
look him up the next day." No response. "Do you remember
this at all?"

"I do remember your asking." A deep sigh. "I'm sorry,
Ben, I forgot to do it."

"'S'right."

"No, it's not all right. I could have gotten his room key
when he turned it in and we could have tested it for DNA."

"Dorothy, if he's the one, I guarantee you he didn't turn in his room key." Ben continued to stare at the picture. "The guy was heavier . . . older." He closed his eyes, trying to revive a memory. "He was smelly . . . no, not smelly. Sweaty . . . the kind of musty odor you get when you're nervous or you've done physical labor."

Ro was already going down the list of hotel guests on that date. "There's no Kevin Barnes."

"Can I see the list of patrons?"

"Of course." She handed it to him.

Quickly, Ben's eyes scanned down the names. "Nike B. Ravens is an anagram of Kevin Barnes."

"Nike's a girl's name."

"Did you say anything to him when you checked him in?"

"I didn't check him in, Vicks, but I would have noticed the name."

"Well, maybe your coworkers aren't as astute. And if I were looking for a sexual psychopath, I wouldn't be looking for a girl. It's a good dodge."

"Then why use an anagram of the name when he's used his real name before?"

"Because if you're using aliases, it's good not to stray too far from your real name. Otherwise you forget who you are. As for using his true name, the guy is keeping it real once in a while. Probably to confuse the police if they were looking." Immediately he fished out the names that were registered at the Jackson around the time of Ellen's abduction. "Holy shit! Here it is! Karen Bevins." He regarded Ro. "He's using girls' names. I've got to tell George Tafoya—"

"Ben, you've got to tell Shanks."

"And say what, Ro? That you've been hacking the Jackson Lodge registration database?"

"I haven't hacked into anything."

"Not technically, but all this information was illegally obtained. You'll get into trouble. It'll ruin your life. We can't tell Shanks unless we can come across it in some other way."

"You bumped into him on the night of the equinox, right?"

"How would I know his name? He didn't introduce himself." Ben was frantic. "Let me think . . . I should talk to George Tafoya . . . wait. I can't call him."

"Why not?"

"Because his phones are bugged."

"He told you that his phones are bugged?"

"Yes, and probably his house and his car. Maybe even his cell phone."

"Is Lilly's phone bugged?"

"I haven't the slightest idea. But that's a very good plan." He called up Haley. "Hi, is Lilly with you? Do you know where she is? No, never mind, it's not important." He looked at Ro. "Lilly is at the library. Maybe I'll go down there."

"Can you at least wait until JD arrives here so you don't abandon me since I'm helping you out? Unless you want me to leave."

"No, no, no. You're right. Let's see what else I can find out about this dude or Karen Bevins or Nike B. Ravens." Ben paused. "You try to figure out how we can get this name to Shanks without having you arrested."

She said, "How about . . . I noticed him . . . that he was coming in very late on the equinox . . . and it got me thinking. So I looked him up—"

"No, you can't look him up." He thought a moment. "You would have to know who he is . . . his name. And like you said, you didn't check him in. Furthermore, he was registered under a different name."

She blew out air. "Fiction writing was never my forte. I'm a terrible liar."

"I know that firsthand."

She threw a pillow at him. That was her usual behavior when she became frustrated with him. When the doorbell rang, Ben checked his watch and Ro checked hers. She said, "JD isn't due for another hour."

"Be back in a moment." Ben opened the front door. Lisa Holloway was wearing her usual black dress with an irregular hemline and combat boots. She had dyed a purple streak in her hair. Her nails were painted black. Her eyes were ringed with dark eyeliner and her lips were bright blue.

"Hey." He stepped outside rather than invite her in. "What's up?"

"Not much."

"You okay?"

"Yeah, I'm fine." Her eyes furrowed. "Do I look not okay?"

"No, you look . . . like you always do. What's up?"

"I was just wondering if you'd like . . . to get a cup of coffee or something."

"Ro's here. We're working on some stuff together. Then I'm going down to Albuquerque. I have work tomorrow and classes at UNM."

"Okay." She dragged her toe across the porch. "Some other time."

"Sure."

"You wanna go to prom together?" she blurted out. When

Ben didn't answer right away, she crossed her arms over her chest. "Don't feel obligated. Josh Martin has already asked me but . . . I'd rather go with you."

"I'm taking Ro."

Her face was confused. "So who's JD taking?"

"He's taking Ro too."

"You're *both* taking her?"

"Yeah, that was the deal when she started dating JD again, that we'd both take her to prom."

She nodded. "Two dates . . ." She nodded again. "Sweet." She shrugged and started to head to her car. "See you."

Ben held up his hand. "Wait." She turned and looked at him. Ben beckoned her with a crooked finger and she stepped back up onto the porch. He said, "Sure, let's go to prom together. But I'm not going to any after party or any hotel or—"

"You don't have to fuck me, okay?" Her eyes were hard and sad at the same time. "I know you're not interested, okay? Especially after . . ." She averted her glance. "You know."

"Yeah, that was kind of unfortunate."

She faced him. "I'll pay for the limo, your tux rental, and the corsage. Just show up, okay?"

"Don't waste money on a limo. I'll drive. And I'll pay for my own tux rental and I'll pay for the corsage. I was gonna do that anyway, so it's fine. What kind of corsage do you want? Pin-on or wrist?"

"I don't know. I haven't bought my dress." Her voice softened. "Any color you like?"

"Color? You mean you're not wearing black?"

"I'm not going Goth, okay." She rolled her eyes. "I don't want my kids looking at my prom picture and saying, 'God,

Mom, what were you thinking?' I've already said that enough times to myself."

"You and me both." He smiled at her and she smiled back. "There's nothing wrong with a signature look."

"If you don't care, I will probably wear black . . . but not Goth black. There you have it. Are you really going down to Albuquerque, Vicks, or are you trying to get rid of me?"

"No, I'm really going back to Albuquerque. High school is over for me and I've got a major topology test—" He heard muffled footsteps and turned around.

Ro had come outside. "If this was going to take a while, the least you could have done was let me know."

"I'm going." Lisa waved. "Bye."

"Bye." Ben turned to Ro. "Sorry." He walked back into the house and to his room.

She followed. "What was that all about?"

"She asked me to prom."

"Lisa did?"

"Yep."

"What'd you say?"

"I said okay."

Ro glared at him. "Aren't you taking me?"

"JD's taking you."

"I thought both of you were taking me."

"That's what I told her at first . . . that I was taking you and JD was taking you as well. And then I realized how stupid that sounded, so I said I'd take her."

"Thank you very much." She was angry.

"Ro, c'mon. Do you really need two dates? JD's your boy-friend."

"That wasn't my choice."

"Well, it wasn't my choice either."

"Well then, who the hell's choice was it if it wasn't yours?"

"No, no, no." He turned to her. "Don't lay that on me. *You* made the choice."

"I told you I was drunk. I didn't even want to do it."

"But you did it anyway."

"What do you *want* from me, Ben? I said I was sorry about a million times. Obviously, everything I did for you . . ." She took up a pile of paper and threw it at him. "All this shit . . . all my sleepless nights illegally poking into computers, wiggling my ass for disgusting businessmen, working myself to the bone just wasn't enough to atone for my sin! I don't know who's stupider. You or me."

She picked up her purse. Ben caught her by the arm. "Why are we fighting about this? It's ancient history."

"You're an asshole, that's why we're fighting."

"I'm an asshole? *I'm* an asshole?"

"Yes, you're an asshole. You promised to take me to prom and now you're taking Lisa." She turned on him. "She *fucked* him too, you know."

"I know, Ro, I was there." But Lisa wasn't his girlfriend at the time. He didn't point that out. Ro was already too worked up. He let go of her arm. "What are you getting so upset about anyway? In a couple of months, you'll be gone for good and I'll just be a small footnote in your life."

There were tears in her eyes. "Well, then *excuse me* for thinking that maybe as my first love and my first lover, you saw me as something more than a footnote."

"No, no, no. You got it wrong. I said that *I'd* be the footnote in *your* life."

"But what you really mean is *I'm* the footnote in *your* life."

"No, I meant what I said. That *I'm* the footnote in *your* life." He covered his face with his hands. "Can we stop fighting, please?"

"Why are you taking Lisa Holloway to prom? Everyone will just snicker behind your back."

"As long as it's behind my back, what do I care?"

She hit him. "She's a slut."

"She's not a slut. She's just . . . friendly."

"I can't believe you're going with her."

"I'm going with her because she asked me. And because I felt I owed her one from a long time ago. And because you have a real boyfriend and a legitimate date without me. And to tell you the truth, I'm tired of being second in line behind that idiot. I don't enjoy being his straight man and I don't enjoy sitting with you guys and I'm really not going to enjoy sharing you with him at prom. I'd rather go with Lisa, as . . . *friendly* as she is . . . because I'd rather have a whole date with someone I like than half a date with someone I love. I don't want to hang out with your crowd, I don't want to stand in the shadows while you dance with him, and I don't want to be someone I'm not! What I want to do is find the monster that killed my sister so he doesn't do it again. And if it's Kevin Barnes, I'm going to find him and rip him to shreds. And if it *is* him, you've helped me out like nobody else. I love you dearly. You know that. Can we please just stop fighting!"

She looked at him. "I love you too."

Ben smiled. "You know we broke up at the perfect time: before our love could turn into contempt. How good is that?" She didn't answer. He tried out a weak smile. "I'd still love to dance with you."

She remained silent.

"Please, let's get along. It's like two months before you leave River Remez for good." He looked at her and then looked down. "Ro, if it isn't Kevin Barnes, I need your help. You know all the codes and the abbreviations and everything. And if it is Kevin Barnes, you're my eyes and ears at the Jackson. I know that's being selfish, but I can't do this without you, Dorothy."

He had expected her to take his head off. Instead she said, "Even if I hated you—which I do sometimes—I would continue to help you, Vicks. I realize we're dealing with a greater issue than stupid teenage love."

"I knew there was a reason I loved you so much."

"Don't sweet-talk me. I am so . . . pissed at you." She hit his chest. "You threw me over."

"Do you really want me to call Lisa up and tell her I changed my mind?"

"Yes."

"Well . . . I'm not going to do it." She hit him again. "I'd still love to dance with you." No response. "Please?"

She folded her arms across her chest. "I want a prom picture with both you and JD, one on either arm."

"Fine."

"*Two* pictures with both of you. Then I want one alone with you and one alone with JD."

"Whatever you want."

"And I want two corsages, Vicks, one from you and one from JD."

"Done."

"And the one you get me better be bigger and more expensive than Lisa's."

"You are ruthless."

"Yes or no."

"Yes."

"Go with Lisa." Ro waved him away. "I give you my permission."

"Thank you very much, Your Grace."

She looked at the mess in his room. "I can't concentrate anymore." She thought a moment. "I don't have all the registers from the Lodge in Albuquerque—just for some selected days. Let me hunt around a little more."

"No way, no way!" Ben shook his head. "George knows that I obtained the names illegally, but he doesn't know how. We've gotten out of this alive. If you get caught, it'll ruin your life. Please promise me you'll stop."

"Why should I? You don't promise me anything. And even when you do, you renege."

Ben took her in his arms. "It's bad enough that you're still working at the Jackson. You really shouldn't press your luck. You should quit."

"Vicks, if he's onto us—and just maybe he is—he knows what I'm doing there, so . . . maybe it's better that I'm there." She pulled away but kept her arms around his waist. "You know what that crime show says: keep your friends close but your enemies closer."

"Actually, I think Sun Tzu said it in *The Art of War.*" Ro was silent. He said, "I looked it up."

This time she broke away. "I'm hungry. To make up for your sins with Lisa, you may take me out for dinner. You can clean all this up later."

"I should clean it up now. I have to get back to Albuquerque. I've got a big test tomorrow and . . ." Her look made him wilt. "I thought you were going out to the movies with JD."

"We'll catch a later show. And if he gets pissed, I don't care." She was glaring at him, daring Ben to contravene her orders.

Pick your battles, Vicks.

He said, "Where would you like to go eat?"

She picked up her purse, flipped her hair, and tossed him a look over her shoulder. "Kiki's is just fine. Although if you should opt for something better, I wouldn't say no."

CHAPTER 6

WEAPONS WEREN'T HIS thing. If it couldn't be done with the hands and the brain, it was a cop-out. Still, there was something thrilling about holding a killing machine in one's hands. Something so powerful, so strong, yet so compact. Weapons were the ultimate combination of art and mechanics.

He knew he was taking chances. It wasn't that he wanted to be caught—that would be disastrous—but it seemed that over the years he'd needed more and more to keep up the thrill. It was like sex. The act was fine, but sometimes the foreplay was even finer. And as he got older, it seemed he needed more and more foreplay, hence the weapon. It produced a thrill, holding something potentially lethal. It gave him power.

And that's what it was all about really.

Power.

"STOP SQUIRMING." LAURA Vicksburg put down her phone and adjusted the camera attachment. "If you stop moving, I can finish quicker."

"I'm not moving on purpose. The tux doesn't fit." Ben was annoyed. "Why are you even doing this? There's a photographer at the prom. I promise I'll order extra photos."

"He or she will not have a mother's love. And stop glaring at me. It wrinkles your forehead."

His father, hiding behind a newspaper, was laughing. Haley put up her hand. "Wait." She straightened his clip-on bow tie. "I can't wait for my prom."

"Want to go instead of me?"

She ignored him. "We have morp in two weeks, but it's not the real thing. It's, like, homemade decorations and weak punch. And we're not allowed to wear strapless or minidresses or gowns. That doesn't leave too much in the fashion department."

"You've hit on something," Ben told her. "Prom is really all about chick fashion."

"You just realized this?" Haley patted his cheek. "You really do look handsome, Ben. You clean up very nicely." She backed away and his mother took another picture.

"Can I go now?"

"Where are your six friends, Grumpy?" Laura waved her hand. "Yes, you can go now!"

"If I had my choice, I'd rather take you or Haley or even Lilly . . ." He looked at his sister. "Where *is* Lilly? I never see her anymore."

"We're going shopping together this weekend for dresses." She looked peevish. "She's going with Ezra to morp. She has a life without me."

"I'm just used to seeing her, that's all. No need to get snippy."

She stuck her tongue out. Laura's eyes had turned wet. "Promise me you'll *try* to have a good time. I know this isn't your thing, Ben, but you won't regret it. It's what . . . you should be doing at your age."

Ben nodded, knowing exactly what she meant.

This first time should have been Ellen's moment. He was a piss-poor substitute, but he was all that Mom had.

LISA DECIDED TO do a modern twist on her usual garb. The dress was black lace but had an underlay of gold. Supersexy and contemporary and very short, like a baby-doll nightgown. Her long legs were encased in seamed stockings held up by a garter belt that peeked from under the micromini hemline. Her shoes were ultrahigh heels and they glittered like the stars.

Ben complimented her. She complimented him. Her mom took pictures while criticizing Lisa's dress (too short), her makeup (too much), and her hair ("you should have done an updo"). Had she been Ben's mother, he would have taken drugs too. On the ride over, Lisa was sulky and silent.

"You look great," he told her.

"Thanks." She was fiddling with her hair, which had been tied in an elaborate braid. "My mom's a bitch." Her eyes were hot. "God, I can't wait to get out of there 'cause it's either I leave or I'll commit homicide."

"If she meant to embarrass you in front of me, it didn't work. You look superhot." He parked the car and helped her out. "Take it from me as a guy: you couldn't do any better."

"Should I have done an updo?"

"You should let your hair loose. Guys love long hair."

She began to undo the braid, her carefully designed coif falling over her shoulders in waves.

"Perfect," Ben said. "Should we go in or would you like more time?"

"I suppose we have to take the plunge."

Ben took her hand and together they walked inside. The gym wasn't exactly transformed—it still smelled of sweat and dirty socks—but it did look festive. There was bunting and banners, there was colored lighting, and there was a disco ball. Onionfeather—the band—was dressed in retro suits with skinny ties: white jackets and black cuffed pants that showed their socks. There was a full-sized buffet table with desserts and punch and coffee. The dance floor was half filled with couples gyrating to terrible music. The guys were in rented tuxes and the girls glittered like tinsel. Ro was holding court near the coffee urn. JD had his arm around her waist. Ben sighed. The girl was an absolute knockout, wearing something long and slinky, with silver and gold threaded through it and a big slit that revealed a good deal of leg. The entire dress showed off that incredible body.

"Balenciaga," Lisa said.

"Pardon?"

"Ro's gown. It's designer. You can't even get the label here. She must have bought it in New York or something. There's one thing I can guarantee you: it must have cost a fortune."

"Waste of money."

"Not on her." She turned to him. "You know she told us like the first week she came here that she was approached at sixteen to model for the Katy's Intimates junior catalog. That's lingerie, in case you didn't know."

"Oh, I know all about Katy's Intimates."

"I bet you do. But her mother didn't want her to do it and then they moved to River Remez. She's still bitter."

Ben laughed. "I . . . did not know that."

Lisa smoothed out her dress. "Some of us just have to be happy with the H&M catalog." She raised her eyebrows and began pointing around the room. "That dress, that dress, and that dress. They're from Forever 21. That one's H&M. Those two are Ross Dress for Less—"

"Lisa, you look hot. Let's get our picture taken."

They waited in line for the photographer, and when they were done, Ro took Ben's arm, glaring at Lisa while smiling at the same time. It was a feat. "My turn."

"Ro—"

"Go ahead," Lisa said. "You two look nice together."

"Thank you," Ben said.

Ro's whisper was more of a growl. "I hate it when she's nice. It means she's planning on fucking you."

"Will you please stop?"

"She looks like a blow-up doll."

"You're nasty."

She said, "Where's my corsage?"

"In the trunk of my car."

"Go get it."

"I agreed to buy you a corsage that was bigger and better than Lisa's. Which I did. But I didn't agree to give it to you so you can embarrass her, which you've already done by look-ing so hot and classy. So you win, Ro. Can we all try to get through this civilly?"

"As long as you agree that I've won."

When it was their turn in front of the camera, Ro turned

on the fake wattage. When it was over, Ben said, "It's no contest, okay." He kissed her cheek and broke away, trying to find Lisa. But before he could get to her, JD cornered him near the popcorn machine.

"Man, you don't even have to take anything off," he said. "Just slam her against the wall and shove it in."

"You have the soul of a poet."

"Get it while you can, dude. Girls get hot when you look fly."

"More penguin than fly." Ben checked his watch. "How much longer?"

"Around three hours."

"What the fuck do you do here for three hours?" When JD pulled out a plastic bag filled with dried vegetable material, Ben laughed. "Put it away, dude. You need that scholarship."

"They wouldn't have the balls. I'm the finest thing that ever happened to this dump." He looked around. "I lit up before I got here. Makes the food taste a hell of a lot better. The rest is for the after party. Believe me, Vicks, I've got a lot of tricks up my sleeve." He smiled. "Are you gonna be there?"

"Not a chance."

"She's practically flashing you." He furrowed his brow. "Tell me righteous, dude. Are you gay?"

"Seriously? You're really asking me that?"

"Then why turn down pussy? Even if it's not number one pussy, it's still pussy. And she's good, dude. She's certainly had enough experience."

Ro was walking toward them. Ben smiled. "Have fun at the after party, but wear a condom. Oh right. I forgot. You carry those in your car just in case you want to fuck other guys' girlfriends."

"Vicks—"

"I'm just sayin' . . ." He walked away and went looking for Lisa. She was happily chatting away with Shannon Stork. But she was perceptive. She took one look at his face and excused herself. "You okay?"

"Just bored."

"Do you wanna dance?"

The music was off-key and earsplittingly loud. "Sure, let's dance."

"We can sit it out, Vicks." She smiled. "Or we can sit out the entire prom."

"No, no . . ." Ben sighed. "I'm just being a jerk. Sure, let's dance."

"Vicks, we can go. All I wanted to do was show up with you. This isn't my idea of fun either."

"But they haven't crowned the king and queen yet."

"Be still, my beating heart."

Ben laughed. "Do you really want to leave?"

"I wouldn't mind some air. It's kind of stuffy in here."

"Sounds like a good idea." Ben paused. "No tokes or snorts or pills, please. I'd like to graduate."

"I'm clean and sober."

"Perfect." When they got outside, Lisa took his hand and started pulling him away from the gym. "Uh, what's going on?"

"Just come."

They crossed the quad, walking to the front of the school toward the administration building. "Where are we going exactly?"

"It's a surprise."

"I don't like surprises."

"Well, you'll like this one." She took out a key and opened

a door to the administration building. It was deserted and dark, but since there were windows to the parking lot, some lamppost illumination and starlight streamed through.

"Uh, how'd you get a key to the school?"

"I used to have a lot of friends with iffy ethics. Is it my fault that the stupid school never bothers to change their locks? C'mon!" She led him to the stairwell, and in near blackness, they climbed to the second floor.

Ben had a sneaking suspicion where they were going. And when she turned right and left and zigzagged across the hallway, he knew. She stopped right in front of the math supply closet, took out another key, and opened the door.

"Lisa, c'mon."

"You c'mon."

"No, this isn't right."

"What are you afraid of?" She pushed him into the closet and closed the door. "I know you're not gay."

"This isn't right. It isn't respectful."

"I know. It's very sleazy." She started fooling around with his tux's zipper. "Listen to me, Vicks. I'm not doing it for you. I'm doing it for *me*. It's important to me to give you a different memory—other than the *unfortunate* one, okay?"

"Lisa, you don't have to do this."

"But I want to do this." She dropped to her knees, and in a matter of seconds, Ben's "No, Lisas" became "Oh, Lisas." It didn't take long. Five minutes later they were in the dark hallway, alone, silent, and awkward. Instead of feeling relaxed, Ben was tense.

Lisa, on the other hand, was very matter-of-fact. "I need a bathroom. Wait here, okay?"

"I'm not going anywhere." He was on the floor, sitting against the hallway lockers. When she came out of the bathroom, she called his name.

"Over here."

She looked around and sat by his side. Her breath had turned minty. She massaged his neck. "You okay?"

"I'm fine." He was suddenly annoyed. "I'm not a virgin, by the way."

"I know."

He turned to face her. "You girls yak with one another?"

"All the time."

He was quiet. Then he said, "What'd she say about me?"

"That you were big." She patted his knee. "She wasn't lying."

Ben's face went hot. "What else did she say?"

"Who listened? Ro was rubbing my nose in it because she knew I liked you. Well, the joke's on her now." Her eyes held his. "And don't look so scared. I don't expect anything from you, Vicks. All I wanted was bragging rights about nailing you."

"Shouldn't I be bragging about nailing you?"

"Nah." She waved him off. "I'm easy. But you're not." She leaned her head against his shoulder. "I used to feel bad about it—being so . . . slutty. But then I found out that Shannon was not only doing JD when she was going with Weekly, she was also doing Salinez because she found out that Chelsea was doing Weekly. And then, of course, Ro did JD while she was going with you." She shrugged. "I mean, if everyone is a skank, why be embarrassed?"

"Your logic is impeccable." Ben regarded her face. He lifted her chin and kissed her minty mouth. They started making out. The order of events was backward, but it felt nice, so what the hell.

Lisa purred. "She also said you were a good kisser."

"Just good?"

"Well, maybe she said great." Her hands drifted to his crotch. "You want to do it? I mean *really* do it?"

"No, no. This is fine."

"Your words don't match other parts of you."

"That is true enough." Ben pulled her hand away and kissed it very gallantly. "No, Lisa, although you are gorgeous and I am still horny, I will be a gentleman and pass. So remember this moment. There are nice guys in this world."

"You're a dying breed."

"That is probably true but I'm not dead yet."

"Some other time, then, but don't wait too long." She sat up. "In a month I'm gone. My dad can't wait for me to come and my mom can't wait for me to go."

"Where's your dad? Houston?"

"Dallas. But I'll be dorming at school. You should think about UT, Vicks. It's not that far from New Mexico and Austin's a great city."

"Yeah, it *is* a great city."

"Why are you hanging around here? You should be at MIT or Harvard."

Ben just laughed.

"What's so funny?"

"Nothing at all." He took her hand and pulled her up. "Wanna go back to the gym before we both get expelled?"

"Nah, let's just get out of here for good. I'm hungry."

"Sure. Where do you want to go?"

"Kiki's. I want to run into Ro and let her know we were up to something."

"You girls are very catty."

"Vicks, that's what prom is all about. Looking hot so the boys leer at you and the girls give you dirty looks. In that regard, I consider my senior prom a big, big success." She kissed his nose. "And it's all because of you."

"I am happy to have fulfilled your revenge fantasy."

"It wasn't a fantasy, dude. I really did blow you."

Now, how do you respond to that? Ben laughed again. Hand in hand, they walked out of the school and toward the parking lot, which was filled to capacity. It took him a while to remember where he parked. When he found his wheels—the car had been blocked by a limo—he pulled out his keys. But as he got closer, Ben stopped dead and yanked Lisa back. Blood rushed to his brain. His heart was going haywire. "My tires are flat."

Lisa dropped his hand. "Wow."

Ben walked around the car. "All four of them."

"Someone pranked you—let the air out."

He knelt down and looked at the squashed rubber. "This isn't a prank. They're cut."

"What?" There was fear in Lisa's voice. "You mean like someone slashed them?"

"Yep. All four of them." It kicked something into his brain. He felt his head go light. "Oh my *God!*"

He took off toward the gym, did a U-turn, grabbed Lisa's hand, and dragged her with him.

"What's wrong, Ben?"

He didn't answer. Couldn't get the words out. When they arrived back inside, Ben scanned the room, but he couldn't

find Ro anywhere. He did see JD talking to Weekly and Salinez and ran up to them. "Where's Ro?"

"Hey, Vicks." He was smirking. "How'd it go?"

Apparently, his dread wasn't apparent in the dim light. Ben
grabbed JD's shoulders tightly and enunciated very clearly.
"Where? Is? *Ro*?"

"In the bathroom or something. What the hell is wrong
with you?"

Ben raced to the girls' bathroom and flung open the door.
There were a few gasps and a few screams, but he saw her in
a corner, talking to Shannon while putting on lipstick. Before
he could get a word out, she was glaring at him. "Where've
you been?"

Ben hugged her tightly. Lisa followed him inside. He was
about to offer an explanation, but horror seized his insides.
He began to shake as he took out his cell and called home.
Thank God for speed dial. He was sure that he couldn't have
come up with his own phone number right then. Haley answered and relief washed over him.

"Where are you?" he shouted into his cell.

"Uh, you called me," she answered.

"Are Mom and Dad home?" Someone asked him to leave
the girls' bathroom. Ben took the conversation outside. To
Haley, he said, "Mom and Dad are home, right?"

"Yeah."

"Lock the doors and don't open them, no matter what."
He heard a voice in the background. "Who's there with you?
Griff?"

"For your information, it happens to be Lilly. We're looking at dresses in the fashion mags for morp."

"Lilly's there? Even better. She's sleeping over, right?"

"Yeah, of course." A pause. "Ben, what's going on?"

"I'll call you later." He hung up.

Ro emerged from the bathroom. "What is wrong with you?"

Lisa said, "Someone slashed all the tires on his car."

Ro gasped and brought her hand to her mouth. The color drained from her face. "Slashed? Like with a knife?"

"Yeah, like with a knife."

Lisa said, "Ben, you need to call the police."

Ro said, "Ben, call Shanks."

Call Shanks.

His thoughts exactly.

CHAPTER 7

HERE SEEMED TO be as many people around the car as there were inside the gym. A gaggle of girls had gathered in a circle, worried looks on their faces, rubbing each other's arms to keep warm and yakking away with one another. The guys chose to say nothing. Instead they walked around the car, examining the situation, nodding as if they were having profound thoughts. Ben distanced himself and made phone calls. Within a half hour, he had a genuine powwow: Mom and Dad, Haley and Lilly, two squad cars from the River Remez Police, the girls' and boys' VPs, and the school's illustrious, fuming principal, Mr. Beltran.

"Whoever did this is not going to get away with it!" He too was orbiting the car, eyeing the damage. "Not on my watch." He looked at Ben. "You have no idea who did this?"

Of course he had an idea. But he wasn't going to share it. "It was probably random, sir." *Liar, liar, pants on fire.* "I'm never in school anymore. Who'd even care about me enough to piss me off?"

"Well, we'll see about that."

As soon as Ben saw Sam's car pull up, he knew he was in for it. Shanks stormed through the yellow crime-scene ribbon and surveyed the compromised car. After a thorough look at four flat pieces of rubber, he said, "What do you know about this?"

Ben threw up his hands.

"Don't give me that bullshit."

"Talk about blaming the victim."

Within moments, Shanks was surrounded by Ben's parents and the principal. Mr. Beltran said, "Do you have any ideas about this, Detective?"

Sam eyed Ben. "We haven't had a recent rash of slashed tires, if that's what you're asking."

"I'm talking about punks and vandalism. What about those idiots who spray-painted the Palace of the Governors?"

Ben turned so his hot face wouldn't be noticed. Sam said, "That was Santa Fe. I'll check with them. Maybe they've had some similar property crimes."

"You do that," Beltran said. "One of the things that makes this community great is the people. If we let them down, what do we have?"

"A bunch of let-down people," Sam answered.

Beltran bristled. "Just find out who did this. It would be a sad state of affairs if the school district had to resort to policing their own property. Let's not waste any more taxpayer dollars, okay?"

Shanks kept his expression flat. "I'll give it my full attention, Mr. Beltran. Last thing I want to do is deal with angry parents."

After the principal left, Sam pulled Ben away from the crowd, and none too gently. "Okay, Vicksburg, spit it out!"

His parents followed. Dad wagged a finger in Sam's face. "Why are you coming down on him, Sam?"

"Because he knows something about this."

"I don't know anything!" Ben insisted. "Why are you yelling at me?"

"I'm not yelling, I'm asking. And I'm asking because you've been up to something. You know how I know that? Because you're always up to something."

"Why are you connecting this juvenile act to what I do?"

"First of all, it's not juvenile. Juveniles spray-paint. Juveniles key cars. Juveniles even steal cars. But juveniles generally do not slash the tires of random people. And if they do, they don't slash all four tires. To do that, it takes muscle. It takes time. It takes deliberation. Are you honestly telling me that this was random?"

"I'm honestly telling you I don't know who did it. I parked my car and went into my prom. When I came out with my date, my tires were cut."

Sam softened his tone. "The uniformed guys handle things like this. I'm a detective. You called me down and you must have had a reason for it."

"Actually, Ro called you."

"I thought you didn't see her anymore."

Mom said, "She's been at the house for the last few weekends. They're doing something that has to do with my daughter's incident."

His own mother was ratting him out. Ben looked around. The crowds had thinned a bit. Haley and Lilly were talking to Ro.

Sam said, "Should I be talking to Ro? Was she your prom date?"

"No. I went with Lisa Holloway." Ben pointed her out. "She was with me the entire time. Maybe she saw something that I didn't."

Shanks eyed him suspiciously. "You stay here while I get a statement from her."

As soon as Shanks left, William Vicksburg turned to his son. "What the hell is going on? And be honest because this is scaring the crap out of your mother and me."

Mom burst into tears. "What have you gotten yourself into?" She was openly sobbing. "I haven't suffered enough?" She stepped away and tried to get control of her emotions.

"Ben, does this have something to do with Ellen's murder?" Dad didn't wait for an answer. "You and I are going to have a serious talk."

"Dad, I will tell you everything I know." Ben lowered his voice. "But do you honestly think that this is the work of a sexual psychopath? Slashing tires? C'mon!"

"Do you *know* who did it, Ben? And I don't mean who slashed the tires."

Ben knew he meant Ellen's murder. He was beginning to feel very uncomfortable sitting on the information, no matter how it was obtained. He was going to have to tell Shanks everything. And that was going to happen tonight. "No, I don't know who did it, Dad. If I did, he'd be dead. But I have some ideas."

His mother butted in. "What are you talking about? Ellen?"

"Nothing," Dad said.

"Now you're keeping information from me too?"

Dad weighed his options. "He has ideas about Ellen."

"About who did it?"

Shanks was still talking to Lisa. Ben said, "I don't know who did it. That's the truth. I have lists of names . . . of who it might be."

"And you haven't told the police?"

Ben regarded his parents—his father and then his mother. "I got the names illegally."

His father licked his lips. "What did you hack into?"

"I didn't hack into anything. And if you ask how I got the names, I won't tell you. I'd rather go to jail—"

"Ben, stop being so damn melodramatic. That's Haley's department."

"It has to be Ro," Mom said.

"No, it's not Ro," Ben lied. "She has nothing to do with anything. She was just there for moral support. I didn't hack into a computer system. But what I did wasn't legal."

Laura shook her head. She wasn't buying it. "Where does Ro work, Ben?"

"Ro works?" Dad said.

"She does. She got a job when they broke up. And now they're seeing each other again. They lock the door to his room. They're in there for hours. And I know it's not about sex."

Ben's face went hot. "Mom!"

"What do you do with her, Benjamin?"

"Nothing."

"Six hours every Sunday, you two sit around and do nothing?" Mom was furious. "Where does she work?"

"She's a waitress."

"*Where?*"

"Ask her."

"I'm asking *you!*"

"She works as a cocktail waitress at the Jackson Lodge."

Mom turned pale. "You hacked into the database at the Lodge and found *his* name in the registry. And you haven't told us? You haven't told *Shanks*?"

"I don't know his name, Mom! If I knew his name, I'd tell the world!"

"Who are you even looking for? Why do you think he stayed at the Jackson?"

"It's a long story, Mom."

"Then it looks like we're staying up all night."

Ro had materialized. Ben's mother stared at her. "Lovely dress, Dorothy."

"Thank you." Ro's eyes were on the ground. Then they looked up at Ben's dad. "I'm eighteen now. And I'm hiring you as my lawyer."

"Done," Dad said. "What's going on?"

She kept her voice very low. "I overheard you, Mrs. Vicksburg, and you're right. We do have information from the database. We don't know exactly who we're after, but we have ideas." She turned to her ad hoc lawyer. "I didn't hack into anything, Mr. Vicksburg, because I was allowed to use the computer system when I worked the desk. But I went beyond my duties as a desk clerk. I've been printing out data: names of guests starting from roughly six months before Ellen's murder and going forward. Ben and I have been going through the names one by one by one."

Ben's father was stunned, half in disbelief and half in admiration. He said, "What makes you think that the son of a bitch stayed at the Jackson?"

"Los Alamos puts its scientists up there because the Jackson gives them discounts. If there's a scientific meeting that involves more than a couple of people, the lab uses that hotel. There are smaller hotels in the city of Los Alamos, but the Jackson's the biggest that has a deal with the lab. And since I couldn't take a job everywhere, I picked the Jackson."

"You think he's a *scientist*?" Ben's mom asked.

"Ben thinks it's someone with an affiliation with Los Alamos." Ro turned to Ben. "You haven't said anything to your parents?"

Laura was throwing her son dagger eyes. "What . . . is . . . going . . . on?"

Ben took a deep breath and let it out. "Over the years I've been looking at things that were similar to Ellen's case."

"I know that, Benjamin. What have you found out?"

"Similar cases that have taken place near other national labs—geographically. I have told Shanks. He knows my theories. But I have no idea if I'm right or wrong."

Dad said, "How did you find out that this hotel deals with Los Alamos National Lab, Ro?"

"It was very high tech, Mr. Vicksburg. I made phone calls."

Ben said, "It's my fault. She did it for me."

Ro's face remained impassive. "No, Ben, I did it for Ellen."

Laura's eyes overflowed. "Oh dear."

Ben said, "Dorothy, I'm so sorry I got you involved in this mess."

"I'm not sorry at all. But I don't know where to go from here." She smiled at Ben's parents. "I'm open to ideas."

"Well, it's clear you can't tell anyone without compromising yourself. Furthermore, even if you did tell Shanks, he couldn't use the information because you obtained everything in an illegal manner. Ellen's case is still open. We could suggest that Shanks go back and get a subpoena for all hotel registries at the time of the incident. If you figured out some names, he should be able to do the same thing."

"Why didn't he go to the hotels when it first happened?" Laura asked.

"He did, Mom. He investigated every single hotel in the area and looked at the names of people staying in town around the dates of the abduction. But he didn't know he was looking for someone associated with the labs. Also, it could be that the perpetrator's name wasn't on any local guest list."

"Or not in a form he recognized," Ro said. When Ben glared at her, she said, "The jig is up, Vicks. Just come clean."

"*What?*" Ben's dad asked.

"It's possible he could be using aliases."

"Like women's names," Ro added.

"You know this for a fact?"

"No. That's why we're looking at the data from way before and way after the incident. Shanks can't get access to that data without reasonable cause."

"I want to see your files."

"Bad idea, Dad. You work for the government. No one would benefit from you being disbarred."

"Cut the sarcastic shit."

"William, please."

Dad said, "Stop trying to stonewall me, Ben, I don't like it."

Shanks was done interviewing Lisa and was walking toward them. Ben said, "We'll continue this conversation at home."

"What conversation?" Shanks asked.

"Sorry, Sam," William said. "Privileged information."

"What the hell is going on?" When no one answered him, Shanks took Ben's arm. "You're coming to the police station. We're going to have a nice talk, Vicksburg."

Ro said, "He won't admit to anything there because everything is recorded. But he may tell you stuff off the record if he knows what's good for him." She smiled widely. "How about if we go to Ben's house? I'll make a nice pot of coffee and Mr. Vicksburg—the senior Mr. Vicksburg—can tell us what to say and what not to say so no one ends up in prison."

"Just go home, Dorothy," Ben told her.

"Uh, let me think about that, Vicks." She was still smiling. "No."

William turned to Laura. "Go home with the girls and I'll meet you there." To Shanks: "The kids and I will come with you."

"Dad, I have to wait for the tow truck."

Shanks said, "I'm impounding your car."

"Sam, I have finals. I have to get to Albuquerque."

"Take a bus." He shook his head. "Ro's right. The kids aren't going to talk at the police station. Mind if we use your house? That way I can also see what they've been up to."

Dad put his hand on Sam's shoulder. His eyes grew watery. "Just like old times."

Ben said, "You don't have to get involved, Dad. I'll tell him everything."

"Maybe *I* need your father, hotshot." Ro punched his shoulder. "God, I hate you right now."

"Someone slashed my tires and you hate me?"

"You ruined homecoming by cutting out on my special day, you ruined the winter dance by not going with me, you ruined the spring fling with your slugfest, and now you've ruined prom. Grad night is my last hurrah in this godforsaken place. It would be nice to have one event here that you didn't spoil."

"I don't believe you," Ben said. "Let me remind you that I saved you from a very bad Christmas Eve and I took you out to a very nice and expensive dinner for your eighteenth birthday. I also gave you exactly what you wanted as far as birthday presents are concerned. And while we're talking about people spoiling things, guess who spoiled Valentine's Day?"

She yanked him aside and whispered furiously, "That was awful. You know how remorseful I feel. Everything I've done has been for you because I feel so ashamed. You call yourself a nice guy. *Stop* it already."

Her eyes were pure wrath. "I won't mention it again," he told her. "Just go home, Dorothy. I'm trying to save your ass."

"My ass doesn't need to be saved by you. And I'd like to remind you that you weren't making any headway in your 'research' until I helped you out."

"All true, but what does that have to do with anything? I don't want you involved!"

"Too late for that because I'm already involved!" She hit him again. Abruptly, she burst into tears. "Now JD is taking Lisa to the after party and he's probably going to bang her."

"No, he won't." He took her in his arms and kissed the top of her updo. "I promise you he won't."

"Why?" Her eyes were ablaze. "Did you already bang her?" She pushed him away. "Where the hell were you two for so long?"

"I didn't bang anyone. All I'm saying is that JD is loyal to you—"

Shanks broke in. "Sorry to interrupt your little lovers' spat, but there's work to do. Shall we go?"

Ro dried her eyes on the back of her hand. Then she slipped her arm under Ben's. "Let's."

CHAPTER 8

STEWING AND FEELING violated, Ben said nothing as his father sifted through his carefully constructed files, reading what had been meant for his eyes only. He squirmed and sighed, showing his resentment, but his father was uninterested. Ro held his hand and glanced at him in understanding. At long last, they had reached a truce.

Shanks, in the meantime, had gone back to the police station to get his own files and they were waiting for him to return. He hadn't looked at any of the purloined material because as of yet, no one could figure out how to legitimize the files. Shanks knew that if he nabbed someone, he'd have to justify his investigation under oath. The saving grace was the life that all this activity had injected into Ellen's stalled case.

William Vicksburg shook his head. "The police can't use any of this stuff. It was obtained illegally. Who are you two looking at?"

Ro pulled out Kevin Barnes. "Him."

William began to read the data. "He's not a scientist, he's a lawyer."

Ben said, "An immigration lawyer who works for the government getting visas for its foreign scientists. He was at the hotel on the vernal equinox, Dad. I bumped into him. He smelled dirty—wet and musty—like he had just done some gardening. And this was at midnight."

The man paled. "Oh Jesus! We've got to tell Shanks." He wagged a finger. "Son, you are not going to start searching the mountains again."

"No one in the area was reported missing, Dad. I don't think he did anything, although I don't know that for sure."

"So why was he here?"

"Reliving something maybe."

"If this is the guy, I'll kill him myself."

"You'll have to stand in line," Ben said.

Ro said, "No one is killing anyone." She turned to Ben. "How'd you find out he was an immigration lawyer? I couldn't find anything on him except that he's a lawyer."

"George Tafoya told me. He knows him from the lab. He thinks he's weird."

"George Tafoya thinks he's weird?" William said. "*How?*"

"Nothing he can put his finger on."

"Get me George's phone number."

"You can't call him up," Ben said. "His phone lines might be bugged."

"Bugged?" his dad said. "He told you his phone is bugged?"

"He thinks his entire house is bugged. Whenever we talk, we go out and drive in my car. I told him everything I know about Barnes. He told me to back off and let him poke around."

Dad said, "Exactly how many people have you enlisted for help?"

"Just Ro and George. And of course, Shanks."

"What else haven't you told me?"

"We think that Kevin Barnes is using aliases," Ro said. "Specifically girls' names so he's less likely to be noticed."

"How did he check into the Jackson using girls' names?"

"We don't question things like that, Mr. Vicksburg. It would be bad for business. We just smile and do the job."

The doorbell rang. Ben got up. "Must be Sam."

"I'll get it," William said. "Don't tell Shanks any of this. I've got to think of a way to make this all legal. And certainly do not tell your mother any of it. I'll tell her in my own time."

Ben looked at Ro, who said, "The jig is up, Vicksburg. You've been officially outed."

"I'm happy to let the experts do their thing."

"I wonder if that's true." She stood. "Shall we join the others?"

"I suppose we have to."

Ben's parents were having a powwow with Sam. Haley and Lilly were on the couch in their pj's, looking very scared. Shanks noticed it. "Might be better if the girls weren't here."

"I want to know what's going on," Haley said.

"Fair enough," Shanks said. "After all your family and you have been through, you deserve to know. But first let me find out what's going on, okay, Haley?"

Lilly tugged on Haley's sleeve. "They'll tell us when they

know. Let's continue on with our search for the perfect morp dress."

Laura was still fuming at her son. Ben asked her, "You okay?"

"I have a terrible headache."

"I'll get you an Advil."

"What I have can't be remedied with pills."

"Mom, I'm really sorry. But at least we're getting somewhere."

There were tears in her eyes. "Ben, our family has suffered horribly. In a single stroke, our lives were in shambles. A wound can't heal if you keep picking at the scab."

"I know. I'm sorry for all the misery I've caused you."

"You didn't cause me misery. *He* did. I just want some of the pieces put back together, even if the clay pot is badly damaged. Is that too much to ask?"

Ben's dad said, "Laura, why don't you lie down? I'll catch you up in the morning."

"What do they need you for, William?"

"One of us should be here. And Ro hired me as her lawyer. I have to stay."

"So now you're involved?"

"Do I have a choice?"

"No, I suppose not." She walked out of the living room.

Shanks was already sitting at the dining room table, booting up his laptop. Ro said, "I'll make some coffee."

"I'll make it." Ben got up and started a pot. Ro was smoothing out her prom dress. It was then that Ben realized he was still wearing his rented tux. "I'm going to change. You want some sweats, Ro?"

"That would be nice."

They went into his room and he tossed her sweatpants and a sweatshirt. "You've contacted your parents?"

"It was all I could do to keep my father from charging down here."

"He's welcome to join the gang."

"Not on your life, Vicks. I also told them I'm sleeping over."

"Why? I'll take you home."

"I'm not going out in the dark and neither should you. We don't know where he is. Can I take a shower in your bathroom? My makeup is itching my skin."

"Of course. You can sleep here. I'll use Ellen's room."

"That's okay with your mom?"

"Sometimes I sleep there. Sometimes my mom sleeps there. You know . . ."

"Yes, unfortunately, I do know."

When they came back into the living room, Ro had changed into sloppy clothes, her wet hair in a towel. Without the dress and the makeup, she looked about fifteen, especially with the sprinkling of freckles across her nose.

Shanks was staring at his laptop screen. He opened up a briefcase. "Over my many, many years as a cop, I've learned to only ask questions if I want to hear the answers. Right now, I'm interested in getting information without landing either one of you in jail."

"Same goal here," William said. "I'm here as Ro's lawyer."

"That's fine." Sam took out a piece of paper. "Here is a list of scientists that I have been looking into since Ben told me his theory about the killer being involved in the labs." He handed a sheet of paper to Ro and the same one to Ben. "Anyone strike your fancy?"

Ben scanned the names. Some were the people whom Ro and he had been looking into. "How'd you get these names, Sam?"

He gave Ben a long, hard look. "What do you think I do with my time, Vicksburg? Throw paper airplanes across the squad room?"

"Don't take offense. You know me by now."

"Yes, I do." He tousled the kid's hair, an act that was more appropriate three years ago. In Sam's eyes, Ben was still a kid. "These names were chosen because the men on this list have been to three out of the four labs for business. We've investigated all of them, and by our thinking, none of them seems like a suitable candidate." He paused. "But some of them do travel a lot. If you're brilliant and happen to be a sexual psychopath, it's a good deal for you. Talk to me about these names."

Ben took a pencil and checked the names he recognized. To Ro, he said, "How are you doing?"

She made a face. "I remember looking up Peter Chesney and Neville Armand . . . Paul Arons . . . Michael Swit. I know we eliminated them, Vicks, but I don't remember why."

"Neither do I, but if these guys were at all of the labs—"

"Three out of four," Sam corrected.

"At the times of the murders—"

"I didn't say anything about that," Sam said. "What I told you was that they've been to at least three of the four labs."

"Katie Doogan?" William asked.

"Katie Doogan and two others—Julia Rehnquist, who was buried near Lawrence Livermore, and Jamey Moore, who was found not too far from Oak Ridge National Lab."

The elder Vicksburg turned to his son. "You knew about

other murders?" When Ben didn't say anything, he said, "I suppose you've been doing this because I haven't done anything. My bad."

"No, that's not it." Ben put his hand on his father's shoulder. "I started doing it so you didn't have to."

"Can we stick to the case here?" Shanks said. "So you've seen some of these names."

"Some . . ." Ro was still looking at the names. "Why don't you like them as the bad guy?"

"Age, rank, and serial number. They don't fit the profile. Their time is accounted for. They didn't rack up a lot of miles on their rentals. They didn't stay in strange places and they don't have a lot of unexplained absences. Milton Ortiz and Derek Whitecliffe agree. What do you think?"

Ben said, "If you don't like them, that's good enough for me."

"A rare compliment." Sam took the list away. "So . . . for the time being, we'll put them on the bottom." He turned to the kids. "Don't either of you tell me more than I'm asking for."

"Just phrase your questions in a yes-or-no format," William said.

"Do you two have lists of more names?"

"Yes."

"Obviously, I'd like to look at your research, Ben, but if you've gotten the names in a suspicious manner, I can't. Should I look at your names?"

"No."

"That's what I thought. Did you hack into anything, Ben?"

He looked at his father, who said, "No, he did not."

Sam said, "When Ben told me his lab theories, I called up hotels in the area that deal with Los Alamos. Then I got a court order that allowed me to look at the guest lists from those hotels for certain dates. Now I know the Jackson deals with Los Alamos." He looked at Ro. "And I know that you work at the Jackson. Am I right about that?"

"You are correct," she said.

Ben was stunned. "Why didn't you tell me you got lists from the Jackson?" he asked Shanks.

"Because you're not a cop, Vicks, and you're not privy to the same information that I am. And while I could get a court order for some dates, I couldn't exactly justify looking through three years' worth of registry. But unlike you, I can get court orders for hotels in addition to the Jackson. So I have some advantages. The way I figure it, you have some advantages and I have some advantages." Sam smiled. "I'm going to show you a lot of lists of names. I shouldn't be showing them to you. But we're not going to tell anyone, right?"

"Our lips are sealed," Ro said.

"Will, does this make you uncomfortable?"

"Not at all."

"Great." Sam opened a briefcase and pulled out sheaves of paper. "It's a long list. I want you to point out anyone who you think I might want to investigate further."

It was a long roster of names, presented in alphabetical order. Kevin Barnes hadn't made the cut. Ben cleared his throat and handed it back to him. "Do you have the original rosters? The ones directly off the hotel computers?"

"This is the original list. I just alphabetized it."

"It isn't complete."

"Yes it is."

"No it isn't, Sam. It's only men."

His eyes widened. "You're *shittin'* me."

"Do you have the lists from before you winnowed them down to men?"

"They're not organized."

Ro said, "We know who we're looking for."

Sam rubbed his forehead. "Hold on. Let me bring up the files. I'll link them all together . . . it's forty-five pages."

"That's okay."

"They're alphabetized. That should help you out." He showed the kids his screen. "Knock yourself out."

Ben and Ro sorted through the names. She spotted one first. "Venika Berns . . ."

"Who?"

"This one." Ro pointed it out. "And Senna Berkiv. And here's Karen Bevins again."

"Eva Birnskin," Ben said.

Ro scrolled down and down and down. "Oh, here's one. Anne V. Kerbis."

"What are you looking at?" Sam stared at the names. "They're all anagrams." He looked at their faces. "Who?"

Ben said, "The name is not on your list, so do you really want me to say something out loud?"

"I should be able to figure it out." Shanks was talking more to himself than to anyone else. "It's an odd combination of letters . . . V-I-K . . . is it Vik . . . wait, don't answer."

Ben said, "I could write an algorithm that would spit out all the possible combinations of names."

"How long would it take you?"

"There might be something I could download off the Internet. Give me about a half hour."

"Go. I'll keep working at this."

Ro yawned. Ben said, "Do you want to go to bed?"

"Not on your life." She smiled at Mr. Vicksburg. "Do you mind if I stay over? I don't feel like traveling the open roads."

"Of course, honey." William stood up. "I'm going to check on my wife."

"Sure, sure," Shanks said.

Ro said, "I think I'll lie down on the couch for a moment and dream about a real prom . . . where there's a disco ball and a king and a queen and they dance together while everyone applauds."

Shanks was muttering to himself. "Vik . . . Kiv . . . Ben . . . is it Ben?"

Ro said, "It's not Ben."

"Don't tell me."

"Stop asking me."

"I'm talking to myself. Ben . . . Benk . . ."

Ben said, "I'll go try to figure out an algorithm."

Shanks went on, muttering to himself until a half hour had passed. Ben returned with a printout in his hand.

Shanks said, "Kiv . . . Kev . . . Kevin? Is it Kevin?"

"It's very warm in here." Ro made a point of fanning herself. "You must be very warm as well. As a matter of fact, Detective, I think you're sizzling."

"I'm sizzling," Ben said.

Shanks said, "Okay, it's Kevin. Kevin what?"

Ben handed Shanks the printout. He spotted the name right away. It was the combination that made the most sense. "Kevin Barnes." When neither of the kids said anything, Shanks grinned. "Okay. Now we're cooking with gas. He's not the football player."

"Unlikely."

"There's an art dealer, a shop owner, a lawyer—"

Ben cleared his throat. Shanks looked up and then back at the screen. "Why would I be interested in a lawyer?" More taps on the keyboard. "I can't even find out what kind of lawyer he is."

"Just off the top of my head, it might be immigration," Ro told him. "He might get foreign visas for visiting scientists, but that's just a guess."

Shanks was stunned. "How'd you find that out?"

"Just a guess."

"Kevin Barnes works for the national labs?" No one spoke. Shanks closed his laptop and stowed it in his briefcase. "I'm going down to the station house to make some phone calls."

"Who are you going to call?"

"There are just a handful of people you know who could give you that information, Vicks. Specifically people who work for the lab."

"If you're thinking about George Tafoya, don't call him. His lines are bugged."

"What?"

"Honest to goodness. When we talk, we talk in my car."

Shanks just shook his head. "What is he doing for you? Specifically?"

"He said he'd poke around quietly. He told me to stop doing anything I'm doing. And now I've told you everything I know. Can I come back to the station house with you?"

"Absolutely not." He stood up. "This guy . . . whoever he is . . . you think you know something about him. But after tonight, I suspect he knows even more about you." His eyes turned to Ro. "And you." Back to Ben. "I know you can shoot. You might want to go down to the range."

"I was thinking about doing that tomorrow . . . if I get a car."

"What about you?" Shanks was addressing Ro. "Will you be joining him?"

"I don't know how to shoot," Ro told him. "I don't believe in guns."

Shanks licked his lips. "Young lady, maybe it's time to change your religion."

CHAPTER 9

I T WAS AN idiotic thing to do, so unlike him. He was, above all, methodical and calculating and conservative in thought as well as action. He planned meticulously. Something that impulsive was way beyond his understanding of himself.

Why did he do it? He obsessed about his actions as he drove through the darkness, through fog and shadows, until the wee hours of the morning were upon him. Why had he done something so moronic when he knew the kid was onto something? As soon as the girl took the job . . . something was up. He could tell.

Maybe he did it to scare the little shit, let him know that his actions were not without consequences. He knew the kid wouldn't give up—after going in and out of the police station for years—but sometimes you had to show someone who was boss.

He drove on and on, through miles and miles of darkness:

north through New Mexico, passing near Farmington and the
Four Corners until he slid over the border into Colorado. As
soon as he got to Denver, he'd camp out for the night. He had
driven by mountains and flatlands and areas that were re-
mote and perfect for his passion except they were far away.
The next day he'd pass the Great Salt Lake and drive on until
he reached Idaho.

It was two days of driving, but none of that bothered him
much. He loved to drive as much as he loved to hunt. Not that
he expected to find anyone on this lonesome highway and at
this time of night. He didn't even want to find anyone because
then the temptation would be just too much.

Once every nine months: his season, his quota, his passion,
his obsession. Any more than that, he'd be making a spectacle
of himself.

BEN AIMED AND peeled off six shots in rapid succession. He
pushed the button and the paper felon came forward, pierced
like a sieve: two between the eyes, two elsewhere in the face,
and two in the top half of his head.

JD studied his handiwork. "You've been practicing?"

"Here and there."

"Remind me not to piss you off."

"Too late for that." They both laughed. Ro was not amused
with ther camaraderie. Nor was she happy to be at a shooting
range. She fiddled with her earmuffs. She examined her nails.
She alternated between being bored and being sulky, talking
in monosyllabic grunts.

JD put his paper felon on the line and pushed the button.
Mr. Criminal was about thirty yards away. He loaded his pistol and took aim, sighting down to the target. His nose was

just about healed, but there was a slight tilt as well as a chink in the bridge. He'd been playing contact sports since he was five, but it took a girl to screw up his perfect Roman slope. JD claimed he liked the result, that the asymmetry made him look tougher.

Ro said, "When is this going to be over?"

JD put the pistol down. "What's your problem?"

"The *problem* is I'm bored. Let's just leave."

"It's not as easy as it looks," Ben said. "We're doing this for your protection."

JD said, "You could act a little grateful. I spent a fortune on a tux, a corsage, a limo, a room, and a great bottle of champagne, and you crapped out on me last night."

"I'd much rather have been with you than where I was." She glared at him. "And may I add for the record that you looked very happy to be with Lisa."

"I didn't screw her." JD looked at Ben. "Can't say the same for him."

"I didn't screw her either," Ben said. "Don't get me involved in your spat." He turned to Ro. "You didn't have to come here."

"You insisted I come."

That was true. "I thought you might want to learn something."

"I hate guns!"

"Your loss," JD said.

Ro knew she was acting bratty, but it was a cover-up. Secretly, she was fascinated that the two guys in her life were doing something she absolutely abhorred, and doing it for her.

JD sighted down to his target and emptied the chamber. When he was done, he'd hit two in the face, two in the body, and missed two altogether. "He'd still be dead. That's all that matters."

Ben said, "Give it a go, girl, even if it's just this once."

"A gun in my hand is a weapon for someone else. I could never shoot it. I'd freeze."

"Which is exactly why you should learn to shoot a gun," JD said. "So you won't freeze."

Ro didn't say anything. Instead she gave both of them the full force of her steely eyes. It was weird. When she first started at Remez High, all she wanted was to rule the student body, be adored, and as an afterthought, she hoped that JD and Vicks would get along because she really did like them both. Now that they were friends again, it irritated her. Sometimes it seemed that they enjoyed each other's company more than hers.

"Fine," she said. "I'll try it."

JD put another paper felon on the line. He started at ten yards. He gave her his gun and stood behind her. He showed her how to hold the weapon, how to brace it with both hands to avoid kickback as much as possible. He said, "See that little thing sticking out? That's the sight. Line it up with where you want to shoot."

"This thing is heavy."

"Only because you've been holding up your arms so long." His body was close to hers. "Okay, aim for the chest. That's a much bigger target than the head."

"I can hit the head."

"Give it a whirl, then."

She took a shot. The kickback brought her hands up and she didn't even hit the target. She was pissed. "What the hell happened?"

"Physics," Ben told her. "Bullet goes forward, your hands go back. You've got to brace your entire body so that your hands remain steady. Try it again."

She emptied the chamber. All her shots were wide. "This sucks. I suck." She handed JD the empty gun. "Put some more bullets inside. I want to try again."

JD smiled. "Sure thing, sugar."

"You should try my gun," Ben told her. "It has a little less kickback. Might be easier."

"I can handle this one, thank you very much," Ro barked. "I just need practice."

"We created a monster," JD said.

"Nonsense," Ro said. "I still loathe guns. But I have my pride. I will quit as soon as I get a bullet on the target paper."

After another try, she managed to hit the paper but not on the target area. JD held out his hand for the gun.

Ro balked. "Give me another round of bullets. Just let me get one on the body."

"Ammo ain't cheap."

"Just give it to me."

Another round, and she hit the body—twice.

By the time they left, she had peeled off a clean head shot and felt good about it.

Ben thought, *Good for her, good for JD, and good for me. Good for all of us good guys.*

A WEEK LATER Ben was cleaning up three years of an obsession; it was liberating, to be sure, but just like a drug addict, he had twinges of longing. Just one more file; just one more fix. The shredder was going full force. When he was done, the family would have a hell of a compost pile.

"You know, you never answered my question," Ro said to him. She was wearing jeans and a T-shirt and heels. She looked good, as always.

"What question?" As usual, he was listening with half an ear, rereading the file on Kevin Barnes, trying to figure out his next move. "I sure hope we have this right." He looked at her. "Do you think we have it right?"

"Probably, but now it's Shanks's problem." She ripped the file out of his hand and placed it in the shredder. "Stop second-guessing yourself and answer my question."

"What question?"

"On prom night, you disappeared." She was couching her anger in a saccharine-sweet smile. "You were gone for quite a while."

"That's not a question."

"Okay. How about this? Where were you?"

"I was dealing with slashed tires, Ro. I wasn't looking at my watch."

"I'm just saying that it took a long time to examine four flat pieces of rubber."

"What do you want me to say?"

She walked over to him until they were nose to nose. Her eyes were smoldering. "You don't have to say anything be-cause I already know." She pushed him hard. "You dumped me as a date after you promised to take me to the prom. And then you go ahead and screw that skank?"

"I told you I didn't screw her."

"To paraphrase someone we *both* know: You may not have screwed her, but you did something! Because her description of you was way too accurate to be chance!" She pushed him again. "Okay, bud." She wagged a finger in his face. "Now we're *even*!"

"Not quite."

"You're right. We're not even. *You* didn't take on a menial, thankless job and suffer through sleepless nights just to help *me* out. As of right now, you owe me one, Mr. Big."

Ben liked the moniker. It made him smile and that made her angrier. She threw something at him and it whizzed past his head. It crashed into the wall and fell with a thud.

"Okay, okay," Ben said. "We're even."

"No . . . we . . . are . . . not!" This time she threw his calculator.

Ben caught it with one hand. "Okay, now that's expensive. Can you stop destroying my room?"

"This is the deal. I want both you and JD to take me to grad night! And if you stand me up again, I will kill you."

"What about Lisa?"

"The poor dear will just have to go stag." She kissed him hard on the mouth. "Understood?"

He was breathless from her kiss. Whenever he felt out of control, he obsessed about one thing. "Can we finish up with this? It's making me anxious. Plus, the solstice is only a few days away."

She broke away and plopped down on the papers that were covering his bed. "Ben, it's over. Shanks is monitoring the situation. You should be writing your speech for graduation, not playing detective when we have a real detective. And stop trying to wriggle out of grad night. You're going."

He changed the subject. "What kind of speech should I be writing?"

She was incredulous. "Aren't you valedictorian?"

"Salutatorian."

"Salut . . ." She frowned. "How'd that happen? You're the smartest person in the school."

"JD's done way more for the school than I have. I'm fine with it."

She was quiet. "That doesn't seem fair."

"Ro, I don't give a rat's ass. I am so over high school. I don't even know why I'm going to graduation. It's meaningless. And so is grad night. Just go with JD. I'll stay home. I'm tired of tailing after you two lovebirds."

"We're not lovebirds. We're dates of convenience, and as soon as we graduate, it's so, so over. How can I ever be serious with someone who cheated on me?" She realized what she said and put her hand to her mouth. "Strike that."

Ben laughed.

She walked over to him and played with his curls. "I hate to admit this, but you're right. It's stupid for me to have two dates for grad night. Or any date at all, for that matter. Let's all go together as a group: you, me, JD, Lisa, Shannon, Chelsea, Mark, and Weekly. It's fun that way."

"Great." Ben winced. "It'll be one big happy orgy because, apparently, there has been lots of swapping that, in my perpetual haze, I've not been aware of."

She slapped his shoulder. "Stop it." Then her eyes misted up. She blinked back tears. "I'll miss you, Vicks, even with all your quirks and craziness. I've never met anyone like you."

"I'll miss you too, Dorothy." He meant it with every fiber of his being. "But right now, I'm still here and I'm still obnoxious. I've got three years of a fixation here. Help me clean it up."

She said, "You're still speaking at graduation, right?"

"Yeah, I think I welcome everyone."

"What are you going to say?"

"It's like a couple of sentences. I'll wing it."

"You can't wing it, Vicks. You'll have to say the same thing at rehearsal and at graduation."

"We have a rehearsal?"

"Yes, we have a rehearsal." She mocked his voice.

He put down a stack of papers. "When?"

"In three days, Mr. Space Cadet, the day before graduation."

"That's June twenty-first. It's the *day* of the solstice. I can't be there. I'll be watching Haley and Lilly."

"You have to make it or the school won't graduate you."

"Then I won't graduate—"

"Vicks, stop it!" She put her hands on his shoulders. Her voice was soft. "Griff and Ezra will watch the girls. We'll keep them locked up in the house until we come back. They'll be fine."

"No way—"

"Shanks is on it. Albuquerque is on it. You're *done* with this." She stared at him. "I'll be really upset if you don't come to graduation." She paused. "And if you're with the girls . . . who'll be watching me?"

He hadn't thought about that. "Have JD drive you to rehearsal. Tell him to take a gun."

She pushed him away. "Anytime you don't want to deal with me, you palm me off on JD." She picked up her purse. "I'm leaving."

"Wait, wait, wait." Of course, what she said was true. He said, "Okay. I'll come to rehearsal. I'll work it out with the girls."

"Your parents will be home, right?"

"Maybe, but I kinda didn't want them dealing with this."

"So let the girls go to my house. My mom should be home. And we'll emphasize to the boys that they have to be with them at home with the door locked the entire time."

"Let them stay at my house. It's closer to the school."

"I'm down with that."

"Does Griff know how to shoot?"

"The guy is not going to come knocking at your door, Ben. That's just stupid."

"Why am I not reassured?"

"I know you're worried, but it'll only be a couple of hours." She put her purse down and kissed him like she did way back when. "Please come to rehearsal. I really want us to go through graduation together."

Ben was quiet.

"I know we can't go backward," Ro said. "After graduation, we'll all be scattered across the four corners of the globe. And I'm looking forward to the future. Within a few months at college, I'll be pledged with the top sorority and I'll be dating the best-looking guy on campus. But . . ." She blew out air. "You can only have one first love . . . and you'll always be my first love."

He kissed her back and there was instant electricity. Dear Lord, protect him from being seventeen. "And you'll always be my first love."

"So, my first love . . . you'll come to rehearsal with me?"

It was against his better judgment. "I'll go for a couple of hours, okay. That's the best I can do."

"Fair enough." A sad smile. "When I'm gone, think of me from time to time."

"Ro, it's the *not* thinking about you that'll be difficult." He suddenly felt very blue. "How the hell do I move on when you've set the bar so high?"

"I hate it when you say things like that." She was choked up. "It makes me think about what I'm losing."

"You'll always have me here." He pointed to her chest. "And I'll always have you here." He pointed to his own heart.

She wiped her wet eyes. "Now it's my turn to say let's get back to work." She threw another pile into the shredder. It made a god-awful sound that had Ben cringing.

But his mind was still on the conversation.

She was his first love, no doubt about that.

And she cheated on him, no doubt about that either.

There was first love.

And then there was true love.

CHAPTER 10

BACK IN NEW Mexico, he broke into a sweat and it wasn't because of the warm weather. He shouldn't have come back. After his stunt with the tires they were onto him, and he'd have better luck elsewhere.

But compulsion was compulsion and he knew that nothing was going to satisfy him except a hit in this territory. So why did he take a chance on doing something that he'd ultimately find hollow?

It didn't have to be a certain person. Any female that fit the categories would do. But it would be extra-special sweet to do it right under their proverbial noses, prove that lightning could strike twice, and just maybe it would give him the same thrill that she gave him three years ago.

She had fought like a tiger, scratching and clawing and screaming, but she didn't have a chance. Eventually he had subdued her by sheer force. It was because of her spirit that he *decided to start using chemicals to get from point A to point B to point C . . . well, they were dead by point C—limp and lifeless, unable to respond in any way.*

Some guys got off on the fight. He got off on the helplessness. He was ashamed to admit it, even to himself, but he sometimes liked it better when they were dead than when they were alive. He could take his time, whisper things to the girls that he really wanted to say, let them know that he did care about them. That it wasn't personal . . . just . . . it was who he was.

He had passed the Four Corners on the rez, passed Shiprock, and was going into Farmington. He'd be in Albuquerque by evening, ready to set up shop. He knew better than to check in at the Jackson Santa Fe—pretty little Dorothy wasn't there by chance—so he'd hit the Jackson down south, where he still had business at Sandia NL. That way the government would be paying for his room and meals and he could go in and out of Santa Fe without being noticed.

That was if all went as planned. And when things didn't go as planned, well, that was okay too.

Creativity spawned excitement. And that's all he wanted in his dull, dull life. A little fun now and then.

RO WAS CHIPPER while Ben was pissed off and anxiety-ridden. She zipped across the threshold with Griffen following her like the tail to her comet. She had on a bright pink polo shirt that screamed summer. All it did was remind Ben of the significance of the day.

"I don't like this plan." Ben closed the door. "I should be here."

"Stop worrying." She sighed heavily. "We've been over this a thousand times."

Ben looked around. "Where's Ezra?"

"Sick," Griffen said.

"So there's just the three of you?" He shook his head. "Uh-uh, I'm staying home."

"Vicks, Griff is here, the girls are together, and Shanks said he'll make at least three drive-bys."

"I'm not going unless they wait at the police station."

"And I told you I'm not waiting at a police station," Haley said.

She seemed as pissed off as he was. It was the time of the year when she and Ben became orphans. Their mother was barely functioning, managing just to work and sleep. Their dad, on the other hand, was all work. Both of them were as absent as they were absent-minded. Ben and Haley were left to fend for themselves, and since Ben drove, Haley was dependent on him. He became bossy. She became defiant. Nothing worked for either of them.

Haley said, "I've got a ton of work to do for my final papers. And Mom said something about leaving early from work."

Ben said, "She has a doctor's appointment."

"Oh . . ." Haley's complexion darkened. "I thought maybe she actually wanted to spend some time with me."

"She does, Haley." Ben exhaled "She just can't function right now." Silence. "You haven't said anything to her about today, right?"

"God, don't you trust me at all?"

"I'm sorry if it comes across like that."

Haley was somewhat mollified. "Honestly, it's stupid that she doesn't know."

"I wanted here her, Haley. Dad overruled me."

"You haven't told your mom about what's going on?" Ro was genuinely surprised.

"The official anniversary of my sister's death is in spitting distance. She's been in a dark place for days. My dad told me that he doesn't want to unnecessarily worry her."

Ro made a face. "But she knows about the slashed tires. She knows that Shanks was grilling us about Barnes. You need to tell her what's going on. She won't wilt, you know."

"You've never been with her at this time of year." Ben looked at his sister. "Should I tell her?"

"Call Dad and ask him again."

He phoned his father. The conversation was very short. "Don't tell Mom, but he'll be here in an hour or so to oversee, okay?"

"Oh please," Haley shot back. "Call him back and tell him we're fine."

"None of this would be necessary if you guys would wait at the police station."

"And what would Mom think about that?" Haley looked at him with hard eyes. "Ben, we're *fine*. I mean, like how long are you going to be gone? Like two hours? I mean, like, c'mon!"

"Here, here," Ro said.

To Lilly, Ben said, "You okay with this?"

"I can study anywhere." She gave a weak smile. "If you have to go to rehearsal to go to graduation, then go to rehearsal. We'll be fine."

"Can we go already?" Ro was tugging on Ben's T-shirt.

"I'm halfway done with college. Why do I need to graduate high school?" To Ro, he said, "Go on without me."

"I don't believe this!" She was angry.

Lilly stepped in. "Ben, the graduation ceremony isn't for you. It's for your parents. You owe it to them."

Ben knew she was right and that stank.

He wasn't meant to be the oldest child, to be the first one to go to prom, the first one to wear a cap and gown or go to college or get married or have kids or experience any of those milestones. He was born second in line. He should have *been* second in line. Totally wrong but what could he do?

Ben turned to Griff. "You don't answer the door for anyone, right? Even if he says he's Shanks. Even if it *is* Shanks . . . well, if it is Shanks, you call me first. No one goes through that door unless I say so!"

"Dude, I hear you."

"Don't dude me right now," Ben said. "It doesn't inspire confidence."

Griff turned serious. "It's a little embarrassing that you don't trust me."

Ben took his arm and spoke in a low voice. "Griff, he killed four people."

"I'm on it, Ben. Besides, the guy would have to be a moron to come to the house."

Sometimes you've just got to let go. Ben said, "Did you preprogram your cell phones with the numbers?"

"We all did: yours, Shanks's, your dad's, my dad's, and nine-one-one."

"And you'll keep the lines free at all times, right?"

"I got the memo." Griff was staring with his big blue eyes. "I can *handle* it."

Ben finally saw what he wanted: genuine concern in Griff's eyes. The past year the boy had not only grown taller, he had filled out. He had broader shoulders and muscle in his arms. If he kept going this way, he'd make varsity football. In an arm wrestling match, Ben wouldn't be surprised if Griff could take him down. But in a life-and-death struggle, Ben had an advantage over any of them. He had the passion because he knew what he was fighting for. "I'm counting on you. Don't let me down."

"I got it, Vicks."

Ro was pushing Ben out the door. "See you guys. Lock up!" She dragged him to her car. "Will you relax?"

"That is *out* of the question." They got into her Explorer and he pulled out a gun from a boot holster. It was only a little mouse gun, but it was better than nothing. Ro's eyes went wide. He shrugged. "Just in case."

"You're nuts."

He stowed the gun in her glove compartment. "Look, I know I'm being ridiculous, but it's the way I'm wired, okay?" He took out his phone.

"Vicks, c'mon!"

"I just want to make sure that Haley's keeping the line open."

When she answered, she said, "I'm still here."

"Keep the line open."

"I can't if I'm talking to you." She hung up.

He didn't feel right about leaving them, but as long as they toed the line—stayed inside the house with the doors locked—he supposed that they would last a few hours.

That's what Ben told himself over and over and over.

FIFTEEN MINUTES INTO the hour, Haley put down her laptop. "How much longer is that damn truck going to beep?"

Lilly looked up from her workbook. She furrowed her brow as she listened to the incessant *wheep, wheep, wheep* in a high-pitched range. "I hadn't noticed it until you said something."

"How could you not notice it?"

"I was concentrating."

"Well, bully for you."

Lilly forced her lips shut to prevent herself from saying something she'd later regret. It wasn't that Haley was grumpy, it was that she was selectively grumpy. With Griff, she was all smiles. Lilly was a third wheel, again. She got up and went to the window. "It's street repair. The truck is hauling away broken asphalt."

"So why is it beeping?"

"It does that every time it backs up."

"Well, it's driving me crazy! I hate studying to begin with and I've got four finals and a paper." Haley regarded Lilly. "Did you do the English paper yet?" She didn't wait for an answer. "Of course you did. And I bet you already studied for finals?"

Lilly sighed. "How can I help you, Haley?"

"By not being so condescending. You and my brother are really a pair." She stood up. "I'm going to the library."

Griffen said, "You know you can't do that."

"Why? Because Ben said I can't?" She made a face. "Who made him lord and protector?"

"Haley—"

"I understand where he's coming from." Her eyes got moist. "She was my sister too, you know. He acts like he's the only one who's suffered. Just because I'm not hunting around for some phantom killer doesn't mean I don't care or I'm inferior."

Lilly said, "Haley, he's not trying to be superior, he's just worried about your personal safety."

"He's bossy."

Griffen said, "You know we're not going anywhere. Put cotton in your ears or something."

"Let's look at this logically," Haley said. "The library is like ten blocks away. If we all go together and we all stay together, it's probably even a better place to be because it's public."

"Why didn't you say anything to him about the library when he was here?" Griffen asked. "I promised him I'd look after you two."

"So look after us in the library. We'll all stay in the same place at the same table." Haley looked at Lilly. "You just said you can do work anywhere."

"It's not a problem for me," Lilly said. "But if he comes back and finds us gone, he'll freak. Why don't you call him up and tell him your plans."

"How about if we go to the library *first* and then I'll call him up and tell him the change of plans? Because if I call him now, he'll come rushing home and I don't want to deal with him because he'll be pissed. He's always pissed. It's hard being with someone so pissed off."

Tell me about it, Lilly thought.

"With my mom being a zombie and my dad never around, things suck, okay? I know that Ben's being protective, but you know he truly likes bossing me around."

"That's not fair," Lilly said.

"Earth to Lilly. Ben is not God."

Lilly felt her face go hot. Griffen broke in. "Haley, let's just stick with the plan, and when he comes back, we'll all go to the library, okay? Let's just take a break and—"

"I have way too much work to take a break, okay?"

"Jesus! Sorry!" Griffen threw up his hands. The truck continued to beep every time it backed up into the roadway.

"I'm sick of Ben saying jump and we say how high. I'm going with or without you."

Lilly said, "Haley, you know that if you go, then we all have to go."

"So come with me. You know . . . like, strength in numbers."

Griffen said, "You're not worried even though this guy has killed other girls?"

"If it's the guy Ben thinks it is—and there's no proof of that yet—he killed in three other cities. It's been three years. He's not coming back here. It would be stupid."

Lilly said, "What about Ben's slashed tires?"

"It was probably a prank."

"Haley, no one slashes four tires for a prank."

She shrugged. "I don't see why I have to rearrange my life just because Ben says so."

"Because it makes sense? Why are you picking now of all times to be rebellious?"

"I'm not being rebellious." Haley zeroed in on Lilly. "Ben is not my father and I'm not his child. Stop insulting me."

"Could everyone just chill?" Griffen said. "You're just fighting because you're tense. That's normal—"

"Stop psychoanalyzing me, Griff. It just makes me even angrier." Haley was red-faced with moist eyes. She scooped up her books. "This guy has destroyed my family. I'm not letting him destroy me. I'll see you all later."

Griffen picked up his laptop. "We'll all go together."

"Fine, we'll go together," Lilly said. "You should call Ben and let him know."

"Later."

"Haley, stop acting stupid."

"Excuse me?" Haley glared at her. "I certainly know whose side *you're* on."

"I'm not taking sides. This isn't an election."

"I am so gone."

"Wait, wait." Griffen took her arm. "Just wait, okay?"

"Fine."

Haley tapped her foot until Griffen and Lilly had gathered up their belongings. Within minutes, they were out the door and on the street. The first day of summer had turned out to be spectacular. The sun was strong, the sky was a rich teal blue, and the air smelled of lavender and roses. The trio walked down the hillside, the mountains in the distance boasting an array of colors from deep greens to earthy rusts. Birds had roosted in the treetops and bees flitted from sage plant to sage plant.

With the warmth on her face, Haley felt better. The trip to the library was an easy walk, and fifteen minutes later the group reached the building without incident. They found an empty table, sat down, and Haley settled in, taking out her laptop and her books. Griffen sat next to her and Lilly sat across the table from them.

Lilly whispered, "Before you forget, you should text Ben and tell him where we are."

"You do it."

Such a baby, Lilly thought. "Fine, I'll do it." She texted him, then put her phone ringer on vibrate and slipped it in her purse. Finals would be over in ten days along with her first year of high school.

How time flies.

CHAPTER 11

THE LINEUP WAS in alphabetical order, which would have been great if Ben had actually been at the back. Instead, because he was salutatorian—a title akin to the country's vice president and equally meaningful—he had to march in the front of the line, but behind JD. The order of importance was not lost on JD's ego and he ribbed Ben mercilessly.

At the beginning of lineup, the boys' VP made the announcement to turn off all cell phones, that anyone caught disobeying the edict would miss graduation—clearly an incentive for Ben to keep his phone on the loudest ring possible. Instead he played the semigood citizen and put his phone on vibrate and in his pants pocket, where he could check it at regular intervals.

The rehearsal was clearly not going to be an hour. After thirty minutes, the faculty was still arranging the students. The sun was hot and everyone was sweating and fanning themselves with their hands. In the chaos, Ben sneaked a glance at his phone messages.

The text message from Lilly set his heart racing.

SHIT!

He pulled out his phone. JD said, "What are you doing, Vicks? Put that away."

Ben heard his voice but not the words. He read Lilly's message. "FUCK!"

Heads turned in his direction.

"What's wrong?" JD said.

The boys' VP said, "Vicks, what are you doing? Put that phone away."

"I've gotta go, sir."

"What's wrong?"

"I . . . have to pick up my sister at the library."

"Can't someone else do it?"

"No! No one else can do it. I am the only one who can do it and I have to go *now*!"

"Is she sick?"

"No, she's just very stupid."

"This is very poor timing on your part," the veep told him. "You know if you miss rehearsal, you can't attend graduation."

"With all due respect, sir, *screw* graduation."

He jogged away, trying to call Haley and trying to find Ro at the same time. "Answer the phone, you stupid idiot!" Her cell rang twice and then went to voice mail. At that point, Ben's head got fuzzy. He didn't know if it was heat or fear, but his knees buckled. He managed to catch himself before he hit the ground. Ro came over to him. "Ben, what's wrong?"

"I need your car keys!"

"What?"

"Haley went to the library. I can't reach her. Give me your fucking keys!"

"You're in no state to drive—"

Ben grabbed her purse and rooted through her belongings. She was pulling it back by a strap. "Vicks, you have to calm down."

"Don't tell me that!" He yanked her purse away from her, catching her off balance. She stumbled back and fell to the ground on her butt. He pulled out the keys and tossed her back her purse. "I knew I should have stayed back."

He took off, but she ran after him.

"Vicks, wait! Wait! . . ." A pause. "WAIT."

When he got to Ro's car, the temptation was strong to just hop in and speed away. But she looked so pathetic, panting and wheezing. He threw open the passenger door and dove into the driver's seat. He took off before she could fully close the door. "The kids went to the library."

"What? Why?"

"'Cause they're idiots. Call up your brother."

She already had her phone out. "It's going to voice mail."

"I can't believe how fucking stupid they are. Call up Lilly."

Ro went through the contact list until she found the number.

"Voice mail." Ben saw Ro wipe her eyes. She said, "He couldn't have kidnapped all three. Goddamn them! How could they do this! How could they be so damn stupid!"

Ben glanced at her. It was rare for Ro to swear. She was red-faced, sweating and crying at the same time. She was texting with shaking hands. By leaving with him, Ben knew she'd miss the graduation ceremony. She was as upset as he was and that made him get a grip. She said, "Should I call Shanks?"

"Hold off. I'll be there in five minutes."

"I'll try my brother again." Silence. "I'm going to kill him! I am sincerely going to kill him!"

Every second was interminable. Finally, he pulled into the library lot, found a space, and jumped out of the driver's seat. Ro was on his heels.

Since the library wasn't the proper place to start screaming out names, Ben's eyes were in frantic search mode. The public reading room wasn't all that big, and within a few moments, he saw Haley, sitting at a table, typing on her laptop.

He didn't know whether to kill her or hug her.

Walking over, he scream-whispered, "What the fuck!" He glared at Griffen. "Is this what you call *handling* it?"

"She stormed out of the house. I had about two seconds to decide and I thought it was better if we all went together rather than split up."

Ro hissed at him, "Why wasn't your phone on?"

"It was. I had it on vibrate—"

"You didn't answer it."

"I probably didn't feel it." Griff sighed. "Honestly, Ben, what should I have done? Tied her up?"

"That would have been a great idea!"

They were promptly shushed by the librarian, who told them to take it outside.

Ben sat next to his sister. She was blushing, sweating, and had yet to speak. He lowered his voice. "Why did you *do* this to me, Haley? I know I can be a tyrant, but you gotta read the metamessage. I only wanted you to be safe. Now we're both gonna miss graduation because I panicked and left rehearsal!"

Her lower lip trembled and her eyes teared up. "I'm . . . sorry. I just wanted to get out of the house."

"You wanted to assert your independence because I'm

bossy . . . which is fine any other day except today. You know you totally screwed me!"

She was trying to hold back sobs. "The truck was beeping and I couldn't concentrate and that house has so many bad memories sometimes!" She wiped her tears on her sleeve. "I'm sorry."

He sincerely wanted to strangle her. Instead he threw his arms around her and hugged her tightly. "It doesn't matter. Just as long as you're okay. That's all I care about."

"I'm so sorry!"

"Forget it." To Ro, Ben said, "Go back to rehearsal and tell them I was stealing your car. Everyone saw me acting like a maniac. You'll be fine."

Her eyes were wet as well. "It's fine. I don't even care anymore. I'll drive everyone back. I'm just glad for a happy ending."

"Sorry, Griff," Ben told him. "You did the right thing."

"No, I should have insisted—"

"Let's just get out of here. I feel like I'm gonna puke and I'd rather do it outside." Ben got up and looked around. "Where's Lilly?" The question was met with silence. Haley's eyes went to Lilly's purse and open laptop. A stack of books and papers sat next to the computer.

Haley couldn't speak. Griffen stammered out, "I was studying . . . I . . ."

Instantly came the sinking feeling in the pit of Ben's gut, just like when they got the phone call from his father three years ago.

"Do you know where Ellen is?"

Ro stammered out, "I'll check out the bathroom."

"Yeah . . . phew! That's it!" Haley hit her head. "She

said she was going to the bathroom, that I should watch her purse."

Ben's heart was racing. "How long has she been gone?"

"A few minutes—"

He caught up with Ro. Through the door, he heard her call Lilly's name.

"Is she there?"

Silence.

"Ro, is she—"

"I hear you!" Ro threw open the door. "She's not here!"

"Oh God!" Panic set in once again. Ben ran back to Haley and grabbed her shoulders. "She's not in the bathroom. How long has it been since she left?"

When Haley couldn't speak, Griffen said, "Maybe five minutes. I guess I shoulda gone with her."

Ya think? Ben said, "Just five minutes?"

"Maybe a little longer. I wasn't paying attention—"

"Lilly!" He shouted her name out loud. Everyone turned around. "We have a lost girl. *Lilly!*"

Everyone around them started yelling out her name, but after a minute it was crystal clear that she wasn't in the building. The fact that her purse and computer *were* in the building meant only one thing in Ben's mind.

Ro's voice was trembling. "He couldn't have dragged her out the front door."

She was right. Unless there was an alternate escape route, Lilly had to be somewhere in the building. Ben backtracked to the bathroom, and to his horror found an unlocked emergency exit. When he opened it, there wasn't a single chime or beep to let anyone know that the barrier had been breached.

The exit led right to the library's parking lot, where the light hit his eyes like a nuclear blast. After a moment to adjust, he scanned the asphalt, but no one was there. He didn't recall exactly how many cars had been parked when he came in, but he distinctly remembered a white compact that was no longer there. There was an empty spot with a few drops of fluid where that white compact *might* have been. The liquid should have dried up very quickly in the direct sun. Ben figured that at most the car had been gone for less than ten minutes.

Ro suddenly materialized, the other two kids on her heels. They appeared shell-shocked. "Gimme your keys," Ben barked to her.

"Where are we going?"

"I don't know where I'm going, but I'm looking for a white compact, a Toyota or a Honda."

"There must be a million white Toyota or Honda compacts."

He didn't bother to answer, needing to marshal all his energy for the hunt. His mind was reeling like a movie in reverse. "It was four-door . . . not a Honda. It was a Hyundai . . . probably an Elantra." Brain snapping to the present, his eyes scoured the lot until he found what he was looking for. He pointed to a video camera.

"Ro, call up Shanks and meet him here at the library. You tell him what's going on—"

"I'm coming with you, dude."

Too frantic to argue, Ben said, "Okay, come with me. Griffen, *you* wait here for Shanks and show him that video camera. Tell him to put out an APB for a white Hyundai four-door compact that's probably an Elantra. Tell him to call me if he finds the car or if he sees anything else on the tape. Even if he doesn't see anything, tell him to look for that car." He grabbed Ro's hand. "Let's go."

"Anything else?" Griffen shouted to his back.

"Yeah. Tell him the motherfucker's got Lilly!"

CHAPTER 12

HE WAS LIKE a chicken without a head, all impulses but without a working brain behind it. Ben knew that the fiend would end up burying her in the dead of night, near the River Remez in the mountains. The trouble was Ben didn't have a clue as to where he'd do his monstrous activities. In all of the cases, the kill spot had been different from the burial spot.

Where, where, where?

Ro was talking to Shanks in a calm, cool voice that belied her panic. Finally, she hung up the cell. "He's on his way to the library. He put out an APB for a white Elantra."

"God, I hope I'm right."

"Where are you going?"

"North. Toward Los Alamos. It's the only thing I can think of right now. He's familiar with the areas around the lab. Any ideas? I'm open."

Suddenly Ro hit her forehead. "God, I'm an idiot!" She turned to him. "When we take the reservations at the hotel, we take the license plate of the rental car." With shaking hands she started punching in numbers. A few moments later she said, "Hi, Tom, this is Gretchen Majors . . . I'm fine . . . yes, it *is* a beautiful day."

Ben looked at her and whispered, "What *the fuck*?"

She shushed him. "Good to hear. Uh, I need your help. Can you look up the license plate of a guest for me? I got a call that he's stranded and he doesn't—"

"Get to the point!"

"Shut up!" she whispered. "Kevin Barnes, but he could be under the name Karen Bevins or Eva . . . I don't know why but I do know he uses aliases."

Another interminable pause. *"Hurry up!"*

She ignored him. "I really don't know why he uses false names, but I need to get the license . . . I got a call from someone at the airport . . . I don't know why they didn't call the hotel. I gave him my card and maybe that's why . . . Yeah, I had my cell on it."

"Goddammit, Ro! He's got Lilly—"

"Shut up!" She turned to her phone. "No, not you. I'm talking to my dog. Yes, I know giving out your cell is against policy. I'm sorry. But if you could look up that plate, please?"

She was really winging it. *C'mon! Hurry up!*

"Yeah, he might be staying elsewhere but he usually stays at the Jackson Santa Fe or the Jackson Albuquerque. Could you check with Albuquerque? Thank you so much. I'll wait." She turned to Ben. "I'm doing something illegal. He's doing something illegal. Don't say a freakin' word."

"What's taking him so fucking long?"

"Vicks!"

"It's LILLY."

"I'm just as nervous as you are, so shut up! Hi, Tom, I'm still here . . . Uh, yeah, that's probably the person I'm looking for."

"What's the alias?" he shouted.

She plugged up her free ear with her finger so she couldn't hear Ben. "Thank you, Tom. That's a white Hyundai Elantra, right? Good. Would you happen to know what rental company he used? Avis? Great. And would you happen to have the license plate?" She began scribbling something down. "That really helps. Thanks, Tom, I owe you one." She ended the call.

"You got the *license plate*?"

"I did."

"I love you. Call it in to Shanks."

"I will, but right now, I've got a better idea." She made another phone call. "Hi, this is Gretchen Majors from the Jackson . . . Yes, I'm calling because I need a location on a car that was stranded . . . a white Hyundai Elantra." She gave the person on the other end the license plate. "The customer called me from the spot, but in his panic he forgot to tell me where he is. I don't know why he called me. I must have given him my phone number . . . I'd do it myself, but I'm busy with something else, so if you could just give me the location . . . thank you, I'll wait."

Ben was drowning in tension. He couldn't breathe as the seconds droned on, his heart like a steam drill. His eyes were blurry, which was especially bad because he had just entered the highway at top speed, racing to nowhere. Finally, he heard her voice.

"Route 501 toward Los Alamos . . . No, I don't understand why the car is still moving. He said he was stranded."

Ben's instincts had put him in the right area but now that he knew he was close, he had an even bigger sense of urgency, putting pedal to the metal. Both he and Ro were jolted backward and Ro gasped. But she continued to sound professional over the phone. "I really don't understand it either. I'll get to the bottom of it and call you back. Thank you very much." She hung up. She was clutching the door, her complexion something in between white and gray. "You heard what he told me?"

"I did."

"So you know where he's going?"

"I know what route he's taking. Call Shanks."

"I'm a step ahead of you."

Ben's brain was on overdrive. The fact that *his* car was still en route somewhere was a good omen. "After you speak to Shanks, call back the guy at the desk and check up on the car's location."

"Vicks, I've used up my goodwill. I won't get any more out of him. But Shanks can call back and get a bead on him."

She was thinking way more clearly than he was. She clicked off her phone. "Shanks's number goes to voice mail. Nine-one-one?"

"Text him first."

She did. Thirty seconds later her cell rang. Without saying hello, she said, "I got his license plate and a rough idea where he is." She gave him the information. "The car is on the move. Avis has a locator on the vehicle. They can give you the exact point-by-point location. Last time I checked, the car was moving down—"

She stopped talking. Ben could hear shouting over the line, even though the phone wasn't on speaker. Ro was stuttering. "But . . . but . . . but . . . No, I don't know where we are, sir. Ben's driving." More screaming. "I'll tell him, sir. Yes . . . yes . . . yes . . . thank you. Bye." She hung up. "He wants you to go back to River Remez pronto and let the police handle it."

"Fuck that." He exited the highway heading toward 501.

"Do you know where we're going?"

"I know exactly where we're going. I hope that's exactly where *he's* going." Suddenly he was seized with dread. He banged his fist against his head. "Oh shit!"

"*What?*"

"The road to the Los Alamos highway is guarded by national security. There's a checkpoint we have to pass. I'm sure the motherfucker got through easily because he has a security badge."

"So we can't get through?"

"No, we *can* get through. It's not a problem . . . unless the guards have been notified and they've closed off the road. Then we're screwed. Not to mention that I'm so nervous I'm probably going to be questioned. The guard's gonna ask for ID. Do you have a New York driver's license?"

"I have a local driver's license."

"Under Gretchen Majors. Right. But do you have a New York driver's license?"

"Yeah, I've got that too."

"Use that one." They were approaching the stop, the roadway narrowed by concrete barricades and continuing on the other side of the checkpoint. Ben brought the car down to a crawl. "Okay. This is the story. We're going to the Caldera to hike. We're in casual clothes, so it's plausible. Just play along, okay?"

"What's the Caldera?"

"Stop asking questions and just go along with it."

"I'd like to know what it is so if they ask me questions, I can answer them without looking stupid."

"I don't have time for a fucking history lesson."

"God, you don't have to shout."

"I'm fucking nervous."

"Well, join the fucking club," Ro shot back. "Jesus, you're terrible under pressure." Then she burst into tears.

Ben swung the car over to the curb, but didn't turn off the engine. "The Caldera is the cone of a dormant volcano. It's now wide-open space where people hike. I'm sorry I'm shouting, but any minute, those guys are gonna get a call from Shanks about the Elantra. And then they're going to block off the road. And we'll be too late. Let's hold it together for another minute, and then once we get past the security guards, you can swear at me all you want."

"You're right." She dried her eyes. "Sorry."

"I'm sorry too. Let's just . . ." He was still panting. "No problem." He pulled away from the curb and up to the checkpoint. Rolling down the window, Ben was greeted with a blast of hot wind in his face. He put on his best stupid-teenage-boy grin, the kind of dumb look that a dude has when he's with a good-looking girl. It probably came out halfway between a leer and a sneer. "Hello, sir."

The man was wearing a brown uniform; he had a military crew cut and suspicious brown eyes. "Where are you headed?"

"To the Caldera for a hike."

"Little late in the day."

It was four P.M. "We've got at least three hours of good daylight. I just want to show my friend around New Mexico. She's from New York."

The officer peered in the window. Ro smiled and waved. Ben tried to control his tension, hoping that he'd have just a minute before the guard's walkie-talkie buzzed. He smiled again. "Beautiful day." It came out as suck-up and he immediately regretted talking. He had never been good at chitchat.

"It's hot."

"Not as hot as it will be in a month. Besides, the Caldera is usually a few degrees cooler."

"True." The officer asked for ID and Ben showed him his license. Then he checked their laps to make sure their seat belts were fastened. "Try to get back before dark."

"I will. I know the roads are dark after sunset."

"So you go there often?"

God, just close your fucking mouth, Vicksburg. "I used to board around the area in the winter. Now I go in the summertime and hike. It helps me think."

The officer continued to stare at Ben and Ro. Then he waved them on. "Go ahead."

"Thank you." Ben slowly pulled onto the road. As soon as the checkpoint was out of eyesight, he punched the accelerator.

The road was two lanes and sinuous, cutting through the mountains. The temperature was at least ten degrees hotter because the elevation had dropped and the afternoon sun was strong, seeping through the front windshield as they went northwest toward Los Alamos. After a few minutes, the lab buildings came into view. They were low-slung and set back from the road, white buildings with white signs that had LANL and identifying sector numbers in blue lettering. There was no indication of what went on inside, but since the buildings were only closed off by a chain link fence, the structures were probably not the homes of bunker busters. There were dozens of little buildings in the area, all through the Sangres, bleeding into the western Jemez Mountains. Ben had traveled these roads hundreds of times to get to the San Ildefonso and the Santa Clara pueblos, but never in his life had he traveled with such purpose and urgency.

He slowed the car as both of them hunted for a white Hyundai Elantra, his head whirling as they searched. Once the Elantra stopped moving, it meant that the monster had taken Lilly inside one of those buildings. And then they only had minutes before it was too late. "Ro, call Shanks and tell him that we're on top of the guy. Tell him that if he stops the car and takes her out, it's all over. We need a *location*!"

"Got it." She phoned Shanks while peering out the window. He heard Shanks's voice over the line, but then Ro disconnected her cell and punched his shoulder hard. *"Stop!"* She rolled down the window and pointed. "What about *that* car?"

A white Elantra sat behind the gate of a high chain link fence. There was barbed wire on top, so climbing it was a last-resort option. The building wasn't marked with a lab sector sign. It was two stories and might have been used for storage. But seeing as this was Los Alamos, who knew what was inside.

Ro's cell rang again and it was probably Shanks. In the distance, Ben heard sirens.

"Get out of the car!" he ordered.

"What?"

"Just do it! And stay way back from the gate!"

She jumped out of the passenger seat. He slammed the car into reverse, then backed down the road. He shoved the gear back into drive with one foot on the brake and the other on the accelerator. He pressed down and the engine roared, then he steeled himself for the inevitable, gluing his head and neck and back against the seat and the neck rest. As he lifted his left foot from the brake, he depressed the accelerator to the floor and the car shot forward like a ball from a cannon.

It smashed through the chain link fence with that spine-tingling sound of metal against metal—warping, scraping, and gouging. Ben had crashed into the Elantra and sent it hurling into a tree. When that happened, the windshield of the Explorer cracked and the airbags deployed. He braked hard, and the beast came to a halt.

He was in one piece and that was all that mattered. He somehow managed to open the glove compartment and grab the gun, worming himself out of the hunk of metal that had once been Ro's Explorer. By the time he was free, Ro had caught up with him. The two of them raced toward the building.

Coming from the inside was the sickening sound of desperate screaming. The door was secured, so Ben took aim, shot the lock, and rammed the door with his shoulder. The barrier didn't collapse but enough of it broke away from the hinges that he could crawl through the splinters. Inside, it was dim, some light coming in from a few windows. The afternoon sun was sinking fast.

"*Lilly!*"

Another shriek.

"LILLY!" Ben's voice was raw. "Get the fuck away from her!"

Then he realized that the only thing more sickening than the screaming was the sudden silence. Ro yanked on his T-shirt. "It was coming from this way."

They wound and wound their way in the encroaching twilight. The horror scene was tucked into a corner. Ben's knees weakened and his gorge rose.

Lilly's throat had been cut, blood oozing out of the wound. Her hands were around her neck, trying to stanch the flow. She was in shock, her black eyes trembling in their orbs. Her entire body was seized with the shakes. Ro ripped off her T-shirt and knelt down, wrapping the cloth around Lilly's neck while Ben called 911, stuttering out an approximation of where they were and what had just happened. He heard his own voice speak, but he was disembodied, trapped in a nightmare, in a horrific, disorienting daze, until he heard Ro's voice. "She's alive." Ro was gently pressing her shirt against her neck. "It's deep but it isn't spurting. She's gonna make it if I have to rip open a vein and give her a transfusion on the spot! Just hang in there, Lilly. You're gonna be fine. Help is coming, baby, help is coming!"

A distant wail turned louder. They could both hear sirens. Ben dropped to his knees and held Lilly's clammy, bloody hand. He felt fingers wrap around his. To Ro, he said, "What can I do?"

"Barnes!" She looked up. "Go *get* him!"

Ben froze, looking back and forth between Ro and Lilly.

"I've got this, Ben. Help is seconds away. Go get him! Go! *Go!*"

As if to propel him forward, Lilly let go of his hand. His legs found their strength. Gun in hand, he stood up and took off to parts unknown.

CHAPTER 13

HIS BODY WAS slowly returning from the shock, his brain kicking into logic mode.

Ben took in his surroundings.

The first floor of the building was around twenty-five hundred to three thousand square feet, roughly a five-hundred-foot square. The second story was a catwalk that went around the entire perimeter. Every square inch appeared to be taken up by something, mostly boxes that were piled, stacked, and pushed against the wall.

Boxes meant hiding spaces—good for him as protection, bad for him because they could hide a monster known as Kevin Barnes.

The building had a front entrance and a set of back double doors that were still locked from the inside with a double iron bar across the jamb. As far as he could tell, those were the only two ways in or out. But Ben didn't know the building and

Barnes probably did. It was also possible that he had escaped through the front when Ben and Ro were busy with Lilly. He could be long gone, but he could also be within reach.

Take nothing for granted.

Into the bowels of the warehouse. Ben knew he couldn't get a good sense of the layout from the first floor. There were too many boxes breaking up his sight line. He had to go up. A metal staircase was in the corner of the back wall, near the locked and barred double doors. He tiptoed upward, pausing to make sure that each step was silent. When he reached the second story, he immediately hid behind a wall of cardboard. He crouched down, scanning the lower level. He couldn't see everything because of all the obstacles, but he could see enough to orient himself in relation to the building. Most importantly, he could see the back doors. He suspected that Barnes was doing exactly what he was doing. Barnes's goal was to get out. Ben's goal was to stop him.

The sirens kept getting louder and louder until the wailing finally stopped. The lull was followed by a surge of humanity bursting through the front door. First the police, then three EMTs with doctor's bags and equipment. Ben could hear Ro shouting to them and the cops shouting back. The police began to fan out inside the warehouse, taking up positions on the lower floor and upper area with two of them keeping watch over the double doors in the back. If Barnes was still inside, there was no way that he could make it through those babies. The only way he could leave was through the front entrance.

The police were calling out Ben's name, wanting him visible and out of their way so they could continue with the manhunt without shooting him. The smart thing to do would be to say something and wait for them to retrieve him. Get the hell back to safety. Let the pros be the pros. Live to see another day.

But that train had long left the station. Ben had become a heat-seeking missile, homed in on a target and with a predetermined trajectory. Barnes was out there and Ben *had* to be the one to bring him down. He owed it to Ellen—to Katie and Julia and Jamey, and now more than ever, to Lilly. He had to go one-on-one, knowing full well there was a good chance that it would end badly for him.

Ignoring their pleas to come down to safety. After a minute or two, they stopped calling his name, focusing on the monster. They started calling out to Kevin Barnes.

Kevin, you're surrounded.

Kevin, give yourself up.

Kevin, don't make this more difficult than it needs to be.

Kevin, it's over.

It was over for him, but not for Ben.

Feeling the weight of the gun in his hand.

He was not a vegetarian. He ate meat and fish and animal protein and never thought much of it. But he also wasn't a hunter. He wasn't even much for fishing. Sport killing didn't hold much interest for him. If he could get flesh from a grocery store, that was fine.

But this was different. It wasn't bloodlust. That waste of space simply didn't deserve to live. Even if a jury would decide otherwise, Ben had decided long ago that taking Barnes's life would be a righteous killing. He had no trouble imagining what Barnes would look like with a bullet exploding his brain. The thought didn't bother him. Rather, it excited him, feeding him with adrenaline. His vision became clearer and more focused. The hardest thing for him to do was not to react too quickly.

Patience . . . patience.

More people were storming the warehouse. Within twenty minutes, police were everywhere, including Sam Shanks—Ben could hear him yelling out his name. There was concern in Shanks's voice but also anger. He was pleading and chastising at the same time. But Ben remained rooted.

Either catch me or watch me shoot him dead.

They'd arrest him for murder.

Whatever.

He didn't know anything about SWAT procedure, but he figured that the cops would divide the area into sectors. That meant a lot of inch-by-inch searching, clearing each space until they found predator and prey.

When the cops stopped shouting Kevin's name, the space became quieter, but not silent. Ben could hear the static of radios and muffled voices, but sound became dampened, like a mute had been applied to an instrument. There was a good chance he could be shot by accident. All it took was one wrong step.

Slience wasn't just golden, it was a necessity.

Standing up from a squat, taking soundless steps, trying to gauge the situation, knowing that Barnes was doing the same thing. There was conversation among the cops. When it grew louder, he moved. When the talking got softer, Ben stopped.

Both of the doors were heavily guarded.

He threw himself into the mind of the beast. Suppose he was trapped, surrounded. Would he try for an escape or hang tight? Probably he'd stuff himself into a box and wait, thinking that the police probably wouldn't open every single carton in the warehouse.

Barnes had to be hiding. And if that was the case, Ben had no choice but to flush him out before the police did. To do that, Barnes would need a glimmer of hope for an escape.

Which meant drawing the police away from the doors.

Thinking of a plan, Ben stayed put. Let the police do a little of the work for him. They had started opening boxes, going from the front to the back. Cops had arrived by the dozens, the action concentrated near the front doors. The back doors were harder to open, harder to escape from. And they were guarded by two cops with high-powered rifles. But there was still *way* less going on in the back than in the front. And since the cops were working from front to back, it meant they were pushing Barnes to the rear of the building. If Barnes had any brains in his head, he had to know that his only hope was through the back.

Silently, Ben turned on his heel as he inched toward the rear of the warehouse. There was a cop at the foot of the metal staircase he had climbed, and several cops on the second story in front of the staircase.

Again, Shanks called out his name.

The posse kept searching.

If something was gonna happen, it had to happen quickly. He loaded his gun and stuck it in his back pocket. He squatted down.

Looking around for just the right implement to make the right amount of noise, he spotted a piece of a two-by-four about twenty feet away.

That would work.

Creeping toward the fragment of wood, moving with stealth

and silence until it was within grabbing distance. He stretched out his fingers, seized it, then gripped it in his hand. Still hidden behind the boxes, he stood up, listening to the police clear one area after another. Inching toward the railing of the catwalk, he stationed himself close to the edge, but still blocked from the view of the cops.

Ben hurled the two-by-four across the room until it crashed on the opposite side from where he stood. The noise was a magnet, everyone running to the spot. The backdoor guards temporarily stepped forward and away from their positions.

And that's when the mouse darted out, seconds away from making it to the locked door.

Now or never.

Ben flung himself over the railing—a cat in a tree leaping on its prey. Maybe they'd shoot him in the process, but he was so amped he didn't care.

Flying, flying, flying. His body airborne for what seemed like hours.

His mind at peace with his decision.

CHAPTER 14

FALLING ON HIM with a thud, both of them now on the ground. Immediately Ben tried to land punches but Barnes fought back like a wounded animal, scratching, clawing, biting, punching, kicking. The dance of life and death. A few moments into the fight, Ben felt a sharp stab in his ribs, but it did nothing to slow him down. He clawed at Barnes's throat, getting his hand around the monster's neck. But Barnes bit back, hitting him in the face. He got free and rolled over.

Ben saw the gleam of a knife, but kept going, falling on Barnes, pinning him down. Barnes managed to slip away and tried to get to his feet, screaming for help from the police. But the monster had nowhere to go; he was backed up against the wall. Ben grabbed his waist and took him down, the knife clanking to the floor. Ben quickly kicked it away.

The police were closing in.

Ben had to act and act now. He managed enough leverage to wrap his arms around Barnes's neck. He pulled out his gun, and with that, three years of pain, agony, and fury came spilling out.

"You ruined my life!" He whacked Barnes over the head with the butt. "You ruined my fucking *life*!" Another whack. "You ruined my sister, you ruined my family, you ruined me!" A final whack until Barnes went limp in his arms.

Ben still had Barnes in a headlock. He jammed the gun into Barnes's mouth, bracing himself for exploding brains.

But then time suddenly stopped.

He looked around.

There were weapons drawn toward his face, and people yelling, *screaming* at him to put the gun down.

Not just yet, my friends.

Ben used Barnes's body as a shield. With his back to the wall, the police couldn't come from behind. And with the gun down Barnes's throat, Ben knew they wouldn't move on him until they thought they had no choice.

He realized he was enjoying himself. Exhilarated, in fact. Barnes started stirring, then struggling when he found that the gun was down his throat.

"Make a move and I'll turn your head to pulp." Ben was whispering. "You liked when they were all helpless. How do you like the feeling now?"

He pushed the gun down Barnes's throat until he gagged. "Do it now, Barnes. Beg for mercy like they did. Tell me about your wife and kids and all the other shit. Just maybe I'll change my mind."

Gurgles were coming from Barnes's throat. Ben's voice was a hush. His hands were steady, his mind was clear.

"Nah, I don't give a solitary fuck about your kids and your wife. And I certainly don't give a solitary fuck about your worthless life! I'm just thinking how to do it.

"See, this is what I'm thinking. I've got this little gun with little bullets that'll kill you if I put enough of them inside your brain. But if I only do one or two, they'll rattle around your skull, turning all your gray matter to scrambled eggs, but your lower brain'll still be working. So you'll exist but you won't live. What'll it be, Kev? Death or vegetable?"

A wall of uniforms was slowly advancing. Ben noticed and yelled out, "Get back or I *will* shoot him." When no one stopped, he fired the gun at Barnes's feet and screamed, "Back! Now!"

That did the trick.

Shanks's voice cut through the silence, his body emerging from the crowd. He said, "Son of a bitch, Vicks, you did it. You got him. You made a promise to your sister and you kept it. Everyone else failed, but you did it, kiddo. Now just drop the gun and everything will be okay. We'll take it from here. It's over, Ben."

Silence.

Shanks moved a step closer. "You're about to become a hero—"

"A *hero*? Are you out of your mind?" Ben hoisted Barnes to his feet so that he continued to act as a shield. "This piece of shit is still breathing, Sam. So it ain't over."

Shanks tried another approach. "Ben, you want justice, right? Justice for Ellen and the others. How do you think she'd feel about a justice that sent you to jail? Ben, you can't do this to your parents. You can't do it to your mom and dad and your sister. They need you."

"Nah, they don't," Ben said. "Their lives are ruined anyway. This is exactly what they want. They want him dead just like I do."

"Ben, that's ridiculous—"

"Don't fucking tell me I'm ridiculous."

"Sorry . . ." Sam took a deep breath and let it out. "You're right, Ben. That was a rotten thing to say. I'm nervous, dude. I'm really, really nervous. I'm nervous for me, I'm nervous for you. Sorry."

The warehouse went quiet . . . Barnes was now awake; with the revolver in his mouth, his breathing was labored. Ben knew the SWAT team would charge him in a matter of minutes, so he had a real decision to make.

He heard Ro's voice this time. "Ben, don't do it. I'm begging you."

Ben saw tears on her cheeks. Ro sure cried a lot.

She said, "I love you, Ben. Please, for me, don't do it."

He didn't move.

She kept pleading. "Ben, don't do it. I love you. I need you—"

"No you don't," Ben interrupted. The gun was still down Barnes's throat. "If I went away to prison tomorrow, I'm sure you'd be sad. And you'd write me letters. And maybe you'd even visit me. But then you'd move on. And that would be fine with me. Even if I can't move on, you should, Dorothy. The world doesn't stop just because I checked out a long time ago."

Again the room went quiet. Ro blinked several times. Her voice was one step above a whisper. "Ben, Lilly's still alive. *She* needs you."

With the mention of the young teen's name, Ben's brain returned to earth. "Oh shit!" He shoved the body onto the floor and charged forward. "Oh my God. Lilly!"

Immediately he was pounced upon, bodies of men shoving him onto his stomach, whipping his hands behind his back, holding down his legs as he struggled, screaming for them to let him go. Someone took his gun away. He heard Sam telling him to shut up and stop moving. Over and over and over.

Eventually, Ben got the message and went limp. Pressure eased off his back and he was hoisted to his feet, cuffed and surrounded. A gorilla was on either side of him, but Ben was looking into Sam's eyes. "You gotta let me go to her." Tears down his cheeks. "She needs me. I need to *see* her."

"What you need to do is calm down. You're not in your right mind at this moment."

"I'm okay, I swear. Please take the cuffs off." He was begging. "I need to see her." No response. "Sam, she's *dying*!"

Sam sighed, but said nothing.

"I'm not going anywhere. Just let me go to her."

"I'll take you to her, but the cuffs stay on—" Shanks stared at him and his eyes went dark. "Oh shit." He lifted up the kid's shirt. "You've been stabbed. You need medical attention."

"Tell them to let me go and I'll get attention."

"Let him go," Sam said.

As soon as he was freed, Ben bolted to Lilly, hands still manacled behind his back. A huddle of EMTs was working on her. He bent down, his eyes fixed on hers. Her body was shaking even though she had a blanket over her. There was a pool of blood by her side and blood-soaked gauze around her neck. Tubes were down her nose. Monitors and needles were on and in her arms. An oxygen mask was over her nose. Her complexion was gray.

"You're okay, Lilly, you're okay." Saying it just as much to himself as to her. "Just hang in there, baby. I'm not leaving, okay. You're gonna be okay."

Wide dark eyes focused in on his face. He knew she had heard him. Her jeans and underwear had been ripped off and her panties were soaked with blood. Ben felt like his head was about to explode.

I should have fucking shot him.

Shanks was at his side. "You're a fucking idiot, Vicks, you know that? A stupid, fucking moron!"

"Please just take off the cuffs."

"I have to take the cuffs off because you need medical attention. If you bolt, I will haul your ass into jail now and that will be that."

"I'm not going anywhere."

Shanks took off the cuffs and whispered in the boy's ear. "The stab wound. You got it immediately, the second he jumped on you. You were in fear of your life. You understand what I'm saying, Ben?"

"Yes, I got it." One of the EMTs had lifted his shirt. Sam was still holding his shirt. Ben said, "Just let me go to her."

Shanks finally let Ben go. He said, "I'll be right back."

A gaggle of people was talking all at once, mostly medical conversations. Someone told Ben to get the hell away from Lilly, but then someone countermanded the order and said to leave him alone, that he was calming down the girl and her blood pressure was going up. Her body was still shaking, but when Ben took her hand, her fingers weakly tightened around his.

He whispered to her, "Just hold on. Lilly, you're gonna fine. You're gonna be okay. I'm here for you. I'm not going anywhere."

His T-shirt sported a big wet blob, and blood was dripping onto the floor. He knew he should be hurting, but he was so jacked up he felt numb. The EMTs were talking to some kind of doctor over the radio. Words were being bandied back and forth: "blood loss," "shock," "possible severed vocal cords." Lilly's violent shakes had subsided but she was still trembling. Ben could feel his brain working even if he wasn't at his best. His phone was still in his back pocket. He reached for it and began to look up doctors. The nearest specialist was someone in Dallas.

He pulled his hand from Lilly's. "I'm not going anywhere, honey. Just making a phone call." He stood up from his kneeling position and immediately felt woozy, the room spinning around him. He knelt back down—about a foot away from Lilly so she couldn't hear—deciding he could call from a sitting position. Anything was better than passing out. His breathing was shallow and his ribs began to hurt. The adrenaline was wearing off and pain was replacing the high. He was shaking as he punched in the numbers.

"C'mon . . . answer you motherfu—yes, ma'am, my name is Benjamin Vicksburg. I need to talk to Dr. Jacob Winslow. It's a dire emergency! My friend's neck was slashed . . . no, it isn't a joke. I'd let you talk to the EMTs but they're pretty busy saving her life . . . yes, I will hold, thank you."

The wait seemed interminable. A male voice came on the line. "Who is this?"

"My name is Benjamin Vicksburg. My friend was just viciously attacked and her throat was cut. The EMTs working on her said something about her vocal cords being cut. We need a specialist and you're the nearest one to where we are."

"Where are you?"

"Los Alamos, New Mexico."

"Is this a joke?"

"No, sir, I guarantee you that this is not a joke. I guarantee you this will be in the papers tomorrow morning. She's not even fifteen years old. You've got to help. Can you get a chopper from Dallas and meet us here in New Mexico?"

A pause.

"Hello?"

"I'm still here. If she's with EMTs, put one of them on the line."

"Sir—"

"Put an EMT on the goddamn line or I'm going to hang up."

Ben crawled back to one of the EMTs and put his phone on speaker and up against the medic's ear. He said, "You gotta talk to him. He's a throat doctor that specializes in vocal-cord surgery. Please tell him what's going on!"

The woman looked at him, paused, but then complied. The conversation was brief. The doctor asked questions, the EMT answered. Words were exchanged: Lilly's condition, her neck, her vocal cords, her blood pressure, her core temperature, other technical things. Finally, the doctor asked to speak "to the kid." The EMT pulled back from the phone and Ben turned off the speakerphone.

Dr. Winslow said, "They're trying to stabilize her enough to take her to the medical center in Albuquerque. I have a few colleagues there. I'll make some calls. It'll take me at least three hours to get there."

"Thank you, thank you—"

"What is your relationship to her?" he asked.

"Friend."

"You're not a relative?"

"No."

"Where are her parents?"

Oh shit!

What the hell was he going to tell George and June?

"I'll get her parents down there."

"I can't do anything without her parents' permission. What's her name?"

"Lilly Tafoya."

"Her parents?"

"George and June Tafoya."

"And your name again?"

"Benjamin Vicksburg. As in the Civil War battle."

"And give me a couple of phone numbers where I can reach you or people who are involved in this."

Ben gave him his cell number, but he couldn't think of any other number aside from Haley's. He looked up and Sam was nearby. He shoved the phone in his hand. "This is a throat doctor for Lilly. Please tell him I'm legit."

Sam took the phone. "This is Detective Sam Shanks of the River Remez PD. Who am I talking to?"

Ben went back to Lilly, who was now on a gurney. He took her hand. "I'm coming with you, baby."

Sam went up to Ben and gave him back the phone. "How'd you find that guy?"

"The wonders of the Internet. I'm going with her to Albuquerque."

"To the medical center?"

Ben nodded.

"We need to talk, but first you need to get yourself treated."

"Whatever."

"Not whatever. Now."

They were loading Lilly into the ambulance. "I gotta go with her, Sam. I'll meet you in Albuquerque." Ben climbed inside.

No one bothered to object.

The hatch closed. The sirens blared and the ambulance took off. Ben closed his eyes and prayed.

CHAPTER 15

THEY WERE SEPARATED as soon as they hit the emergency corridor in the medical center—Lilly to the OR and Ben into an ER examining room. Slowly, he took off his clothes and put on a robe.

Suddenly he was a patient.

A nurse swabbed his chest. He hadn't really felt the stab beyond the initial jolt, but he sure as hell felt the cleansing. He was dressed with a temporary bandage to stop the bleeding, although by that point, it had trickled down to a slow leak. With an IV in his arm, he waited on an examining table—alone and utterly depleted.

He reached into the back pocket of his pants and made the hardest call of his life. How the hell did Shanks or any of them do this? The line clicked in. He heard himself talk although he didn't even recognize his own voice.

"George Tafoya, please. It's an emergency."

"Name?"

"Benjamin Vicksburg."

Several minutes later: "Ben, what's going on?"

His throat momentarily seized up. Then he said, "Something's happened to Lilly—"

"Oh my God! Is she *okay*?"

"She's . . . in surgery at the Albuquerque medical center. You and June have to come down—"

"What the fuck happened?" When the kid didn't answer immediately, George said, "Ben, what the fuck happened? Tell me!"

A long pause. "She was attacked, George—"

"How?" Then a gasp. "Is it the guy you asked me about? Kevin Barnes?"

"Yes."

"Is she okay?"

"She's in surgery—"

"Answer the fucking question, Ben!" His voice became clogged. "Is my baby okay?"

"I rode with her in the ambulance. When they took her into surgery, she was alive and conscious. You've got to get down here. The surgeon is going to need your permission to operate on her beyond emergency measures."

"Oh my God! How the fuck did this happen?" Ben heard panting over the line. "Fuck this. June and I will be down as soon as I can figure out—"

"I'm sorry, George." But the line was already dead.

Detective Milton Ortiz came into the room. Ben hadn't seen him since Katie Doogan's body had been found. The detective's eyes went to Ben's bandaged chest and then to his face.

"Sam asked you to keep an eye on me?"

"He asked me to check in on you—make sure you got treated."

"I got treated."

"Are you all right?"

"I think it's going to be a very long time before I'm all right." He swiped at his wet face. "Have you heard anything about Lilly?"

Ortiz shook his head. "Sam's on his way."

"I've got to call my parents. Let them know I'm okay."

"They've been contacted."

"I can talk if you want to ask me questions."

"I'll leave that up to Sam."

"He's mad at me."

"You scared the shit out of him." Ortiz looked at him. "We all know it was self-defense."

With a gun down his throat?

Ortiz went on. "He stabbed you, and you were jacked up, not in your right mind. It was self-defense and that's all there is to it. I don't want to hear anything else. Got it?"

Ben got it. "What'd they do with Barnes?"

"I'm sure he's locked up somewhere, demanding to speak to his lawyer."

"He *is* a lawyer."

"Then I'm sure he knows the ropes."

"I fucked up, Detecive. He got her right under my nose. It's totally my fault."

Ortiz's eyes narrowed. "Son, you listen to me and listen good. You need to put the blame where it belongs. On Kevin Barnes. He did it. He is solely responsible. Not you."

"But—"

"There are no buts, Vicksburg."

Ben didn't answer. Nothing was going to help until he was sure that Lilly would be all right—at least medically. She'd never, ever truly be all right again, and that was on him.

Some guy in a white coat came into the room. His name tag said DR. NORMAN MILLSTEIN. He looked about sixty: steel-wool thinning gray hair and a mustache. He washed his hands, introducing himself, and then he started to peel away the gauze. "You've got quite a fan club out there asking about you. There must be over a dozen kids clogging up the waiting room, wondering if you're okay."

"You mean if Lilly's okay . . . the girl who came in with me. Do you know what's happening with her?"

"She's still in surgery."

"Is she okay?"

"I don't know."

"Do you know who's doing the surgery?"

"There is a team."

"Is she stabilized?"

"I don't know." He took off the bandages. "You need stitches, young man."

"Whatever."

"Not whatever. You may not realize it, but you've got some pretty nasty-looking wounds."

"I know. I hurt."

Ortiz took out his phone. "I'd like to take pictures before you close him up. It may help him down the line . . . with the case."

"Go ahead."

As the detective zeroed in on the wounds, Ben looked

down. He had been stabbed and sliced in several places—nasty-looking gashes.

Ortiz finished up his photo taking. To Millstein he asked, "Do you know if the River Remez police have arrived?"

"Not sure."

He turned to Ben. "I'll go see if I can find Shanks. I know he wants to talk to you."

"Thanks," Ben said, although he didn't know why. After Ortiz left, he said, "Could you find out about the girl?"

The doctor was opening drawers and taking stuff out, preparing to sew him up. He said, "I'll do what I can, but truthfully, you'll know when I know."

"You can't peek in?"

"No, it doesn't work that way." He was holding a hypodermic needle. "This will hurt. Hold still if you can." He started injecting around the wounds. When he saw the boy wincing in pain, he said, "Just a few more."

"It's fine." Ben was angry at Ro, at Haley, at Griff, at the world, but most of all, he was furious at himself. He rarely wasted time on emotions. They just got in the way of everything. But anger was something that came naturally. The adrenaline was definitely wearing off and he was sinking into a deep funk. He also did depression pretty well. The shrink he had seen after Ellen died said that depression was just anger turned inward. It sounded a little convenient at the time. Now he understood.

I should never have left them alone.

His belly and sides started tingling. Five minutes later Millstein started to stitch him up.

"Feel anything?"

"Nope."

It was weird because he could sense the needle going in, but it didn't hurt. As the doctor worked, Ben's wrath began to subside. What was the use of screaming at anyone? They probably felt worse than he did. He had done something—fought back and brought down the monster. Ro had battled for Lilly's life. But Haley . . . poor Haley. Lilly was her best friend. There were no words right now that would comfort her. And Griff? He surely had enough guilt to last a lifetime.

More invisible damage done by that waste of space.

Ben knew that when he saw the kids, he'd have to be a source of compassion and understanding even if he didn't feel that way inside. Because he wasn't about to let that bastard have any more power over him. The idea of seeing George and June was nauseating, but he had to face them as well. If they decided to hate him, what could he do? Join the club. He hated himself.

"You're a good patient," Millstein told him.

"Thanks." Ben was thinking, *I should have killed him.*

Then he thought of his parents, of Haley, and of Lilly, of course. He'd have to be there for them. He would dedicate his life to her recovery. He couldn't do that if he was in jail.

Shanks walked into the room, looking old and weary. Dr. Millstein looked up. "We're a little busy in here."

"He's a detective," Ben said. "He needs to talk to me."

"Not while I'm doing this. You can't move, and if you talk, you move."

"I won't say anything," Shanks said.

Millstein didn't answer, but continued sewing.

"How's it looking?" Ben asked Shanks.

"Nasty."

"Stop talking," Millstein said.

"I meant how's it looking for Lilly."

"I don't know, Ben."

Millstein stopped and regarded Shanks. "Please?" He pointed to the door.

"Let him stay," Ben told the doc. "He makes me feel better . . . someone who looks as shitty and worn out as I do."

Shanks managed a very weak smile. "Stop talking. Let him finish up."

"Thank you," Millstein said.

Finally, the doctor stood up. "I'll be back in a moment."

When he left, Ben looked down at his stomach, a patchwork quilt done by an Amish person on crack. Shanks saw him staring. "You'll have stories to tell."

"It would have been a better story to see his head explode." Ben looked up. "Can you find out how Lilly's doing?"

"She's in surgery, Ben. That's all anyone knows."

"Are her parents out there?"

"They arrived about five minutes ago."

"Have you talked to them?"

"I introduced myself. I told them we had the bad guy behind bars. I don't think they heard me."

"Do they hate me?"

"Don't be ridiculous."

"That's the second time you've told me that today."

"Ben, I want to tell you something." Shanks bit his lip. "You know you saved her life. If you had waited for us . . . for the cops to break down that door, she would have been long gone."

"I'm sure George and June don't see it that way."

"George and June are completely focused on Lilly. I guarantee you they're not giving you any thought. But when they do, they'll be very grateful."

"If she's okay, maybe." Silence. "I don't even know what okay means anymore. How can she recover from this?"

"The human spirit is very resilient if you give it a chance."

"Yeah . . . right." Ben rubbed his forehead and felt a pull on his stitches. As soon as the anesthetic wore off, it was going to hurt whenever he moved. "If she doesn't make it, I'll kill myself."

"She made it down to the hospital," Shanks said. "That's step one."

"I just want to wake up six months from now and be normal. Or as normal as I was before all this happened. I'm so frickin' tired of living a nightmare!"

The doctor walked in along with Ben's parents. Laura's eyes immediately started watering. Ben said, "Mom, please don't."

"Oh my God!" She turned her head and stifled a sob. Even his dad had watery eyes.

He asked, "Are you all right?"

"I'm talking and walking, Dad. So I guess the answer is yes. How's Haley? She really needs you two more than I do."

Laura had managed to calm herself down. She kissed her son's cheek and Ben took her hand. He said, "I'm fine. Go tell Haley that I love her and I'm glad she's okay. Tell her that."

William wiped his eyes. "I love you, son."

"I love you too, Dad."

After washing his hands and gloving up, Millstein said, "I'm going to need a little elbow room. He should be out in about a half hour."

"You're not keeping him overnight?" William asked.

"It's not necessary. But someone will need to bring him in tomorrow to re-dress the wounds."

"If I need to sleep somewhere, I'll stay at Grandma and Grandpa's."

Laura said, "There is no way you're going to go there looking like this. It'll kill them."

"Mom, they're going to find out."

"Ben, you're coming home."

"That's stupid."

William said, "Laura, you can't hide this from them. It'll probably be in the papers. It's news, honey. We'll have to prep them."

Laura started crying again. Millstein said, "Maybe it's better if you two wait outside."

Shanks stood up. "Let's give him some room."

Laura handed Ben a bag of clothing. "Sam said he'll need your clothes."

"Yeah, right. Thanks."

"Let's go," his dad said.

The three of them left. Millstein started cleaning the wounds. Ben felt a faint sting and told him so. "I'll give you some pain medication." He unwrapped some gauze. "I'm going to mummify you now. It's the only way that the bandages are going to stay on." As the doc worked, the quiet was haunting. Millstein stood up. "I need some more gauze."

As soon as he left, Ro peeked her head through the door. Her eyes were wet, swollen, and red-rimmed. "Hi."

"How's Lilly?"

"No word."

Ben couldn't think of anything else to say. He beckoned her in with a crook of the finger and she came over. She looked him up and down, covered with gauze, his face and arms splotched with blood. Her own shirt was bloody red, evidence of her heroism. Her hair was matted, her face was drained of color. If there was such a thing as a zombie, she was it.

Ben licked his lips. "You did good."

Water fell from her eyes and rushed down her cheeks. Her voice was a whisper. "It's all my fault." A pause. "You must hate me."

Ben smiled. "I will admit . . . that I've been thinking a lot. And . . . I will admit . . . that I went down that road. That if it hadn't been for that stupid rehearsal, this wouldn't have happened. And if you hadn't insisted that I go, this wouldn't have happened. But then . . . honestly, probably something else would have happened. Because he wasn't going to stop. So . . ." It was getting hard to breathe. "We could do the blame game. Or . . . we can put the blame where it belongs . . . on a psychopathic serial killer . . . and save ourselves a lot of misery. So let's hate the monster and not each other."

She wiped her tears. "That's kind of you to say."

"Ro, we're all sick about Lilly. That's what we're all thinking about. But it's still better than thinking about a burial. And that's because of you."

Millstein came back in and regarded Ro, who immediately burst into tears. The doctor waited a few moments until she had regained some control. Then he said, "He'll be out in a little bit. It would be better if you waited outside."

She kissed his cheek. "Are you okay?"

"Sure."

Millstein cleared his throat and she left. He finished up about a half hour later, giving Ben an armful of medication along with several prescriptions. Ben put on his new and blood-free clothes—jeans and a T-shirt—but his sneakers were still blood-spattered. Pain was seeping in where before it had just felt numb.

Numbness wears off quickly.

Pain lasts a long, long time.

CHAPTER 16

DOZENS OF PAIRS of eyes were upon him. Ben figured that there must have been around forty people, although who they were barely registered. But they included people from the pueblo—some of them outside doing a healing chant. His mother relieved him of the bag of medication along with a bag of bloodstained clothes. "Sit down, Ben."

"I'm okay."

She was pulling vials out of the bag. "Sit down!"

"I'm fine." But he wasn't. He hurt, but he didn't want any pain medication. Nothing to dull him. His eyes scanned the faces around him and his eyes eventually landed on Haley. She saw him and looked away. To his mom he said, "One moment."

Limping over to his baby sister—each step agonizing—Ben put his arm around her, taking her to a private corner. "Don't talk, okay?" His breathing was labored. "It's hard for me to talk, so you've got to listen. It's no one's fault except his." She kept shaking her head no, her eyes pouring out tears. "Haley, blaming ourselves is a waste of time. We've got to keep it all together, okay? Whatever happens, we can't let him fuck us up any more. If he does that, he really wins. And everything that happened today will be for nothing. So let's just . . . hold it together until we get some news about Lilly, okay?"

Haley bit her lip and wiped her eyes. "Okay."

Her voice was a mouse squeak. Ben kissed her head, and when she started to hug him, he gasped in pain. "Oh my God. Sorry."

"I'm fine. Just . . ." He pointed to his cheek. "You can kiss me here."

She did and they both walked back to the group. Ben looked around for an empty seat and the whole waiting room stood up. But then he saw George and June and Lilly's two half brothers in a corner by themselves. June was facing the wall, rocking back and forth. Lilly's half brothers were talking to George. His eyes were downcast, but when he looked up, he noticed Ben. He made the first move. They met in the middle of the room. George's broad face was drawn and colorless. His dark eyes were piercing as they regarded Ben's face.

"No one is telling us a fucking thing . . . just that she was attacked and she's now in surgery. What the hell is going on?" When Ben tried to talk, the words jammed in his throat. George said, "Are you going to man up or stonewall like everyone else? I know it's bad." Tears ran down his cheeks. "Just tell me *something*!"

Ben pointed to his throat. "He cut her."

George's voice grew faint. "Her cut her throat? Dear God! How bad?"

Ben tried to think of something positive. "Like I said . . . she never lost consciousness. She was staring at me on the ride over. And she knew it was me." Ben's voice cracked. "She held my hand. They got her here, George. That's the main thing."

"Did she say anything to you?"

Ben ran his tongue along the inside of his cheek. "No."

"Could she talk?"

"I . . . don't know." He looked down. "There's a neck specialist flying in from Dallas. You'll need to sign some stuff so he can operate."

"I know. They told me that."

"He's a vocal-cord specialist. She was hurt in that area, so they called him down."

He stared at Ben. "What else did the monster do?" When the boy didn't answer, he said, "Was she—"

"Yes." Ben looked away and George swore under his breath. "How'd he even get to her? I thought she was studying at your house. I was going to pick her up from there."

"They walked over to the library. I think he was stalking them—"

"He got her in the *library*?"

Ben nodded.

"The *public* library?"

"There was an emergency exit near the women's bathroom. Most of the time they don't bother to lock it. I think he waited until one of them went to the bathroom."

"He was waiting until Lilly went to the bathroom?"

"I think if it had been Haley, he would have taken her instead." Ben looked down. "I should have killed him when I had the chance."

"Yeah, you damn well should have killed him. Why the hell didn't you?" When Ben was silent, George said, "I don't know what I'm saying. I'm not in my right mind now." His eyes went to Ben's red-stained arms. He lifted the hem of Ben's shirt and looked at his bandaged body. "What the hell happened to you?"

"I'm fine."

"Did you fight him off?"

"I don't remember what I did, except I stuck a gun in his mouth. Other than that, it's all one big nightmarish blur."

"How'd you find out where he took her?"

"Ro managed to track him using her hotel connections. We got there ahead of the police. We called in the police."

"And you're sure it's Kevin Barnes?"

"Yeah . . . it's him."

"I'll kill him. I'll fucking put a gun to his head and shoot his brains out." He paused. "I should have taken you more seriously—confronted the bastard." He shook his head. "This is my fault."

"No, it's not your fault. It's not my fault either. It's Kevin Barnes who did it."

The big man blew out air. "You're right. I should be thanking you . . . you and whatsherface."

Ben smiled. "Ro Majors. She kept her . . ." *Alive.* "She kept Lilly going until the paramedics came."

"Thank her for me, will you? I can't talk to anyone right now."

Ben glanced at his watch. It was eight in the evening—those had been both the fastest and the slowest four hours that had ever passed in his life. They both saw a nurse approach June. George moved in to intercept her and Ben tagged along.

She said, "These are consent forms for Dr. Winslow."

"That's the throat doctor. Is he here at the hospital?"

"Yes."

"Can I talk to him?" George asked.

"He's getting ready for surgery, Dr. Tafoya. He needs your permission before he can do anything."

"What's going on with my little girl?"

"I don't know, sir."

"C'mon!" There was desperation in his voice. "You must know something."

"I'm sorry, sir, but I honestly don't know anything."

George sighed, grabbed the clipboard, signed it, and shoved it into the nurse's chest. Then he walked back to June.

Ben shrugged at the nurse. "He's not himself."

"He's well behaved compared to others. I've been screamed at, cursed at, spit at, name-called, grabbed, shaken, and occasionally a few people have tried to land a punch in my face. Stress brings out all sorts of hidden demons. How are you feeling?"

"I'm still here, so I guess that's good news." Ben smiled, she smiled, and then he turned and went back to the crowd.

His presence brought the soft conversation to a halt. The faces began to take on names—his parents and grandparents; Ro and Haley, of course; but also Griffen, JD, Weekly, Mark Salinez, Lisa, Shannon, Chelsea; Mr. Beltran, the principal; Tom Gomez. Lilly's grandmother and grandfather. Ben's cousin Henry was there, looking completely sober. If there was ever a time to get hammered, Ben felt it was now. Shanks was sitting next to Ben's father. He offered the kid his chair, but Ben shook his head. Within a few minutes, conversation picked up again—something along the lines of whether or not the school should hold graduation. JD, Weekly, Griffen, and Salinez got up and left. Ben wondered where they were going but was too tired to ask.

He went over to the far wall, away from everyone, and sat down on the floor, legs straight out in front of him so as not to pull his stitches. Ro brought him a chair and walked away. He managed to stand long enough to sit in it, stitches burning and pulling and his whole body enveloped in pain. He threw back his head, looking up at an acoustical-tiled light green ceiling.

For just a little while he needed to be alone.

Everyone respected that.

You don't bother the injured wolf.

HALF AN HOUR later Ben went over to Shanks. "Where is he? Barnes."

"Locked up. Have a seat, Vicks."

Ben sat down. Shanks's jaw muscles were working overtime. He looked like he was chewing on imaginary gum.

"Is he talking?"

"Barnes? Of course not."

"No bail, right?"

"He's a suspect in four murders. Not a chance."

"What's gonna be his story?" A pause. "He's not gonna plead guilty."

"I have no idea what his story will be," Shanks said. "They've just finished processing him, Ben. Then he has to talk to a lawyer. Then he has to be officially arraigned. These things take a while."

"If I were him, I'd say that he heard screaming, went in,

and was trying to help Lilly, and that we scared him away. And he stabbed me because I scared him."

Shanks whispered, "And this is your rebuttal story. You found him . . . on top of Lilly and he started cutting at you with his knife. That's why you have those gashes. You ran after him, jumped him, and he stabbed you. And you do have a stab wound. It was at that point when you took out your gun. In fear for your life. Got it?"

"Sounds good except I beat him up."

"He was wielding the knife. You were in fear for your life. It's the total truth, son . . . maybe not in that exact order, but the truth. Case closed. Stop talking about it, all right?"

Ben nodded. "You can legally take his DNA now."

"Yes we can."

"You must really feel sorry for me." Shanks looked at the kid, who said, "The old Shanks would have said, 'Thank you for reminding me. Otherwise, I would have forgotten about that.'"

Shanks smiled. "We put a rush on it, but it'll still take about twenty-four hours. The judge already agreed to hold him without bail until the tests come back. As soon as we get the matches with the other murders, he's a goner. It's over." Shanks ran his hand through his messy hair. "I'm going to need a statement from you when you're feeling better."

"I can do it now. It's torture just to sit here and wait. Go get a pad and paper."

"I'll be right back." As soon as Shanks left, Ro came over. Ben's dad got up. "Take a seat, honey."

"Thank you." She sat down and put a hand on Ben's knee.

"Looks like I fucked up grad night, Dorothy." He shrugged. "Sorry about that."

She let out a sad laugh. "God . . . was I ever *that* superficial?"

"All the time." When she slapped his leg, Ben said, "Okay. I know you're all right. You're hitting me."

Ro smiled with wet eyes. "She's gonna make it, right?"

"Of course." JD, Weekly, Salinez, and Griffen had returned. There were cotton balls taped to the insides of their arms. "They gave blood?"

"Yeah," Ro said. "My turn." She stood up.

"I'll go with you," Ben told her.

"You stay put."

"I'm okay."

"Ben, there are like thirty people in this room who are all willing to donate. Just sit down and concentrate on making more of your own erythrocytes, okay?"

She got up and JD immediately took her place. He was wearing the same shirt and jeans that he had on for graduation rehearsal. "You okay?"

"I'm fine. Why does everyone keep asking me that?"

JD lifted Ben's shirt, looked at the bandages, and let it fall back down. He wiped his hand across his mouth. "How bad was it? I mean, how bad was she?"

"She'll recover . . . I hope."

JD turned away. He said, "We should be graduating tomorrow. It was my day, Vicksburg. I fucking knew you'd figure out a way to upstage me."

Ben laughed and it hurt. "I'm the man, dude."

JD laughed too. "Yep, just for today, you *are* the man. Do you hurt?"

"Kills."

"You need anything?"

"Nah."

"How about something to eat? You want a Doogie burger or something?"

"If I put anything in my stomach, I'll puke."

JD nodded. "Did the doc give you meds?"

"Yeah."

"Pain meds?"

"Yeah, my mom's got the bag."

"What'd they give you for pain?"

"I dunno. Probably Vicodin . . . maybe OxyContin. I really don't know."

JD raised his eyebrows. He whispered, "Wanna get high together?"

Ben didn't know if he was serious, but the comment made him smile. "I'll tell you what, JD. Whatever I don't use, it's yours. My graduation gift to you."

"Cool."

Shanks had come back with a yellow legal pad and a pen. JD stood up. "If you need something . . ."

"I'll let you know."

Shanks walked Ben into a secluded spot with a couple of empty chairs. "Walk me through the day."

Ben did so, with the modifications suggested to him by Ortiz and Shanks. The entire recitation took longer than he thought it would and wore him out.

Shanks said, "You did good."

"You're satisfied?"

"I am. You were clearly acting in self-defense and you were in fear for your life. I—and everyone around me—will recommend that no charges be brought against you."

"You're sure about that? Barnes is going to tell a different story."

"His DNA is going to put him at the scene of four murders. There were forty cops there to witness what happened and to back you up. A little girl is fighting for her life." Shanks closed his notebook. "There are things in life you'll worry about. This won't be one of them."

CHAPTER 17

LIMBO IS DEFINED as the place between heaven and hell, but it's way more hell than heaven. The waiting was interminable, but the group kept saying if it was taking this long it must be good news.

At midnight—around eight hours after the attack—two surgeons dressed in green scrubs, still wearing caps and shoe covers, came out of a locked door and looked around the waiting room. George bounced up and so did June. The surgeons spoke to the Tafoyas, who kept nodding—no wailing. Ben took that as a good sign.

George looked around, eyes falling on Ben. He motioned the kid over, then put a protective arm around him. One of the surgeons was tall and graying, and had piercing blue eyes. "Are you the kid who called me? Vicksburg?"

"That was me. You're Dr. Winslow?"

"I am. That was quick thinking on your feet."

Ben had a thousand questions, but knew better than to ask any. Not with Lilly's parents around. George said, "She made it through the surgery. She's in guarded condition."

Relief did not even begin to describe Ben's emotions. "Guarded is good, right?"

"It's a very good outcome considering what she went through," Winslow said. "She's in recovery. We'll transfer her to the ICU and then you can see her. That's going to take a couple of hours."

Ben couldn't help himself. "What about her . . . you know." He touched his neck.

"Her vocal cords?" Winslow said. "There was damage, but not as bad as it could have been. Vocal cords aren't really cords like a string. They are more like an accordion. I can't say anything definite, but I'm optimistic. She'll likely need another operation—maybe two—and vocal rehabilitation."

"But she'll talk again?"

"I'm optimistic."

"Enough questions," George said. "Go home, Ben. Take care of yourself."

June was staring at Ben with dry eyes. "George is right. Go home. And thank you, Ben."

"Honestly, I'm gonna stick around. Do you guys need coffee or anything?"

"No. If you're not going home, then go back to your crowd. Give us a moment to digest all this shit." George kissed the top of the boy's head. "You know how grateful I am to you and whatsherface, right?"

"Right."

"Okay. Go away."

"What should I tell everyone? They're gonna ask."

"Just tell them that she made it through surgery. Everyone should leave and give us some peace and quiet. It's hard looking at everyone with them pretending not to see me. Tell them all to pack it in, including the tribe. I don't need their fucking incantations. I mean, if they want to do it in Santa Clara, that's fine. I will appreciate the community support later on, but right now, I'm too sick to deal with anyone, including you. So go away."

"I'm leaving."

He was greeted by expectant faces.

Ben gave a thumbs-up, which was answered by spontaneous smiles and sighs of relief. "She made it through surgery and is in guarded condition. That's all I know." He rubbed his eyes. "George wants everyone to leave. Our presence is making him nervous."

Slowly, people started to gather up their belongings. Henry came up and he and Ben fist-bumped. Ben's grandparents came over, his grandma saying, "Are you coming to the house, Benny?"

"Eventually. I'm gonna stick around here for now."

Ro said, "You just said everyone should leave."

"I'm not included in everyone." To his grandma: "I'll be here for a while. I'll call you to pick me up when I'm ready, okay?"

"When will that be?"

"Tomorrow morning, probably."

"Benny, you need to rest."

"I know, I know. Go. I'll call you later." He turned to Ro. "George says thank you for what you did with Lilly."

"He did? I didn't think he even knew my name."

"He didn't. He called you 'whatsherface.'"

"Okay, that figures."

The crowd had thinned to Sam Shanks and the families—Ro's as well as Ben's. Ben looked at Griff. "No long faces, okay, dude? We're all just doing the best we can. And it's gonna be okay."

"I'm staying with you," Haley said.

Ben knew this was something she had to do. "Okay, Hales. Stay with me. A little company might not be bad."

"I'm staying with her," Griff said.

"And I'm staying with you," Ro said to Griff.

"And we're staying with you," Ro's dad told them.

Ben's dad said, "Mom and I are not leaving without Haley and you, Ben. What if you start to bleed and you need help?"

"Dad, I'm in a hospital."

His mom said, "If you stay, we're staying. End of discussion."

"Whatever. Do what you want."

The group was silent for a few minutes, but eventually people started to talk—slowly at first, then the pace picked up. Shanks got coffee and doughnuts. He took some over to the Tafoyas, who joined the crowd until they were all chatting away about things both big and trivial. From graduation to Ellen's childhood. From Ro's college choices to Gretchen's illness. And of course, they all told stories about Lilly. It was nonsense talk, but it was serious conversation. There were a lot of wet eyes interspersed with the occasional smile and even a chuckle or two.

Just passing time.

AS SOON AS Lilly was moved to the ICU, the powwow started to break up. June and George immediately left to be with their daughter. George's sons left for Las Cruces. Griff and his parents called it a day. Shanks needed to get back to River Remez to begin his paperwork. And Ben's parents insisted that Haley go home and get some sleep.

It was down to Ro and Ben. Since Lilly was still alive, it was a safe bet that graduation would go on and that was okay because life goes on. At the ceremony, there would probably be the requisite moment of silence, and even though it was nonsense, it made people feel better, so why not?

It was five in the morning when Ro called a taxi to take her back to River Remez. Ben walked out and waited with her by the curb. Sunrise was coming—a new day filled with a new hope. And after three years of the chase, perhaps it was in the cards to finally see a little light.

"Sorry about your car."

"It's collateral damage," Ro said. "You're not going to come to graduation, are you."

"Nope. Looks like my parents will have to wait for Haley."

"What about your speech?"

"You can talk in my place. People would much rather look at you than at me."

"They want to see you."

"They want to see a freak."

"More like a hero."

"You're way more of a hero than I am."

"So from one hero to another . . ." She wiped away tears. "Come to graduation. If you won't do that, at least come to grad night. Allow yourself one teeny bit of high school. It won't change anything. But just maybe it'll make you feel a little better to be, like . . . normal."

"'Normal' is not on my vocab list. Besides, I can barely move, let alone party."

"We'll rent a wheelchair."

Ben kissed her softly on the lips. "Have fun, honey. Really. You deserve it."

Her cheeks were wet. "It's so ironic. I've always been such an attention hog. Now that everyone's gonna be focused on me, I don't know if I'll be able to handle it."

"You have to handle it," Ben told her. "Someone has to be the socially adroit one." They both saw the cab coming down the street. "You'd better have fun, Dorothy. That's an order. I'll want to hear every detail about graduation and grad night, okay?"

"Okay."

"I mean it. Who got stoned, who got arrested, who got drunk and puked on himself, and most important, who banged whom."

"Well . . . that just about sums up high school." She dried her eyes. They kissed again and then she slipped into the cab, disappearing from sight.

Slowly and painfully, he made his way inside to the waiting room.

Everything he had done—all that research and running around and all the promises and hours and toil and sweat and even getting knifed—he had told himself that he was doing it for Ellen. But truthfully, he'd been doing it for himself. If he ever wanted to look in the mirror without flinching, he couldn't let that bastard win. And now that Barnes was caught, and Ben had won, he was floundering, more than a little lost. Superfluous to everyone except maybe Lilly. And Ben needed her way, way more than she had ever needed him.

HE HAD FALLEN asleep in a chair and woke up with a start around two hours later. It was a little before eight in the morning and he stank. Feeling like shit, he went into the men's room and washed his face and arms and scrubbed his hair with liquid hand soap. The water was pinkish as it flowed down the drain. He stuck his head under the hand dryer and shook out his hair like a wet dog. Then he bought coffee and muffins for the Tafoyas.

Since he wasn't allowed into the ICU, he left the goodies at the nurses' station. The nurse on duty said she'd tell George that he dropped by and that he was still here. Ben was convinced that George would never get the message, but an hour later he showed up. "Go home."

"I've got an appointment. They're gonna change my bandages. What's going on?"

"She's still heavily sedated. But . . ." A deep exhale. "She's improving. Her blood pressure is coming up." He paused. "We're trying to keep it real—no false hopes—but I'm . . . I'm optimistic." George shook his head. "You're not going to leave until you see her."

"I'm a mule, George. You should know that by now."

"Okay, Ben, this is the deal. If I let you see her, will you leave?"

"After they change my bandages, yes."

"And you'll go home to River Remez."

"Actually, I'm going to stay with my grandparents. It's closer and I've been living there anyway. They're just waiting for me to call so they can pick me up."

"Great. Stay there. Recuperate. Take care of yourself and let us take care of Lilly. That's the deal."

"I promise I'll leave and rest up for a while. But I know

myself. I'm gonna come back. I think my grandparents got me a tablet for a graduation present. I'll bring it with me. It'll keep me busy for hours."

"You don't need to be here, Ben. You need to take care of yourself." Ben didn't answer and George dry-washed his face. "I'm talking to a wall."

"Yes, you are."

"There can't be more than two people in the ICU. June won't leave. That's a given. I suppose I could use a few minutes to take a piss and just organize my scrambled brain. I want to check in with work and get that out of the way. I'll see if June will allow you to visit."

"Is she mad at me?"

"No." George was taken aback. "Why on earth would she be mad at you?"

"I left them alone in the house, George. I shouldn't have gone to graduation rehearsal—"

George cut him off. "No one's mad. You're family. Don't be stupid. Wait here while I ask June if it's okay."

As soon as he left, Ben closed his eyes, but the images were too awful and too bloody. Instead he stared at nothing. George returned around a half hour later. "June says okay, but just for a few minutes." A pause. "Ben, she's doing better but she looks bad. You've got to steel yourself, for June's sake. Keep it up-tempo."

"Got it."

George had taken ten steps before Ben managed to stand up. He turned around and saw Ben struggling. "Sorry." He came back. "Lean on me."

"I'm okay. I just move *slowly*."

Together they crept over to the ICU. Ben was in a lot of

pain but it felt right. He wasn't supposed to be okay while Lilly was not okay. The nurse had him gown up and cover his feet and head. The ICU room was glassed in. Ben could see a body on the bed with tubes running in and out all over the place. Machines were beeping and chiming. The beat of his heart only added to the rhythm. He went inside.

June was sitting next to Lilly, her delicate fingers wrapped around her daughter's limp hand. She had looked up when Ben came in, but then her eyes went back at Lilly's face. She was a small woman to begin with, but the psychic pain had somehow made her diminutive. There was an empty chair—George's seat—and Ben took it.

Lilly had tubes in her nose and mouth and an oxygen mask over her face. Her neck was completely wrapped in white bandages and gauze. Her left hand was on a board attached to the bed railing and there were needles in her arm and wrist and a couple of IVs dripping clear liquid. Her complexion was gray, as if all the life force had been sucked out of her.

Keep it positive, Vicksburg. But keep it real.

He had wanted to tell her that everything would be all right, that she would be fine and things would go back to the way they were. He had wanted to tell her how beautiful she looked, healthy and rosy and full of spit and fire. He had wanted to tell her all of that. But it wasn't true, and deep inside Lilly would know it wasn't true. She always had a great bullshit detector.

"Can I talk to her?" he whispered to June.

She turned, her eyes reaching deep within his soul. "A few minutes."

He ran a finger across Lilly's ashen cheek. "Hi, hon. It's Ben."

For just a moment she opened her eyes, but then the lids fluttered and closed. Her heart rate quickened. Then it slowed until the intervals between each beat lengthened. The monitor read a sluggish forty-five beats per minute, but she was sedated.

Keep it positive, keep it real.

Again he touched her cheek. "We got him, honey." Her heart rate sped up a bit. More than hearing him, he knew she understood. "We got him and he's behind bars. He's never, ever gonna get out and he's never, ever, ever gonna hurt anyone else again. It's over and done with. He's toast. Your job is to just get well."

Ben paused to keep the emotion out of his voice.

"You just get well and heal up so that I can give you and Haley a hard time like I always do. We're all here for you, Lilly—anything you need and anything you want. I'm here as long as you want. I'm not going anywhere. Right now, I've got nothing but time. So when you wake up and you're better, if you want to hang out and annoy me, I'm here, okay?"

No response. But her blood pressure was stable, her breathing was stable, and so was her heart rate. So that was as good a response as anything.

"I know your dad wants to come back and be with you here in this room. And since there can only be two people with you, I gotta leave the ICU. But I'll be close. I'm gonna stay with my grandparents so I can come back and forth easily. So . . . so . . . I guess I'll talk to you in a little bit. Because your dad wants to be here and we can't have more than two people in the room . . . I think I already said that.

"Take care, hon. Get well . . . get well real soon. I'll be waiting." Ben looked at June. "Thanks."

She leaned over and kissed his cheek. Then she continued her vigil.

George was just outside the ICU. He helped Ben walk back to the waiting room, offering him coffee and a croissant once the kid was seated.

"Thanks. I actually *am* a little hungry." Ben nibbled the croissant.

"Call your grandparents."

"I'll go to the house as soon as I get my bandages changed."

"When's that?"

Ben looked at his watch and took out the vial of antibiotics. He swallowed a pill dry. "At ten. In an hour." He took a sip of the coffee. It felt warm and soothing. "I'll leave when that's done. Thank you for letting me see her." Another sip of coffee. "You know, she opened her eyes for a second."

"She *did*?"

"Just for a second. But she did react to my voice. Her heart rate went up. She heard me, George. And I really, really think she understood what I was saying."

"You kept it positive?"

"I kept it positive."

George dry-washed his face again. "I've got something in my car that I've been carrying around for months."

"What?"

"Just wait here."

"Sure. Where else would I go?"

George was back about five minutes later, carrying a manila envelope. "This is Lilly's graduation present to you. And today is officially your graduation, whether you're there or not." He handed Ben the package.

"What is it?"

"Just open it."

The flap had been taped shut. Ben ripped it off and pulled out a stack of paper. The first thing he saw was a letter from the California Institute of Technology congratulating him on his acceptance. He hadn't applied to Caltech. He hadn't applied anywhere except St. John's and UNM. Looking at George, he said, "Excuse me?"

"It was Lilly's idea. She wanted to make it happen. So a few of us got together and did what needed to be done."

"A few of you being . . ."

"Lilly, me, your parents, of course, Tom Gomez, your teachers who felt you were selling yourself short. Even your principal was in on it."

"You *forged* an application to a major university."

"We didn't forge anything." George was irritated. "You got the grades, you got the scores, you got the National Merit Scholarship. Your teachers in high school and at UNM wrote the recommendations. They certainly weren't forged. I have no idea what your boss at Circuitchip wrote, but I assume it was okay 'cause you got in."

A pause.

"Lilly wrote your essays. Did a damn good job. They sounded just like you . . . actually, smarter than you. And she didn't mention Ellen, even though everyone said she should. She figured you wouldn't have liked that."

"I wouldn't have liked it."

"The only thing that was forged was your signature— courtesy of your dad. Big effing deal."

Ben regarded the letter. "This is ridiculous. I'm not going anywhere . . . especially not now. She needs me."

"Lilly has two parents, Ben. She doesn't need a third."

George weighed his words. "You know you're a little like me, kid. And maybe that's why Lilly always had a thing for you." He paused. "Benjamin, it's time for you to stop being a grown-up and start acting your age."

"I'm not going anywhere," Ben repeated. "I can't leave her alone."

"You're not leaving her alone, you're going away to college. Thousands of kids just like you do it every year. Stop being a baby."

Ben was furious. "Me? A baby?"

"Ben, you're fine as long as you're facing death in the eye. It's life that gives you problems."

Ben was too angry to talk, then a few moments passed and a cooler head prevailed. Ben said, "George, I can't leave her now. It'll break her heart." Silence. "She *loves* me."

"I know she does. I've seen enough of her doodling: 'Ben,' 'Benny,' 'Benjamin' written across the insides of her notebooks . . . all the hearts with your and her initials in them. The true question is, do you love her?"

"Of course I love her."

"I mean, do you really *love* her?"

"George, she's not even fifteen yet."

"Well, she won't be fifteen forever." When the kid didn't answer, George said, "Ben, if you love her, you'll go to Caltech. She *wants* you to go."

Dumbfounded, Ben stammered out, "That was then. This is now."

George stared at the kid with wet eyes. "If you want to do something for her—something very, very important for her—*blaze* the fucking trail. She chose Caltech for you because *she* wants to go to Caltech. She wants to go to L.A. She always wanted to learn how to surf."

George looked upward.

"After what happened, I should never let her go. Never, ever, ever. All I want to do is hold her hand and tell her I love her. And June . . . pssh . . . she's superprotective to begin with. If it's up to us, we'd keep her under lock and key forever. What good will that do? We'll cripple her.

"But if she has a guardian angel out there, someone who can take care of her if she needs it down the road, maybe . . . just maybe . . . June will relent and let my beautiful daughter spread her beautiful wings. That monster took a lot from her, but he didn't take her brain. He didn't take her soul. If you want to help her, get yourself educated and help my daughter to do the same."

Ben was still looking at the letter. "I can't believe my dad forged my signature."

"Stop making a federal case out of it."

"This is going to cost a fortune."

"Your parents would mortgage the house if they had to. Fortunately, they don't have to. There should be another letter inside." George grabbed the envelope from Ben. "Here we go. Work-study. Eighty percent reduction in tuition, room, and board. You'll need to go by the third week in August, Ben. There's orientation and entrance exams to determine your level in math and physics. We've already sent in your acceptance letter. It's a done deal. If you pull out now, you'll expose us all to being charged with fraud."

"I'll just say I changed my mind."

"If you do that, it's like spitting in Lilly's face." George was snorting. "You think about it." He stood up. "You think about what the people who love you did for you. And when you're done thinking about it, you get on that fucking plane and make us all proud."

With that, he left.

Ben had never wanted to go away for college. New situations were torture. He was out of his element at parties and social gatherings. He wasn't a talker or a good team player. He was a loner who lived in his head. He liked numbers more than words and was happiest when he was by himself with a pencil and piece of paper, working on abstract concepts that had nothing to do with real life.

Then he thought for a moment.

He suspected he had just described a lot of the student body at Caltech.

A class full of Vicksburgs. Now, that was a scary thought.

It was Lilly's graduation present to him. Under the current circumstances, he had no choice but to accept.

Lilly, Lilly, Lilly.

Why couldn't she be like most girls her age? Why didn't she just hang up posters of rock stars, chase boys, shop for makeup, and call it a day? Why did she have to be so much like him?

CHAPTER 18

B **EN KEPT A** diary, so he would remember.

DAY ONE

Ninety-six hours after being viciously attacked, Lilly celebrated her fifteenth birthday by being moved from the ICU to a room in the special-care ward. Her vitals were stable, but she still had a fever and she still needed oxygen and a glucose drip. She hadn't eaten because she couldn't swallow, let alone talk. Disoriented, confused, and loopy from the medicine, she needed time to even realize she was in a hospital. She became agitated. She had to be sedated a number of times. She moved in and out of consciousness, her eyes scanning her environment, soaking in whatever she could.

There were so many tests; in and out and in and out. That in itself would tire out a normal person, let alone someone as compromised as Lilly. June yelled each time they took her away. She yelled when they brought her back. Ben had to keep on reminding himself that despite everything, Lilly was making progress. She had some moments of lucidity. And she recognized people. When he talked to her, he was positive that she knew who he was.

DAY TWO

The nurses liked to keep the number of visitors in her room to two. June was a fixture. George, Haley, and Ben took shifts. Lilly began to have longer periods of consciousness and became aware of her surroundings. At one point, when Ben was visiting her, she was coherent enough to understand that she had neck surgery and couldn't talk. She lifted her hand and pantomimed writing in the air.

Ben hunted in his backpack and took out a notebook of lined paper and a pencil.

She wrote: ???????

June became paralyzed, but recovered quickly. She told Lilly that she had been in an accident. That her throat had been injured, so she needed to rest her voice and try to recover.

Her eyes narrowed, and Ben knew that look. She didn't fully believe her mother, but she didn't argue. She lay silently until she fell asleep. She seemed a bit more peaceful when she slept. That is, until they woke her up to change her dressing.

Dr. Winslow was there. He talked to June. He talked to George. He told them that Lilly was making remarkable progress. Then he patted Ben's shoulder and told him that he had done a good job.

After fucking it up in the first place.

DAY THREE

When he arrived at nine, Lilly was up and watching TV. Her fever was down and she no longer needed an oxygen mask. The IV was dripping and she was being fed through tubes, but without the mask, she looked healthier than before, even if her complexion was still wan. George finished up his coffee, stood, and said, "I'm going to go in to work and try to clear my desk for a few hours. You'll stay with June until I get back?"

"Of course."

George kissed his daughter's forehead and Ben took his chair beside the bed. He leaned over the bed so Lilly could see him and she gave him a slight wave. Then her eyes went upward to the TV. She didn't initiate any contact for a while. Then she picked up a tablet Ben had brought for her, wrote something, and handed it to Ben. *What kind of accident?*

Her voice wasn't working but her mind sure was. Ben showed the tablet to June, who was momentarily stymied. Ben said, "Do you remember the ambulance?"

She snapped her fingers and pointed to the tablet still in June's hands. Her mom gave it back to her.

No.

"Okay. You were in an ambulance and I was with you when they took you to the hospital."

I remember you.

"Right. I was with you the entire ride."

She wrote and showed Ben the tablet: *What happened?*

June blanched when he showed her Lilly's words. She said, "It was a car accident, Lilly. A very bad accident. We'll tell you everything once you're completely better. All that matters is that you get better."

Lilly lifted her eyes back to the TV. When her mother spoke to her, she refused to engage her. At some level, she knew that June wasn't telling the truth.

DAY FOUR

Lilly's eyes were moving back and forth when Ben came into the room. She sensed his presence before he spoke, already writing in her tablet.

What happened?

Her mother was furious with Lilly's insistence on knowing. She said, "Ben got in a car accident. You're very lucky to be alive."

He'd take the blame. Not a problem. But Lilly didn't buy it.

She wrote: *Why isn't Ben hurt?*

"I *was* hurt." Ben leaned over and lifted his T-shirt. He had healed sufficiently to have equal amounts of pain and itch, but was still bandaged up. Lilly slowly lifted her free hand and touched the gauze. "I was hurt, but not nearly as bad as you were. Lilly, it was all my fault. When you get better, when you truly, truly get better, I hope you'll forgive me."

She didn't answer, but he could almost smell things percolating in her brain. She looked away and stared at the wall until she closed her eyes and fell asleep. While she napped he went down to the cafeteria to get lunch for June. When he came back, Lilly was up again.

"Hey." Ben spoke so she knew he was in the room. "Just went to get your mom and me some lunch. Do you mind us eating here?"

She wrote: *Tell me about the accident.*

June was smoldering. She couldn't figure out why Lilly

wouldn't let it go. It was what made her a fine math mind. Ben took a bite of an apple. "I was driving Ro's Explorer and plowed into a chain link fence." All of that was true. "The windshield shattered and pieces flew all over the place." True too. "Your throat got cut." That was true, although it had nothing to do with the car. "You almost died. If Ro hadn't been there, you *would* have died. She saved you. Do you forgive me?"

Her eyes were boring into his. *I forgive you. But I don't believe you.*

Ben didn't say anything and neither did June. She took the tablet away. "You need to rest."

Lilly didn't argue, but they knew she was angry. When Ben talked, she wouldn't respond with any kind of gesture or written word. Eventually, she fell back asleep and so did June. Neither one woke when George came in. Ben got up and left.

DAY FIVE

Haley wanted to hang out with her best friend without her brother horning in. Ben relinquished his vigil, spending the day with Ro at his grandparents' house, filling out an excessive amount of college forms. After a lot of deliberation, Ro had decided on the University of Pennsylvania.

It was the first time he'd been alone with her since *that* day. He owed her for saving Lilly's life, for allowing him to catch a monster, and he owed her big-time because she had dealt with everyone—all the phone calls and questions, the media—TV, radio, and newspaper interviews. She allowed Ben to remain in the background. She allowed him to heal.

She said, "Do you think if I wrote up what happened at Los Alamos Brown would reconsider?"

"Ro, after what happened at Los Alamos, you could get in anywhere. You caught a serial killer."

"*We* caught a serial killer."

"You can take all the credit. I certainly don't give a shit."

"The way I figure it is that if the school didn't want me for who I am before this happened, then screw it!"

"Brown didn't reject you. You're on the waiting list. If you want to go, let them know what happened. At the very least, send them one of the million articles and let them see what you're made of."

She sat back and blew out air. "How's Lilly?"

"Getting better." Ben regarded her. "Did you know about this collusion behind my back?"

"Of course. Lilly told me. I thought it was a great idea, although in the back of my mind I thought you'd never go. Now, of course, you have to go."

Of course, she was right.

Suck it up, Ben.

He was filling out forms for a roommate. It creeped him out—someone sleeping where he'd also be sleeping. He'd never gone to sleep-away camp for precisely that reason.

"You could have told me."

"Right." Ro looked at him. "You know, maybe you'll actually like it."

"Maybe." And that was as much of a concession as he was going to give her. "Will you text me from time to time?"

"I'll text you every day . . . until I get a boyfriend. Then it might be every other day."

"Ha ha." *Suck it up, Ben.* "I'll miss you."

"I'll be back for holidays. Griff decided to spend another year here, so my fam is staying on."

"How's he doing?"

"Feeling guilty like the rest of us. But by staying here, he and Haley figure they can be there for Lilly."

"I should be here for her."

"She needs her peers, not someone overprotecting her like her parents. Do her a favor and learn the ropes at Caltech so when she gets there, she'll have a tour guide."

"That's what George said."

"He's right. Go try to salvage whatever teen years you have left, Vicks. That's what I'm doing."

"You're more resilient than I am."

"Bullshit. What's your ideal roommate?"

"Besides you?"

"Good answer." Ro got up and peeked over his shoulder. His roommate requests were nonexistent. "Should I fill it out for you?"

"Sure. That way I'll have absolutely nothing to do with this fiasco and a lot of people to blame."

"Or thank."

Ben looked at her. "Thank you. For everything."

"You're welcome." She grabbed the application out of his hands and began to fill it out. "You want a mixed floor?"

"No. If it were up to me, I wouldn't even want a mixed dorm."

"C'mon, Vicks, have some fun. Besides, I'm sure the girls are just like the boys there."

"No mixed floor." He looked over her shoulder and tried to see what she was writing, but she covered the sheet.

"I want it to be a surprise."

"No thanks. I've had enough of those."

"Yeah, but not good ones. This'll be a good one. I know what's good for you. Now sit down or pace or go away."

Ben smiled. "Seriously, I will miss you."

"I know. I'll miss you too." Ro looked at him with dewy eyes. "It's probably better this way. I can't deal with any more intensity. I want to go back to my former superficial life."

"Don't you know you can't go home again?"

"Yeah, but I can go to college. And I don't even have to reinvent myself. I'm a legitimate hero. I now deserve all the adulation that comes with it. I am invincible." When Ben laughed, she pouted. "I'm serious."

"I know. That's what's so funny, but also charming. It must be wonderful to know who you are."

"You'll get attention too, you know. While I know you'll never relish it like I do, don't brush people off. Try . . . talking about it even if it's just a sentence or two. It'll make the people you're talking to feel important and it's a lot cheaper than psychotherapy."

He was about to protest, but what would be the point? "I'll try."

"As my dad always says: 'Good enough for government work.' And it's good enough for me."

DAY SIX

When Ben arrived at the hospital in the afternoon, Haley had been with Lilly all morning. This time she'd brought Griffen. The three of them were watching TV. Haley and Griff left when Ben came in and Lilly seemed to be in a good mood. She was down to one IV drip and just a nasal tube. Haley said she had actually managed to swallow some juice. She coughed, of course, but she kept at least half of it down.

The graph was on the upswing.

Lilly's largesse did not extend to Ben. When she saw him, she scribbled on her tablet. *What really happened, Ben?*

Of course June was there. Ben showed her the message and again she took the tablet away. "You were up all morning with your friends. You need to rest."

This time Lilly wasn't about to relent. She kept snapping her fingers until her mother gave in and gave her the tablet. *I want to talk to Ben alone.*

"No," June said. "You need something, you talk to me."
You're not telling me the truth.

"I'm telling you what you need to know." June looked at Ben. "You should leave now."

He got up but Lilly slammed her free hand onto the bed railing. Then she grabbed her mother's arm. June gave her the tablet. She wrote: *Stop treating me like a child.*

"Should I go?" Ben asked June.

"Yes."

Lilly threw the tablet at her mother's chest, where it landed with a thud. For the first time ever, Ben saw June cry, although it was silent. Big fat tears ran down her cheeks. Ben touched June's arm and she looked away.

"Can I have a word with you, please?" When they were out of Lilly's earshot, he whispered, "I can handle this. I'm not gonna overload her with details."

"What are you going to tell her?"

"That she was attacked. She knows it wasn't a car accident. Give me a chance, okay?"

June wiped her eyes. "Just a few minutes—and nothing, *nothing,* about the rape."

"Fair enough."

She left the room, but lingered outside and that was certainly her right. Ben went back to Lilly and handed her the tablet.

I feel bad.

"Do you want me to call the nurse for more pain medication?"

Not that kind of bad. I feel bad for throwing the tablet at her. I know she's worried.

"Are you worried?"

Should I be worried?

"You're going to need more surgery, Lilly. And voice therapy." When she didn't answer, Ben said, "I'm so sorry."

She still didn't answer. Then she wrote: *What happened?*

Ben exhaled. "The truth? You were attacked. But we got the guy who did it. He's behind bars and he's never going to see freedom again. So you're safe. Absolutely safe."

Lilly's hand went to her neck. *He cut my throat?*

"Yes."

She didn't write anything for a few minutes—a very long time to sit in tension. Finally, Lilly scribbled, *I don't remember.* Tears fell onto her cheeks. Ben pulled out a Kleenex and gave it to her. *I don't remember anything!*

Barnes had no doubt knocked her out in order to get her into the car. It wasn't surprising that she had no recollection of the kidnapping. "That's a good thing, Lilly. It's a self-protective thing."

Who was he? Ellen's killer?

"Yes."

You caught him?

"The police did, yes."

How did you get hurt?

"He stabbed me with the same knife that he used to attack you. We're blood brothers . . . blood siblings." A small smile played on her lips. "You're not going to have to testify, if that's what you're worried about. We got his DNA matched to my sister and three other murdered girls. There might even be more. So like I said, you're safe. He's never getting out."

So you fought him off?

"I fought with him, yes, but by that time the police were all around, so he knew he was doomed. My only regret is that I didn't shoot him when I had a chance."

You had a gun?

"I did."

Again she didn't immediately respond. Then she wrote: *I'm glad you didn't shoot him. Why ruin your life?*

"That's what everyone kept telling me. Lilly, you should know that Ro saved you. She kept you going until the ambulance got there."

You were with Ro?

"Yes."

She paused a long time. *This happened the day before graduation, right? The graduation rehearsal.*

Ben's eyes moistened. "So you do remember that day."

Only that we went to the library. Another protracted silence. *Nothing after that.* A pause. *Except your face. I remember your face.*

"We were in the ambulance together speeding off to the medical center. I was talking to you and you were looking at me the whole time." He stood up. "Now that's enough questions. Don't ask me anything else 'cause I won't answer you. I'm gonna go get your mom, okay?" She held his arm. "What is it, hon?"

She waited a few moments, then she wrote: *Am I still a virgin?*

Fury swept through his body. His vision went blurry for a few moments. "Unless you know something that I don't, of course you are," he snapped. "Stop asking silly questions."

She held his chin and brought his face in front of hers, staring with big, black eyes. Determined eyes, but he certainly wasn't going to be the one to tell her.

The sad truth was he didn't need to tell her, because deep in her heart, she already knew. She could read his eyes and that made him feel low. But Lilly was always one to throw a curve ball.

She managed a smile for his benefit. She picked up the tablet and wrote one word.

Dang.

DAY SEVEN

With her fever gone and her vitals stabilized, Lilly was allowed to go home. June and George had fixed up her room with enough medical equipment to staff a small hospital—IVs, oxygen tanks, monitors, and a fridge filled with juices and sports water. Even though June took a leave of absence from her job, she and George hired a full-time nurse for Lilly.

Outside the house were banners and balloons welcoming Lilly back home. Inside the living room, there were more flowers than were blooming outside in the garden. As she was wheeled out of the hospital, Lilly smiled and waved, and then George made an announcement.

No one was permitted to visit her until after the weekend.

The no one extended to Ben. That was okay with him. The Sabbath was a day of rest.

CHAPTER 19

THE SUMMER PASSED in a heartbeat.

A nationwide scan of missing girls uncovered possible links to three more victims whose bodies had yet to be discovered. In exchange for the whereabouts of the bodies and of course with the permission of all of the families involved, the D.A. took the death penalty off the table. Barnes was allowed to plead out the seven murders and the attempted murder for seven life sentences without the possibility of parole. Ben figured it was good that he hadn't whacked him. It gave three other families a chance to bury their dead.

Before he could blink, he was at the Sunport in Albuquerque, standing in the security line with Ro and JD and other kids from his class, waiting to catch planes, to take the next step. Families were fussing over their children and Ben's mom and dad were no exception. Ro's mom had actually wanted to come and help move Ro into her dorm, but Ro insisted that after all that had happened, it would look funny to have her mommy there.

It was never an expectation that JD's parents would help him move into his dorm. It wasn't an expectation for Ben's parents as well, although his grandfather really wanted to come. Ben figured he was more curious about Caltech than he was concerned about Ben, but that was Grandpa Ed. Parents' weekend would come very soon and Grandpa and Grandma were invited. His buddy Grant was going to meet Ben at the airport and show him around L.A. Ben knew he'd be in good hands.

Ben was healed but still a little raw around the edges. He couldn't bike or run or lift weights, but he did take lots of long, long walks alone, thinking and planning and just trying to figure it all out. He couldn't move as fluidly as he wanted, but with a little time and patience, he knew he'd be fine.

Three weeks before, his classmates had thrown him a surprise eighteenth birthday party. He hated surprises, but this was a nice one and he had a good time—it was his last chance to say good-bye to everyone who was leaving.

As they got closer to security, Ben gave his parents a semi—bear hug good-bye. His mom had dry eyes but his dad did not. Then it was Ben's turn to take out his laptop and remove his shoes.

"Bye." Another series of hugs all around. "I'll call you went I get to L.A."

Ben, JD, and Ro passed through security, then checked for their respective flights. Ro was going to Philadelphia via Midway, JD was going to Durham via Baltimore, and Ben was going straight to L.A.

The Sunport was pink and green with little booths selling turquoise jewelry and knickknacks that were supposed to remind people that they were in the Southwest. JD was going to a bigger town, although Durham was still small compared to many other cities. The adjustment wouldn't be too hard, especially since he'd be breathing football, parties, and girls—there would be no time to be lonely. Ro had lived in or near a big city almost her entire life. She was going back to her roots.

Ben was alone—a small-town boy going to the big city for the first time. Ro and JD had regular backpacks, while Ben had a wheelie bag. He felt like a six-year-old, but better to feel infantile than to rip something open.

The boys sat with Ro between them. While Ben began fussing with his laptop, JD and Ro carried on a semiprivate conversation revolving around JD's football games and Ro's choice of a sorority. Ben thought about navigating life without a quest.

Within a half hour, there was a boarding announcement for the flight to Baltimore, and that's when JD got up. He hugged Ben first.

"Take care, Vicks. And when your start-up offers its IPO, let me in on it."

"You'll be the first one I call."

"And when we make it into the finals, give me a call and I'll wrangle you a ticket."

"I'll be there, James David, making sure you don't do anything felonious in the after-game celebration. Take care."

Ben took his wheelie and went over to his gate, giving JD and Ro some privacy to say their good-byes.

Five minutes later Ro sat down next to him. "I have a little time."

"You want to sit by your gate? You're leaving first."

"This is fine. I'll hear the boarding announcements."

"What boarding group are you?"

"C."

"I'm C too."

"I'll probably get seated next to a sleazy guy or a wailing baby. God forbid there should be a cute guy on board."

"You never know."

"I guess I'll see you around Thanksgiving." She fiddled with her chipped nails. "You'll be home, right?"

"Of course. If it had been up to me, I would have never left home."

He laughed and so did she. It was strained for both of them.

She said, "It's really time for both of us. Although I have my doubts how much four years of parties, drinking, and sex can help me become productive."

"I see what your priorities are."

"And what are your priorities, Vicks?"

"Getting up in the morning."

She hit him. The first garbled boarding announcement for Midway came across the loudspeaker. She stood up and so did he.

"I'll walk you over."

"It's just across the aisle."

"I want to be with you."

"That's different." She put her backpack on and took his arm. She said, "So you'll come visit me in Philadelphia?"

Ben couldn't help it. His eyes moistened.

Ro said, "Okay, okay, you don't have to visit me."

He hugged her tightly. "Of course I'll visit you."

She leaned her head on his chest. "I will never, ever find another boy like you, Benjamin Vicksburg. You are an original. I love you."

"I love you too."

She broke away. "Let's talk when we get settled."

"Good idea. And tell me what you think of Grant when you go for a weekend in Boston. He's already planning a million things."

"You know, you don't have to set me up. I think I can do okay on my own."

"I'm not setting you up. It's his idea, Ro. He's dying to meet you. That boy knows a good thing when he sees it."

They heard the boarding announcement for the B group. Ro said, "I'd better stand in line."

They walked hand in hand up to the gate until her group was called. Ben said, "Knock 'em dead, Dorothy. Philadelphia will never know what hit it."

"Philadelphia is just the start, baby. Because once you're in the majors, there is no going back." She broke away and handed her ticket to the airline attendant. "Bye, Vicks. Go out and own the world." She pranced down the Jetway: tall, proud, and full of herself. Ben wouldn't have wanted it any other way.

Back in front of the gate for the Southwest flight to LAX, Ben was alone until his group was called. The flight was full, but he managed to snag an aisle seat next to a mother and a four-year-old kid who was already bouncing in his seat. Ben didn't care. He liked the energy.

Before he stuffed his wheelie underneath his seat, he retrieved a college guidebook, well-worn and dog-eared, that took him back to an earlier time. Ellen and he were sitting at the breakfast bar at their house, just the two of them. It was before school and their mom was busy getting Haley dressed. He was wolfing down sugar cereal, listening to Spotify on his phone—a recent gift for his birthday. Ellen was drinking juice and munching on toast. She wore a red T-shirt and jeans, and her hair was in her eyes as she studied the book.

"I've found it, Benny." He hadn't heard her initially because of his earbuds. She hit his arm and he took them out.

"Huh?"

"I said I found where I want to go to college."

"Where?"

"Bryn Mawr."

"Bryn Mawr?" With his usual tact at fourteen, he said, "What's so good about Bryn Mawr?"

"Well, it's near Philadelphia."

"What's so good about Philadelphia?"

"It's near Bryn Mawr."

He had laughed. That much he remembered. "That's crackass." He checked his watch. He was meeting his buds before school started. They often did that. Also, he liked to bike when the roads were clear. He picked up his backpack and Ellen handed him the book.

"You keep this. I don't need it anymore."

He tucked the book into the pocket of his backpack. "Are you really going away to college?"

"Of course I'm going away to college," she answered.

Something came over him. Even at fourteen, he knew he'd miss her when she left. "Then I guess I'll have to visit you in Philadelphia."

She gave him a thousand-watt smile. "I'd like that, Benny."

That was the last time he ever saw his sister in the flesh. At least it had been a good memory. And perhaps because it was, he was able to keep his promise. Holding her book, he paged through until he found Bryn Mawr. She had checked it off with a smiley face, writing: *This is it!*

Her writing made him smile.

And then it made him cry.

Instead of her, he was the one going off to school—for all the people who believed in him, all the people who worked so hard—family, teachers, mentors, and friends. But most of all, it was for Ellen. Always and forever.

The four-year-old was looking at him. Embarassed, Ben wiped his face. His phone beeped: a text from Lilly. R U there?

He texted back, Just sitting on the plane, waiting to take off.

There was a pause.

I envy you.

So you come join me, hon. Least you could do since it was your idea.

Another long pause.

I don't know, Ben . . . I've got a long road ahead.

And what could he say to that?

She texted, I'm scared, Ben. I'm scared of EVERYTHING.

He replied, So come join me at Caltech and I promise I'll hold your hand.

What if therapy doesn't work? What if I can't talk ever again beyond a squeak? I can't even scream for help.

So come join me and I promise I'll be your voice. Your brainpower is still off the charts. You have no excuses, young lady.

Another pause.

I may have the brains, Ben, but I no longer have the heart.

Again, his eyes went wet.

So take my heart. You own it anyway.

He could picture her face, and see her eyes moisten with

tears. They had spent a lot of time together once she was out of the hospital. At first, the conversations had centered around her: what she needed and how she felt, questions asked and answered, until there was nothing left to tell her. The endless writing seemed to exhaust her. So to fill in the silences, Ben began to talk about himself. And as he talked, she began to answer with an occasional mouthing of words. And the funny thing about lipreading is you concentrate very hard because some words look alike if you're not paying close enough attention. It means looking intensely at someone's face. And when you really look at the face, you notice a lot more.

And the more he looked at Lilly and read her mouthed but unspoken communication, the more he truly understood Lilly Tafoya. It was like meeting her for the first time. And talking about himself . . . it was like he was meeting himself for the first time as well.

He confided in her, things that he hadn't admitted in a long, long time. And as he did, she ceased to be just his little sister's best friend. Lilly Tafoya became *his* friend.

Girlfriend?

Not yet.

But like George said, she wouldn't be fifteen forever.

Ben saw his future. Lilly would come to school with him. If she couldn't talk, he'd shadow her in class if she wanted. And if she didn't want it, he'd still be around in case she changed her mind. And they'd get educated together. They'd get advanced degrees. Eventually, they'd go back to New Mexico, where, like her parents, they would probably wind up with jobs at one of the many labs. They'd get married—two ceremonies: one in a church and the other at the pueblo. They'd go to local sports games, take long walks in the mountains, play Scrabble and video games. They'd be on school boards and community boards and make the system better. They'd throw birthday parties and block parties and holiday parties. They'd make a family together, a life together. They'd grow old together.

For most guys his age, this was surely a vision of hell. To him, it was exactly what he'd wanted for the last three-plus years: a chance to live a normal life.

She still hadn't texted him back, so he texted her again.

I've got to turn off the phone. They're making announcements and the flight attendant is giving me the stink eye.

He was about to press the off button when his phone chimed. He looked down at the text.

I love you, Ben.

A huge smile planted itself across his face.

"Sir, you have to turn off your phone."

He looked up. The flight attendant, a woman in her fifties with short blond hair and muddy blue eyes, wore a very stern expression.

"She just told me she loves me." He showed her the text.

The woman sighed and rolled her hand in the air as if to say, *Hurry up.* He texted Lilly back but didn't push the send button. To the flight attendant, he asked, "'I love you too' or 'I love you, Lilly'?"

"'I love you, Lilly,'" she whispered.

"Yeah, I thought so." He pushed the send button. Once he saw that the message had gone through, he turned off the phone and stowed it away.

Then, for the first time in what seemed like a very long time, he sat back to enjoy the ride.